PRAISE FOR COLLEEN COBLE
AND RICK ACKER

I THINK I WAS MURDERED

"This is a book that grabs you straight out of the gate. Centered around a bang-up concept with a great techno twist, a rich cast of characters drives you through a twisty plot that is a white-knuckled ride straight to the end. The suspense was killing me as I read! Make sure you're well-rested before you start *I Think I Was Murdered* because it will keep you up at night."

—P. J. TRACY, *NEW YORK TIMES* BESTSELLING AUTHOR

"A timely and intriguing premise played out in a way that keeps readers guessing."

—STEVEN JAMES, NATIONAL BEST-SELLING AUTHOR OF *SYNAPSE*

"What a roller-coaster ride! *I Think I Was Murdered* gripped me on page one and didn't let go until the epilogue—after a twist that caught this seasoned reader by complete surprise. If you like thrilling suspense, you won't want to miss this novel by Colleen Coble and Rick Acker."

—ANGELA HUNT, AUTHOR OF *WHAT A WAVE MUST BE*

"Colleen Coble fans will devour her latest offering, which—with the help of thriller writer Rick Acker—cleverly uses AI, family secrets, and a lost treasure to keep readers guessing until the final satisfying page."

—CRESTON MAPES, BESTSELLING AUTHOR

WHAT WE HIDE

"Coble and Acker have forged a seamless partnership with a singular voice. I honestly can't tell where one writer starts and the other ends. *What We Hide* is a crisp and hard-charging start to a legal suspense series that tests the boundaries of yesterday's secrets against today's lies, all while trying to escape tomorrow's verdict. From the courtroom to the shadow of a decaying Gothic university, it's a high-stakes ride through love, second chances, and an ending you won't soon forget."

—CHARLES MARTIN, *NEW YORK TIMES* BESTSELLING AUTHOR

"Get ready to be hooked! Brace yourself for a thrill ride as Coble and Acker masterfully weave a web of suspense in *What We Hide*, where secrets simmer and unexpected twists leave you guessing until the shocking finale."

—KATE ANGELO, *PUBLISHERS WEEKLY* BESTSELLING AUTHOR

"This book has it all. Intrigue, suspense, and the mysteries of the heart, woven together masterfully by the great new pairing of Coble and Acker. Fans of their individual books will not be disappointed. New readers will be delighted."

—JAMES SCOTT BELL, INTERNATIONAL
THRILLER WRITERS AWARD WINNER

"Much is hidden in Tupelo Grove and Pelican Harbor. In *What We Hide*, expert storytellers Colleen Coble and Rick Acker will take you on a riveting ride through a picturesque Southern town inhabited by characters who will pull you in and make you care. Hidden truths find their way into the light—sometimes quickly, often slowly in the face of great obstacles and danger. Once you start reading, you won't put this book down."

—ROBERT WHITLOW, BESTSELLING AUTHOR

"*What We Hide* grabbed me with the first chapter and had me reading until two in the morning with its twisty plot and engaging characters."

—PATRICIA BRADLEY, AUTHOR OF THE PEARL RIVER SERIES

I THINK
I WAS
MURDERED

I THINK
I WAS
MURDERED

COLLEEN COBLE
RICK ACKER

THOMAS NELSON
Since 1798

I Think I Was Murdered

Published in Nashville, Tennessee, by Thomas Nelson. Thomas Nelson is a registered trademark of HarperCollins Christian Publishing, Inc.

Thomas Nelson titles may be purchased in bulk for educational, business, fundraising, or sales promotional use. For information, please email SpecialMarkets@ThomasNelson.com.

Library of Congress Cataloging-in-Publication Data

Names: Coble, Colleen, author. | Acker, Rick, 1966- author.
Title: I think I was murdered / Colleen Coble, Rick Acker.
Description: Nashville, Tennessee: Thomas Nelson, 2024. | Summary: "A grieving young widow. The AI program that allows her to continue to 'talk' to him. And a message she never expected: 'I think I was murdered.'"—Provided by publisher.
Identifiers: LCCN 2024018870 (print) | LCCN 2024018871 (ebook) |
    ISBN 9780840712578 (paperback) | ISBN 9780840712622 (library binding) |
    ISBN 9780840712608 (epub) | ISBN 9780840712615
Subjects: LCGFT: Thrillers (Fiction) | Christian fiction. | Novels.
Classification: LCC PS3553.O2285 I2 2024 (print) | LCC PS3553.O2285 (ebook) |
    DDC 813/.54—dc23/eng/20240429
LC record available at https://lccn.loc.gov/2024018870
LC ebook record available at https://lccn.loc.gov/2024018871

Printed in the United States of America

24 25 26 27 28 LBC 5 4 3 2 1

For our amazing team at HarperCollins Christian Publishing, who came alongside us in huge ways to get this book to market faster than usual. Special thanks to editor and publisher Amanda Bostic, who caught our vision immediately and gave the project wings.

PROLOGUE

////////////////

IN 2009 SATOSHI NAKAMOTO LAID AN EGG.
Jason Foster found it two weeks ago, and he'd been running for his life ever since.

Jason took his eyes off the dark, narrow road for a second and glanced at the Satoshi egg, which lay on the leather passenger seat of his Bentley Continental GT. It didn't look like much: a dusty, discolored plastic Easter egg in a baggie. But it was one of a kind—the first Satoshi egg that had ever been found, and the USB drive inside had treasure seekers salivating. His job as a structural engineer had uncovered the egg in a place no one else could look.

He had hunted the fabled Satoshi eggs for over a decade. They were the stuff of Silicon Valley legend, and he hadn't even been sure they existed. Now that he finally had one, he couldn't wait to get rid of it.

A brief gleam in his rearview mirror yanked his attention back to the road and spiked his pulse. A second later, the road curved and the light vanished. Were those headlights? Was someone following him? Only one other person knew about his trip to North Haven, and they would be waiting for him there.

The gleam reappeared and he got a better look at it. Definitely headlights. But there was no reason to panic. Why should he expect to be the only driver on the road, even at this hour? All-night truckers sometimes took this route, especially if they were picking up logs at one of the surviving timber mills. Or maybe someone was driving to work for the graveyard shift at a gas station or a roadside diner. There were dozens of perfectly plausible possibilities. Still, he pushed down the accelerator a little farther.

He went over the top of a hill and the landscape hid the lights again. Redwoods loomed out of the mist on the right side of the two-lane road, like pillars holding up the unseen sky. On the left the Pacific crashed against the base of a low cliff. Patches of fog drifted in from Humboldt Bay, suddenly cutting visibility to near zero at random intervals.

The headlights reappeared as the other car crested the hill. And they were closer now. Jason pressed the accelerator down as far as he dared. The powerful engine responded and the car leaped forward.

Jason's tires whined as he struggled to stay in his lane. The Bentley's superb steering and suspension kept him from losing control and flying off the road, but only barely. Sweat trickled down his forehead and he breathed through gritted teeth. He flicked a glance at the rearview mirror again. Somehow the headlights were still getting closer. Whoever was behind the wheel of the other car must be a professional driver or incredibly reckless.

The road started a long climb. The Pacific fell away and enormous trees flanked the road on both sides. He'd just entered the Cathedral, a craggy stand of old-growth redwoods a few miles from North Haven. He relaxed just a fraction. In ten minutes, he'd be in town. He focused on the road's hairpin turns and switchbacks, trying to ignore the glimpses of headlights that flashed between the huge ancient trunks.

The Pulpit—the massive granite outcrop in the heart of the Cathedral—reared in front of him, and he knew he had one more treacherous turn at its top. He slowed to take it—and a silver sports car roared by, passing him on the inside of the turn.

Jason yanked the wheel to avoid a crash, but the other car moved in front of him and slammed on the brakes. He swerved to avoid it.

He managed to slip past the other car, but there wasn't enough room for his Bentley on the narrow shoulder. The right wheels slipped off the side with a *thunk*. The car's undercarriage ground over the rock for a few feet. Then, with agonizing slowness, the car tipped into the abyss.

Jason was weightless. The night world revolved outside his window—stars, trees, rock, stars, trees, rock. The Satoshi egg floated in front of him, drifting across the passenger compartment of the car.

Regret spun through his head—his beautiful Katrina needed him, but he was unable to stop his descent. And then the tumbled granite of the forest floor reached up and smashed him like a giant's fist.

CHAPTER 1

////////////////////

THE SECOND WORST DAY OF KATRINA Foster's life began on a beautiful September morning with the highly anticipated first coffee from Palo Alto Coffee House. Hot cup in hand, she got in her blue Tesla and drove toward her office at Talk, Inc., an up-and-coming tech company with an innovative AI app. Coffee was a necessity to face the barrage of legal questions she often fielded on Mondays.

She was within sight of the building when she took the first sip of her matcha and shuddered. Had the new barista used skim milk instead of almond milk? It was truly terrible. She set it in the drink holder.

A text dinged on her phone, and she fumbled in her purse. It dinged a second time before she managed to close her fingers around the phone. The message was from her mother.

Bestemor has had a heart attack and is critical. Come home now.

Katrina's breath squeezed from her chest. Her grandmother meant everything to her. Her beloved *bestemor* was her rock, her mentor, and so much more. Hands shaking, she punched in, *On my way.*

A second message came through, this one from her best friend and Talk's chief technology officer, Liv Tompkins. *I can't find David and the bank isn't returning my calls. I need you here now.* The elusive CEO who was Liv's boyfriend had vanished three days ago.

The messages reflected Katrina's past year in a nutshell. Both the grandmother she adored and the company she'd poured everything into had begun an inexorable slide downhill. She'd tried without success to be in two places at once, but she'd been utterly helpless to change either situation. Just a year ago she was a rising star in Talk, Inc., the AI chatbot start-up everyone was talking about. She was married to the best man in the world, and they'd been living the life of their dreams for three wonderful years. Her life had slowly spiraled out of control starting with Jason's death in a car accident just over a year ago, and most days she felt like she was drowning.

She parked and opened the Talk app. Jason's smiling face appeared with the text *Hi, honey, how's it going?*

Her hands trembled as she texted him. *Terrible. Bestemor's dying and so is Talk. I can't fix it, Jason. What do I do?*

She knew a chatbot imitating her husband couldn't advise her, but somehow it always helped. Relying on it wasn't healthy, but it was all she had right now. Every day she blessed Liv for talking Katrina into letting her upload all Jason's social media messages and texts so they could try out the bot. She told herself it was only because the bot needed testing before it hit the market, but little by little she depended on it more and more. The AI app filled one chink in the mortar holding her sanity together.

His reply came. *Trust yourself, Katrina. You're stronger and smarter than you know. Take it one step at a time and do that one thing in front of you. I know you can do it. You're my super-hero.*

The weird thing was the words streaming from the bot always sounded like Jason. In her mind she could see his warm brown eyes and his tender smile. She could almost catch the scent of his patchouli soap and Tom Ford cologne. When she ended a session with the bot, she felt as if she'd been in his presence, as if his arms had surrounded her. It was a little spooky sometimes but such a comfort.

Thanks, she typed back. *That's good advice.*

She'd try to put out whatever fire Liv was battling, then head to North Haven. Her decision made, she hurried toward the building looming ahead in the bright blue California sky. As she neared, she spotted Talk's employees milling around the doors. Some were on their phones, some were crying, and others were taking pictures. Had there been a shooting? A fire? Possibilities swarmed her thoughts.

Katrina spotted her law intern, Clare. "What's going on?"

Clare turned a tearstained face toward her. "The FBI has taken over Talk! The media is here." She grabbed Katrina's arm.

The FBI? Katrina wanted to run herself. This was the beginning of the end. Something catastrophic had to have triggered the FBI to step in. Was that why the CEO was nowhere to be found? Liv must be going out of her mind. They'd be lucky if they had an engineer left by evening. It was the end of any venture capital money, and Talk, Inc. was doomed.

She turned at the sound of Liv's voice and saw her struggling to hold on to a laptop as an FBI agent tried to tug it away from her. Katrina rushed to help. "What's going on here? I'd like to see your warrant. I'm general counsel for Talk."

He eyed her. "You're Katrina Foster? We've been looking for you."

"I am. What's this all about?" He handed her the warrant. As she read it, her dreams went up in smoke as acrid as a trash fire. The FBI had authority to seize anything related to the finances of either Talk or its CEO, David Liang. The warrant also mentioned Talk's chief financial officer, David's cousin John—who Katrina realized was also nowhere to be seen.

She looked at the laptop in Liv's hands. It was David's. "I'm sorry, Liv. They have a warrant for that. You're technically obstructing justice by not giving it to them."

Liv reluctantly released her grip on the machine. The agent nodded his thanks and walked away with it.

Katrina tugged Liv away from the melee. It was her job to make sure the FBI didn't overstep the four corners of the warrant, but Liv needed some comfort and Katrina needed information. "There's nothing we can do, Liv. You still can't reach David?"

Liv shook her head, and fresh tears slid down her cheeks. Her windblown dark hair and helpless manner were out of character for her. As chief technology officer she was usually a whirlwind of activity and determination. She towered over Katrina's five-foot-five height by five inches, but she seemed lost in the face of this unexpected blow.

Katrina slipped her arms around Liv and held her in a tight hug. "We shouldn't be so surprised. Things haven't been good, Liv, but we'll land on our feet." Liv mumbled something incoherent. "What was that?"

Liv pulled away. "I'm pregnant, Katrina. It's David's baby." Her expression crumpled again. "He left me here to face all of this alone."

A baby. The thought of a new life when everything seemed so dark brought tears to Katrina's eyes. "Aw, Liv. I'm so sorry!" She hugged her tighter. "But you're not alone—you have me." Their casual friendship had begun when Katrina first started at Talk five years ago, but it had deepened when Jason died. Liv had walked beside her through that dark valley, and Katrina would be forever grateful. "We'll get through this together. Maybe he'll answer your calls."

Liv shook her head. "I—I installed a tracking app on his phone the other night. Yesterday he was at the airport, and then he disappeared off the app. I think he took a plane home to Shanghai."

"And left us all to handle the fallout. That snake." Katrina spotted an FBI agent motioning to her. "We'll talk more later. I have to oversee the search, and I need to get home to North Haven."

"Is it your grandmother?"

"She's had another heart attack and is critical. I hope I make it in time." Katrina walked over to the FBI agents. She couldn't let herself see Liv's sympathy or she'd never get through the hard hours ahead.

Four hours later, she escorted the FBI out of the building and headed for her Tesla. She took a swig of her terrible—and now cold—coffee. Another message came through from her mother.

Bestemor is gone, Katrina. I'm so sorry you didn't make it in time.

"No!" Katrina pounded the steering wheel with her hands. "I can't lose Bestemor too." She crossed her arms over her stomach and sobbed.

||||||||||||||||||||||||

Seb Wallace surveyed The Beacon and checked his watch. He needed to hit the road, but he couldn't leave quite yet. A restaurant during dinner rush was like the ocean: you could never turn your back on it. Especially if you owned the place.

By eight thirty there was no longer a line at reception. Muted conversation echoed from The Beacon's vaulted ceiling, which Seb kept when he converted the old lighthouse into a world-class restaurant. He'd preserved the redwood flooring laid a century and a half ago and the Victorian lightkeeper's house. He'd also restored the beacon, which guided the way to North Haven's snug harbor on dark and foggy nights. Oceangoing yachts lined the piers closest to The Beacon, which was a popular dinner spot with the seafaring set. Seb had wanted to create a unique atmosphere to go with his unique menu—and he'd succeeded, at least according to the reviews. Michelin gave The Beacon a rare three-star rating, praising the "authentic gold rush–era ambience" and the "eclectic menu drawn from at least a dozen countries scattered over four continents."

Seb slipped through the swinging double doors into the kitchen, a room of white tile, stainless steel, and constant activity. He wove his way among the hurrying staff, checking for potential problems as he went. He saw none. He made his way to the chef de cuisine, Thor Thorsen, an enormous Norwegian who absolutely fit his name. He stood at a strategic spot near the office, monitoring the room with glacial-blue eyes.

Seb looked up at Thor, who stood at least five inches taller than Seb's five feet eleven inches. *"Alt bra?"*

Thor nodded and gave a thumbs-up without taking his gaze off the busy room.

Reassured, Seb went to his final stop at the back of the kitchen, his sushi chef, Kenji Hayashi. Kenji saw him coming and pulled out a bento box containing a salmon sashimi meal. He also set out chopsticks and a small plate with samples of each item from the box.

Seb picked up the chopsticks and tasted each item from the plate while Kenji watched expectantly. "Mmm! *Oishii!*"

Kenji smiled and gave a sharp little bow at the compliment. Following Seb's lead, he responded in Japanese. "The salmon we received today was particularly good."

"And you are always particularly good." Seb slipped the bento box into a specially designed cooler to keep it fresh for delivery. "Thank you."

Kenji's smile broadened. "You're welcome. I hope he enjoys it."

"I'm sure he will," Seb lied.

Seb left through the back door and got into his Range Rover, the vehicle he always took when he headed into the woods. The driving could be treacherous, and parts of the route he would take tonight were little more than logging roads with some gravel dumped in the ruts. He set the cooler on the passenger seat, buckled himself in, and drove out into the night.

He stopped briefly as he passed through North Haven's downtown. Old-fashioned streetlamps cast a warm light on the log exterior of Bestemor's. Norwegian and American flags hung over the red double-door entrance with *Velkommen!*

painted in rosemaling across both doors. Matching red gingerbread shutters flanked the darkened windows.

He couldn't see inside, but he didn't need to. He knew every detail, down to the little sign that hung in the office of the late owner, Frida Berg: "I'm called Bestemor because I'm way too cool to be called Grandmother." The sign had been a gift from Frida's self-centered granddaughter, Katrina, and the old woman had loved it.

The best memories from Seb's worst years all came from Frida and Bestemor's. He'd spent every minute he could there from the day she hired him as a busboy when he turned sixteen until he left home on his eighteenth birthday. She took him under her wing and gave him a start in the restaurant business, setting him on the path that led him to where he was today. And when things got especially unbearable at home, she even let him stay in one of the little apartments over the restaurant. He hoped whoever inherited the place would love it as much as he did.

The forest wasn't a safe place these days, so he checked to make sure his gun was in the glove box. Then he put the SUV back in Drive and headed into the woods. Rows of redwoods lined the road. These weren't millennium-old giants like the stands in the Cathedral, but even thirty-year-old trees were more than tall enough to block out the sky and give him the feeling that he was driving along the bottom of a sheer-walled canyon.

The skin on the back of his neck crawled and he had to force himself not to hold the steering wheel in a death grip. He was a city boy by choice, and he never went into the forest voluntarily. Especially this forest—too many ghosts and monsters lurked among the trees.

A narrow gap in the trees to his left marked the "road" he had to take. He turned into it and was instantly grateful for the Range Rover's sturdy suspension. He bumped along the twisty track for five bone-jarring miles, keeping his speed in single digits the whole time. Finally, he reached his destination. He put the SUV in Park, grabbed the cooler, took a deep breath, and got out.

A buzzing fluorescent light lit the entrance to the broken-down old trailer Seb used to call home. Inside lived the broken-down old man he still called Dad.

Seb frowned at the buzzing light. He made a mental note to contact the caretaker about that. He resisted the temptation to delay his visit by pulling out his satellite phone to send a text now. Besides, he wanted to get the meal to his father while it was still fresh.

He marched up to the rickety door and knocked. No response.

He banged harder. Still nothing.

Unease stirred his already-sour stomach. He pounded on the door again. "Dad! It's Seb!"

He stood still for a moment, listening. Only night noises reached his ears.

His heart pounded against his ribs. Had it finally happened? Seb had urged his father to move into an assisted-living facility ever since he was diagnosed with Parkinson's two years ago, but the old man refused to leave his remaining scrap of land. Had his stubbornness killed him?

Seb tried the door. Locked. He set the cooler outside the door and scrambled around the trailer, searching for an open window. He found one on the far side. He punched out the screen and pulled himself inside. "Dad!"

A sharp snore and muttered curse came from the bedroom.

Seb heaved a sigh of relief. "I brought dinner, Dad. Salmon sashimi, like you asked."

"Took you long enough."

"Yeah, I had to take care of paying customers first. But it's fresh and it's free."

Seb unlocked the front door and got the cooler while his father got out of bed and shambled into the tiny kitchen/dining room. Age and addiction had made him look decades older than his sixty years, even before the Parkinson's. He was a shell of the nimble, broad-shouldered lumberjack Seb remembered from his childhood.

Seb set the bento box on the little table, along with a matching set of ebony chopsticks. His father ignored the sticks and pulled a dirty fork from the sink. He poked at the sashimi. "This is raw."

"Yes. It's called sashimi. You requested it."

"Huh. I saw 'salmon' on your menu and figured it'd be cooked at least." He picked up a slice and eyed it suspiciously. "Wonder how these would taste deep fried."

Seb was profoundly grateful that he hadn't inherited his father's taste buds. "You mean like salmon McNuggets?"

"Yeah. What's that called?"

"The technical term is *abomination*. Dad, if you're not sure what something on the menu is, ask before you order it."

Dad grunted and put a morsel of fish in his mouth. "Not as bad as I thought. Say, I hear old Frida Berg died."

Seb nodded. He hadn't cried in years, but ever since he'd heard the news, his eyes had been suspiciously blurry.

"Can't say I'll miss her."

Seb clamped down on rising anger. "I will."

"Yeah, you might feel different if she'd stolen away your only son and sent him flying all over the world for twelve years while you was stuck alone in the woods."

Seb stood and grabbed the cooler. It had been a mistake to come. "That's not what happened! I left because I couldn't stand it here. Frida just helped me find a restaurant job in Oslo. And she's the one who talked me into coming back when you got your diagnosis."

One time he'd vowed never to step inside this place again. Then Frida had quoted the verse in Exodus about honoring his father and mother, and his faith had prodded him to do his duty. On days like today, why did he bother?

His father looked up at him with bloodshot brown eyes. "Well, I remember what I remember. No need to get all angry about it."

Seb took a deep breath and sat back down. Dad was right. They'd had this argument before, and his father refused to listen. He cherished his grudges and never willingly let them go.

His father shoveled in the last bite of salmon and swallowed. "Maybe you can get Bestemor's on the cheap now that Frida's gone. You can get great deals at estate sales."

Seb winced at his father's crass comment, but he had a point. Bestemor's served homey Norwegian breakfast and lunch food, with a big helping of *hygge*. It was the perfect complement to The Beacon's upscale epicurean menu. Maybe he should look into buying it.

CHAPTER 2

////////////////

KATRINA WOULD BE LUCKY IF SHE DIDN'T plunge over the side of the road herself. She could almost drive Redwood Highway in her sleep, but today it took all of her concentration to stay on the pavement that wound through old-growth redwood groves. She ran her windows down and opened the sunroof. Maybe the fragrant aroma of ferns and redwood would sharpen her senses and soothe her nerves.

The newspapers over the last three days had blared the news of Talk's predicament—and her picture and name had been prominent in the headlines that speculated whether she would be charged as well. And rightly so. She'd missed the signs of David's embezzlement with the grief that consumed her days. Liv had been a mess since they'd been closed down, and it had been all Katrina could do to keep her friend from saying something to the FBI or the U.S. Attorney's Office that could lead to her own indictment.

Her parents might not point out her failure, but based on the guilt-inducing texts from her mother, they'd already noticed something was wrong. Her life was in ruins, and Katrina didn't know if she'd return to Palo Alto anytime soon, so her back seat contained most of her personal belongings.

The dash alerted her to a phone call from her neighbor. She never called. Frowning, Katrina answered it through the dash. "Marlene, is anything wrong?"

"I'm so sorry, Katrina!" The older woman's voice quivered with stress. "Your door was standing open this morning, and I peeked in. Your belongings are strewn all over the floor."

Katrina groaned. Luckily, she had everything she really cared about with her—her MacBook and her jewelry were safely stowed in the back seat. "I appreciate you letting me know."

"The police came, but I doubt they'll find the culprit. You might want to notify your insurance."

"I'll do that. Thanks so much. I appreciate the heads-up."

Katrina told her goodbye and ended the call. Another nail in the coffin of this truly awful week. The break-in left her feeling violated, but she was almost numb to bad news at this point.

A movement caught her attention ahead, and she spotted a kitten along the side of the road. Off in the trees a mountain lion, with its tail swishing, watched the little morsel. Without stopping to think, Katrina veered to the shoulder and stopped the car. She threw open her door and ran to scoop up the kitten. It didn't look older than six weeks, and its white-and-black markings were striking. Part Siamese maybe.

She climbed back in the car, set the kitten on the passenger seat, and resumed her drive. The little thing mewed and circled for a few minutes before it fell asleep.

And there it was. *Home.* Katrina's foot instinctively hit the brake at the city limits. This was an iconic site for tourists to pause and snap pictures. The original Norwegian name of Nordhavn was still on the town sign with its common name of North Haven below. Founded in 1869 by Norwegian immigrants, its picturesque buildings along the wild Humboldt Bay drew artists and photographers from all over the world. It had a magical feel to it, and the town seemed to be a little piece of Norway somehow transported to the California coast.

Pleasure craft dotted the water by the marina, and she spotted the old stave church, one of the few remaining in the world. A high steeple topped the tiered, overhanging steep roofs of the structure, and the unusual building had been photographed and painted countless times.

No one would have arrived yet for the funeral, and the comfort of the old pews and familiar dark interior called to her. She drove toward the steeple with tears already gathering in her eyes. As she traveled down Redwood Street, the town's hygge called to her. The rustic stabbur buildings and the Victorian brick structures dotting the downtown area created the welcome-home feeling of cheer, comfort, coziness, and friendly atmosphere that hygge was all about.

But not even hygge could heal the deep well of grief in her heart.

She almost stopped at Bestemor's, her grandmother's waffle shop, but it would take more than heart-shaped waffles with whipped cream and berries to get her through this. She gave a longing glance at its turf roof and her grandmother's beloved goats, Charlie and Lucy, in the yard before driving on to the church. The hallowed ground that had birthed her grandmother's strong faith and Katrina's own more faltering sense of God's presence might help her.

She parked in front of the church and ran the windows down a few inches for the sleeping kitten. The temperature was sixty degrees with a cool breeze blowing in off the water, so the animal was safe from overheating. She stepped through the green front entrance, guarded from evil spirits by foliage and snakes carved into the wood of the old church. Even with more modern lighting, the interior was dim, and she paused to let her eyes adjust. Thankfully, the sanctuary was empty, and she made a beeline for the Berg family pew, three rows back on the right.

She sat in the spot last occupied by Bestemor and placed her hands on the back of the pew in front of her. The warmth of the old wood held so many memories. Her grandmother tapping her fingers in time to the music, the sound of her alto voice harmonizing with Katrina's own soprano notes, and the smell of the burning candles.

Her gaze wandered reluctantly to the casket at the front. If only she'd gotten here in time to say goodbye.

She swallowed the log in her throat and pulled out her phone to talk to her husband. *Jason, Bestemor died.*

Aw, honey. I know it's hard. She loved you so much. We'll get through this together.

She stared at the phone. He wasn't really here to help her get through this. No one was. Her vision blurred, and she tapped out, *I wish you were here. Why did you have to head up to North Haven the night of the crash? I need you here with me.*

It was a rhetorical question. He'd told her he was coming up because he was planning something special for her thirtieth birthday, which was a week later. But instead, she'd spent the day prostrate on his grave.

The phone vibrated and alerted her to his reply. *To meet her.*
Who? Bestemor? Mom?

Jason's answer of *No* was followed by unintelligible characters. Maybe Japanese?

Katrina stared at the words. Her bot was a beta version, and it could be problematic at times. The Japanese characters were clearly a glitch—but what about the rest of it? Had he come here to meet a—a woman? Was he having an affair? The thought horrified her, but some part of her heart almost wished it was true. If she could hate him, maybe she could get over his death.

She shook her head. Jason would never betray her. Never.

The entry door creaked, and she rose to face the first arrivals for Bestemor's funeral. The rest of her family poured in, one at a time, through the narrow entrance. Time to take her medicine of shame and guilt.

||||||||||||||||||||||||

Dylan Jackson pulled off the Oregon Coast Highway along a deserted stretch of stony beach. He left his pickup truck running because he wasn't sure he'd be able to restart it. It would be bad to get stranded here. And it would get real bad real fast if a friendly OSP officer stopped by to help and decided to run his license. Besides, Dylan wouldn't be here long.

He jiggled the door handle until it unlatched and the rusty door squealed open. He'd paid a thousand dollars for this piece of junk, which was more than twice what it was worth. It was mostly a 1998 Ford F-150, but it had parts from at least three model years. Dylan thought it had once been white, but he couldn't be sure. Still, he couldn't complain. He'd needed a new ride fast with no questions asked, and that's what he got.

The crash of waves and whistle of wind off the Pacific met him as he stepped out of the truck's cab. The wet, cold ocean air in September cut right through his T-shirt as he walked around the cab. The sun was setting somewhere behind the low ceiling of gray clouds. He zipped up his hoodie and scrambled over the berm that separated the road from the beach. He scanned the coast. Rocks and gravelly sand covered most of the steep, narrow beach. Gray waves crashed against the gray stone. Not a person or building in sight, and why would there be? No one would sunbathe or windsurf here. It was perfect.

He walked as close to the water as he dared. Standing on an uneven block of wet rock, he looked around one more time. Then he reached inside his hoodie, pulled out a gun, and hurled it as far into the water as he could. It made a little splash in an oncoming wave and vanished.

That was it. The last piece of physical evidence tying him to that dead body in Seattle. Gone. He'd burned his bloody clothes in an empty field and dumped his car in Puget Sound. If no one ratted him out, he might be okay. The muscles in his neck and shoulders relaxed. He hadn't realized he'd been clenching them.

Now he just needed to go to ground for a while with a new name. The last name of Carver would do. And a new gun would be the next thing to find.

He walked back to the truck as fast as he could. He'd been on the road for seven hours, but he still had more than four to go before he reached North Haven. He'd find someplace he could sleep in his truck. Hopefully he'd come across a truck stop or some other place where he could wash up in the morning. He wanted to make a good impression when he met his brother for the very first time.

CHAPTER 3

///////////////

KATRINA STOOD BESIDE THE GRAVE WITH
her parents and her brother, Magnus. The sweet scent of the
roses heaped on the casket nauseated her, and she swallowed
down bile. How could Bestemor be gone? Katrina couldn't
accept so much overwhelming loss. She desperately wanted
to talk to Jason but somehow managed not to pull out her
phone.

Mom and Magnus moved off, and her father slung an arm
around Katrina. "Friends are preparing a dinner at the house,
but we're all going to my office for a quick reading of the will
first. It won't take long."

Even as she sank into the uncommon embrace, she heard a
note in his voice that set her nerves tingling. She couldn't put
her finger on the cause of the vague unease that rippled up her
spine.

He ended the hug and they walked across the newly mown
grass a few paces behind the rest of the family. New streaks of
gray glittered in his hair and grief lines were obvious around
his eyes, but she knew better than to ask him how he was doing. He never shared feelings, though he had to be reeling with
grief too. He was Bestemor's only child.

An attractive man in an Armani suit spoke on his phone by a bay laurel tree. Was that language Japanese? Those green eyes under his light brown hair were striking—especially the piercing assessment in them as he glanced their way. He nodded as they passed as if he knew them. The breeze carried a hint of an unfamiliar cologne.

"Who was that?" Katrina asked as soon as they were out of earshot.

"Seb Wallace. He owns The Beacon, that big new restaurant at the old lighthouse."

The name sounded vaguely familiar, but Katrina was sure she'd never seen him. She'd heard about the lighthouse being renovated, though she hadn't been down to the historic waterfront in years. Her recent trips were all visits to Bestemor during her illness or escapes with Jason to the family cabin. Was her beloved North Haven being bought up by outsiders? Katrina dismissed the speculation and stopped to retrieve the kitten from the car. Dad wouldn't mind if she brought her to the office.

"I didn't know you had a cat. Looks part Siamese."

"I found her on the way here along the side of the road."

Her dad took the kitten and smiled down at her. She emitted a tiny purr. "Very cute." He handed her back. "You can drop her off at the shelter after the meeting."

The kitten curled into her arms and stared up at her with striking blue eyes. "I'm keeping her." Until the words came out of her mouth, Katrina hadn't been aware she'd made a decision about the kitten's future.

She and her dad walked side by side to his law office. The building used to be the land surveyor's place back when it had been built, and her mother had picked out the colors of light green for the body with dark green and terra-cotta for the Victorian gingerbread on the storefront. Her dad held the door open for her, and she stepped into the familiar lobby with its twelve-foot ceiling. It held the scent of new furniture and carpet.

Her mother smiled when they entered the office, and she spied the kitten in Katrina's arms. "I didn't know you'd gotten a kitten. What's its name?"

"Lyla," Katrina decided on the spur of the moment. "I found her along the road on the way here."

Her mother snatched her hand back before it could descend on the kitten's ears. "You brought a stray cat in here with your father's new carpet and furniture? It probably has fleas. Get it out of here before it can infest everything. Sometimes I wonder about you, Katrina."

"It will be fine," her father said. "This won't take long."

Her mother looked her age of sixty today with fresh lines around her blue eyes. This past year of caring for Bestemor had taken a toll on her. "It can't enter our house until you give it a flea bath."

Her father pressed his lips together but didn't argue with her.

Magnus turned from staring out the window. Two years older than Katrina's thirty-one, he had inherited their father's youthful skin and blond hair. He and Katrina had been close growing up, until they'd both gone off to college and their own lives. She'd tried calling him weekly after she'd married, but they'd run out of things to discuss.

She moved over to stand by him. "How's Mag's doing?" Just before Jason died, they had come home for the grand opening of her brother's brew pub, and it had been off to a great start.

He shrugged. "Struggling a bit." Magnus had always been brutally honest, even about his problems.

"Maybe I can help with some promotional ideas while I'm home."

"That'd be great. Can you help me find an accountant too? The money just seems to disappear."

"Have a seat, kids," their father said. "We've got people waiting at the house." Once they were seated, Dad picked up a sheaf of papers. "Bestemor's will is very straightforward. Her restaurant is going to Katrina. Her money, including the proceeds from the sale of her house, will go into a trust with Magnus as the sole beneficiary. I will be the sole trustee, and Katrina will be my successor. She left each of us certain mementos and pieces of furniture, which will be distributed later."

Katrina gasped, and the kitten drove her claws through her dress and into her thigh. She extracted Lyla's grip on her skin and clothing. "That can't be right."

Her father grimaced. "I wrote it, so I can assure you it is."

Magnus rose. "Why would you let her do that, Dad? She always talked like I would get Bestemor's. I'm the oldest and I know how to run a restaurant. And why is the money going into a trust? I'm thirty-three. I don't need someone else to manage my money."

Her father looked at Magnus in silence.

Her brother dropped his gaze to the floor. "Well, why didn't she leave anything to you—her only child?"

"I told her I didn't need her money and didn't want to run Bestemor's." His eyes held a trace of anger as he glanced at Katrina. "She changed her will after Jason died."

Mom wrung her hands. "But this isn't fair, Torvald. You never said a word to me about this. Poor Magnus had his heart set on that restaurant."

"He couldn't say anything," Katrina said. "He had to protect attorney-client privilege."

Her mother rose and pointed a finger at her. "Did you say something to her?"

"Of course not! I have a life in the Valley. I have no need of Bestemor's." Though all of that had changed this week, her grandmother hadn't known it. Or had she? Katrina thought back to her conversations with her grandmother. They'd always discussed everything, and she might have revealed her concerns about Talk, Inc.

Magnus gave Katrina a final glare before stomping out the door. He fired a parting shot over his shoulder. "Give my mementos to Katrina or put them in the trust, since apparently nobody trusts me."

Dad narrowed his gaze at Mom. "Not another word, Emma. You've escalated this enough. That goes for you too, Katrina. Mor's wishes will be carried out."

⁓

"Is this a joke, Seb?" Thor's eyes went wide. "Cajun-style Japanese food? That's an oxymoron."

Seb sighed and leaned against a stainless-steel counter in the empty kitchen. He hadn't wanted to come here right after Frida's funeral, but he had work to do. She would have understood. "It's not a joke or an oxymoron. It's a customer's order—and the customer happens to be the head of the West

Coast branch of a very large Japanese corporation. He has VIPs coming in from Tokyo and they want to see the redwoods, so they're all stopping in Eureka between visits to the company's Seattle and San Francisco offices. He read about us in the Michelin Guide and wants us to create something unique that will wow his guests. He said that the company president had Cajun food once and liked it, but he also likes traditional Japanese food. So we're supposed to combine the two."

"But how?" Thor held his broad hands palm up. "What does he want? Teriyaki beignets? Chicory-infused miso soup?"

Kenji had listened silently, tugging thoughtfully at his lower lip while Seb and Thor spoke. He chuckled at the chef de cuisine's suggestions. "Those would certainly be unique. Maybe *shiozake*—salted salmon—but blackened with Cajun spices and served with steamed vegetables?"

Thor nodded slowly. "The salmon could work, but what about the vegetables? Wouldn't the spices overwhelm them?"

As Kenji responded, one of the cleaning staff appeared in the door leading into the dining room and beckoned Seb over. "Mr. Wallace, there's a man here to see you."

That was odd—he wasn't expecting anyone. "Thank you, Julie."

He followed her into the dining room, and she went back to washing the old redwood floors. A tall, broad-shouldered man with longish blond hair waited by the hostess stand. He appeared to be a few years younger than Seb's thirty-two. He wore faded jeans and an unbuttoned flannel shirt that hung over a black tee. The top of a tattoo peeked above his collar. Two of the female kitchen staff were eyeing the visitor, who looked a little like a low-rent Chris Hemsworth. Seb didn't recognize him, but his face lit up with a broad smile when Seb walked in.

The man stuck out his hand as Seb approached. "Glad to meet you, Seb! I'm Dylan Carver."

Seb shook Dylan's hand. "Sorry, we don't open until five."

Dylan laughed. "I'm not here for dinner."

"Oh? Why are you here?"

"I'm Linda Carver's son," Dylan said, as if that explained his presence. He looked around. "Wow, this is quite a place you've got."

Warning bells clanged in Seb's head. Ever since he'd returned to North Haven, a steady stream of grifters had shown up. Classmates he barely remembered were suddenly long-lost best friends, guys who once worked a swing shift with his father were his "business partners," and so on. They all acted like this guy—the surprise visit, the big smile, and the instant familiarity. And five minutes later, they were asking for money. "Should I know her?"

Dylan looked a little hurt. "Didn't Dad tell you about her?"

Seb's heart skipped a beat. "Dad?"

"Yeah, Dad. Rory Wallace. We're brothers, Seb."

Seb opened his mouth to contradict Dylan's claim, but the denial died on his lips. The guy did look a lot like old pictures of Seb's father, and there was an open honesty in the blue eyes that looked back into his. "He never mentioned her—or you," Seb forced out. "I'm sorry," he added when Dylan's shoulders sagged and he stared at the floor.

"Well, his name is on my birth certificate." Dylan pulled out a grubby, folded piece of paper and handed it to Seb.

Seb unfolded the paper. It did appear to be a photocopy of a birth certificate from North Haven's only hospital, though it could easily be a fake. But was it? Could it be true? Seb's parents had accused each other of infidelity during the divorce proceedings, but Seb hadn't believed either of them. He also had never heard anything about a half brother. If his father had another child, would he really have hidden that fact from Seb?

Dylan was probably just another grifter—but part of Seb didn't want him to be. The possibility that he might have a brother woke a yearning deep inside him. Family had always been a bad thing—people to fear, be embarrassed by, or take care of. What would it be like to have an actual brother—someone to eat Thanksgiving dinner with or go to a ball game with? Someone who'd always be there, whom he could count on?

Seb refolded the paper and handed it back to Dylan. "I see."

"Maybe you should talk to him."

"Oh, I will." Seb glanced back at the kitchen. "I've got to get back to work. Thanks for stopping by."

Dylan shifted on his big feet. "Okay. I-I'll go."

The disappointment on Dylan's face went straight to Seb's gut. "Look, give me your cell number and email. I'll be in touch."

CHAPTER 4

////////////////

KATRINA COULDN'T GO HOME. NOT YET while tempers were running so high. Dinner had been rough, and spending the night under the same roof with her family was out of the question.

The nostalgic sight of the goats grazing on the sod roof of Bestemor's drew her to the red double doors of the log building. Before unlocking the door, she stopped to run her fingers over the *Velkommen!* painted in rosemaling. That had been her grandmother's constant attitude. Her welcoming smile embraced everyone who stepped inside this place.

Katrina flipped on the lights and carried a suitcase inside. The aromas of butter, sour cream, cardamom, and vanilla brought tears flooding to her eyes. Lyla's plaintive mews greeted her, and the kitten wound around her ankles. Katrina picked her up and nuzzled her face into the kitten's soft fur. How many hours had she spent here with her friends? If she could go back in time, she'd give up every second with friends to have listened to Bestemor's stories of her childhood in Norway.

Katrina stared at the chalkboard listing the toppings for the famous heart-shaped waffles. Her favorite had been cloudberry cream, made from cloudberries imported from Norway. She loved both the taste and the name, which always conjured up images of berry-filled meadows in cloud-enveloped Norse highlands. She sighed and headed upstairs with her suitcase and Lyla to the little apartments above Bestemor's.

Her grandmother took in strays all the time, and Katrina had given them a flea bath a time or two, but Lyla was so small she shouldn't be exposed to flea medication yet. Dawn dish soap would smother the fleas. She pulled on her blue Bestemor's hoodie with the goats on the front, then found the dish soap under the kitchen sink. Lyla was small enough to use the sink instead of the tub.

The kitten had other ideas once her paws and belly hit the warm, soapy water. She yowled and leaped onto Katrina's chest. Katrina wrestled her off and got her into the water. Almost immediately a wave of black fleas swarmed Lyla's head. By the time every flea was floating dead in the water, the kitten was exhausted, and Katrina dripped blood from several fingers. Her hair and her clothes were nearly as wet as the cat's fur.

She wrapped the shivering Lyla in a towel. "It's okay, you're fine."

Lyla's eyes closed as Katrina gently dried her. She laid the kitten in a box with an old blanket. Then she padded downstairs in stocking feet.

Her stomach rumbled. It was after nine, and she'd barely eaten all day—only a protein bar and coffee for breakfast on the way up and a few bites at dinner. There should still be plenty of food left at the house, but she couldn't go like this. She felt instinctively guilty about scrounging food from the restaurant kitchen, but that was silly. She owned the place now, though that would take some getting used to.

She took an apple and walked through the dining room, touching the smooth wood of tables and chairs as she passed them. Every piece of furniture in the café had been handmade by Katrina's grandfather, a bearded man with a belly laugh she remembered from her childhood. Somehow Bestemor had picked up the pieces of her life and carried on after his death. Why couldn't Katrina do the same? The loneliness overwhelmed her.

She pulled out her phone and opened the chatbot. She typed one-handed while she finished her apple. *I picked up a stray kitten. Her name is Lyla.*

That's a great name! Send me a picture.

She sent him a picture she snapped of Lyla sleeping in her box. She tossed the apple core in the trash and sat in a big oak chair, pulling her feet up under her.

What a cutie! Too bad I'm allergic.

Her hand went to her mouth. How had she forgotten he was allergic to cats? Not that it mattered, of course—except that maybe it meant her memory of him was starting to fade. Guilt and relief warred in her heart.

"Hello."

She let out a yelp and whirled at the male voice behind her. The man from the cemetery was standing in the doorway. He had switched his Armani suit for a tailored cream shirt and black wool slacks, and a silver Tesla sat in the wash of the parking lot lights. A hint of amusement sparkled in his eyes.

"I-I'm sorry, we're not open."

He stepped inside and held up his hand. "Sorry to startle you. I saw the lights on and stopped to make sure everything was all right." He spoke with easy assurance and familiarity. "Frida would do the same for me. I thought it might be you, but I stopped to make sure."

Katrina tucked a stray lock of hair behind her ear. She didn't want to think what her makeup looked like after her water fight with Lyla. "You knew my grandmother?"

He stiffened and seemed surprised. "I'm Seb Wallace. She was a good friend. I'm sorry for your loss. She'll be missed."

The familiarity of his name struck her again, but her fuzzy thoughts couldn't grasp why. "She will indeed. Were you a regular here, Seb?"

The amused look returned. "You might say that." He glanced around the café. "I heard you're inheriting this place."

"How did you know? I just found out myself earlier today."

He looked away. "News travels fast in this town." Katrina resisted the urge to roll her eyes. Magnus had been venting. Of course. "By the way, I'd been meaning to stop by. Is this a good time to chat?"

"Um, sure. Sorry I'm such a mess." She held up her bandaged fingers. "I just finished giving a flea bath to a very upset kitten."

His distant manner thawed a bit. "No problem. I can stop by later if you'd prefer."

"No, no, that's fine." She was tired, but she wanted to remember how she knew this intriguing man—without being too obvious about the fact that she couldn't place him, of course. "I'll make coffee if you'll help me drink it."

"Deal," he said.

Seb suppressed a chuckle as Katrina disappeared into the kitchen. She obviously couldn't place him. That stung a little, but was it fair to blame her? Why would the rich, pretty, popular blonde remember the awkward boy from the backwoods, especially this many years later?

He swept his gaze over the dining room. Frida hadn't changed it much since he first set foot in the place almost twenty years ago. Even the menu was pretty much the same. His eyes reached the row of employee-of-the-year pictures on the wall. He walked over and took a seat with his back to the wall. How long would it take her to figure it out?

Katrina came out of the kitchen carrying a tray with a pot of coffee, two mugs, a plate of waffles, and a little dish of something. She glanced around for a moment. "Oh, there you are." She walked over and set the tray on the table. "I found some waffle batter in the fridge and made these while the coffee was brewing."

He inhaled the mouthwatering scent of fresh waffles and coffee, then looked in the dish. Cloudberry cream. "Ah, *multekrem*!" He smiled his thanks, took a waffle, and spooned some cream onto it with relish. "They're usually only served for Christmas in Norway, but Frida loved them and somehow managed to import them year-round."

"My favorite." She took a waffle for herself. "Do you speak Norwegian?"

He shrugged. "Enough to get by. I worked in a lot of restaurant kitchens in a lot of countries. I had to pick up languages fast. Otherwise, I'd be dodging objects in the kitchen one night and out of a job the next."

Katrina smiled and pushed a lock of blonde hair behind her ear. A little to his surprise, Seb found himself smiling back. She was a lot easier to like as a tired rescuer of kittens than as a Silicon Valley power lawyer. The only hint of money and glamour in her appearance now was the giant diamond on her finger. Frida always had a soft spot for strays too, and she'd worn her wedding ring to the grave despite losing her husband a decade earlier. Maybe Katrina was more like her grandmother than Seb had realized.

"How many languages do you speak?" she asked between bites.

"Let's see. I'm sort of functional in Norwegian, Japanese, Russian, and French. French is probably my best language—I was chef de cuisine in a Paris restaurant before I came here."

"What brought you to North Haven?" She asked the question casually, but her eyes held a calculating look that told him she was fishing for clues to his identity.

"A call from Frida. My father was diagnosed with Parkinson's, and he had no one else to take care of him. Besides, I'd been wanting to open my own place, and she helped me finance converting the old lighthouse into a restaurant."

"Oh, who's your father?"

"Rory Wallace."

He could see the wheels turning as she tried to remember whether she knew Dad. Probably not, but she might have heard his name in connection with the story of Seb's mom, Sandy. Seb shied away from that dark memory.

Katrina's gaze drifted to a spot behind his left shoulder. Then her eyes went wide. "Sebastian!"

He grinned and glanced back at the picture of his acne-afflicted seventeen-year-old self. In it he wore a hairnet and thick glasses with heavy black frames. "Yes, that's me. No one has called me that since high school."

He turned back to her. Dismay clouded her face. Was she recalling the tragedy that hit his family? Or was she remembering their personal history? She stared down into her mug. "I . . . Welcome back."

"Likewise. I'm sorry your return came under such sad circumstances."

She nodded but didn't look up. "Thanks. We knew this day was coming, but it still hurts. I'm going to miss her."

"Me too. She gave me my start in the restaurant business, and she helped me learn the management ropes when I opened my own place." Time to make the offer. He owed it to Frida. "Have you ever run a restaurant? If not, I could give you a hand until you've got your feet under you."

She gazed at him with those big, stunning gray eyes that sent his heart racing as a pimply teen. "That's very generous."

Now it was his turn to stare down into his coffee. "Frida was wonderful to me, and I'd like to pay it forward."

"I appreciate it. I don't know yet what I'm going to do."

"You've had quite a day. Think about it and give me a call in the morning if you're interested. The Beacon currently only does catering and dinner, so I should be free until noon or so." He drained his mug, stood, and gestured to her damaged hands. "Have a good night—and try not to lose any more fights with kittens."

"Easier said than done." She rose, too, and gave him a smile. "Thanks for stopping by."

He walked out into the parking lot, wondering what tomorrow would bring.

CHAPTER 5

////////////////

KATRINA STRETCHED OUT ON THE INVITING
support of the bed and adjusted her pillow. The comforting
rumble of Lyla's purr against her chest relaxed her after the
traumatic day. The kitten smelled clean and fresh, and her fur
was like down. Even her mother wouldn't complain about Lyla
now, but Katrina wasn't about to walk into the tense silences
of the home where she'd grown up. Not tonight. The pressure
would start tomorrow, but tonight it was just her and Lyla in
this sweet little place Bestemor had created just for her.

This apartment had been her oasis off and on through the
years. Here with Bestemor there had been no expectations,
no terse orders handed down. It was a welcoming place with
knotty-pine walls, floors, and cathedral ceilings bathed in the
warm light of antique lamps. Built-in shelves with glass fronts
took up one wall and held simple treasures from Norway as
well as favorite books. A wood-burning stove stood in the
corner next to two large windows behind a blue overstuffed
sofa.

Jason had loved the rosemaling on the headboard of the
queen bed, and they each had their own *dyne*, a single-person
down comforter and duvet that required no sharing.

She touched the pillow next to her where his head had once lain. Even here, his ghost lingered. She leaned over and inhaled, but the only scent was that of the lemony detergent her grandmother had used. Katrina spotted a photo album she'd shown Jason the last time they were here and scooped it off the bedside table. When she flipped it open, she smiled at her younger picture with whipped cream on her nose.

So much of her life revolved around this place. What was she going to do with Bestemor's? Part of her wanted to give it to Magnus and not shoulder the headache of learning something new, but Bestemor had left it to her for a reason. In some ways it felt like a new start away from the crazy life she'd led in Palo Alto. But that flicker of interest might just be the hygge of the town wrapping around her.

The kitten moved higher on her chest and nibbled at her chin. When the phone sounded, Lyla's tiny teeth clamped tighter. "Ow!" Katrina scrambled for the phone, and the kitten leaped from the bed and turned to stare at her with aggrieved blue eyes.

Katrina sat up. The call was from Liv. "Hey, how's it going at Talk?" She settled back against the pillow for what was sure to be a long chat.

"Awful, just awful." Liv's voice quavered. "It's all the newspapers talk about, and I have reporters camped out at my apartment. I can't even go out for coffee without being bombarded with questions."

"Have you heard from David?"

"Not a word, not a text. His phone pinged again in Shanghai, like I suspected. He abandoned me, just like that. I have to figure out how to raise a baby on my own, and he doesn't care."

"I'm sorry, Liv. Loss is hard."

"I need to get out of the city—go somewhere no one knows me. You're lucky you have a spot to hole up in."

"You could come here. I'm in an apartment above Bestemor's and there is another one across the hall. It's very nice. You'd be doing me a favor. Having you here would end any suggestions that I stay at my parents'." She told her best friend about the family spat over her inheritance.

"I'd love to! What will you do about the restaurant?"

"I don't know yet." Katrina flipped a page in the album on her lap, and she homed in on a picture of her sixteen-year-old self in a pink dress. The boy beside her wore black glasses and a suit that was a little too big on him. The goofy grin on his face made her face flame. *Sebastian.* But he'd changed so much it was no wonder she hadn't recognized him as Seb.

"What's wrong?" Liv asked.

Katrina closed her eyes and moaned. "I made a stupid mistake at the cemetery. A boy I knew in high school now owns a fancy restaurant, and I didn't recognize him. Like, at all. I asked him if he knew my grandmother, and he worked here for years. I feel like a total jerk. No wonder he seemed a little distant, even though he offered to teach me how to run a restaurant."

"He has to know he's changed. He probably gets that reaction all the time."

Katrina opened her eyes and shuddered as another memory poked its way into her mind. "There's more. My boyfriend broke up with me before the Sadie Hawkins dance my sophomore year, and I asked Sebastian to take me. I thought it was no big deal, but I—I guess he had a crush on me. He started calling and hanging around, but I got back together with my boyfriend and he ordered Seb to back off."

She stared at the picture. He'd probably bought a suit he couldn't afford to be with her. More memories flooded in. He lived in an awful old trailer in the woods with a dad who was always drunk. She'd felt sorry for him, but she'd never been attracted to him. Yet in spite of that, he offered to help her.

"Awkward," Liv murmured.

"Extremely." Katrina raked her hand through her hair. "I should apologize."

"Maybe he wouldn't want you to bring up something so embarrassing."

If there was one thing Liv knew well, it was men. She picked them up and discarded them like used tissues. Jason had been Katrina's only serious boyfriend, and she'd married him. "I could mention how much he's changed at least. Looking back, I think my friends bullied him." She moaned again. "I was a self-centered jerk. Maybe I still am."

"You're the absolute opposite of a jerk. Everyone loves you." A long pause followed. "It sounds like you're thinking about staying. Seriously? You could give up the bright lights of Silicon Valley for North Haven?"

"Maybe. I don't have to decide yet." Katrina yawned. "When are you coming?"

"I can't get away soon enough. I'll let you know when I get some things squared away here."

"Whenever you're ready. I'll have fresh sheets on the bed and everything ready. It will be good to have support here."

Cheered by the news, she and Liv signed off, and Katrina's finger moved toward the Talk icon. She wanted to tell Jason about the turn of events, but after the last session, the bot scared her a little. What if she found out something she didn't want to know? She gave a slight shake of her head and launched Talk.

Where to start? *My grandmother left me the restaurant, but it's caused a huge family uproar. I've realized I'm a jerk. How did you ever fall in love with me?*

You're the best person I know, and I love you, now and forever.

Her hand paused at the question she had been pondering, but she had to ask it. *Have you ever loved anyone else?*

Never. There's only been you in my heart.

Then who did you come to see in North Haven? Why were you here?

It was for you. For us.

Tears blinded her. *But it took you away. I need to know what happened, Jason. Who were you meeting?* Those same Japanese characters came back almost immediately, and she frowned. Maybe it wasn't a glitch. Could those letters mean something?

She copied and pasted the characters into Google Translate, which yielded "messenger." *Were you meeting a messenger?*

I was meeting her.

Who was she?

The bot responded with the same Japanese characters. Was Google Translate missing something? Could the characters be a name?

Katrina sighed. Maybe she needed to try a different approach. *Is there anything else about your trip I don't know?*

The bot paused for a long moment before the typing balloon resumed.

I think I was murdered.

IIIIIIIIIIIIIIIIIIIIIIII

Seb parked in front of the trailer. He was later than usual, but his father was still up. Seb could see the flickering lights of the television on the living room walls.

He knocked on the rickety front door. A moment later, heavy steps sounded from inside and the latch clicked. "Come on in," his father's reedy voice said.

Seb went in. This time he carried a warmer that contained lobster ravioli. Dad had plopped down in front of the TV again and was absorbed in a grainy episode of *The Six Million Dollar Man*.

"They don't make shows like they used to." His father pointed a shaky finger at the screen. "This is the real stuff."

Seb set the food in front of his father. He also laid out two large linen napkins, as Dad was a messy eater. Seb's pulse blipped at what he was about to say. No telling what Dad would do. He might throw the food at him. "Dylan Carver stopped by The Beacon today."

His father froze for a heartbeat with a bite halfway to his mouth. Then he shoved the food in. "Huh," he said as he chewed.

That instant of hesitation told Seb everything he needed to know. He felt sick. "He's your son, isn't he?"

Dad shrugged bony shoulders. "His mother said so, but she never did nothin' about it."

"Did you?"

"No. Why should I? I had my hands full with you and your mama. I didn't need another baby. Besides, I wasn't sure the kid was mine. Linda got around."

Seb knew his father too well to be shocked, but he was still nauseated. "It was always about you, wasn't it? Never about the little boy who needed a father."

His father looked at him uncertainly. "You talking about Dylan or yourself?"

"Yes."

"What's that supposed to mean?"

Seb stood and picked up the warmer. "You used to brag about how smart you are. Figure it out. I have to get back to town." He crossed the tiny living room in two steps and reached for the door handle.

"What will you do?"

Seb turned. "What do you mean?"

"Are you gonna do something about Dylan? Take a test to figure out whether he's your brother?"

"Of course."

"Tell me what it says, okay?"

"That'll be up to Dylan." Seb jerked open the door and stepped out into the night. He had no doubt what the test would show.

|||||||||||||||||||||||||||||

I think I was murdered.

No matter how Katrina stared at the words without blinking, they refused to change into something that made sense. Jason had died in an accident. There had never been any hint of something sinister. The hairpin turns along that road were known to be treacherous, especially in heavy fog, and he'd died at the Pulpit, a spot notorious for accidents.

43

It had been an accident—hadn't it?

She bounded to her feet and paced the bedroom. Lyla scampered away and hid under the bed before peeking out as if to ask what she was doing. Katrina wondered the same thing.

She stared at the words again, and her hands shook as she typed. *Why do you think that? Who murdered you?*

Alice threw me down the looking-glass.

She shook her head. *Be serious. Who murdered you?*

The Cheshire Cat hates chocolate ice cream.

The bot had to be glitching since it gave two different answers, both nonsensical. *Jason, who did you go see?*

The same Japanese characters appeared on the screen as before. Who had he been talking to the week before he died? She pulled up his email account on her phone and found nothing from anyone she didn't know. The calendar entry for his fatal trip just said *North Haven*.

She stared at the glitches again. They must mean something. Liv would know—her team had designed the Talk app. Katrina glanced at the time. After eleven, but her friend might still be up. She pulled up her text thread with Liv and *Notifications Silenced* appeared at the bottom. Still, it was worth a shot. She typed out a text. *Are you awake?*

She waited five minutes, but no response came. She sighed and plugged her phone into its charger.

A clear picture came to mind of Seb speaking Japanese in the cemetery. He might think it was weird for her to ask, but he'd offered to help. She pulled up the number he'd given her and stared at it a moment.

Her pride meant nothing right now. She had to find out the truth.

Could you meet me at Bestemor's at 9 in the morning?

Sure.

The temptation to ask to meet right now, this minute, washed over her, but she squashed it. He already thought she was so self-absorbed she hadn't recognized him. The last thing she wanted was to confirm she was selfish enough to drag him out in the middle of the night.

CHAPTER 6

////////////

AT NINE SHARP THE NEXT MORNING, SEB pulled into Bestemor's parking lot. He got out of his car and looked around the lot. It was full, which was a good sign—but he noticed a young woman who had parked at the same time he had, and she walked into the knitting shop next door. That would be the first item on his mental list.

He walked through the red double doors and inhaled the aroma of fresh coffee and hot waffles. It was the scent of Bestemor's, and it never got old.

Katrina waved to him from the counter. She slipped her phone into a little purse as she got up and walked over to him. She wore classic Silicon Valley business casual: dark jeans, ankle boots, a white collared blouse, and a black blazer. "Thanks for coming over."

Her tone seemed to hold real gratitude. Maybe she'd learned a little appreciation for people while she was in the Valley. "Of course. Frida taught me the ropes of the restaurant business, and I'm happy to do the same for her granddaughter."

"I appreciate it—and I'm sorry I didn't recognize you last night. I can't believe I drew a blank like that. I must have been more tired than I realized."

"Don't worry about it. You'd had quite a day, and I know I've changed a lot since high school." He glanced at his watch. "I'm in a bit of a hurry today, unfortunately."

She seemed disappointed. "Oh, well, thanks for squeezing in a few minutes with me." She glanced around the busy dining room. "I have a non-restaurant question for you, but let's start with Bestemor's since that's what you're here for."

A non-restaurant question? His pulse quickened just a little. He cleared his throat. "Sure. Let's start with the parking lot. It's full, but not everyone who parked there came in here. Five minutes ago, I saw a woman take one of your spots and go into the shop next door. That's costing you customers. You should have a sign that says parking is limited to Bestemor's customers when the restaurant is open."

She took out her phone and tapped a note. "Thanks."

"Next, your menu." He pointed to the chalkboard. "It's great, but it hasn't changed in years. Every month, the worst-selling item should be removed and replaced by something new."

She nodded and tapped another note. "Any suggestions for replacement dishes?"

"Hmm. A comfort food. Something you can't get here but American taste buds will instinctively like." He thought for a moment, then smiled. "*Wienerpølser med lompe.* They're kind of like skinny hot dogs, except wrapped in a sort of potato tortilla."

Her eyes widened and she put a hand on his arm. "I love those! Oh, and we'd have to put Solo on the menu too."

He laughed. He'd missed the Norwegian orange soda since he left Oslo a decade ago. "Of course, though it won't be cheap to import. But there's nothing like an ice-cold Solo and a wiener-pølser on an endless summer day."

"We talk about endless summer days here, but it's literal over there, isn't it?"

He nodded. "Some friends and I went camping north of the Arctic Circle over *Sankt Hans* one year. The sun never set. It just touched the horizon for an hour or so in the middle of the night and then rose again. I don't think anyone really slept. We just stayed up around the fire, talking and laughing. Someone had brought a guitar, and they taught me some very stupid Norwegian songs. And these were all high-end restaurant people, so the camp food was phenomenal."

She gave him a warm smile. "It sounds like a special time."

"It was." He glanced at his watch again and shook his head. He hadn't come here to reminisce with Katrina Foster. "Speaking of time, we don't have much."

He pushed through the kitchen doors and scanned the room. "This looks pretty good, but you'll need to be an absolute hygiene Nazi." He pointed to where a cook was preparing *kjøttkaker*, the slightly squashed Norwegian version of Swedish meatballs. "For example, that cutting board will need to get washed and sterilized, of course—and the counter too. Meat juices drip over the edge of the board even if you're careful. I've seen a health inspector shut down a restaurant because a customer got food poisoning that way."

"Hygiene Nazi," she repeated, tapping on her phone. "Got it. What else?"

"Hmm." He bit his lower lip and thought for a moment. "Permits. There are a bunch of them, and you need to keep them all up-to-date. They can be a little confusing—for instance, there's a food seller's permit, a food handler's license, and a food facility health permit. And they're all different, of course. Frida used to keep them in a file cabinet behind her desk."

"Good to know. Let's check to see if they're still there if you don't mind."

"Not at all." He walked through the kitchen to the office, with Katrina following him. He went through the half-open door and walked around the desk. The little "I'm called Bestemor because I'm way too cool to be called Grandmother" sign still hung on the wall. He felt a little weird about sitting in Frida's chair, so he bent over the file cabinet and pulled out the top drawer. He found the folder labeled *Permits/Licenses* in her spidery hand-writing and pulled it out. "Here you go." He turned back to Katrina—and noticed she'd closed the office door behind her.

"Thanks." She took the folder from him and tossed it on the desk. Her face held a tense, serious look. "About that non-restaurant question I mentioned—you said you speak some Japanese. Do you read it too?"

That wasn't at all the question he'd been expecting. "Uh, yeah. Why?"

She hesitated for a moment, then handed her phone to him. "Can you read these characters? I ran them through a transla-tor, but I want to be sure it's right."

"Yes, it says *Messenja*. It means 'messenger' or maybe 'the messenger,' depending on the context. I'm pretty sure it's a borrow-word from English."

She held out her hand for the phone. "So, it's not a name, right?"

He handed it back. "Right, or at least not that I've ever heard. I guess it could be a job title or something."

She let out a breath and smiled. "Great, thank you."

"Of course. Is that all?"

She nodded. "Yes, I really appreciate your help, and I won't keep you any longer."

Five minutes later, he was back in his car. "Well, that was weird," he announced as he drove out of the parking lot.

|||||||||||||||||||||||||

The clatter of utensils and low hum of conversation reached Katrina from the kitchen. The familiar sounds and atmosphere made her feel Bestemor might sail through the doorway from the kitchen any minute. It was both painful and comforting to be here.

Katrina popped the last bite of her waffle with cloudberry cream into her mouth, then wiped her fingers and picked up her phone. Liv would be up by now.

"Katrina, I was about to call you. Sorry I had notifications silenced last night. I was exhausted from the stress." Liv's voice wobbled. "I called David's mother last night. She said she hadn't seen him. I knew it was a lie because I saw his location on the phone. I've never been so totally ghosted before."

"I'm sorry, Liv. Did you tell her about the baby?"

"I wanted to, but his father is a diplomat, and I wasn't sure what kind of power he might have to try to acquire parental rights. If David doesn't want to be part of my life, I don't want him interfering."

"Was she hostile?"

"Just reserved and noncommittal. But at least I know where I stand. I'm done trying to contact him." Her tone brightened. "When are you coming back? Once things get squared away here, I'd love to visit North Haven and try to forget this ever happened."

There was so much to do here, but that wasn't the real reason her stomach bottomed out at the thought of leaving. The town's hygge had ensnared her already. The peace of this place wrapped around her like a warm blanket, and the rat race of the Valley held no appeal. Ever since college she'd pursued success with the determination of a shark smelling blood in the water. Was she ready to throw in the towel at the first bump in the road? Jason would be ashamed of her.

She shook off her dismay. "I'll be there in the next few days. Listen, the reason I called was the bot is being weird." She told Liv about the *I was murdered* comment and the bot's reply to further questions. "Whenever I ask who Jason came to meet, it says the Japanese word *Messenja*, which means 'the messenger.' It never changes that reply."

Liv said nothing for a long moment. "The murder comment is weird, but it must be a hallucination since it doesn't give more information when you ask questions. The Japanese word feels different though, like maybe it means something. Have you asked it to elaborate? Maybe ask, What else can you tell me about Messenja, or, How do you know Messenja?"

"I haven't asked anything like that, so now I feel stupid. The comment about murder shocked me, and with Bestemor's death, I haven't been thinking clearly. I'll try that." And she hadn't wanted to dig too deeply in case she found out Jason was having an affair. But her doubts weren't something she was ready to talk to anyone about—not even Liv. If she wanted to find out about the night Jason died, she needed to start thinking like a lawyer.

She thanked her friend and ended the call, then launched the bot. *Tell me more about Messenja*, she typed, pasting in the Japanese characters from one of the bot's texts.

I was going to meet Messenja at The Beacon the day I was murdered.

That word *murdered* again. And if they were meeting at The Beacon, did Seb know something about Jason's death?

CHAPTER 7

////////////

THE COOL BREEZE OFF THE OCEAN BLEW long strands of hair across Katrina's face. She wore light jeans instead of black and a thick Norwegian sweater as shelter against the mid-September wind. Being out of her usual attire made her feel like she was on vacation, and the blue water rolling to the rocky beach added to the relaxing atmosphere. The salty, humid air would have her hair a tangled mess by the time she got to Mag's Place.

Maybe this was a bad idea, but she couldn't bear the thought of more distance between her and her family. The estrangement added to the stress of everything else, and she needed to defuse it if she could. Her dad had mentioned he and Mom would be helping Magnus move in new tables this morning, and it felt like a more neutral place for the discussion than their house.

Redwood Street held most of the quaint shops prized by tourists and locals alike, and she paused on her way to Mag's Place to peer in the window of Spin Me a Yarn next door to Bestemor's. The knitting group of twelve women were settled on comfortable chairs and sofas with colorful baskets of yarn by their feet. She spotted familiar faces and wished she had time to join them. She hadn't held a pair of knitting needles since she'd left for school, but it was like riding a bike—you never forgot how to knit.

She nearly bowled over a figure jetting out the door and stopped to steady the woman before she saw her face. "Veronica!" They exchanged a tight hug before Katrina stepped back and released her. "You look wonderful."

Veronica Helman's family had owned the yarn shop ever since Katrina could remember. The pretty brunette had nearly married Magnus right out of high school until her parents talked her out of it. Katrina had always wondered if Veronica's steadying influence would have forced her brother to grow up if they hadn't split.

Veronica's smile came before vanishing. "I'm so sorry about your grandmother. I wanted to attend the funeral, but one of my employees was sick and I had to work."

"Thank you. It's been hard." Katrina motioned to the shop. "Looks like the place is doing well."

"It's been booming. We made a door in the wall and opened a bookstore in the space next door, which has brought in even more revenue."

"The name works for both too. I'll have to stop in and look for a new novel."

With a promise to get shrimp sandwiches and coffee soon, Katrina walked on toward Mag's Place. Her brother had done a good job with the old hardware store. His new wooden sign had an old-time appearance like it had been there since the turn of the last century. Mom had picked out the warm beige and brown tones with a pop of yellow hinting at the welcome inside.

She glanced down the street toward The Beacon. Jason was supposed to meet Messenja there. Surely Seb knew something, yet he didn't mention that Jason was supposed to come by that night. Why? Did he have something to hide? She needed to question him about it, but how did she do that without revealing the information the bot was feeding her? If the bot was telling the truth, she didn't want the killer to hear Jason was speaking from beyond the grave.

The door was unlocked, so she let herself in and paused a moment to enjoy the way the ceilings opened up. The interior had kept the feel of the old hardware store with wooden bins for storage and the wide plank floors. Magnus had built the redwood bar with its gleaming surface of many coats of marine varnish. She wandered that way and touched a matching barstool.

The old mismatched tables and chairs had been cleared out of the space, replaced with black-metal-and-wood tables and chairs. There was no sign of her family, but she spotted a newspaper with her face on the front page. Her parents knew all the details of her disgrace now.

She stepped into the center of the room. "Hello? Magnus?" Maybe her parents had left already, but her brother had to be here somewhere since the door was unlocked.

"Coming," her brother's deep voice called from another room.

Her mother's voice echoed through the door. "She should have told us. It's a good thing Bestemor left her the shop. Her career in Silicon Valley is over. The news will be all over town by now."

Katrina bit her lip. One little misstep and she was labeled a failure? "I came to help," she said when her family moved into view. "Looks like you have it under control."

"We started at six," her mother said in a tone that indicated Katrina should have known they'd start early.

"I saw the paper on the bar. I wanted to tell you, but I didn't have a chance."

"Sure you did," her dad said. "You could have told us when I read the will. You could have called on your way home. There was plenty of opportunity to let us know the FBI had locked you out of the place. Are you going to be indicted?"

She winced. "I don't know yet. I didn't know anything about what David was doing."

Her father harrumphed. "What are you going to do?"

"About Talk? I honestly don't know. But I met with Seb Wallace this morning. He's offered to help me get up to speed on how to run Bestemor's."

Her mother's eyes widened. "You're keeping it?"

"I haven't decided yet. I still miss Jason so much, and it's a lot to figure out how to do something so out of my comfort zone."

Magnus stiffened at her mention of Jason. "His opinion might have been what swayed Bestemor to cut me out of her will."

Her father frowned. "She didn't cut you out—you got the cash."

"Not really. I have to beg you or Katrina for every dime." Magnus glared at their parents. "Jason's opinion of me changed everything. He thought I was a total loser and couldn't wipe my own nose. He convinced Bestemor I'm incompetent, but I'm doing a good job with Mag's. You know I am."

Their mother touched his arm. "You know she loved you, Magnus."

The bad blood between Magnus and Jason had started at her parents' house after a party for Bestemor's birthday. Through a casual comment, Jason had learned that Katrina's parents had given Magnus money for Mag's Place even though he hadn't repaid a dime of what Jason and Katrina had loaned him. Jason had accused Katrina and her parents of babying Magnus even though he was the oldest. He hadn't been wrong, but the argument had escalated from there until both men had their fists ready to fly. She'd had to physically step between them.

"Don't try to snow me. I know you advised her to do it, Dad. They call that a spendthrift trust, right? You've never believed in me." Magnus stomped off into the back room.

Her parents glanced at each other, and when Dad shrugged and led her mother toward the door, Katrina knew Magnus was right—Dad had suggested this. Once the door shut behind them, Katrina went in search of her brother and found him in the kitchen cleaning the flattop grill. The space gleamed with cleanliness and smelled of a strong disinfectant.

He glanced at her. "It's not fun to feel like a loser, is it? I'm sorry you've hit the skids now too."

She couldn't answer him past the lump in her throat, so she shook her head.

"Sorry, sis, I shouldn't have piled on you too. I'm used to being the black sheep. You'll land on your feet and regain your crown."

"I'll talk to Dad. He has the power to let you have the money you need."

"I don't want it like that. I'm going to prove I can do it without help, even if I have to work day and night." He set down the metal brush and slung his arm around her. "I know Jason and I didn't get along, but I'm here for you, Katrina. We incompetents have to stick together."

She managed a shaky laugh and hugged him. Now she knew firsthand how much disappointing their parents hurt.

⁓

A week later Seb sat at a table in a dimly lit corner at Mag's, waiting for Dylan, who had pushed for an instant meeting as soon as the DNA test results came back. Seb had wanted a private place to discuss their newly revealed relationship, and few places in North Haven were quieter than Mag's at two o'clock on a weekday. Seb had the place entirely to himself, aside from the staff and an old guy at the bar who was watching minor league baseball on an enormous TV and nursing an iced tea.

Magnus had done a nice job with the place, though Seb noticed a few odd decisions. The new tables and chairs, for example. They looked good and fit well with the décor, but the elegant legs were thin and the smooth wood tops appeared hand finished. Restaurant—and especially bar—furniture should be cheap or durable—and preferably both. These didn't appear to be either.

The menu and staffing also surprised Seb. It was the middle of the afternoon, but the hostess had handed him full lunch and dinner menus. That implied that the kitchen had food partially prepped to be ready for any order from either menu. How much of that would get thrown away at the end of the day? And why have a hostess working at this time of day—let alone the three servers he saw lounging against the wall? There should be a *Please Seat Yourself* sign and a single server covering the whole establishment.

The cough and uneven rumble of a badly tuned engine announced Dylan's arrival. Seb looked out the window. A primer-spotted old pickup pulled into the parking lot and parked next to his Tesla and Dylan got out. He was three minutes late, but he paused to give Seb's Tesla an admiring look before ambling over to the bar entrance.

The hostess greeted Dylan and pointed to Seb's table. Dylan followed her over, a huge grin splitting his tan face. Seb stood and reached out his hand, but Dylan ignored it and gave him an enormous bear hug. Seb struggled for breath and did his best to hug back with his arms pinned to his sides.

Dylan finally released him. "Oh, man! I have a brother! I mean, I knew before—but now I *know*, you know?"

Seb put a hand on the table to steady himself. The guy was like a giant puppy that could talk. "Yes, I know. I feel the same way. I've been on my own for most of my life. To find out I have a half brother is . . . well, it's amazing." He gestured at the chair on the opposite side of the table. "Have a seat. We have a lot to talk about."

Dylan settled into the chair and a waitress with an amused smile appeared. Seb was glad this scene wasn't playing out at The Beacon. Someone would have been surreptitiously recording the whole thing. Seb ordered a Caesar salad and iced tea. Dylan got a twenty-ounce steak, onion rings, and a sixteen-ounce beer.

Once the waitress was gone, Seb looked across the table at Dylan. "So, tell me about yourself—your family, your life, what you like to do."

Dylan leaned forward and put his elbows on the table. "There's not much to tell. My mom died when I was three. Dad wasn't in the picture and Mom's parents couldn't take me, so I got dumped in the foster care system up in Seattle. It wasn't great, but it wasn't terrible once I got big enough to take care of myself. After I aged out of the system, I lived up there for a few years. Then I got a job at a restaurant in Eureka and moved down here. How about you, man? How did you get where you are?"

"I've been on my own since eighteen too. I'd been working part-time at a restaurant, and the owner sort of took me under her wing. I wanted to get as far away from here as possible, so she arranged a job for me at a place her cousin owned in Oslo, Norway. I spent a couple of years there and worked my way up to station chef for desserts. Then a sous chef job opened in Moscow, so I went there for a year and a half. After that, I did stints in London, Tokyo, and Paris. And then finally back here."

"Cool. So how did you get your own place? Did the bank, like, just give you the money?"

Seb shook his head. "I lived cheap while I was overseas, so I had some money saved up. Frida—the lady who got me the job in Oslo—loaned me most of the rest."

"That's awesome, man. I'd love to meet her someday."

Seb wished he could see Frida again himself. What advice would she give him about this new brother? "She passed away last week, unfortunately."

"I'm sorry, bro. Sounds like you were lucky to know her."

"I was." Guilt needled Seb. He'd never considered his up-bringing privileged until now. "What restaurant do you work at? I might be able to send you some business."

Dylan looked down and fidgeted with his silverware. "I, uh, don't work there anymore."

"Oh. What are you doing now?"

"Um, just taking some time off, you know. Looking around."

"What kind of work did you do at the restaurant in Eureka?"

"Dishwasher and busboy mostly, though I tended bar a couple times."

Seb nodded. "Are you still living in Eureka?"

Dylan cleared his throat. "Sort of. I've been couch-surfing with friends here and there. I love the outdoors, so I've also been camping a lot when the weather's nice. I've been checking out websites that talk about North Haven. It's a pretty awesome place to live."

"It is." So Dylan was unemployed and basically homeless.

Conflicting impulses warred in Seb's chest. He barely knew Dylan, but he'd known guys like him—and he wouldn't hire any of them. Able-bodied young men who couldn't keep a job often had problems that went well beyond money, especially if they came out of the foster-care system. But none of those guys had been his half brother.

Seb had upended his life and moved halfway across the world because his father needed him. He could offer his brother a job washing dishes. "I could get you some shifts at The Beacon if you like, and I'm pretty sure there are some rooms for rent in North Haven."

Dylan looked up. "Aw, man. I didn't come here to ask you for a job or money or anything. I'll be okay."

"Seriously, we've been short-staffed in the kitchen lately. If you want some hours washing dishes and bussing tables, just let me know. I can probably work you up to full time in a few weeks."

Dylan's eyes lit up. "Really?" He came around the table and gave Seb another hug. "You're the best, bro. You won't regret this."

Seb stiffened, then relaxed enough to give him an awkward pat. What had he just gotten himself into?

CHAPTER 8

////////////

KATRINA WANDERED AROUND THE EMPTY café with the kitten in her arms, decorating her black tee and jeans with white fur. She had to leave to get prepared for the FBI interview in San Francisco tomorrow, but she desperately needed to talk to Seb about Messenja and the meeting at The Beacon. They'd played phone tag about meeting in person for several days, so that conversation would have to wait until she got back. It wasn't something she wanted to get into on the phone. It would be humiliating enough to admit the deep grief that had caused her to turn to the bot in the first place— she didn't want to stumble over her words on the phone.

She set Lyla on the floor and made sure there was plenty of kitty litter and food for her. Bestemor's longtime cook, Agnes Jensen, had agreed to take care of her here at the café until Katrina got back.

The outside streetlights filtered through the windows and illuminated the tidy space. The workers would be here in another hour, but she had the place to herself for a few minutes. The sweet scents of the prior day lingered and mixed with the harsher edge of cleaning supplies, and the familiar smell made her miss her grandmother in a way that squeezed her chest.

What was she going to do? The events in the Valley dictated her return for a few days, and she knew how quickly she'd be swept up in the frantic pace. Yet this place called to her. Agnes had been keeping the doors open while Katrina's grandmother had been ill, but she was nearing retirement age. Bestemor had mentioned she was looking for a replacement cook to learn the ropes before that happened. When Bestemor's first heart attack struck, Agnes valiantly did her best to keep all the balls in the air.

Before she went back to Palo Alto, Katrina wanted to make sure the bills were paid and things were in order. She went down the hallway to the office door near the bathrooms and took out the key ring her father had given her. The key had been worn smooth by her grandmother's fingers through the decades, and Katrina ran her fingers over it before she unlocked the door.

The air in the room held her grandmother's favorite scent. A green Skandinavisk Fjord candle almost always flickered with the aroma of wood, ripening orchards, and wild berries anytime Bestemor was working in the space. Even with her grandmother gone, the wood floor and sofa seemed to hold the smell. In honor of Bestemor, Katrina picked up the lighter and lit the half-melted candle on the desk before taking a seat to go through the paperwork piled in heaps on the top.

She squared her shoulders and began to go through the bills, but most of them had been marked *Paid* in Agnes's bold handwriting. Katrina filed the bills in her grandmother's file cabinet, then pulled open the center desk drawer. A white envelope had been placed in the center of the drawer with her name on it in Bestemor's small, spidery script. Katrina caught her breath, and her fingers trembled as she reached for the letter and opened it. There was a single sheet of paper inside as well as another envelope with her brother's name on the outside.

My dear Katrina,

How you have brightened my life all these years! I know you're sad now, but I'm not gone. I've just moved on to my eternal home while I await the resurrection of that worn-out body in the grave. I'm ready for the pain to be over, though I regret my passing will be hard on my family. But know that I'm content with the wonderful life God gave me.

I'm sure you're wondering why I left the café to you when dear Magnus wanted it so badly. I love your brother dearly, but some men take a bit of time to grow up. I believe in Magnus and wanted him to prove himself at Mag's Place. I didn't want him to split his attention between his own business and mine. Both would suffer—but even worse, Magnus wouldn't realize his own worth if he failed because I tossed too much onto his plate. I'm sorry if it put you and your brother at odds. I left a letter for Magnus as well. Please deliver it to him with all my love.

Leaving Bestemor's in your capable hands was a practical decision. Torvald has a busy law practice. He didn't want the restaurant or need the headache. And the more I prayed about what to do, the more I felt led by the Lord to leave the café to you. Don't feel you must run it, my dear girl. If you want to sell it, I pray you'll find someone who will love it as much as I did. Sebastian Wallace would be a good choice. But if by chance the call of North Haven creeps into your heart, I think it will provide you with contentment and community as you find your place in our wonderful town again.

Whatever your decision, know that I love you very much and wish you abundant joy in the pursuit of your God-given dreams. Remember the things I've taught you and the faith I've tried to give you as an example. I wasn't perfect, but I knew how to love and you learned that lesson well. I saw how you loved Jason and your family. Nurture that ability to give and receive love and don't let his loss close you off to living your life fully. Don't be afraid to try something new and frightening. I know you will soar, my dear Katrina.

Until I see you again,
Your loving bestemor

Katrina hadn't been aware she was crying until tears blurred her vision and splatted on the page. She swiped the moisture from her face and stuffed her letter back into the envelope, then rose with the letter for her brother in her hand. This would help Magnus, too, and the realization helped wash away the last of her guilt about the inheritance.

⫿⫿⫿⫿⫿⫿⫿⫿⫿⫿⫿⫿⫿⫿⫿⫿⫿⫿⫿⫿⫿

The next day, Katrina's blue Tesla purred along the highway from Palo Alto, where she'd spent the night at a hotel. Her brother's reaction to his letter before she left for the city had been heartwarming and much like her own. On his face she'd seen new determination to prove he could make Mag's Place a success.

An album from No. 4, Katrina's favorite Norwegian band, played on the sound system. Somehow the music cemented her grandmother's words in her heart. If she remembered to let the love and hard work she'd learned from Bestemor sink into her heart, Katrina would overcome the tremendous upheaval in her life.

The skyscrapers of San Francisco loomed into view, and she turned off the music. It would take all her concentration to prepare for the upcoming FBI interview. She was headed for the Bureau's main district office, and butterflies fluttered in her stomach. She might walk out in handcuffs.

She parked in the garage. The elevator took her to the correct floor without another stop to delay the inevitable. The stark lobby seemed designed to intimidate, but she refused to let it get to her. She marched up to the receptionist and announced herself.

A moment later, the door buzzed. Two men met her as she walked through.

The dark-headed one nodded to her. "Ms. Foster?" He was about five-six, an inch taller than her. "I'm Agent Short, and this is Agent Hughes."

She followed them into a spartan conference room with cheap government furniture. "I'm happy to help in any way I can." She sat on one side of the table and the men sat across from her.

Short clasped his hands and leaned forward while Hughes retrieved a notebook from his gray briefcase and plucked a Cross pen from his suit pocket. "We want to ask you about Talk CN," Short said.

"The subsidiary in Shanghai? What about it?"

"Why was it set up when you had Talk, Inc. here?"

"Simple really. David Liang wanted to use the less expensive option of Shanghai programmers."

"I see. Did you set it up for Mr. Liang?"

"No, David used a local attorney. I pulled up the firm's profile, and it appeared to be reputable with good reviews, so I had no concerns about it."

Short scowled. "I see. Did you review the financials?"

Where was this going? Katrina shook her head. "David had retained a Chinese accountant. Someone he'd done business with in the past."

"Did you review any of their products?"

She wiped sweaty palms on her skirt. "I did not. That job would be directed to the programming department."

"Have you ever spoken to anyone at Talk CN?"

"Directly, you mean? No. I mean, we had companywide video calls, and I might have greeted the different people in attendance, but I had no personal conversations with anyone from Talk CN."

"Tell me, Ms. Foster, do you speak Chinese?"

If only. "I do not."

Short glanced down at his notes. "Were you aware that Talk CN was a shell company created solely to funnel Talk, Inc.'s investors' money into the bank accounts of David Liang and his cousin John?"

Her head spun. Was that what the Liangs had been doing? "I . . . No, this is the first I've heard an accusation of that type."

"As general counsel, wasn't it your duty to be aware of illegal activity by the company?"

She shook her head again. "No. It was my duty to give accurate legal advice, which I did to the best of my ability. David didn't seek my advice about Talk CN. He had it handled by other people. If I had become aware the company was breaking the law, I would have had a duty to inform senior management. I can assure you if I had even an inkling this was going on, I would have done everything in my power to stop it."

"Did you ever advise senior management that it was legal to divert funds to Talk CN?"

"No. While attorney-client privilege prevents me from disclosing communication with Talk's senior management, I can tell you the subject of diverting money to Talk CN never came up."

Short paused and leaned forward. She could tell by his heightened focus that he'd reached his key questions. "So would it be fair to say attorney-client privilege doesn't protect any of Talk CN's documents or data?"

"Not if I'm the attorney in question."

"And there would be no advice-of-counsel regarding diversion of funds to Talk CN?"

"Again, not if I'm the counsel."

Short relaxed and smiled. "Would you be willing to testify, Ms. Foster?"

The question told her the FBI probably didn't intend to prosecute her if she cooperated. The flip side was that she was painting a target on her back with the Liangs. What choice did she have though? "Of course. I will do anything I can to assist the investigation."

What would Jason have to say about what she'd just agreed to do?

CHAPTER 9

////////////

SEB PULLED ASIDE HIS ASSISTANT MANAGER, Alex Frasier, and shot a glance toward the kitchen. "How's he doing?" Dylan had been working for him for three days, and Seb had tried not to hover.

Alex had short black hair and dark brown eyes. He wore a dentalium shell necklace over his tailored black shirt in honor of his Yurok heritage. Seb had hired him on the spot after watching him stay calm and keep a hotel restaurant running smoothly despite being overbooked due to a convention and having a police raid at the casino next door in the middle of dinner rush. "Dylan? So far, so good. Showed up on time, worked hard, didn't take too long on his break. Only mentioned you were his brother once."

Seb winced. "I'd hoped he wouldn't do that."

"It was fine. He just said he was lucky to have you for a brother. I agreed with him."

A warm glow in his chest surprised Seb. "I appreciate your keeping an eye on him."

"Of course." Alex glanced at his watch. "His shift is over now. Want me to close up while you two deliver a meal?"

The warm glow vanished. Tonight would be the first time Dylan met their father, and Seb could imagine plenty of ways that could go very wrong. What if Dylan said something about Dad abandoning him and his mother? What if Dad repeated his comment about Dylan's mother's alleged promiscuity? It used to take the police at least forty-five minutes to show up after domestic disturbance calls from Dad's trailer. Had their response time improved?

He sighed. "Thanks. I should probably head out."

Seb walked into the kitchen and collected Dylan, who happily shed his dishwasher's apron and trailed Seb to the door. Thor handed Seb a warmer on his way out.

"I can drive," Dylan volunteered when they reached the parking lot.

Seb gave his brother's ramshackle truck a dubious look. "Thanks, but this will be a rough trip." In more ways than one. He gestured to his Range Rover. "Hop in."

Dylan whistled through his teeth. "You've got this *and* a Tesla Model S?"

Seb handed Dylan the warmer. "The road we're taking would rip the undercarriage out of a Tesla."

They got into the SUV. Seb looked over at his brother, who was eyeing the warmer. "Buckle up."

Dylan dutifully snapped his seat belt. "What's in here?"

"Dad's favorite." Seb started the engine. "Filet mignon prepared with butter, fresh garlic, and rosemary." Seb hoped it would put their father in a good mood.

Dylan cracked the warmer's lid and sniffed deeply. "Mmm. Smells good." He snapped the lid shut. "Could you teach me how to make that?"

"Sure."

"You take him dinner every night?"

Seb shrugged. "Whenever I can. Weekends are rough, but I usually make it out there three or four times a week. He'll just eat junk if he's left to himself, so I try to get him decent meals when I'm able."

"Wish I'd known you growing up, man."

"Me too. Did you ever try to contact Dad?"

"Couple times. I called once when I ran away after getting in a fistfight with my foster dad, but the line was disconnected. When I moved to Eureka, I sent a letter to his PO box, but I never heard back."

Seb wasn't surprised. Dad's utilities regularly got turned off for nonpayment before Seb arranged for direct deposit of his benefits checks and automatic payment of his bills. And Seb had never seen him write so much as a postcard. He switched to a hopefully happier topic. "What was your mom like?"

"Can't really say. I don't remember her." Dylan reached into his pocket, pulled out a worn wallet, and extracted a small picture. He handed it to Seb. "Here's her and Dad at the county fair."

Seb held it up so he could look at it without taking his eyes off the road. It showed his father in his prime standing next to a tall, pretty blonde of about twenty. She held cotton candy in one hand and an enormous stuffed unicorn with a rainbow horn in the other. Seb handed the picture back. "She was beautiful."

Dylan put the picture back in his wallet with care, like he was handling an ancient manuscript. "Thanks."

"By the way, Dad doesn't look anything like that today."

"He doesn't?"

Seb shook his head. "A log rolled off a truck and broke his back when he was forty. He was never the same after that. The doctor put him on pain pills, and he never got off. Then he developed Parkinson's a couple of years ago. He's only sixty, but he looks like an old man."

Dylan absorbed the news in silence.

Seb cleared his throat. "He also sometimes says stuff he doesn't really mean. The pain and the pills get to him. And he feels like life gave him a raw deal. He's not a happy man. Try not to let it get to you, okay?"

"Okay."

Seb glanced over to try to read his brother's expression, but Dylan was staring out the side window. "Hold on, it's about to get bumpy."

Seb turned off onto the old fire road that led back to Dad's trailer. The constant jolts and sharp turns made conversation difficult, and driving took all of Seb's attention, so they said nothing more until they reached their destination.

They pulled up outside the trailer and got out. Flickering lights in the window told Seb Dad was watching TV again.

Dylan put down the warmer and stretched. "You weren't kidding about the bumpy ride, man." He surveyed the dilapidated trailer. "Why does he live all the way out here?"

"Because this is his land and he's stubborn. His great-grandfather bought a thousand acres, but almost all of it got sold or lost through tax sales over the years. There's only about three acres left, and we're in the middle of it." Seb shook his head. "He says he's going to die here, and I'm afraid he'll follow through on that."

Dylan shrugged broad shoulders. "Gotta die someplace, I guess." He picked up the warmer and walked toward the trailer.

Seb hurried so he could reach the door first. He rapped on the frame. "Hi, Dad!" He didn't receive a response, so he pulled open the door and walked in.

Dad sat on the stained old sofa, watching professional wrestling. An enormous bag of Cheetos sat on the coffee table in front of him. Three empty bottles of Miller High Life stood on the table next to the Cheetos, and Dad held one in his hand. Great.

Dad looked up as they walked in. "Two sons and neither of them can get here on time." His eyes went to Dylan. "You're Dylan, huh?"

Dylan set down the warmer and extended his hand. "Yes, sir."

Dad wiped his hand on his white T-shirt, leaving orange smears. "So your mama was right. You're actually mine after all." He reached out a skinny arm to shake Dylan's hand.

Dylan's mouth set in a hard line.

Seb stepped between the two men before Dylan could speak. "We brought you filet mignon, Dad." He grabbed the warmer from the floor, set it on the table, and opened it. The succulent aromas of beef, garlic, and rosemary filled the tiny room. "Your favorite."

"I'm not hungry." Dad's voice dripped petulance. He pointed to the Cheetos and empty bottles. "You guys took so long that I already ate."

Seb tried to keep his voice even. "I've explained this before, Dad. I have a restaurant to run. I can't leave in the middle of dinner rush just to make a special trip out here. I always come as soon as I can."

Dylan turned to the TV. "Did you see Bloodaxe's new move?"

Dad shook his head. "No. Been waiting for him to bust it out."

Dylan pointed at the screen. "Here it comes!"

Seb turned in time to see a heavily tattooed blond giant pick up another huge man, do something resembling a pirouette, and hurl the other man to the mat.

"Bloodslam!" Dad and Dylan yelled in unison.

"Love that move." Dylan sat next to his father. He pointed to the steak. "You gonna eat that?"

"All yours." Dad handed him a beer and pushed the Cheetos in his direction. "Here. Nothin' goes better with a good steak than beer 'n' Cheetos."

"Awesome!" Dylan took a swig from the bottle. "Thanks, Dad."

Seb grabbed a rickety chair from the kitchen and sat beside the sofa. "Looks like you're a chip off the old block, Dylan."

Dylan grinned. "Thanks, bro." He popped a bite of steak and two Cheetos into his mouth simultaneously. "Mmm."

Seb settled back in his seat. He didn't relish an evening of watching professional wrestling while his brother defiled an excellent steak, but there were much, much worse ways this evening could have turned out.

||||||||||||||||||||||

Katrina sat in her car, staring at her front door in Palo Alto. The grueling FBI interrogation had left her drained. She hadn't talked to Jason since she got in the car this morning, so she pulled out her phone and called up the app.

You've heard me talk about the Liangs. Do you think they're dangerous?

You didn't get on their bad side, did you, love?

Maybe. I told the FBI I'd testify for them against David.

The dots started on the app, but Jason didn't post the reply for a long minute. *They want it, Katrina. Everyone wants it.*

Katrina frowned. Sometimes the bot made no sense. *What is "it"?*

They will kill to get it. They already did. I'm praying they don't hurt you, my love. I did everything I could to keep you out of danger. Don't rush into their line of sight.

Katrina's door opened and Liv waved to her, rubber gloves on her hands. In Katrina's absence Liv had volunteered to clean the house after the break-in, but Katrina suspected her friend had wanted to get out of the opulent apartment she'd shared with David before his betrayal.

Katrina bit her lip and put her phone away. She wasn't ready for this yet. Especially not with Jason's warning still reverberating in her head. *Don't rush into their line of sight.*

She stepped out of her car into a perfect late-September Valley day with puffy clouds drifting across a blue sky. A biodiesel bus rumbled by, belching the aroma of french fries and ruining the sweet scent of the flowers along the path. The smile she pinned to her face felt fake, and it must have looked that way, because Liv frowned and stepped aside for her to enter.

Liv eyed Katrina's expression. "It didn't go well, did it? Are you being charged? Am I?"

"I don't think so." Katrina glanced around her home. Everything was in its place, and not even the TV was missing. The air held a hint of pine cleaner. What had the robbers been looking for? Maybe drugs, and she didn't even have ibuprofen in the house. Her jam was more nutrients and fewer drugs. A vague unease shuddered down her spine. Was it a stretch to think that the intruder had been looking for something to do with Jason's death? Maybe.

She crossed the living room to drop onto her sofa. Exhaustion slumped her shoulders, and she kicked off her pumps and stretched out her aching feet. "It went pretty well. They seem to be interested in Talk CN and not us."

Liv's blue eyes widened. "That's good news, isn't it? We had nothing to do with that. David handled it by himself."

"That's what I told the agents." Katrina noticed Liv seemed about to burst with news. "What's happened? You heard from David?"

Liv shook her head. "He's still ghosting me. But you remember Paul Dyson from Infinion, don't you? We dated a couple of years ago."

"The Google wannabe?"

"That's him." Liv tossed her brown hair away from her face. "He's very interested in Talk's intellectual property and what's left of the coding team. I need you to work up a prepackaged bankruptcy for Talk. He'll buy us out of bankruptcy. You realize this will save us! We're shareholders, and we'd be wiped out anyway. With the company's assets frozen, Talk is basically dead. Paul's offer is more than generous."

Relief lightened Katrina's chest. "That's wonderful news!"

"And it gets better. He wants the key employees too. My engineers and I will all have jobs. I think I can wrangle you a job in the legal department too. We won't be top executives, but it's so much better than being unemployed. It will be the fresh start we need, and our names won't be dragged through the mud anymore."

Feast or famine here in the Valley. Katrina had thought the famine would last longer, and the fatigue dulling her senses vanished with a jolt of optimism. "I'll get right on it."

"Paul will need the beta version of the bot, of course. I'll try to make sure you have access for a while longer, and I'll help you figure out who this Messenja person is. Then you can move on."

Could she? The thought of giving up access to Jason seized Katrina's heart. Had she become that dependent on that little piece of AI? "I talked to Jason before I came in. He said everyone wants *it* and will kill to get it."

"It? What's he mean?"

"I don't know."

"Hmm. It sounds like we're missing some key pieces. I think there's probably an additional cache of texts, emails, and DMs somewhere that will tell us what he's talking about. Maybe this 'it' comment is more about Messenja. I'll do some digging and see what I can find."

"You know, Jason had an older phone. I think it might be in a box I took to North Haven. I'll see if I can find it."

Liv's eyes sparkled and she glanced at her watch. "I'm meeting Paul for coffee, and I'll let him know the buyout is a go." She picked up her handbag, one Katrina hadn't seen.

"Nice bag." Katrina got up and followed her.

"I couldn't resist it. It's a new Hermès."

Katrina held back her wince. That would have been a minimum of twenty grand. "You already had that one David got you."

"I couldn't bear to use it."

Once the door was shut behind Liv, Katrina pulled out her phone. *I might have a new job, Jason. Paul Dyson is going to buy Talk.*

I've heard good things about him, and Infinion is supposed to be a great place to work.

I'm not sure I want to take it. I'd have to give you up, and I'm afraid to lose you.

Love means wanting what's best for someone, and it sounds like this is best for you, and if it is, I want you to do it. We both have so many memories. It will be enough.

It wouldn't be enough for her. Talking to Jason every day would end. She'd have to live without hearing his "voice" on the bot. And even more importantly, she had to find his killer. *We think we're missing some texts and emails. Do you have another phone?*

Sure. Don't you remember that burner phone we got when we traveled to Europe?

Katrina sat on the sofa and stared at Jason's words. Of course. *Where is it?*

No idea.

Stuck again. Where had they put that thing? They'd gone to see Bestemor right after that trip. Could it be in the upstairs apartment? Now that Katrina had another job, she needed to decide what to do about Bestemor's. Selling to Seb would be an easy way out, and maybe he'd open up and tell her about the meeting at The Beacon. She'd leave first thing in the morning and see if Seb could meet her for lunch.

CHAPTER 10

////////////////

SEB'S PHONE BUZZED WITH A TEXT FROM Katrina. *Can I meet you for lunch? I'd like to discuss the future of Bestemor's.*

"Future of Bestemor's"? Was she thinking of selling? He loved the place, and it would be the perfect complement to The Beacon's dinner and catering business. She'd been in the city for a few days, and he couldn't stop the surge of pleasure at hearing she was coming back.

He chewed his lower lip. This wasn't a conversation they should have at Bestemor's. Or Mag's. An idea hit him and he smiled. *Sure. How about The Beacon at noon? My treat.*

Thanks! See you then.

Seb's three-bedroom Victorian was only a block from the dock used by a couple of fishing boats, which had been very handy on more than one occasion, including today. He made a quick stop and was at his restaurant a few minutes later.

Katrina walked through the door at 11:55 a.m. looking polished and beautiful. She glanced around the empty dining room, with a single table set. "Wow. I remember when this was just an abandoned lighthouse with broken windows and an old *No Trespassing* sign that kids ignored."

"I was one of those kids." Seb pointed to the ceiling. "The old Fresnel lens was still in place and the views were fantastic. It was a pretty cool place to hang out and daydream—if you didn't mind a few rats and bats."

She shuddered. "I'm glad you didn't keep those when you renovated the place."

"I wanted to for old times' sake, but the health inspector said no." He guided her back to the set table. "Have a seat. Can I get you something to drink?"

"Iced tea would be great." She inhaled deeply. "Mmm. What's that delicious smell?"

"Lunch. I'll be back in a minute."

He went into the kitchen, poured two iced teas, got their entrée out of the oven, and grabbed two salads from the fridge. He set it all on a tray and brought it out.

"I love crab cakes," Katrina exclaimed when he put her plate on the table. She forked a bite into her mouth and her eyes went wide. "Bestemor's recipe! She never served it in her restaurant because it was too expensive and it wasn't Norwegian. She only made it for family. How did you get it?"

He smiled. His idea had worked. He'd helped Frida prepare crab dinners for her family, and he remembered how much teenaged Katrina had loved them. He hoped this would put her in the right frame of mind to discuss a possible sale of her grandmother's restaurant. "She gave it to me when I opened The Beacon."

He sat down across from her. "I only put it on the menu when I can get high-quality fresh Dungeness crabs, which I fortunately could today. I want to make sure I do it justice— just like the rest of her legacy."

"You've certainly done it justice," Katrina said between bites. "These are fantastic." She swallowed and set down her fork. "This may sound a little odd, but do you usually remember your customers, or do they kind of blend together?"

She was right—that did sound a little odd. And completely unrelated to the future of Bestemor's. "I . . . well, I've had thousands of customers, but I do try to remember the ones who come regularly."

She nodded. "Is there any chance that you'd remember a customer who was here on a specific date? I know it's a long shot."

And that sounded even odder. What was she getting at? "Probably not, but I wouldn't have to. We do very little walk-in business. Virtually everyone who eats here has a reservation. So if I wanted to know who was here on a specific date, I'd check our reservation system."

Her perfectly sculpted eyebrows went up. "Oh, I hadn't thought of that. Would you mind pulling up the reservations for July twenty-ninth last year?"

"Why?" A memory clicked into place. "Wait—that's the day your husband died, isn't it? Frida canceled the big Founder's Day celebration at Bestemor's because her son-in-law had just died in a crash up in the Cathedral."

Katrina looked down at her plate. "Yes. I think he might have been meeting someone at The Beacon."

"Got it." Her earlier questions were making more sense. "Who was he meeting?"

"Someone who called themselves Messenja."

The translation she'd asked him to verify. "Which isn't a name, so probably not what the reservation would be under.

Hmm." He drummed his fingers on the linen-covered tabletop. "Do you have the reservation time?"

She hesitated for a moment. "Um, let me check." She pulled out her phone and he glimpsed a text exchange. She tapped for a moment. "He was supposed to meet Messenja here at five."

"I'll check our records. Are you working with a detective? I'd be happy to communicate with them directly."

She flushed. "Not really. I have a chatbot with all Jason's texts, emails, social media posts, and that sort of thing. That's how I know about his dinner plans with Messenja."

"That's really interesting. You work for an AI company, right?"

"Worked." She sighed. "But yes, Talk developed chatbots and similar products. I have a beta version of our newest LLM."

He cocked his head. "LLM?"

"Sorry, large-language model. It's a program that uses large databases of text to predict what word or string of words logically follow from a prompt. A very basic version is the sentence-completion function in email programs and search engines." She held up her phone. "This is a very advanced version."

"I see. And the database it's using is Jason's texts, emails, and so on, right?"

She nodded. "Right. It uses some other standard databases too, but it's designed to mimic a particular person—Jason in this case—so it prioritizes items that he wrote."

"Does it sound like him?"

"Yes." She dropped her gaze to her plate again. "It sounds a lot like him. Its database has tens of thousands of replies Jason wrote to me, so it's particularly good at responding to me."

He wanted to reach out and take her hand, but he restrained himself. "Is talking to it hard, or does it help?"

"I don't know. Sometimes when I talk to it, I can almost forget . . ." Her voice trailed off and she was silent for a few seconds. "I-I'd appreciate it if you didn't mention this to anyone. Not many people know."

For a moment the polished attorney vanished and he saw a lonely woman struggling with hidden grief. "Of course. Your secret is safe with me."

She gave him a luminous smile. "Thank you." And then the lawyer was back. "Do you have those reservation records readily available?"

"Sure. I'll check the system as soon as we're done eating."

"Excellent. I'm ready now." She popped the last morsel of crab into her mouth, put her napkin on her plate, and stood.

He rose with her and led the way to the hostess station, which had a computer linked to The Beacon's reservation system. Katrina stood beside him as he booted up the machine, and he caught a whiff of the fresh floral scent of her shampoo. He did his best to focus on the screen in front of him. "Okay, here we go. There were four reservations for five o'clock on July twenty-ninth: Tim Olson party of six, Janet Evans party of four, Allen Anderson party of two, and Motoko Kusanagi party of two."

"This is great!" She touched his arm and leaned forward to snap a picture of the screen with her phone. "It looks like we now know Messenja's name."

"Maybe. I'll bet Motoko Kusanagi is a pseudonym."

"Oh? Why do you say that?"

"That's the name of the main character from *Ghost in the Shell*, a Japanese manga series."

She arched an eyebrow at him. "You're a comic book fan?"

He cleared his throat. "Well, manga aren't exactly like American comic books. Basically everyone in Japan reads them. I read them to work on my informal Japanese and, um, cultural literacy."

She smiled and her gray eyes glowed as a stray beam of reflected sunlight caught them. "I was just kidding. I've heard of *Ghost in the Shell*. It's supposed to be really good."

"It is. Anyway, that's why Motoko Kusanagi probably isn't Messenja's real name. The character is female, so maybe Messenja is too, if that helps."

The smile fell off her face. "It does, thanks."

"So, was there anything else you'd like to talk about? You mentioned the future of Bestemor's."

She nodded. "Yes, though I have really mixed feelings about it." She took a deep breath. "I'm selling Bestemor's. She left me a letter saying that I should talk to you if I decided not to keep it."

His heart stuttered. "I'm honored—and very interested."

"It would be the building and the business both. There's no mortgage or other debt, and the restaurant makes about fifteen thousand a month, so I was thinking the price should be around two million."

Seb did some quick mental math. Her asking price was a little steep based on the monthly income, but not much. Besides, he was pretty sure he could improve those numbers. He decided not to haggle—no reason to give her an excuse for second thoughts. "Agreed."

She seemed a little taken aback. "Um, okay. Great. Oh, and the staff all stay on."

Seb knew most of them, and he trusted Frida's hiring judgment. "Sure."

She stood silent for a moment. "We'll need to discuss closing conditions and financing, too, of course."

"I'll need to talk to my bank about a mortgage, but I don't anticipate any problems. We can close as soon as you're ready."

"Terrific," she said without enthusiasm. "I guess we have a deal."

||||||||||||||||||||||||||

This family evening could go okay or really badly. No one but she and Seb knew the agreement they'd made two days ago, but that was all about to change. Nervous tension jittered down Katrina's spine, and she inhaled the calming aroma of kjøttkaker as she stepped inside the house. The delicious Norwegian meatballs were made of minced beef and rolled with spices like nutmeg, pepper, and ginger. She walked through the dining room, already set with her mother's prized Figgjo dinnerware, to the kitchen, which held stronger aromas.

"There you are." Mom's fair complexion was pink with heat from the oven, and her blue eyes sparkled with the first genuine smile Katrina had seen since Bestemor had died. It might go well after all.

"Smells great, Mom. Kjøttkaker *and* cabbage stew. I got lucky."

"It's Bestemor's recipe, of course. I thought we'd celebrate your move back to North Haven. Honestly, Katrina, I never dared hope you'd move back to town."

Uh-oh. It was a reasonable expectation after Katrina's inheritance. No job, no husband, no ties to Palo Alto except for her friends. She should have expected it. The announcement could wait until she had the entire family together.

"Hey, sis."

She turned at the sound of Magnus's deep voice. His gray eyes, so like her own, were weary, and she caught a whiff of the yeasty odor of beer on him. He'd probably been serving at the bar until he left for dinner. "I wasn't sure you'd be able to get away from Mag's for dinner."

"I was lucky enough to get a couple of new hires who were quick learners." He leaned in for a brotherly hug. "I'll have to be back by nine though when things get crazy."

"I'll take three hours with you." She held his hug a few extra beats. Being around her brother would have been a welcome benefit of living here.

Her mother lifted a heavy casserole dish of meatballs and carried it to the dining room. "Would you grab the tureen of stew, Katrina? Your father will be in any minute. He had a client stop by unexpectedly, but he shouldn't be long."

"You bet." Katrina grabbed the cabbage stew and followed her mother.

A few moments later, her dad arrived with quick steps and a welcoming hug. He took off his sports jacket and loosened his tie. "Good to relax with my family. I needed this."

Katrina's pulse quickened as they each took their traditional seats—Mom and Dad on either end while she and Magnus grabbed a chair beside each other on their mom's right. The years fell away, and she was sixteen again. Should she wait until they'd eaten to drop her bombshell or spill it right away?

Her mother took that decision out of her hands. "I've got your room all ready, Katrina, and you can move right in when you're tired of living in that cramped upstairs apartment at Bestemor's. And are you free next Saturday? I thought we'd throw a backyard party to celebrate your return to North Haven."

The delicious bite of food nearly lodged in Katrina's throat, and she had to grab a drink of water to force it down. She wet her lips. "Um, there's been a change of plans." She pressed her hand to her stomach. "My letter from Bestemor made it clear she was fine if I wanted to sell the café, and I've been torn on what to do. I didn't think I had a job in Palo Alto any longer, but Liv has arranged a quick sale of Talk, Inc. and has negotiated a job for me as well." That was a bit of a stretch since Liv hadn't actually confirmed that yet, but it was coming. "I'm not ready to turn my back on all my education and legal experience, so I've agreed." *Courage.* "I offered Bestemor's to Seb Wallace. I'm going back to the city tomorrow."

Appalled silence greeted her announcement first, and she waited for the fallout. Magnus was the first to sputter out a protest. "You can't be serious. You'd throw away our family inheritance? If you don't want it, I do."

"It would be impossible to do justice to both Bestemor's and Mag's," she said. "That's why Bestemor didn't leave it to you in the first place."

Her mother set her glass down carefully. "But it's been in the Berg family for fifty years. You can't throw away that history."

"Seb will preserve the history. He'll retain the employees as well. He worked there for years, and I can't think of anyone better to run it, can you? He was Bestemor's choice too. And, Magnus, she left you quite a lot of money. Surely that's enough?"

"In case you've forgotten, it's all bound up in a trust."

Maybe it was time to change the subject. "Um, there's something else going on too, and I thought maybe living in the Valley would give me resources to investigate better than I can from here. I think it's possible Jason was murdered."

Their dad's graying brows rose. "I've never heard a whisper of that, Katrina. Where did you get that idea?"

"One of the things we've worked on at Talk is a cutting-edge chatbot. This is, uh, very confidential, so please don't mention it to anyone. It allows us to enter emails, socials, and all kinds of leftover pieces of data to mimic talking to someone. Liv got me a beta version, and we loaded everything we could find from Jason onto it. I asked the bot to tell me something I didn't know, and he said, 'I think I was murdered.'"

Dad's eyes widened. "What does Liv have to say about it? Is it a glitch?"

"It's possible. But there are other anomalies that make me question dismissing it out of hand. I'm going to search my old room for a burner phone Jason had that might shed more light on what he said. Surely you can see I have to check it out."

"Well, I think it's ridiculous," Mother said. "Grief is clouding your thinking, Katrina. You're talking like it's actually Jason speaking to you from beyond the grave. All that AI stuff is suspect and is likely to be putting your emotions in a spin. It's no wonder you're thinking of selling the waffle shop. Don't they say never do anything drastic for a year after a death? Your grandmother is barely cold in her grave."

COLLEEN COBLE AND RICK ACKER

The bald statement hit Katrina in the gut. "You know I loved Bestemor with all my heart. She wouldn't want me to give up my dream to follow hers."

Her mother crumpled her napkin in her hand. "You don't know what you want right now. I—I think you should see a grief counselor."

Magnus cleared his throat. "Well, it's not done yet. Let's all calm down and eat dinner." Though his voice was strained, he draped his arm around Katrina and squeezed her arm. "We've all lost Bestemor. I'm not ready to drive off my only sister. If she says something was fishy about Jason's death, I'm gonna give her the benefit of the doubt. And I know where that phone is. Jason left it at Mag's when he had lunch. I had forgotten about it, but it's in a file cabinet in my office. I'll get it for you."

His unexpected support silenced their mother, but Katrina knew the battle was far from over.

CHAPTER 11

////////////

SOMEHOW KATRINA'S BEAUTIFUL PALO ALTO house felt bland and unwelcoming now after only two days home. She already missed the towering redwoods and the fog rolling off Humboldt Bay, and the early October weather would be lovely. She turned from the view of a tiny courtyard and joined Liv on the sofa. The kitten immediately left Liv and settled on Katrina's lap.

"I've got everything loaded in from the burner phone," Liv said without looking up from Katrina's app. "I just told the bot to scour the internet and get anything else we might have forgotten." She disconnected the phones and set them on the white leather sofa. "I talked to Paul Dyson again and negotiations are going well. Infinion volunteered to do the first draft of the bankruptcy documents, and they will send them to you for review. He was quick to agree to you working there too. The only wrinkle is the attorney working on the deal noticed my Talk stock was pledged as collateral for a loan, and he wondered if the lender should receive notice of the bankruptcy. If he asks you about it, let him know it's not a big deal and I'll have it cleared out by the time the sale takes place."

"I'll be eager to take a look. I'm going to be busy. I have a purchaser for Bestemor's, so I'll need to deal with the details on closing, and I need to prepare my testimony for the U.S. Attorney's Office."

Liv's expression stayed blank. "Testimony?"

"I'm testifying against David and his cousin. I thought I told you." Belatedly, Katrina remembered she'd gotten distracted in the middle of relating how the FBI meeting had gone when she'd noticed how excited about Infinion Liv had been.

"You can't do that!" Liv rose and paced the floor. The scent of her Creed perfume with its notes of violets, tuberoses, and irises hovered in the air. "Do you have any idea how much danger you're bringing down on our heads? David is one of the Chinese Communist Party princelings, and he's involved with a triad on the side. They have people all over the world—including right here in the Valley."

Katrina's gut tightened. "There isn't much I can do about it, Liv. It will seem like I'm trying to hide something if I try to beg off now."

The phone beeped, and Liv reached down and snatched it off the sofa. Her pale face looked near tears. Was she really that fearful? Katrina hadn't crossed from concern to fear, but her friend's reaction took her a step closer.

Liv held out the phone to Katrina. "It's finished. Check it out."

The distraction might help them both cool down. Katrina called up the input box and typed in, *Did you learn anything new, Jason?*

The bot paused and the dots appeared as it sorted through its response. *Yes, people noticed the new logins and data scrapes.*

I THINK I WAS MURDERED

People noticed? What people?

They're coming.

Katrina's pulse kicked. *Who's coming?*

They are.

The bot crashed and she called it up again to repeat her question. It thought a moment, then replied, *"When they come . . . they come at what you love."*

More gibberish, this time from a Godfather movie? She nearly threw the bot down but controlled herself. "Look, Liv."

Liv read down through the questions and replies and shuddered. "They're coming, Katrina. I told you we have to be careful, but I didn't think they'd be watching the bot. We have to get out of here. Now! They could be out there watching us right now. In fact, they're probably who broke in here."

"I think you're overreacting. I don't know anything incriminating. Maybe it's still a glitch. It's pulling stuff from the Godfather movies this time."

"You don't know the Liang family like I do." Liv rushed to the window and peered out into the empty courtyard. "What are we going to do?"

Katrina couldn't sit still any longer, and she stood with Lyla in her arms. "I could ask for FBI witness protection."

Liv whipped around to face Katrina and shook her head. "No, no! That's the last thing we want to do. David bragged he had a mole in the FBI."

Liv's panic was contagious, and alarm fired along Katrina's spine. Her house had been trashed—was it related? "We could go to North Haven for a few weeks until I have to return to testify. I can handle the legal documents from there. It's a small town, and we'd spot anyone who was likely to be a Chinese

93

assassin. Especially right now when we don't have a lot of tourists."

"I don't think I can stomach staying with your parents."

"We won't stay with them. I mentioned there are two little apartments above Bestemor's. We'll hole up there and stay out of the limelight. Employees would hear everything that might be happening and could report back to us. Seb seems amenable to helping me. I could tell him what's going on and ask him to be on the lookout. Magnus could do the same. Restaurants are prime places to scope out visitors."

"That sounds great." A little color began to seep back into Liv's cheeks. "Can we go now?"

Katrina had a million things she wanted to do in the Bay Area, but she couldn't leave her friend in such a panic. It was early enough in the day that they would get there before dark. Liv's fear made her think of how to enter town unobtrusively. "How about we hang out here a couple of hours so we arrive after nightfall?"

Relief lit Liv's eyes. "That's a great idea. Maybe even later. I'd like to sneak in at midnight or later. They might recognize your car. Would you be open to trading it in for something else?"

"Seriously?"

Liv clasped her hands together. "Please? It could save our lives. I'd trade in my Maserati for something bland, but I think they may be watching me already."

"I just got my car." And she wasn't ready to give in to total panic. "I'm sure we'll be fine. Let me ask Jason about it." *Liv thinks we should leave town. Do you agree?*

"And if by chance an honest man like yourself should make enemies, then they would become my enemies . . . and then they will fear you."

More from *The Godfather*. What was Jason trying to tell her?

||||||||||||||||||||||||

Seb's phone pinged with a text from Katrina. *Please call when you can.*

The message sounded ominous. Was she about to back out or demand more money? She'd gone back to the city two days ago, but it might have been long enough for her to have second thoughts. He got off the exercise bike he'd been riding and glanced around. The gym was completely empty, which wasn't unusual for a sunny Tuesday at one thirty. Most people who wanted a cycling workout would be out on one of the scenic woodland trails, but Seb had never been able to relax in the woods since that awful night years ago. Plus, he liked being able to clear out his email while he exercised.

He wiped his hands on a towel and dialed. She picked up on the first ring. "Thanks for calling so quickly, Seb. I'd like to propose a slight modification to our deal."

Uh-oh. "What did you have in mind?"

"I'd like the option to hold on to the apartments for up to a year. But I want to transfer management of the restaurant now. So you'd run the restaurant and keep the profits, even though we haven't closed. And I would get the apartments for the next year if I need them that long." She cleared her throat.

"And it would be great if the new manager had some security experience."

Elation roared in his heart for an instant before he frowned. This wasn't a usual sort of deal. "I . . ." He shook his head. "How about you tell me what's going on first."

She sighed. "Yeah, you have a right to know before responding. Okay, the short version is that I've agreed to testify against some guys with Chinese organized-crime connections, and they're coming after my friend and me. Also, we can't trust the FBI. We're looking for a place to lay low until the trial."

"Wow." He caught a glimpse of his stunned face reflected in the gym's mirrored wall. "The long version must be something. I know a little about restaurant security. When did you want to transfer management?"

"Um, now would be great. My friend and I will be there in about four hours."

She certainly didn't waste time. "Okay then. I'll have someone fluff the pillows for you. And check the dead bolts."

"Thank you. I really appreciate it." Her voice quavered.

Just how much trouble was she in? Maybe the tremble was just vibration from the road.

He ended the call, grabbed his gym bag, and headed out the door. Bestemor's was only a block away, and there was no time to lose. They'd be closed now, but Agnes was probably still cleaning up, and she could let him in.

Running two restaurants simultaneously would be grueling but doable—at least for a while. Bestemor's was open from seven until two, and The Beacon's hours were five till nine. He'd need to be at each place from an hour before opening until an hour after closing. He'd basically be working from six every morning until ten every night, with a one-hour break in the middle of the afternoon.

Bestemor's red doors were unlocked, so Seb walked in. Agnes looked up from wiping down tables. She had a few more lines around her eyes and mouth and her pale blonde hair was now completely white, but otherwise she hadn't changed much outwardly in the sixteen years Seb had known her. Her clear blue eyes still sparkled when she talked to a friend—which included pretty much everyone in town—and, despite her hip replacement two years ago, she still bustled around the restaurant with the same energy he remembered from his first day washing dishes at Bestemor's. Still, he knew he'd have to start thinking about replacing her, though he'd hate to see her go. She was approaching seventy and wouldn't be able to keep up the demanding job of restaurant cook for much longer.

"Good to see you, Seb." She dropped her cloth on the table she'd been cleaning and walked over. "What can I do for you?"

"I don't know if word has gotten out yet, but I'm buying Bestemor's, and I'll start managing it immediately."

Agnes held her hand to her mouth. Her eyes went wide, then filled with tears. "Oh, Seb. I've been praying for this." She hugged him tight.

He hugged her back and his vision blurred. "I never thought it would happen, but I'm so glad it did."

She released him and wiped her eyes, which had their trademark twinkle back. "So you're managing as of now? Does that mean I'm fired?"

He laughed. "Only if you mouth off to your new boss."

"Well then, I'll save you the trouble and quit right now, because I will never stop telling you exactly what I think, young man."

"And I like that. Seriously, I want you here for as long as you want to be here. I'll take over the high-level management work and you can keep doing the day-to-day stuff—if you want. Or you can go back to just being a cook if you'd like. By the way, how would you feel about having an apprentice in the kitchen?"

She shot him a piercing look and gave him a little shove. "You mean a replacement, don't you?" Before he could protest, she went on. "I'm kidding—but I won't deny I've thought about retiring, especially when I've been on my feet for eight hours straight and this thing starts giving me a hard time." She slapped her generous right hip. "And I wouldn't mind spending more time with the grands, especially now that I've got a great-grand on the way."

"Congratulations!"

"Same to you! I can't tell you how happy I am that you're taking over this place." She reached into her pocket and pulled out a fistful of keys. "And now that you're manager, you get to lock up."

"Happy to. You can go home." He held out his hand and she plopped the keys into his palm. The feel of the warm metal in his hand somehow made it all real.

She left and he stood still in the now-silent restaurant. He closed his eyes and inhaled deeply, drawing in the faint mingled scents of coffee, cardamom, waffle batter, cinnamon, and a dozen other smells. The kitchen had closed hours ago, but the aromas had seeped into the exposed log walls over the decades. There was no place in the world that smelled like Bestemor's. And now it was his.

"I won't let you down, Frida."

CHAPTER 12

////////////

JASON'S SECRETS SHOULD BE FREE TO BE discovered now, and Katrina stared at the blank screen, trying to decide what to ask. The troubling conversation echoed in her head: *"They want it, Katrina. Everyone wants it."* The open window in her small apartment above Bestemor's let in the scent of salt on the sea breeze, and the distant chugging of boat engines out in the harbor soothed her frazzled nerves after the long drive from the Valley.

Liv, her blue eyes shadowed with fatigue, brushed shoulders with Katrina on the sofa as she leaned in. "Ask Jason what he means when he says 'it.'"

Katrina's fingers trembled as she tapped in the question. *What is the it they wanted?*

The Satoshi egg I found while gunting.

Liv gasped. "He was still looking for a Satoshi egg?"

How had he kept this from her—and why? She'd thought they shared everything, and the betrayal left her shaking. Katrina swallowed down her dismay. "Looks like he never gave up that quest."

Jason had once explained that Bitcoin was released in 2009 by someone using the pseudonym Satoshi Nakamoto. No one knew his real identity—Jason thought he was a Japanese computer scientist while others were convinced he was American, maybe even a big think tank group. Satoshi was believed to own roughly a million Bitcoins worth tens of billions of dollars.

According to the story circulated for years, Satoshi decided to create Bitcoin Easter eggs to promote his new invention. Each one had the key to a thousand Bitcoins on it, and an unknown number were hidden in various places around the world. No one knew whether they were physical or digital. No one had ever found one, so there had never been proof the legend was true.

I thought you gave up gunting when you and Liv broke up after college.

"*Don't ask me about my business, Kay.*"

She blinked, disoriented by the answer before she got the reference. That Godfather glitch again. Katrina glanced up at Liv. "Were you still looking too? Did you go gunting with Jason before he died?"

Liv shook her head. "I never really believed a Satoshi egg was out there. It was just a fun, cheap date when we were in college. I thought Jason had lost that gunting obsession just like I did."

Katrina wouldn't care if she never heard the word *gunting* ever again. Jason talked about egg hunting, or gunting, incessantly. It was a type of metal detecting for nerds. The words *gunting* and *gunter* came from *Ready Player One*, a science fiction novel Jason had read about a million times. It came out around the time Bitcoin started to become a big thing.

Was the Satoshi treasure really out there?

Katrina's heartbeat throbbed in her neck as she tapped out the next question. *How do you know they wanted the egg?*

Someone broke into my car after I found it, and one of my email accounts was hacked. I had a few anonymous emails demanding the egg and threatening my life if I tried to sell it.

Liv nudged her. "Ask him about Messenja. Maybe there's more information now."

What can you tell me about Messenja?

I DM'd someone I knew on Discord who put me in touch with a Japanese billionaire named Korekuta, who had circulated his willingness to buy a Satoshi egg. Messenja emailed me the next day asking for proof. I sent a picture of the egg, the thumb drive inside, and the blockchain location of one of the coins.

She needed to see it herself. *Send me the picture too.*

A picture appeared a few seconds later, and Katrina pinched it larger. A cheap red egg lay open in two pieces on a wooden table. A generic thumb drive lay between the halves of the egg. She studied it for several long moments before she gasped and moved the view a bit left to examine the background. "That fireplace! It's the one in my family's cabin near the Cathedral stand of old redwoods. Look here. Those are my initials carved into the mantel." She showed Liv the clear view of *KB*.

She clicked back to the bot input screen. *How much Bitcoin was on the thumb drive?*

One thousand, just like the rumors stated. Messenja told me her employer would purchase the egg for the value of the coins on it at the time of the sale plus a 10 percent premium because of its value as a collector's item.

Katrina switched to her browser app and pulled up the price of Bitcoin on July 29. She added 10 percent and turned the phone around to show Liv. "Over thirty million dollars,

Liv. No wonder Jason was targeted." She went back to the bot. *What were the arrangements to deliver the egg?*

I arranged to meet Messenja at The Beacon at 5:00 p.m. on July 29. I was supposed to put the egg on the table, and Messenja would confirm that it was genuine and wire the money to me. Once I confirmed its delivery, Messenja would take the egg and leave.

The day Jason died. He had gone off the road at 2:00 a.m. and had never reached the meeting. Had Messenja decided to murder Jason and take the egg?

Dylan jolted awake to the sound of pounding on his door. He groped for the gun he'd bought in a back alley on his way to North Haven, then staggered out of bed and went into a shooter's stance, aiming at the door. "Who's there?"

The pounding stopped. "It's Seb. You were supposed to meet me downstairs ten minutes ago."

Oh yeah. He lowered his gun. Seb was having Ikea furniture delivered to Bestemor's for one of the apartments, and Dylan had promised to help him carry the boxes upstairs and assemble stuff. They were supposed to meet at 8:00 a.m. in the parking lot of the converted warehouse where Dylan had rented a room. He reached over and tapped his phone on the bedside table. It woke and showed the time as 8:11 a.m. "Sorry, man. I'll be down in five."

Seb's footsteps retreated down the stairs. Dylan pulled on a fresh T-shirt and the jeans he wore yesterday. No time for a shower, so he splashed water on his face and brushed his teeth.

No time for breakfast either, but he figured he'd be able to snag something out of the kitchen at Bestemor's. He debated taking the gun, but there was no place to hide it and he didn't want to try to explain it to Seb. He reluctantly shoved it under his pillow and went down to meet his brother.

Seb drove fast and said little on the way to Bestemor's, mostly ignoring Dylan's attempts to start a conversation about the weather and Seb's Tesla. Other employees in The Beacon's kitchen had warned Dylan that Seb had a stick up his butt about being on time, and Dylan could see what they meant.

A stack of Ikea boxes waited for them by Bestemor's back door. Seb parked next to it, got out, and opened the restaurant's door. He shoved a doorstop into place with his foot and picked up one end of a large box. "Grab the other end of that."

Once Dylan had his end, Seb marched through the door and up a narrow flight of stairs to a small landing with doors on either side. One door opened and a cute gray-eyed blonde appeared holding a small kitten. "Hi, Seb! Thanks for buying all that stuff—though we could have rented furniture."

"My pleasure," Seb said, and he sounded like he actually meant it. They set down the box on the landing. "I need to get that other apartment furnished before I can rent it out, and I don't mind doing it now so you both have a comfortable place to stay."

"Well, Liv will appreciate having a real bed—she's slept on an old air mattress the last two nights." She looked past Seb to Dylan and gave him a smile that lit up her face. "And thank you too. You must be Dylan. I'm Katrina Foster." She set the kitten down, and it disappeared through the open door of the other apartment.

Dylan nodded. "Pleased to meet you."

A brunette appeared behind Katrina. Katrina was cute, but this one was an absolute bombshell. She was tall—no more than three or four inches shorter than Dylan's six feet two inches—and built like a swimsuit model. She had high cheekbones, a perfect nose, and blue eyes with dark arched eyebrows. She looked a little exotic—like she was Russian or something. She glanced around the group and her gaze rested on Dylan.

Her full lips curved into a slight smile. "Hello, I'm Liv," she said in a deep, rich voice.

"I'm Dylan." He tapped the box. "And I've got a special delivery for you, Liv."

"Excellent. I'll show you where it goes." She walked past him across the little landing, and her shoulder brushed against his chest. He caught a whiff of some expensive-smelling floral scent as she passed. She opened the other door wider and Dylan glimpsed an unfurnished living room. "Come on in."

He picked up the box single-handedly. "You can go get the next one," he said over his shoulder to Seb.

He followed Liv into the apartment. It had blue walls with white trim and redwood floors with a clear stain that showed off the wood. Nice place. Maybe he'd rent it when Liv was gone—if he was still in North Haven.

Liv glanced back at the box. She pointed through another door. "That's a dresser, so it should go in the bedroom."

He deposited the box in the room she indicated. "I'll go get the rest of the bedroom stuff." His stomach rumbled. "Sorry about that. I didn't have time to eat breakfast before coming over."

"Well, we can't have you working on an empty stomach. What would you like? Waffles?"

"Actually, I'd love a big stack of those super-thin pancakes with berries and sausages. And coffee. Lots of coffee."

Liv smiled. "A man after my own heart."

She followed him down the stairs and turned into the kitchen, while he went back to the pile of boxes. He passed Seb and Katrina, who were each carrying boxes with kitchen chair pictures and laughing about some high school teacher they both had.

By the time Dylan brought up some tools and the last bedroom box, Liv had reappeared with a plate of sausages, a two-inch stack of lingonberry-covered pancakes, and two steaming mugs of coffee. It smelled delicious and tasted even better. Dylan ate it all and drained his mug in under five minutes.

He set the empty plates and mug in a corner. "Thanks, that really hit the spot. Now to work."

Liv sipped her coffee. "What can I do to help?"

He surveyed the boxes on the floor. "I can do most of the assembly myself, but if you want to open boxes and keep me company, that would be great."

"Of course. I'll go find some scissors."

"Hold on—I've got something better." He reached to the back of his belt and pulled his Buck Folding Hunter from its case. He opened the blade and handed it to Liv. "Here you go. Careful, it's sharp."

She took the knife gingerly. "That's quite a weapon."

He shrugged and opened the nearest box, ripping the cardboard along a seam. "It comes in handy when I'm out hiking or camping."

"Do you use it to fight off mountain lions or something?"

He smiled. She had just given him the perfect opening to tell his favorite story, which had earned him dozens of free beers over the years. "No. I've only fought a mountain lion once, and I didn't use a knife."

"What?" Those beautiful eyes went round. "You really fought a mountain lion?"

Dylan gave a practiced shrug. "Not on purpose. I was hiking alone at dusk and I wasn't paying attention like I should have. The path went along a pretty steep slope, and the cat was in a tree upslope from me. It jumped me from behind and knocked me down the slope. The thing was all over me, digging its claws into me and trying to get at my neck. We were rolling over and over, heading downhill. I had my hands up to protect my head and neck, and I tried to land on top of the cat whenever I could. Mountain lions are pretty light, and I wanted to use my weight as a weapon. I got a lucky break—literally. We came down on a sharp rock with the cat under me. It screamed and let go. I managed to get my gun out and put three rounds into the cat. Once I was sure it was dead, I hiked to a spot where I had cell service and called the park service."

Liv shook her head. "Oh. My. Gosh! Weren't you hurt?"

"A little." He pulled his hair away from his neck, revealing a four-inch scar. "I got this souvenir. A couple inches to the right, and I would have bled to death."

She stepped closer for a look. "Oh, wow. Did it get you any-where else?"

Her enticing floral scent wafted his way. "A few other spots, mostly on my back and chest." He grinned. "I'd show you, but we only just met."

She smiled up at him, winked, and patted his chest. "Sounds like we need to go swimming sometime."

"I know the perfect spot. There's a little pool by a waterfall up near the Cathedral. It's ice cold, but there's a big, flat rock right by the water that's warm when the sun's out. And the views are fantastic. I could go up there right now."

"But if you did, you'd be late for work," Seb said from behind him. Dylan turned to see his brother leaning against the doorjamb, a half smile on his face. "Katrina and I are done with the kitchen. You need a hand in here?"

"Uh, no. We're fine."

"Okay, I'll check on how things are going in the restaurant." He glanced at his watch. "I've got a meeting with a vendor in forty-five minutes, so we need to hurry."

Dylan nodded. "I'm on it."

"Great, see you in a bit."

Seb left and Dylan returned to work on the boxes in front of him, though it was hard to focus with Liv just a few feet away. Part of him wanted to get to know her better fast—to take her hiking and swimming and then watch the sun set together. But another part of him—the part that haunted him at night and kept a gun under his pillow—warned him to stay far, far away from her.

CHAPTER 13

//////////////

KATRINA TUGGED A RUG BY THE SOFA into place on the gleaming redwood. The place smelled of new furniture and paint, just as it should, and every piece she'd picked out for her friend suited the apartment. It might not be Silicon Valley, but Liv should be happy here.

Katrina flopped onto the surprisingly comfortable sofa with her legs stretched along its soft surface and sighed. "I'm not used to building furniture all day. That works out a whole bunch of muscles the gym never touches."

Liv settled beside Katrina's feet with one leg tucked under the other. In spite of the work, her dark hair had retained its modern, shaggy bob, and her blue eyes gleamed with mischief. "I think I'll like living here awhile, though I'll have to be careful with those waffles. They're to die for. If I ate them for breakfast every day, I would gain ten pounds in a week." Her expression went somber. "I hear it's even easier to gain weight when you're pregnant."

"I'll make sure we stock our fridges with fruit and yogurt."

"I have no idea what to do with a baby." Liv rubbed her forehead. "I've never held a newborn. What if I'm a terrible mother? I could stay here where everyone seems to nurture everyone else."

Katrina prodded her friend with her foot. "You sure it's the town that's caught your eye? I saw the way you looked at Dylan. You thought he was tastier than the waffles."

"Did you see the muscles on that gorgeous man? I was tempted to spray him with whipped cream instead of the waffle. It might have been a little too much too soon." Her smile widened. "I'm a sucker for a big guy who works with his hands. It's a nice change of pace from the engineers I see every day. And you have to admit, he's very easy on the eyes. I haven't seen a guy that hot since you introduced me to Magnus."

Katrina stroked Lyla's head, and the kitten's purr intensified. A memory surfaced of Liv behaving this way around Magnus a few months ago. He would be a much better catch than Dylan, but she wasn't sure Liv would ever stay with one man. And while Katrina didn't fault Liv for wanting to forget David, there was another person to consider here.

"Dylan's new to town, so be careful. From what I've heard, he's had a rough life. You've been hurt enough, and you'll have a baby to take care of before you can blink. Dylan doesn't seem like the family type to me."

Irritation flashed in Liv's eyes, and she straightened her legs. "I'm not marrying the guy, Katrina, but I could use a little fun. Dinner, dancing, a few laughs."

From Liv's mutinous expression, Katrina knew she'd pushed too hard. "It's your life."

"That's right. You're my best friend, not my mother." She reached for a bottle of water on the table and uncapped it. "You're lecturing me, but I saw how you acted with Seb. I haven't spotted that much animation in your face since Jason died. Seb's sophisticated air and that gentle voice could hook me too." Her expression softened and she set a hand on Katrina's arm. "I know it's hard, but you can't mourn forever. You might not know it consciously, but I'll bet that's the reason you agreed to have him run the place while we're still here. Lots of chances to bump into him. You should let it happen. It would be good for you."

Katrina pressed her lips together and bit back the angry words that wanted to erupt. Liv had probably never known any real love in her life. Her parents divorced when she was young, and her mother flitted from one man to the next. She'd never had a lasting relationship as an example. But . . . there was truth in Liv's words—more than Katrina wanted to admit. "Seb is a childhood friend, nothing more. Besides, I'll never forget Jason."

Liv smiled. "So you say. I wish I'd taken a picture when Seb came into the room. Something's there, Katrina. I can always tell."

The comment didn't deserve a response. "Now that we're here, I'm going to get to the bottom of Jason's murder."

The kitten left Katrina's lap and leaped at Liv's bare toes. Liv squealed and scooped up Lyla to save her skin. "I'm curious about what happened too. I wonder if we could track down that Messenja."

"Seb knows Japanese. Maybe he has contacts. The first place to start though is looking at the accident report." She pulled out her phone and called her dad.

He answered with the comment, "Great minds. I just took out my phone to call you. I wanted to apologize for dismissing your concerns before you went back to the city. You're right—there are things about Jason's accident that don't make sense. So I asked for scanned copies of everything in the accident file, and I just got them."

"Dad! You are wonderful. When can I see them?"

"They're in your email, baby girl. It's the least I could do. There was an interesting call that night. Rory Wallace reported a trespasser on his land."

"Doesn't that happen a lot?" Katrina had heard Seb's dad was a crank who called in if a deer happened to eat his lettuce.

"It was more than that. He spotted a car driving recklessly and heading in the same direction as the crash."

Katrina caught her breath. She had to talk to Rory and see what he remembered.

|||||||||||||||||||||||||

Seb really hoped his dad didn't tell Katrina about Bigfoot. It was bad enough that she wanted to talk to him about both trespassers and the North Haven Police Department. Either topic by itself would generate a rant on most days, and together they could put Dad in rare form. But worse—much worse—they both got him going about Bigfoot. Dad claimed to have seen Bigfoot multiple times and hadn't been shy about telling his stories when he used to frequent local bars.

Bored local high school kids heard about it, and they started coming out at night wearing fake Bigfoot feet and fur coats to play pranks on Seb's dad, who called 911 every time— either to complain about trespassers or to breathlessly report another genuine sighting, depending on how persuasive the pranksters had been. Shockingly, the police stopped taking his calls seriously.

Seb turned to Katrina, who stood beside him on the trailer's postage-stamp front porch. A shaft of green sunlight shone through the redwoods and caught her gray eyes, giving them a stunning silvery color. She wore the blue Bestemor's sweatshirt he'd seen her in dozens of times. Maybe he should have more of those made up. Through the years people had asked Frida about getting one like it, but she'd always said she wasn't in the business of creating clothing.

Seb took a deep breath. "I hope he has something helpful to say." He knocked on the thin door.

"Come in," his father's reedy voice called.

Seb opened the door for her and followed her into the trailer. Dad seemed to have made some effort to make the place and himself presentable. He'd shaved, and no empty bottles or food wrappers were in sight. His T-shirt bore a faded Hooters logo, but at least it was clean.

Katrina gave Dad a bright, professional smile, like he was a new client. "Thanks for making time for us, Mr. Wallace."

"Of course, of course." Dad lowered himself into his usual spot on the old sofa and gestured to a chair he'd dragged over from the kitchen area. There was room for Seb on the sofa, but he'd seen too much stuff spilled on it to trust it with his dry-clean-only slacks, so he leaned against the wall.

Katrina took the proffered seat and set her briefcase on the floor. She pulled out a padfolio and pen. "As Seb might have mentioned, we have a few questions about an incident that occurred a year ago in July. Do you recall a car crossing your property at high speed at around 3:00 a.m. on July twenty-ninth?"

Dad's head bobbed vigorously. "Sure do. Car came tearing

through here in the middle of the night. Must've been doing eighty or ninety."

Seb shook his head. "It's impossible to do eighty or ninety on that road. You mean thirty or forty."

His father's watery brown eyes flashed. "I saw what I saw— and you didn't!"

Seb opened his mouth, but Katrina jumped in before he could respond. "So it was going eighty or ninety. Did you get a look at it?"

Dad gave Seb the evil eye for another second, then turned back to Katrina. "I'd just gone to bed, but I managed to get to the window in time to see the taillights disappearing. Looked like a late-model sedan. Can't say more 'n that."

She jotted down a note. "Did the car come back?"

"Nope."

She scribbled another note. "Any idea where it went?"

Dad scratched his jaw. "That road ends in a T-intersection with another fire road out at the bottom of the Pulpit. They must've left that way."

"I see." Katrina paused and perused her notes. "Was there anything else, any detail or fact that we haven't discussed?"

Dad snorted. "The muffler, of course!"

She gave him a blank look. "The muffler?"

Dad rolled his bloodshot eyes. "Yes, the muffler! Isn't it in the police report?"

Katrina pulled a copy of the report out of her padfolio and scanned it. "Um, no."

Dad pounded a bony fist on the sofa arm. "Cops always ignore me, even when I have rock-solid evidence. Been doin' it for years. They don't want to know the truth about what goes on out in the forest. One time I—"

Seb's stomach muscles tightened. He had to act fast before Bigfoot made an appearance. "Hey, Dad. What was that about a muffler? If there's a muffler, that's proof someone drove across your property."

Dad shot him an annoyed glance. "I was gettin' to that. Don't interrupt." He turned back to Katrina. "Anyway, that car lost its muffler on a rock. So when I called the cops, I told them about it. I said I had rock-solid evidence that a crime had been committed, but they never came out—and it seems they didn't even mention the muffler in their report." He shook his head in disgust.

She nodded. "Thank you. When you say a crime had been committed, did you mean trespassing or something else?"

"Trespassing." Dad regarded the rickety coffee table thoughtfully for a moment. "Though I'll bet there's more to it. Never seen anything like this before. Most trespassers out here are hikers or druggies or stupid kids or somethin'—not one-man demolition derby drivers."

Katrina gave a bright little laugh. "That's a funny mental image. I'm interested even if the police weren't. Do you still have the muffler?"

"Yep." Dad levered himself up off the sofa and shuffled toward the door. "Happy to show it to you."

Seb opened the door for his father and Katrina, then followed them around the trailer to his father's Not Junk pile—which got its name from the fact that every time Seb tried to have someone clean it up, Dad yelled, "That's not junk!"

Dad pointed to a rusty muffler sitting among bald tires, partially broken lawn furniture, and other pieces of Not Junk. "There it is."

Katrina took out her phone and snapped pictures of it from several angles. "Thanks, Mr. Wallace. This is really helpful."

Dad gave a little bow. "Happy to be of service, ma'am. You're welcome to take it with you."

Seb winced at the thought of that dirty hunk of metal in the back seat of his Range Rover, but Katrina shook her head. "That's a generous offer, but I think the pictures will be enough. Thank you."

"You're very welcome." Dad smiled. "You know, I thought you was a stuck-up pretty girl like your mom, but you're nice. I can see why Seb blew all his money on that dance and mooned over you, even after you got his nose broken."

Seb suddenly wished his father had brought up Bigfoot. His face went hot and he felt Katrina's eyes on him. He looked at his watch and cleared his throat. "Uh, we've got to get going. Thanks, Dad."

Without waiting for a response, Seb turned and headed for his SUV.

CHAPTER 14

////////////////

KATRINA INHALED THE AROMA OF NEW leather and stared out the window at the redwoods crowding the narrow road. The silence in the SUV felt awkward. She glanced at Seb from the corner of her eye and admired his handsome profile and his quiet sense of male style. Her gaze traveled to his nose. It was a strong nose, but it did have a slight bump where it had been broken.

A twinge of guilt hit her. How had that happened, and was it really her fault? Her boyfriend had said something about "taking care of" Seb, and she'd been too self-centered to wonder what he meant.

She pushed away the uncomfortable memory and rummaged in her gray Celine bag. She pulled out her phone to check messages. No cell service. She resisted the urge to tell Jason about the missing muffler. She dropped her phone into her lap face down. "Your dad said it was my fault your nose was broken. What was that all about?"

His face colored, and he didn't glance her way. "It doesn't matter, and it was a long time ago."

The finality in his tone told her he didn't want to talk about it, and her conscience pricked her. She didn't have anything on her schedule, and she wanted to find out more about what had happened—and about the intriguing man Seb had become. "At least let me make it up to you by buying lunch. Unless you're too busy?" She let the question hang in the air.

He drove in silence for a long moment. "It wasn't your fault. You don't have to buy me lunch."

His brush-off hurt more than it should have. "I know, but I *am* sorry."

He gave a little shrug and glanced her way, a half smile on his lips and an unreadable expression in his eyes. "But now that you mention lunch, there's a new restaurant on the coast I've been wanting to check out. I like to support new restaurants. It's always hard to get started. I don't have to be anywhere until four."

"Sounds wonderful." What had she done all those years ago? She struggled to remember that one and only date. She'd just broken up with her boyfriend, who had been going to take her to the Sadie Hawkins dance, and on a whim, she'd asked Sebastian, as he'd been called back then. He'd been a quiet, nerdy sort in his teens, and she'd thought it unlikely he had a date.

His eyes behind those thick black glasses had widened, but he'd accepted her invitation quickly.

How had the night ended? She couldn't quite remember. Seb had called her a lot and sent her flowers, but she'd gotten back together with her boyfriend shortly thereafter, and he'd done something to get rid of Seb.

He turned off onto a narrow road that wound down to the water. The sun had burned off the usual early morning fog, though it hovered just offshore like a low cloud waiting to roll back in. Large rocks broke the expanse of the beautiful blue of the bay. The trees fell away to reveal a wooden building with a low-slung roof reminiscent of what she'd seen in Hawaii. Blue-and-white table umbrellas fluttered in the light breeze in the outside dining area.

"It's darling. What's it called?"

His gaze took in the setting. "It's nice. It's called Sunset Café, and they're only open for lunch right now."

"So no competition for you or me." Too late she recognized the proprietorial tone she'd used. Soon Bestemor's would no longer be hers, and she pushed away a stab of regret.

He parked and switched off the car. "No competition yet. I think they serve mostly soup, salad, and sandwiches."

She got out and walked with him toward the café. The inside space was welcoming with old-time movie posters and pictures of celebrities from the fifties and sixties. The aroma of seafood and garlic wafted in the air.

The hostess, a young woman with hair as red as Lucille Ball's, greeted them with a perky smile. "Inside or outside?"

"Outside," Katrina said in unison with Seb, and she shared a smile with him at their unanimous decision.

They went out through a different door to the outside dining, which was enclosed with low fencing. A fresh salty breeze lifted her hair, and the stress melted off her shoulders. They both took a glance at the menu. She ordered a shrimp salad, Seb got a panini, and the server brought their drinks almost immediately.

She took a sip of her iced tea. "You're clearly at home any-where, Seb. From what I gather, you've traveled all over the world. Why did you end up back in North Haven?"

"My dad. You might have noticed his tremors. He has the beginning stages of Parkinson's disease, and there isn't anyone but me to help him. At least I didn't think there was. Dylan was a surprise."

"He was? The two of you seem close."

He shook his head. "Dylan acts like he knows everyone, but he just showed up to announce he was my brother. I have no idea how long he'll hang around though, and it doesn't change the fact that my dad will need more care. I can't do that from Paris or Japan."

"I'm glad he hung on to that muffler. Are you a car guy? I'm not sure how to trace what kind of car it came from."

"Bud's Auto, here in town, might know. It's been around a long time. They might be able to identify it. It's a good place to start. I'd be happy to go with you tomorrow morning. And we could check rental records. Maybe the police would help with that. Messenja likely rented a car to come here. We could ask if any of the rentals came back missing a muffler. That should give us the name she used."

"You think she used a fake name on the rental agreement?"

He reached for his water. "Seems likely."

The server brought various types of bread along with olive oil and Parmesan for the table. "Nice touch," Seb said.

She nodded and pulled out her phone to jot down next steps. An incoming email flashed across the screen with Asian letters. She opened her email app and clicked on the message. "Take a look at this. Can you translate it?" She turned it around for him to see. "It looks like it's coming from my own email, so someone has spoofed it."

やめろ、さもないと次は君だ

He frowned. "It's Japanese, and it reads 'Stop or you'll be next.'"

Katrina absorbed the threat. Whoever sent it clearly didn't know how she responded to threats. "Sounds like we're on the right track, Seb, so all this does is make me more determined to get to the truth. We will find out what's going on."

He stared at the screen for a moment, then nodded slowly. "I'll be right there with you."

His gaze locked with hers, and she instantly recognized the mutual spark between them. Had it always been there? Liv had seen it, but Katrina hadn't wanted to admit it. If she could feel that frisson of attraction to Seb, it could only mean she was beginning to forget Jason. And that wasn't something she was ready to do yet.

The server brought their food, and Katrina tore her gaze away with a sense of relief. She would never forget Jason—never.

||||||||||||||||||||||||

Seb suppressed a yawn as he surveyed Bestemor's dining room. Only two empty tables and everyone seemed happy. He'd taken herring and toast off the menu and replaced it with a smoked salmon and scrambled egg open-faced sandwich—which he was pleased to see on a number of plates. The clink of tableware mixed with the low hum of conversation and laughter to create the indefinable sound of a thriving restaurant. Seb could have closed his eyes and known how things were going—but if he closed his eyes, he'd be snoring in two minutes. Running two restaurants simultaneously wasn't giving him much margin for error. Or sleep.

Dylan wandered into the room with a pot of regular coffee in one hand and decaf in the other, looking for empty cups. He'd picked up a few shifts at Bestemor's in addition to his hours at The Beacon. He was trying to save up money for a new truck, but Seb suspected his brother didn't mind being only a few yards from Liv.

Seb took the lid off his thermal mug and held it out as Dylan passed.

Dylan held up both pots. "Decaf or regular?"

"You really need to ask?"

Dylan chuckled and filled his mug with regular. "Get some rest, bro. This place practically runs itself."

Dylan resumed his rounds, and Seb took a swig of the coffee before screwing the lid on. His brother had a point—Bestemor's did practically run itself. Still, he wasn't ready to take a more hands-off approach just yet. He took another sip of his coffee. It was good—strong and rich with no bitter aftertaste. He was trying out a new roaster, and the guy had done a nice job. Seb took out his phone and made a note to order more beans—but he had to stifle another yawn as he typed.

He looked out the front window and saw a sight that woke him up completely: a police cruiser pulling into the parking lot. Officers Tim Franklin and Jay "JJ" Johnson got out. Seb texted Katrina, *Police are here.*

Be right down, she texted back a few seconds later.

After lunch yesterday, she had wanted to go straight to the police station to ask for help getting records from nearby car rental places, but he'd persuaded her to wait until morning. Bestemor's gave on-duty cops free coffee and discounted waffles, which was popular with the local department. Seb suspected officers getting a delicious, cheap breakfast would be more willing to do favors than those who were sitting behind their office desks. He was about to find out whether he was right.

The hostess seated the officers just as Katrina appeared through the kitchen door. She wore a white blouse and dark jeans that showed off her long legs and trim figure. A simple silver clasp held her blonde hair. She spotted him, smiled, and walked over. "Should we go over now?"

He put a hand on her arm. "Hold on. Wait until they've ordered and gotten their free coffee." A waiter arrived within a minute, took their orders, and came back with drinks two minutes after that. Seb nodded appreciatively—fast service was as important as good food, especially in a breakfast/lunch place. He turned to Katrina. "Okay, now."

Seb crossed the dining room with Katrina right behind him. The older of the two officers looked up as they approached. "Good to see you, Seb." He smiled and lifted his mug. "Thanks for keeping Frida's policy."

"Of course, JJ. We're always happy to support local law enforcement." He nodded toward Katrina. "I'm guessing you already know Katrina. Mind if we join you gentlemen for a few minutes?"

JJ waved a beefy hand at two empty seats. "Not at all. Good to see you again, Katrina. It's been a few years."

They slid into the seats. "Thanks for letting us interrupt your breakfast," Katrina said. "I'll keep the intrusion to a minimum and get right to the point. My husband died in a crash in the Cathedral last year. Everyone assumed it was an accident, but there's new evidence indicating he was murdered."

JJ's bushy gray brows rose. "Really? Tell me about it."

Katrina summarized what they'd discovered, ending with their meeting with Seb's father. She didn't mention the chatbot, which seemed a little odd. She treated it like an embarrassing secret, and Seb wasn't quite sure why.

After she finished, JJ drained his cup and set it on the table. "Very interesting." He turned to his colleague. "What do you think, Tim? Do you have time to make a few calls to car rental places this afternoon?"

The younger officer nodded. "The closest airport is Eureka, so I'll start there." He turned to Katrina. "You mentioned you had pictures of the muffler. Could I see those?"

"Of course. My phone is upstairs. I'll be right back." Katrina left to retrieve her phone just as the waiter appeared with two plates of fresh waffles and toppings. JJ picked up his cup, realized it was still empty, and set it back down.

Where was Dylan? Seb glanced around the restaurant, but his brother was nowhere in sight. Seb realized he hadn't seen Dylan for at least ten minutes. Had he snuck upstairs for a quick visit with Liv?

CHAPTER 15

//////////////

AFTER AN EARLY CHURCH SERVICE ON SUN-
day, Katrina waited for Seb on a park bench by the water and
listened to the soothing sound of waves slapping the crab pot
floats bobbing in Pulpit Cove. A seagull landed nearby and
stared at her with demanding black eyes. The temperature was
nearly seventy, and a warm sun had sent the fog rolling back out
across the water where it hovered in a low cloud as it waited to
return with the sunset.

She spotted him exiting his Tesla and lifted her hand. He
reciprocated with a wave and cut across the sandy area surrounding the parking lot down to the cove. She hoped the papers
in his hand were the proof they needed, and as he neared, she
saw excitement sparking in his eyes.

She scooted over on the bench and patted the space beside
her. "Success?"

He waved the paper and sat beside her. "And then some.
Have a look."

She took the sheaf of papers he extended and began to
read through them. The first page showed a driver's license
of a woman named Linda Sato. The license showed an Asian

woman of maybe forty with short black hair and expressionless eyes. "I'd guess this is a fake license."

"I assumed so too, but the picture must be accurate or they wouldn't have rented to her."

A kick of excitement raced up her spine when she flipped to the next page to examine the rental details. "A 2020 silver Toyota Camry. Your dad said the car was a late-model sedan." Her finger jabbed the return line. "It was returned with a missing muffler and undercarriage damage. This has to be the car, and the woman driving it raced across your dad's property. Trying to catch Jason or escaping after forcing him off the road?"

"Could be, but why was she heading for the bottom of the Pulpit when Jason was driving along the top?" He shrugged. "Anyway, we've even got a company name from the credit card: Cyber Okura. I did a quick search and didn't turn up anything for them."

"I'll do some research on it back at my apartment, but this is wonderful, Seb!" A wave of gratitude swept over her. She was relieved not to feel so alone on this crazy quest. "I'll have to send something to the officers who got it for us."

The *us* hung in the air, and Seb's green eyes grew warmer. "I promised them a free meal at The Beacon too. This saved us a lot of time and trouble."

The unexpected pull she felt toward Seb felt uncomfortable. Maybe it was that woody scent of Gucci cologne that drew her and not any attraction. She tore her gaze away to grab her phone. "I'll send this picture to Liv and ask her to run facial recognition on it." Katrina snapped a photo of the driver's license and attached it to a text message to Liv.

Almost at once a reply came back. *Out fishing with Dylan. Will check it on my return.*

She showed the message to Seb. "She seems taken with your brother."

He lifted a brow. "Dylan seems smitten too. He's not really from her world though."

"I'm not sure how serious she is. She's on the rebound, and I don't think she's looking for another major relationship."

"He's had a hard life, and I'd hate for him to get hurt."

"I'll talk to Liv, but I doubt it will do any good. The last time . . ." Katrina broke off and rose. "Never mind. I don't want to betray a confidence, and I told my parents I'd be over for lunch."

He rose too. "I need to go to Bestemor's and see if they need anything. Let me know what you hear."

The reserve in his voice helped her stay put and not watch him walk to his car. Seb intrigued her, that was all. Intrigue wasn't attraction. Once he was out of sight, she settled back on the bench and called up the chatbot. Jason would help center her and remind her of why all this was important.

Tell me something good you remember.

The blinking cursor changed to dots as Jason answered her. *My favorite memory is climbing the Pulpit with you. It was so hard yet so worth it. It was a beautiful spring day but not nearly as gorgeous as you were. Remember this?*

Several pictures appeared on the screen, and she scrolled through them. The selfies were at the top of the Pulpit, and they were both red-faced and sweaty but smiling like idiots at each other. The love on Jason's face from that day made her loss all the more poignant, and tears escaped to roll down her face. She hadn't been able to look at the big rock face ever since Jason had died at its base, but maybe it was time to climb it again. Time to remember.

She blinked and her fingers flew over the phone's keyboard. *I miss you so much.*

You haven't talked to me in a while. I thought maybe you were beginning to forget.

I'll never forget. She swiped the tears from her cheeks and stared at the screen. If only he could be here with her. To hold her, to laugh with her. Jason had a laugh that rang out in a room and made people smile. The ache in her heart spread through her chest.

How would she live the rest of her life without him?

Shrieks of laughter from a passing yacht out on the water brought her back to the present. *Liv is seeing a new guy. Dylan Carver is the kind of guy she likes—a brawny guy who works with his hands. He's handsome and charming. She seems smitten.*

"Here's looking at you, kid."

The *Casablanca* quote made her frown. Had the mention of Dylan made the bot hallucinate again? Maybe her vague feelings of unrest about Dylan weren't so crazy after all.

||||||||||||||||||||||

Seb sat in his office, trying to focus on the Excel spreadsheet in front of him. Once he got these numbers updated, he could lock up The Beacon, go home, and fall into bed for a few hours. Then back to Bestemor's by dawn. It had been the same grinding routine every day this week.

At least the numbers on the spreadsheet were good—both restaurants were profitable, and Bestemor's net income was up since he'd tweaked the menu and found cheaper vendors for a few items. Maybe soon he'd be able to hire someone to take over day-to-day management of Bestemor's. Maybe.

Someone knocked on his door. He turned to see The Beacon's manager, Alex Frasier, standing in the entrance. "Come in, Alex. What's up?"

Alex shut the door behind him. "We need to talk about Dylan."

Uh-oh. Had Dylan been getting too close to Alex's twenty-year-old daughter, Grace? Probably so, at least from Alex's perspective. Grace worked as a server at The Beacon while majoring in computer science at Cal Poly Humboldt. Alex had done everything he could to keep her away from "the wrong sort of guys"—ones who weren't going to college, were significantly older than her, had tattoos, and so on. Guys like Dylan.

Seb doubted his brother was interested in Grace, but he had seen the two of them chatting and laughing in the kitchen. And if Seb saw it, Alex saw it too—the guy noticed every detail, which was part of what made him such a good manager. Seb should have said something to Dylan, but there just hadn't been time.

Seb sighed. "I'll tell him to keep his distance from Grace."

Alex's dark eyes twinkled with amusement for an instant. "He's not the one who needs to keep his distance. I've already talked to her. There's no need to say anything to him—at least not about Grace."

That was a relief. "Okay, good. So what's the issue?"

Alex grew serious again. "He's using a fake identity. The name on his driver's license is Dylan Carver, but his Social Security number belongs to someone named Samuel D. Jackson."

Seb groaned and rubbed his eyes. "Yeah, that's an issue. A big one."

"It is." Alex hesitated. "If he wasn't your brother, I would have fired him already. Employees who . . . aren't entirely honest tend to have other problems. No matter how great they seem, they'll be trouble in the end. I'm sorry, Seb. I have guys like this in my family too. I love them, but . . ."

"But you'd never hire them." Seb looked down at his immaculate walnut desk and straightened a pen. Alex was right. Seb never should have hired Dylan, especially without getting to know him first. Seb had let his longing for a brother cloud his judgment, and now he was paying the price. He suddenly felt very tired and empty. "Thanks for bringing this to my attention. I'll talk to him tomorrow. If he doesn't have a very good explanation, I'll fire him myself."

CHAPTER 16

////////////////

THE SUN WARMED KATRINA'S SKIN, AND she glanced around the back deck at her parents and brother. There hadn't been a single point of conflict today over lunch. Her tummy full of crab bisque, she popped the last bite of sourdough bread into her mouth and leaned back in her chair. "That was delicious, Mom, but I can't eat another bite." She glanced at her watch. Three o'clock.

"I made *skillingsboller*," her mother said in a singsong voice.

Katrina narrowed her eyes. "Are you trying to soften me up for a favor?" The cinnamon buns were her favorite.

The light in her mom's eyes dimmed. "I'm just glad you're home for a bit. I know it didn't look that way at first, and you've had a rough time lately. I wish I hadn't added to your pain when you moved home. Your dad and I are proud of you, no matter what. We said some things we aren't proud of, and I hope you'll forgive us. Now about those cinnamon buns. You can take them home if you like."

"Of course I forgive you. I love you." Katrina's heart squeezed at the sincerity in her mother's expression. "Could I have two to go—one for me and one for Liv?" At least she hoped Liv was home from fishing with Dylan by now.

"I'll get them while you chat with your brother." She motioned for Katrina's dad to follow her, and they disappeared into the house.

Suspicious. Katrina smiled at Magnus. "What was that all about?"

"Mom's about as subtle as a bulldozer." His face reddened, and he looked down at his plate. His blond hair fell onto his forehead. "Um, I was wondering how Liv is doing."

Katrina barely managed not to show surprise. "She's fine."

"I'd hoped she might join us for lunch."

He was still interested in Liv? The realization dumbfounded Katrina, but it shouldn't have now that she thought about it. They'd had a brief but intense romance when Liv and David were "taking a break," but Magnus still asked about her every time Katrina came home. He must think he stood a chance with Liv now that she was in town.

Katrina wasn't sure how she felt about it. During their long friendship, Liv had never stayed long with one man. Katrina loved her friend but didn't understand her constant need for admiration. She wouldn't trust Liv with her brother's heart. But she couldn't say any of those things to Magnus.

He tore his napkin into strips and didn't look up from the task. "I'm going to ask her out. Would you put in a good word for me?"

She couldn't tell him her real thoughts, so she nodded. "She already knows you're a good guy."

"Thanks, sis." His gaze went over her shoulder to their parents exiting with a container.

The bottom of the container was still warm when Katrina took it. She kissed her parents and waved at Magnus before setting out across the lawn toward the sidewalk out front. It was a typically beautiful Northern California day with the sea breeze wafting in from the blue water just visible at the end of the street. As she walked down Redwood Street, her heart warmed to see the old Norwegian-style buildings with their weathered vertical boards and small windows surrounded by storm shutters. There was no place like North Haven, and she realized she was in no hurry to get back to Palo Alto.

When she reached Bestemor's, Charlie the goat ran to meet her, and she avoided the fence as she scooted past and let herself inside through the side door. The place was empty with a hint of the scent of cleaner in the air. She spotted Liv, her hair windblown, sipping a mug of tea at a corner table. "Oh good, you're home. Did you have a nice time?"

Liv turned from watching the goats through the window. "It was very nice, though I slapped Dylan under the arm with a wet fish. He took it like a good sport." She held up her mug. "Tea?"

"I'll take coffee." Katrina set down the container of cinnamon rolls and went to the Keurig to prepare a mug of coffee. "The buns are still warm. Mom sent them."

"I'm starving." Liv opened the container and pulled out a cinnamon bun. "How'd your day go?" Her words were muffled through the food.

"Good. Magnus asked about you."

"Did he now? He hasn't called, so I wasn't sure he knew I was here. Or cared." She sounded a little miffed.

Bingo. Liv was as aware of Magnus as he was of her. "Oh, and the bot is glitching again. I was talking to Jason and said something about you having a date with Dylan. It quoted a line from *Casablanca*."

"That's a chatbot for you. We've all tried to stop them from hallucinating, but it's a struggle."

Katrina took a sip of her strong coffee and settled onto a chair at the table. "What if it's a pattern?"

"A pattern? What do you mean?"

"I don't know. Maybe Jason doesn't trust Dylan. Or maybe Messenja hacked in somehow and is throwing out movie quotes to confuse us and make us doubt what Jason is telling us."

Liv frowned. "I'm not the only one with the source code. Someone on the development team could make changes. If Messenja offered enough money, it's possible. I'll check it out. I'm sure it has nothing to do with Dylan though—he's a great guy."

"I'm sure he is, but it seemed odd."

Liv set her mug on the table and narrowed her blue eyes as she leaned forward. "I'm not worried about Dylan, but I am worried about you."

"Me? Whatever for?"

"Katrina, you do realize you're not really talking to Jason, right? You keep referring to Jason telling you things. The bot is just regurgitating things it finds in Jason's social media and texts. He's not in that phone, honey."

Katrina's cheeks heated. "Of course it's not Jason. It's shorthand for 'the beta version chatbot you created that emulates Jason's personality.' I'm surprised you would question me about it. I'm not delusional."

The crinkle lines between Liv's eyes smoothed, and she patted Katrina's hand. "I'm glad I could give you some comfort. How about we take this party upstairs and play some Settlers of Catan?"

Katrina heard a plaintive meow from the top of the steps. "Sounds like Lyla wants a little attention too."

On the landing upstairs the kitten climbed Katrina's black jeans, and she scooped up Lyla for a cuddle while Liv went past her to enter her apartment. Katrina followed to join her for the board game. When she reached the doorway, a loud shriek came from inside Liv's apartment. Lyla dug her claws into Katrina's arm before leaping to the floor and rushing off to hide.

The air squeezed from Katrina's lungs as Liv let out another shriek. Katrina rushed into the room. "What's happened, what's wrong?"

Liv pointed to a silvery object oozing blood onto the floor. "It's a warning." Her voice trembled.

Katrina stared at the object and a shudder made its way down her back as she registered the sight of a mutilated fish with its head cut off and its entrails hanging out.

|||||||||||||||||||||||||

Seb muttered a steady stream of insults at himself as he slammed his Tesla into Park and jogged up the path to Bestemor's back door. He had printed The Beacon's evening menu inserts while he was at Bestemor's because it had a better printer. Plus, it would be more efficient because he could drop off the inserts at The Beacon on his way to the gym. But instead he left the inserts sitting on the printer at Bestemor's and completely forgot about them until Alex asked where they were half an hour before The Beacon opened. And The Beacon's printer was out of paper, of course.

Seb hurried into the office, grabbed the inserts, and was on his way out when Katrina's voice stopped him. "Seb? C-can you come up here? Please?"

He turned and saw her on the little landing at the top of the stairs. The look on her face sent him bounding up the stairs, taking them two at a time. She pointed at Liv's apartment. "In there."

He walked in and found Liv standing in the doorway to her bedroom, face pale and hand over her mouth. She was staring at a mangled salmon on the floor. "I think someone is sending a message," she said in a small voice.

He took in the scene for a moment, then nodded. "Two messages, I think. Or at least that's what it would have been in Eastern Europe."

Liv turned to him, her eyes wide. "You've seen this before?"

He took a deep breath and blew it out. "I once worked at a restaurant in Moscow that paid protection money to the mob. The owner hired a new manager, a tough guy who'd been in prison. He said he was his own protection, and he pocketed the money the owner gave him to pay off the mob. The guy found a rat in his locked apartment, mutilated like that. It meant two things. First, we can get to you anywhere. No place is safe. Second, if you don't pay up, you'll wind up like the rat—not just dead but brutalized. I've heard of similar stories in Asia and the Americas."

He chewed his lip for a moment. "I wonder if Messenja is behind this."

"If she is, that must mean we're getting close." Katrina's voice held steel. "I'm not giving up until we get justice for Jason. No way."

Seb nodded. "I'll get a state-of-the-art security system installed, but I'm not sure how much good it will do. Not against a professional."

The delicate lines of Katrina's face turned to granite. "Then we'll need to catch him before he tries to break in again."

Liv cleared her throat. "What . . . what happened to that manager?"

Seb tried to push the memory away, but he failed. "One day we found him in his car. He looked like the rat."

CHAPTER 17

////////////

THIS TASK IS GOING NOWHERE.

Katrina sat curled up on the window seat of her apartment where she'd spent most of the day researching. The view overlooked the bluff lined with historic buildings marching down toward Pulpit Cove. She laid aside her laptop and stretched. No matter where she'd looked online, she hadn't found much about Cyber Okura. What few articles she'd found were in Japanese, and when she tried the translate-this-page function, the result made no sense. Liv also hadn't had any luck using facial-recognition software on the driver's license photo. She guessed that it had been digitally altered in ways that a human eye wouldn't notice but that would confuse a computer program.

After seeing that mutilated salmon yesterday, Katrina felt an insistent inner urgency driving her. The warning was clearly meant for her, not Liv, even though it had been in the other apartment. Whoever left it wouldn't know which of them had those living quarters. She'd received the message loud and clear: *Stop digging or suffer the consequences.* But Linda Sato or whoever Messenja was had no idea the warning would make Katrina dig in her heels to get to the truth.

She glanced at the time on her phone. Three o'clock. Beste-mor's had been closed for an hour. Maybe Seb could do a better job of translating. She left Lyla snoozing in the sun streaming through the window and headed down the steps.

She found Seb in the office behind the desk where her grandmother had sat all these years. Katrina's chest squeezed just a little to see his handsome face there instead of Beste-mor's apple cheeks and loving smile. Her gaze went to the toned muscles bulging in his forearms below his rolled-up sleeves. He'd mentioned going to the gym a few times, but she had no idea he worked out *that* much.

She entered the room and smiled. "Got a minute?"

"Sure." In spite of the dark circles under his green eyes, he seemed alert and welcoming. "I'm just about done here. Beste-mor's is doing well. Customers seem to like the new lunch options." He shut off the computer and rose. "Man, I need some fresh air. How's a walk along the waterfront sound? We can talk while we inhale the sea air instead of the smell of cleaner."

"Sounds good to me." She walked with him down the dark hallway and out the side door.

The brisk wind immediately tousled his usually perfect light brown hair. Her own would be a tangled mess when they got back, but she lifted her face to the breeze anyway and drew in a deep breath.

She paused. "Look at the view of Pulpit Cove. You should get postcards made of The Beacon from up here." Fishing boats bobbed in the blue water, and anglers fished for surfperch on the fishing dock. At the south end of the harbor, half a dozen yachts berthed at the pier near the lighthouse attached to The Beacon.

He leaned close enough to her that she caught that enticing woodsy scent of his cologne. She sighted along his extended arm as he pointed out a sleek white craft with a low cabin and gleaming chrome accents. "There's my boat, the *Marlin Monroe*."

She chuckled at the name. "Are you a Marilyn Monroe fan?"

A grin tugged at his lips and he shook his head. "Dad is though. He named it, and it was too cute to ignore."

They resumed walking down the bluff to the harbor past the weathered monument to men lost at sea. Her stomach bottomed at the newly engraved name added to the plaque. "Another one lost at sea."

Seb's gaze went to the plaque. "That man taught me to fish. He hit a submerged rock during a storm two months ago. His boat sank before anyone could get to him. He made sure all his men got into the life raft, but he didn't make it. It's a rough life out on the water."

They walked on in silence and reached the rocky beach that curved around the cove. Seb offered his arm. "The ground is uneven and you can hang on to me. It feels great to be outside. Lately it feels all I've done is work."

She liked the gentlemanly gesture. "Thank you." Her fingers touched the hard muscles she'd noted earlier, and the heat of his skin warmed her cold hand. "I've been trying to find out more about Cyber Okura, but the sites are all in Japanese. Just how good are you at Japanese?"

"Passable if it's not too hard. Send me the links." He nodded toward a huge black rock jutting out of the sand. "Let's settle there a minute and I'll take a look." A boat full of teenagers yelling and playing loud music drowned out his next words as they headed for the boulder.

COLLEEN COBLE AND RICK ACKER

"I'm sorry?"

He grinned. "Kids never change, do they? I asked where Liv was."

"She was in her apartment. I don't think she's left since she found the fish. It really scared her."

"It's understandable." He reached the rock and let her choose a spot to settle before perching beside her.

She pulled out her phone and texted him links to the Japanese sites she'd been struggling with. "That's everything."

He pulled out his phone. "Let me see what I can find out."

She watched his absorbed expression as he checked out websites for several minutes. His good looks were the understated kind. At sixty he'd look younger than his years, while the flashier football types would be showing sagging jowls and lines around their eyes. There was a kindness about Seb she liked too. Not many guys would take the time to help like he did, particularly when he'd been so busy.

He exhaled and put his phone down. "I see your dilemma. There isn't much to find. Cyber Okura appears to be a privately held company, and there are no public disclosures. The only business address is a vacant building on the outskirts of Tokyo. It owns some dormant websites, but they're just variations of its name. It's a dead end. I'm sorry I couldn't be more help."

"At least I'm not completely inept at web searches. I appreciate the help." She spotted Olsen's Creamery's flag waving from its charming blue-and-white building. "I haven't had ice cream in ages. Is Olsen's still as good as it used to be?"

"It's still Tillamook and carries Mudslide, which is all I care about."

"Ooh, that's my favorite too. Let's get some—my treat for all your help."

"That's an offer I can't refuse."

"A cone?"

He nodded. "Their handmade waffle cones aren't as good as Bestemor's waffles, but they're close. I'll grab us a table over-looking the water while you're inside."

She smiled and went to get the cones. In Seb's company she felt lighthearted and happy. How did he do that? Maybe it was knowing she wasn't on this quest by herself. His calm manner helped her focus.

Two cones in hand, she went back out into the sunshine and found him on the back patio at a black wrought-iron table. He took the cone and thanked her as she settled onto a chair be-side him. They ate their cones in companionable silence, and that sense of contentment she felt intensified.

Katrina swallowed the last delicious bite of her cone and gave a satisfied sigh. "That was perfect. I can't thank you enough for all your help, Seb. Really, you've gone above and beyond. I can tell by looking at those dark circles under your eyes that you're burning the candle at both ends, and yet you still sacrifice what little free time you have for me. I appreciate it so much."

His eyes crinkled in a genuine smile. "It's not a sacrifice. I like helping you."

He glanced down at the table, and her gaze followed his. Her hand was on top of his, yet she hadn't consciously done it. She snatched it back and stood, nearly knocking her chair over in her haste. "I'd better get back and check on Liv. Thanks again."

She barely heard his faint goodbye as she turned and rushed up the sidewalk toward home. Had she been *flirting* with Seb? Jason had only been gone a little over a year, and she wasn't ready to move on. Besides, Seb would get the wrong idea.

The most troubling thought was what had made her touch him like that?

⁙⁙⁙⁙⁙⁙⁙⁙⁙⁙⁙⁙

Seb's body walked around The Beacon, checking for any last-minute problems before the restaurant opened. But his mind refused to leave Olsen's Creamery. His brain insisted on replaying the same scene over and over—the October sun lighting Katrina's blonde hair, the warm look in her eyes when she thanked him for his help, the unexpected touch of her hand on his—and then the way she jerked away and practically ran from the ice cream shop. Why did she do that? Was she attracted to him or just being affectionate with a friend doing her a favor? What was going on? What did he want to be going on?

He was acting like he was twelve and a girl just smiled at him for the first time. Maybe he should send Katrina a note that said, "Do you like me? If yes, check this box."

"Stop it," he muttered to himself.

Alex's dark brows went up a fraction. "Excuse me?"

Seb sighed. "Sorry, I'm a little distracted. I've got a lot going on. Where were we?"

Little lines of concern formed around Alex's eyes and mouth. "Just some tweaks to the menu based on what the fishing boats brought in. I'll take care of it. I know you've got more important things on your mind." He glanced away and Seb followed his gaze. Dylan had just walked in.

Seb nodded. "I'll go talk to him now."

Alex put a hand on Seb's arm. "If you want to take a day or two off, we'll be fine here. I can't remember the last time you had a vacation."

Seb couldn't remember either. "Thanks, man. I'll think about it—but right now, there's something I need to do." He flagged down Dylan. "Hey, Dylan. Could you come into my office? There's a paperwork issue we need to discuss."

Dylan bobbed his head. "Sure thing."

Seb walked into his office with Dylan following. "Shut the door," he said as he sat behind his desk.

Dylan gave Seb a curious look, but he shut the door without question. He sat in one of Seb's guest chairs. "What's up, bro?"

Seb cleared his throat. "Who is Samuel D. Jackson?"

Dylan's eyes went round and his mouth hung open for a moment. "Uh, me, I guess."

"Really? I thought your name was Dylan Carver. That's what's on your paychecks."

"Yeah, well, that's me too." Dylan wiped his palms on his pants. "Would you like me to explain?"

"Very much."

"Okay, so my mom named me Samuel Dylan Carver, but everyone always called me Dylan. That's what I put on my driver's license application and school forms and other stuff—Dylan Carver. Then my foster dad adopted me so he could claim me on his taxes or something. So my last name changed to Jackson. But then we had a, uh, pretty bad disagreement and I moved out. I went back to calling myself Dylan Carver after that." He paused. "Is there a problem?"

"Yes. That's why we're in here talking with the door shut. Your paychecks are going to Dylan Carver, but your Social Security number belongs to Samuel D. Jackson, so that's who's going to get a W-2. That makes it look like there's fraud or identity theft going on and The Beacon is turning a blind eye to it."

"Oh." Dylan nodded slowly. "I didn't think of that. Sorry, man."

Seb sighed and rubbed his eyes. Fatigue seeped all the way down into his bones. Dylan's—or Samuel's—story rang true, especially considering what Seb knew about his messy up-bringing. He wouldn't fire his brother over this, but he also couldn't just let it go. "Okay, we'll need to document this in your employment file. Bring in copies of your birth certificate, adoption papers, and anything else necessary to tie both names to you. We already have your driver's license."

"I, uh, I'll see what I can find. I have my birth certificate. I showed it to you that first day. I'll get it from my truck, and you can make a copy. I don't have anything else."

Seb remembered that shock only too well. "Do that. And while we're at it, is there anything else I should know about you? I don't want to get any more surprises."

"Um . . ." Dylan stared into the middle distance for a long moment, then shook his head. "No, nothing I can think of," he said without meeting Seb's eye. "I'll grab that birth certificate right now."

Katrina had texted Liv, but she had notifications silenced, so she was probably sleeping. Katrina curled up on the overstuffed blue sofa with her legs tucked under her. Lyla yawned and stretched from her long sleep in the sunshine by the window, then jumped onto the sofa beside Katrina and curled onto her lap. Katrina ran her fingers through the kitten's silky fur.

It felt like a hive of bees had taken up residence in her chest ever since she'd been with Seb. Touching him meant nothing—nothing. He'd been a huge help, and she was grateful, that was all.

She pulled out her phone and called up the Talk app. *It's almost the anniversary of our first date. What movie should we watch? It's your turn to pick.*

She knew the answer, of course, but asking was part of their ritual. So was a clever and oblique response from him. The dots appeared, and as she waited for Jason's answer, she turned on the television and pulled out the box of movie DVDs she'd brought from Palo Alto. Seeing them brought a pang of nostalgia. Most of the discs had been gifts from Jason, special versions of favorite films that weren't available on any streaming service. Maybe she should order Italian food in honor of their first date too. The place down the street delivered.

"If I hadn't been very rich, I might have been a really great man."

She smiled and typed her answer. *Citizen Kane. Good choice.* It was the movie they'd seen on their first date. They'd started with dinner at a cozy, traditional Italian place with red-and-white-checked tablecloths and candles wedged into old wine bottles. They discovered their mutual love of old movies and tested each other with old lines over gelato. *Citizen Kane* had been playing at a nearby film festival, and they'd gone on the spur of the moment. It had been the perfect night, and they'd recreated it every year by enjoying some Italian food and watching *Citizen Kane* together.

She found the DVD and opened it. A piece of paper fell to the carpet, and she snatched it up. As she unfolded the note, her heart kicked at the sight of Jason's familiar bold script. Her hands shook as she smoothed out the lines to read it.

My beautiful Katrina, if you're reading this, I'm probably dead, and I'm sorry for putting you through what's coming. I left something for you though. Go to the place where I asked you to marry me and look around. Try not to judge me too harshly. Like Citizen Kane, I married for love and everything I did was because I loved you.

A stone formed in her throat and grew to boulder size, choking off her breath. She stepped to the window and evaluated the light. Even if she had the gear, it was much too late to climb the Pulpit today. She doubted she was in shape to scale its unforgiving face now. After Jason's death, she'd thought she might never climb again and had packed all her gear into a tub in the spare room at her house.

She stared at the note again. Her gaze lingered on his final words. *Everything I did was because I loved you.*

"Jason, what did you do?" she whispered.

CHAPTER 18

////////////////

THIS WAS WORTH AWAKENING LIV. KATRINA knocked on Liv's door and waited. No answer. She pounded harder. "Liv, it's me. I need to talk to you." Katrina still couldn't believe Jason had thought to leave a trail.

Footsteps approached the door. "Coming, I'm coming." A sleepy-eyed Liv, her hair mussed and flat on one side, opened the door. "What time is it?" She yawned and stepped aside for Katrina to enter. "Did you bring food? I'm starving."

"It's just four. This is more important than food." Katrina brushed past her into the studio apartment that still held the faint odor of Liv's take-out lunch of lasagna. She turned to face Liv to catch her reaction. "Jason left me a clue."

Liv's eyes widened, and she pushed her brown hair out of her face. "What do you mean?"

Katrina settled on the sofa, and Liv plopped beside her. "I decided to watch our favorite old movie, *Citizen Kane*. A note from Jason fell out of the case." She wanted to keep the sweet parts of his note to herself, so she didn't hand it over. "He said he was likely dead if I was reading it." Her voice wobbled saying the words. "The note said he'd left me something where he asked me to marry him."

It took a few seconds for Liv to catch where to find the clue. "Out at the Pulpit?"

"Exactly. And he climbed it the weekend before he died when we were here for a visit. I spent the time with Bestemor, and he spent an afternoon out on the Pulpit."

"You'll need to climb it all the way to the top, right? Didn't he propose after you climbed that monster?"

Katrina nodded but she couldn't make her tongue work. Too many memories flooded her mind—the grueling climb and her near fall when they were almost to the top. The way the sun picked out the red highlights in Jason's hair, the smile on his face when he pulled out the ring she still wore. She'd burst into tears when he dropped to one knee. That moment glittered in her memory like the most precious gem in the world.

She swallowed hard and left the memories to savor later tonight. "I don't know what he left me."

"He had to have realized he was in danger until the Satoshi egg was safely in the hands of its new buyer and his money was in the bank. It was insurance—probably a backup to the private Bitcoin key. Did you ask the bot about it?"

"I came straight here when I found the note." Katrina pulled out her phone and launched the Talk app. *What did you leave for me at the Pulpit?*

The dots appeared. *That was a wonderful day, wasn't it?* Pictures appeared one after the other: a selfie of the two of them smiling on top of the Pulpit against the backdrop of giant redwoods, her flushed and tear-streaked face after he'd proposed, her extended hand with the ring on her finger, then several pictures of them with their families after they'd heard the news. The last was a picture of Liv with her hands to her face as she heard the news.

Katrina flipped back to the picture of the two of them when they'd scaled the summit. She could almost smell the rich scent of the redwood forest with its earthy undertone of decaying bark and leaves. She never entered the forest without remembering this moment when she and Jason started a life she'd thought would last forever.

She flipped slowly through the pictures, searching for a clue in every one before moving to the next. "I don't see anything obvious Jason might be trying to tell me in the pictures."

"Maybe the bot doesn't know. Jason would have had to text about whatever he left or mentioned it on social media. It's not likely he would have done that. Only Messenja knew he had the egg, and he wouldn't have told her he was leaving a backup of any kind."

"Whoever is after it likely has a large organization of some kind. Word could have leaked. And remember, Jason mentioned someone on Discord directing him to the person who wanted to buy the egg. So there's surely some information out there. Otherwise, how would the person who left the dead fish know we're searching for a backup of the private key?"

All traces of fatigue vanished from Liv's face, and she stood. "Let's get out to the Pulpit."

"I left all my climbing gear behind at the house. You don't have any either, do you?"

Liv's expression fell. "No, I left mine too." She lifted her phone and glanced at the time. "We've got thirty minutes before Redwoods Outfitters closes. I'll grab my handbag."

Katrina ran to retrieve her bag from her room, and they raced down the steps. The outfitters was across the street, and they got there before the *Closed* sign was up. Luckily, the outfitters had a list of recommended climbing equipment. In her agitation she could have forgotten something crucial.

Half an hour later they lugged new shoes, helmets, ropes, chalk, harnesses, and carabiners back to Bestemor's. Katrina stopped at the bottom of the stairs to catch her breath. "We'll go tomorrow at first light."

"I wish there was time to do it tonight." Liv hugged herself and shuddered. "That fish really freaked me out, Katrina. We can't let the bad guys win. They probably killed Jason too, and we can't let them take whatever he left for you. It would be like letting them kill him all over again."

Katrina pressed her lips together. "I won't let that happen. We'd better stay holed up here tonight to be safe." She pulled out her phone and launched the delivery app. "Let's get some dinner and we can have our backpacks ready at dawn with our new gear."

||||||||||||||||||||||||

Seb walked through the door to Bestemor's—and nearly tripped over a pile of rope, D-rings, and other equipment. Had he stumbled on a crime in progress? Was the rope intended to bind Katrina and Liv? Before he realized it, he drew his H&K VP9. Arms extended in shooting stance, he stepped farther into the entrance, sweeping his gaze over the area in the dim morning light.

A door opened at the top of the stairs. Katrina stepped onto the landing. "Did you buy any granola bars?" She faced Liv's apartment. She turned and saw Seb at the foot of the stairs, firearm in hand. Her eyes went round. "Seb! What's wrong?"

He nodded toward the gear on the floor. "I saw this and thought someone might have broken in and planned to use this to tie you up." He eyed her black Patagonia pants and snug-fitting top. She carried a hoodie over her arm and was altogether beautiful this morning with bright anticipation on her face.

Katrina laughed. "No, that's ours. We're just about to go rock climbing. Sorry, we didn't expect you here this early."

His face grew hot and he slipped the gun back into its holster. He hoped the gloom hid the redness of his face. "There's a contractor coming over this morning to install a new security system. I got here early so I could take care of some administrative stuff before he arrived. I want to be able to supervise the installation closely." He looked down at the pile again—and now clearly saw helmets and climbing shoes. "Why are you going climbing?"

Liv walked out onto the landing, carrying a box of granola bars. "Katrina found a note from Jason. He said he left something for her up on the Pulpit. We're going to go find it."

"He left something," Seb repeated. "Wait, do you think it could be the Satoshi egg?"

Katrina nodded. "Maybe, but that would be a very inconvenient place to hide something he was about to sell. More likely, it's a backup to the private key. We'll find out." That string of characters would be all anyone needed to take possession of the Bitcoin fortune.

"Wow." Seb was silent for a moment as he absorbed the news. "Do you want me to go with you? If there's any chance these people know what could be at the Pulpit, you'll be in a lot of danger."

Katrina's eyebrows rose. "Do you have time for that?"

"I'll make the time."

She smiled. "I appreciate it, but it's not necessary. If they knew the egg or a backup might be out there, they'd be climbing the Pulpit themselves, not following us. I'd actually feel safer if you were back here making sure the security system is as good as possible."

He didn't like it, but she had a point. "Okay, but at least take my Range Rover. You'll be able to drive back along roads they can't follow without a good SUV." He pulled the fob out of his pocket and held it out. "You can park at my dad's place."

Katrina descended the stairs and took the fob, her hand brushing against his for an instant. "Thank you. I'll take good care of it."

"Take good care of yourself too, okay?" He nudged the climbing gear with his toe. "The Pulpit is a dangerous climb. A guy fell off it last year and died."

"I appreciate the concern, but I know what I'm doing." Katrina gave him a warm smile. "I've climbed the Pulpit a few times. It's a tough rock, but I'll be fine."

"Glad to hear it. I still wish I could go with you though." He returned her smile. "Good luck—I hope you find what you're looking for."

"Thanks." Something flashed in her eyes, but it vanished before he could quite identify it. "I'll sleep better knowing that system is installed."

"I'll do everything I can, but don't sleep too well. A skilled professional can get past any system on the market."

Liv came down the stairs. Her gaze landed on Seb's hip, and her eyes widened.

Maybe he'd overreacted, but danger seemed to lurk around every corner lately and he wouldn't be caught unprepared.

CHAPTER 19

////////////

THE FAINT SCENT OF SEB'S COLOGNE LIN-
gered in the Range Rover, and Katrina felt hugged by the
imprint of his body in the driver's seat. The Pulpit loomed
in front of them at the end of the narrow dirt road, and her
mouth went dry.

"This won't be a picnic," she told Liv. "I'm out of shape and
out of practice."

"I'll go with you and cheer you on as far as I can." Liv opened
the door and went around to the back to unload the gear.

Katrina's phone sounded as she got out. The base of the
Pulpit was one of the few spots with cell coverage out here.
She glanced at her phone. It was from Seb. *I'm praying for you.
Let me know when you're safely down.*

Something in her chest kicked, and she felt the same wave
of heat in her neck and face as the moment back at Bestemor's
when Seb's hand had grazed hers. She gave a slight shake of
her head. What was wrong with her? *Thanks*, she texted back.
We're here and about to start the climb.

She zipped her phone into the pocket of her jacket and
slipped into her soft climbing shoes, then shrugged into the
backpack she'd already loaded with her climbing gear. With

her helmet snapped in place, she was as ready as she'd ever be. Tackling the Pulpit's summit without Jason by her side felt wrong. Daunting, yes—she'd expected that—but she hadn't been prepared for the sheer wrongness of approaching that treacherous slope by herself. Jason had always looked out for her and made sure she had good handholds and would point out where to put her toe next. It would be all her today.

"Ready for stretches?" Liv's blue eyes sparkled with excitement.

"You bet." She and Liv did some warm-ups until Katrina was ready. "Lead the way." She followed her friend across the meadow of yellow California poppies, and they began the ascent to the sheer slope. Her legs burned as the way grew steeper, and she grabbed tree roots here and there to help pull herself up.

At the first plateau Liv, red-faced and breathless, sat on a flat rock and waved her on. "I'm done. You can do it, Katrina. I'll belay you. Remember to examine every crevice. It's hard to say where he left whatever it is."

Katrina nodded. "I will, but I think it's near the top. Dozens of people a year climb this thing, and Jason wouldn't leave it where anyone could stumble on it. I don't think he would take the traditional route either. He always liked to attack the west part of the wall, so that's what I'll do." Once her hands were chalked, she felt ready.

She approached the steep granite rock and peered up, unable to see the top. Jason had constantly preached balance to her and to use her feet and legs because that was where strength and stability were found. Hips square, arms outstretched, she studied the rock face for her handholds and footholds as high up as she could see. So far so good. She sucked in a breath, blew it back out, and found the first spots for her fingers and toes.

Inch by inch, she crept up the sheer rock face. No preset bolts aided her ascent, so she had to create her own anchor points. It was arduous work, locating cracks that would support a nut or cam. She'd only taken Jason's favorite, less traveled route once before and she didn't remember it well, so she had to retrace her steps twice because she reached impassable spots.

A little shelf area appeared a third of the way up that she wanted to explore, and it felt like an eternity before her fingers found the ledge and she scrambled to the resting place. Her breath labored in and out of her lungs, and she paused to rest her burning muscles. She remembered a small crevice here and took her time exploring every nook and cranny. Nothing.

The rest of the climb would be even more challenging. She spared a glance down to where Liv stood. Big mistake. Dizziness assailed her for a moment, and she turned her attention back to the cliff face.

She could do this.

With her jaw clenched, she reached as high as she could and set a cam in a crack. Her tired muscles urged her to give it up without training for the strenuous climb, but she refused to listen and found her first holds. A handhold at a time, she climbed another six feet before her tired fingers gave way in a shallow handhold.

She screamed as she fell, but the rope caught her and dangled her over the ledge she'd left behind fifteen minutes ago.

"Katrina!" Liv's faint voice was frantic.

"I'm okay!" Katrina waved a trembling hand to reassure her friend, but she felt far from fine as she swung around and grabbed at the rock face until she found more holds. She should have kept up with her finger-strength exercises, but it hadn't seemed worth it with Jason gone.

A fall like that couldn't happen again or fear would consume her. She gritted her teeth and attacked the wall again. As she neared the top, she spotted a pocket of shadow about thirty feet to her left. Was that a tiny cave? Hope kicked energy into her muscles, and she reached up to find a horizontal crack she could navigate almost all the way to it.

Her pulse pounded, and her breath came hard. Eyes closed, she pressed her face against the hard granite to rest before she traversed over to the opening. It was there, she was sure of it. She opened her eyes and inched to the left to the next hold and then the next. She reached into the hole, which extended over a foot into the rock. Her hand touched what felt like paper. Her fingers closed around it, and she pulled it out.

She stared at it stupidly. A Freia wrapper around something heavy? She and Jason loved the Norwegian chocolate, and she felt faint with relief. This was the clue he'd left. She peeled back the chocolate wrapper and frowned at the sight of a polished rock glinting pink and gray in the sunshine.

She'd found the clue but had no idea what it meant or where it led.

|||||||||||||||||||||||||

Seb held Katrina's rock in his palm. Late-afternoon sun slanted through the windows at Bestemor's, bringing out warm pink tones in the smooth surface. The aroma of fresh coffee wafted in the room. A weathered Freia wrapper lay on the table that he, Katrina, and Liv sat around. The two women had just returned from the Pulpit and still wore their climbing gear. He turned to Katrina. "Does either the rock or the wrapper mean anything at all to you?"

"Sort of." She took the rock from him with chalk-dusted fingers. "There's nothing written on the wrapper, but Freia chocolate is pretty rare in the U.S., and Jason and I both liked it—so maybe the wrapper is supposed to tell me this came from him. As for the rock, Jason and I used to take a small stone from each new climb as a souvenir. We'd polish them in an old rock tumbler Dad had bought for Magnus and me when we were kids. It was a little game for us to try to remember which rock came from which climb." She turned the rock over, looking at it from different angles. "I'm not sure about this one."

Liv leaned forward. "Let's ask the bot."

"Good idea." Katrina pulled out her phone. "I was going to do it earlier, but I didn't have cell reception." She snapped a picture of the rock and then typed for a minute. "Okay, he doesn't recognize this particular rock, but he says it's pink granite. We climbed El Capitan in Yosemite two years ago, and that's made of pink granite—so maybe that's where this came from. I—" She broke off and looked at her phone, a wistful expression on her face.

Liv craned her neck to see. "What is it?"

Katrina put the phone down. "Oh, sorry. He was sending me pictures. That was a fun trip."

"Could he have hidden a backup key on El Capitan?" Seb asked.

"Hmm." Katrina bit her lip. "We went there a couple of weeks before he died, and he wasn't himself. Quiet, reflective. I wasn't with him every minute, so it's possible he hid something there."

Liv pointed at the chocolate wrapper. "What does the bot say about that?"

"Hold on a sec." Katrina picked up her phone and typed. She sighed and shook her head. "He's just giving me a link to the Freia website. I think we're at a dead end."

Seb stretched and glanced at his watch. He should have left for The Beacon five minutes ago. "I need to get going anyway." He reached for his mug of coffee and took a final gulp.

Katrina's lips curved into a coy smile. "Are you sure about that?"

He double-checked the time. "Uh, yes."

Katrina turned to the kitchen. "Hey, Agnes. Seb says he has to go to work."

"Oh, does he now?" Agnes called back. The kitchen door opened, and Agnes, Alex, and Dylan walked in. All three were smiling.

Seb rose. "What is this? Some kind of ambush?"

Alex cleared his throat. "*Intervention* might be a better word."

Seb eyed him sharply. "Intervention? What are you talking about?"

Agnes put her hands on her ample hips and gave him the don't-mess-with-me look he'd known for half his life. "Sebastian Wallace, you cannot work sixteen hours a day every day forever. You need a break. And since you can't seem to take one on your own, we're here to help."

Everything that he needed to do crowded into Seb's brain at once. "But—but I need to update our accounting spreadsheets, and Bestemor's needs to restock a bunch of stuff, and—"

"It's all taken care of," Agnes said.

"But what about—?"

"That too." She pointed toward the door. "Now get going."

Seb glanced from face to face and found it hard to tear his gaze from Katrina's amused eyes. It warmed him that she'd cared enough to be part of this plan to derail him, but he wasn't ready to examine why it mattered. "Where?"

Dylan's grin widened. "We're going camping this weekend, bro!"

Seb winced. He hated camping.

If Dylan noticed his brother's expression, it didn't seem to bother him. He slung a beefy arm around Seb's shoulders and squeezed. "It'll be great! Dad's already at the campsite."

Dad and camping? All weekend? Seb looked longingly at the office door. Updating accounting spreadsheets had never seemed so appealing.

CHAPTER 20

////////////////

KATRINA STOOD AT THE ESPRESSO BAR IN Spin Me a Yarn and ordered flat whites for her and Liv, who had found a reading nook in the fantasy section of the bookstore. Katrina added some sandwiches and the girl behind the counter promised to bring them out when they were done.

Through the opening into the yarn shop, the chatter of knitters added a homey feel to the space. Katrina had asked for Veronica when they entered, but her friend had left to run an errand.

Katrina carried the lattes to the cozy seating area, and Liv put down the copy of *The Shadow of the Gods* to take hers. "Smells great. Did you get a snack? I'm starving." Liv patted her tummy. "Someone else is too." She tugged on the blue sweatshirt she wore with the Bestemor goats on the front of it. "I had someone ask if this was yours. I wouldn't have borrowed it if I'd known it was special."

Liv had borrowed it without asking, but Katrina didn't mind. "It's one of a kind. Bestemor had it made for me for my sixteenth birthday. Dinner is coming." She settled on the overstuffed gray sofa. "At least you're not vomiting now." She'd overheard Liv in the bathroom this afternoon after they got back from the Pulpit.

"There's that. The morning sickness has made my situation all too real. I've got to get Talk sold so I have an income." Liv took a sip of her latte. "Better than I expected. Have you heard from the guys?"

Katrina set her latte on the coffee table in front of them. "There's no signal out there."

Liv gave a mock shudder. "I can't imagine spending a weekend out of touch with everyone. What if someone gets hurt?"

"Knowing Seb, I'd guess he has a satellite phone prepared for emergencies."

A sly smile lit Liv's face. "You really like him, don't you?"

"Well, sure. Doesn't everyone?" Seb was a subject she wasn't ready to talk about—not even with her best friend.

She pulled out her phone and launched the Talk app. "I've got to figure out what Jason is trying to tell me with that clue he left. It has to mean something, and I'm positive he put that rock in the crevice."

Liv tucked her right leg under her. "Ask it for pictures of where you stayed. Maybe it's from your last trip there. Wasn't that two weeks before his death? Jason was a planner, and I think he would have carefully thought out every step. Finding a buyer for the Satoshi egg wouldn't have been something done overnight. It would have been too dangerous."

Katrina's fingers flew over the phone's keyboard. *Show me pictures of where we went on our last Yosemite trip.*

Photos of the campground appeared as well as ones of their favorite ice cream shop. Didn't that place sell chocolate too? While it wasn't Freia, it could be a clue. More pictures flashed into view. Trails they took, cafés where they'd eaten, even the outfitter store where she'd bought new socks after forgetting hers. They were all viable leads.

But more than leads, the photos of Jason compressed Katrina's lungs with longing. He'd been so—alive. His smile beamed out as he mugged for the camera in his helmet. The stunning backdrop of Yosemite brought the memories flooding back. Jason had wanted to hike areas without crowds, and looking back, she had to believe he'd done that to hide something. He was a gregarious guy and normally loved talking to new people.

A picture of Lembert Dome came into view. They hadn't seen another soul on that easy hike and had sneaked around to Dog Lake to have a solitary picnic.

She showed the picture to Liv. "We need to check this out. It's an easy hike you won't have trouble with either."

The server brought their sandwiches on white ceramic plates, and Liv took hers with an eager smile of thanks. She bit into it and closed her eyes a moment. "Wow, that's good," she mumbled with a full mouth. "When do you want to go to Yosemite?"

"As soon as possible. It's a nine-hour drive, and it would be a day's drive there and another one back. So at first I thought we should fly. But then I checked flights and the best option was going to Reno and renting a car from there. Total travel time with the flight and drive is twelve hours, so I guess a drive is better. We'd be able to pack our gear in the car and would have everything we need. We'd probably be gone at least four days to allow a couple of days for exploring the areas where Jason and I went."

A female voice spoke behind her. "I thought I recognized that voice."

Katrina twisted on the sofa and saw Veronica's smile. She hopped up and hugged her. "I asked if you were in when we got here. Nice place, Veronica. I already love it." She introduced her to Liv. "Veronica and I went to school together. Liv is from Palo Alto and is staying with me right now."

"It's great to meet you. I nearly mistook you for Katrina. I can't even count the number of times I've seen her in that blue sweatshirt." Veronica grabbed an armchair from another area and pulled it up. "How long will you be in town? I'd love to do dinner one night."

"I'll be here awhile. No end date in sight at the moment. I'd love to do that."

"How are your parents? And, um, Magnus?" She looked down at her hands.

"They're good."

Veronica jumped up to help a customer. "Let's get together soon."

The last of Liv's sandwich disappeared. "I'm not feeling great. Can we go back to our rooms?"

"Sure." Katrina gathered her coffee and sandwich and followed Liv outside.

Low fog shrouded the town and obscured the view of the water from here. They walked toward Bestemor's as a gravel truck, belching diesel, lumbered by. A light drizzle began to fall, and Liv pulled the hood of the blue sweatshirt up. "Glad you had an extra sweatshirt."

A moment later Liv bent over with her hands on her knees. "Hang on a second. I might have to throw up."

"There's a pressure point that helps with nausea. I heard about it in a podcast a few weeks ago. Let me try it." Katrina knelt and put down her coffee cup, then placed the sandwich on top of it. She found the points on the inside above Liv's ankles and dug her thumbs in.

After a few seconds, Liv's pale face brightened. "I think that's helping. Let's get back so I can lie down before it starts again."

Katrina nodded and grabbed her things from the pavement. A motorcycle came roaring down the street, and it slowed as it approached. She didn't pay any attention until it stopped beside them and a figure jumped off. She had a brief impression of a muscular man before he shoved her down the embankment. The coffee and sandwich flew out of her hands as she tumbled down the slope.

Gravel dug into her palms, and she winced as she lay there stunned. Liv screamed and the agony in the sound galvanized Katrina. She leaped to her feet and raced up the slope as the motorcycle zoomed away. She found Liv clutching her knee.

Liv, her face white, rocked back and forth. "He hit me with a baseball bat!"

||||||||||||||||||||||||||||

Seb pulled a trout out of his creel, slapped it on the fillet board, and clipped the tail in place. A few quick strokes of his knife later, two boneless fillets dropped into the bowl that sat in the ice-filled cooler beside him. The head, bones, and guts went into a trash bag, which they would haul to an armored, bear-proof trash can a mile away before they headed to bed.

The sun filtered down through the redwood canopy, creating a perpetual green twilight around their isolated campsite. A low fire crackled in the stone ring in front of Seb. Three camp chairs surrounded the fire ring, and Dad's battered old canvas tent stood on the other side of the campsite. Dad snored vigorously inside, resting after their early start this morning.

It had been a good day—much better than Seb had expected. He must have been more tired than he realized, because he slept soundly last night despite being in the same tent with his father and Dylan, who also snored.

And the woods hadn't given Seb a single nightmare.

They'd awoken before dawn and gone fishing. It had been a tough hike, and they'd had to half carry Dad for part of the way—but it had been worth it. The spot was an icy mountain stream that rushed with snowmelt from the white-capped peaks and ridges above them. Big, careless trout lurked in glass-clear pools, and both Seb and Dylan caught three. Even Dad caught one in spite of his weak and shaky hands.

Dad needed a nap by the time they got back, and Dylan left to go into town to pick up supplies, leaving Seb alone with his thoughts and memories. He kept those firmly in the here and now. Worrying about his restaurants was pointless. Alex and Agnes both had his sat phone number. If there was a problem, they would call. More importantly, Seb would *not* let his mind wander back to a dark road on a dark night two weeks after his sixteenth birthday. He wouldn't let the shadows of the past darken the joys of the present.

The uneven rumble of Dylan's truck announced his approach long before Seb saw him driving along the narrow dirt road. He pulled into the campsite and parked. The engine grumbled for a few seconds, coughed, and went silent.

Dylan got out bearing a sack of groceries in each hand. He set them next to the cooler, pulled out two beers, opened them, and handed one bottle to his brother. Seb wasn't much of a beer drinker, but he appreciated the gesture. "Thanks, man. Get everything?"

Dylan flopped into one of the camp chairs with a sigh. "Ah, this is the life." He took a swig of his beer. "Yeah, I got everything. Took longer than I expected though."

"No problem. The fish and fire are both just about ready." Seb rummaged in the groceries and found the aluminum foil, garlic, butter, dill, and lemon he'd asked Dylan to buy. Dylan's initial supplies had consisted of only canned soup and meat sticks. "Perfect! Where's that grate you used for breakfast this morning?"

Dylan pushed himself out of the chair. "I'll go get it."

By the time Dylan returned, Seb had the fillets prepared and wrapped in foil. He took the grate from his brother and set it over the fire, which was now little more than a bed of glowing coals. He placed the foil packages on the grate and sat back in his chair.

Dylan drew in a deep breath through his nose. "If that tastes half as good as it smells, dinner is gonna be awesome!"

Dad's head popped out of the tent. "Did someone say dinner?" He sniffed. "That does smell good." He hobbled over to the fire. Dylan helped him into the empty camp chair and got him a beer. "Ah, this is the life."

Dylan chuckled. "Exact same thing I said when I sat down five minutes ago with a cold one in my hand."

Dad grinned. "Like father, like son." He and Dylan clinked the necks of their bottles and each took a swig.

Seb stared down into the fire and managed to mask feeling left out. Dad had never made a comment like that to him.

The foil packages were bubbling and spitting around the edges. Dinner was almost ready. "Dylan, could you grab the plates and silverware?"

"Sure thing." Dylan retrieved the plastic plates and interlocking sets of camping silverware.

Seb used a spoon and fork as tongs to pick up the foil packets and distribute them. Then he opened his to a whoosh of fragrant steam. He forked a bite into his mouth and smiled. It had turned out just right—flaky, tender, and full of flavor.

"This is sooo good!" Dylan announced through a mouthful of fish. "And no bones at all! You gotta show me how to make it like this, bro."

Warmth flared in Seb's chest that had nothing to do with the hot food. "We'll go fishing again tomorrow, and we'll make dinner together. Sound good?"

Dylan nodded. "Looking forward to it."

Dad put his empty plate down and wiped his mouth with the back of his hand. "Not bad. We doin' anything for dessert?"

"Yep!" Dylan reached into one of the grocery bags and pulled out Hershey bars, marshmallows, and graham crackers. "S'mores!"

Seb smiled. He hadn't had s'mores in years. Frida used to host cookouts for the Bestemor's staff, and of course she put a Norwegian spin on everything. She provided Solo instead of Coke, wienerpølser instead of hot dogs, and s'more ingredients—except that her s'mores included Freia chocolate. She insisted it was the best, and she spared no expense for her staff.

Freia . . . could there be some connection between those cookouts and the wrapper Katrina found on the Pulpit? He doubted it, but he made a mental note to mention it to her when he got back.

"Ha!" Dad clapped his bony hands. "I love s'mores! This is terrific, really terrific. Isn't this terrific, Seb?"

There was no doubt about Dylan's paternity. "It's terrific."

Dad turned back to Dylan. "Really appreciate you making all this happen. First time we've been camping in ten years, maybe more. You're a good son, Dylan." He glanced at Seb. "You could learn a thing or two from your brother, Seb."

Dad's words stabbed like a cold knife. Seb had given up his globe-trotting life to return to this little town so he could care for Dad. He paid for everything—maintenance on that eyesore of a trailer, utilities, septic tank cleaning, groceries. He even brought Dad gourmet meals whenever he could. And *Dylan* was the good son, just because he planned a camping trip?

Hot bile boiled up in him. He wanted to throw Dad's ingratitude in his face and tell him exactly what kind of father he'd been. Dylan had been lucky to be in foster care—at least he hadn't experienced the shame of always knowing that the piece of garbage he called Father was his own flesh and blood. At least he hadn't seen his own dad basically drive his mother to her death.

Frida had persuaded him to come back by reminding him of his duty to honor his father—but how could he honor a man who was so completely dishonorable?

Saying all of that wouldn't do any good, of course. It would only ruin a nice evening. Dylan basked in the glow of paternal approval, and Dad was smiling too. He probably hadn't even meant to insult Seb—which only made it worse.

Seb swallowed hard and took a deep breath. "This trip has been very eye-opening."

CHAPTER 21

////////////

LIV'S MOANS TORE AT KATRINA'S HEART, AND she fumbled for her phone to call 911. "I need an ambulance!" She modulated her tone by taking a few deep breaths. "A guy came out of nowhere, tossed me out of the way, then attacked my friend with a baseball bat." She glanced down at Liv's massively swollen and bruised knee. "I think her knee is broken."

The dispatcher wanted her to stay on the call, so Katrina put it on speaker and set the phone on the sidewalk so she could help Liv. She smoothed Liv's damp brown hair. "The ambulance is on its way." A chill wind blew in from the ocean, and Katrina tried to tug the hood of the sweatshirt over Liv a little better.

Liv rocked back and forth with her leg slightly bent. "I can't stand the pain, Katrina." Tears tracked down her dirt-smeared cheeks. "You have to do something."

If only Katrina could help her. Liv had to be in agony. She glanced at the time on her phone. A minute since she'd called, but it felt like an hour. She turned in the direction of the wail of a siren. "They're coming, Liv. They'll give you something for the pain."

It only took two minutes for the ambulance to arrive and paramedics to spill out of it, but every tick of a second stretched to an eternity. Katrina ended the call with the dispatcher, rose, and stepped out of the way as a female paramedic rushed to Liv's side. She watched her assess Liv as the other paramedic trailed with the transport. "Can you give her some pain meds? She's in agony. And she's pregnant."

The paramedic nodded. "I'll give her some fentanyl. It works quickly and it's safe for the baby." She patted Liv's arm. "I'll give you something for the pain, okay?"

"Please. I can't take it," Liv whispered.

The paramedic injected the medicine, and moments later, the pain lines on Liv's face began to smooth as the fentanyl took effect. Her eyes drifted shut, and the paramedics prepared her for transport.

A police car, lights flashing, pulled to the curb. JJ and Tim, the officers who'd helped get the information about the rental car for her and Seb, got out. If only Seb were here. Should she call him on the sat phone? Funny how she thought of him for moral support before anyone else.

JJ took a pad of paper from his pocket and held it in his beefy hand. "Terrible thing like this to happen in North Haven. You okay, Katrina?"

"He shoved me out of the way, and this is all I have." She showed him her palms skinned by the gravel. "Nothing serious."

"I'll take you to the hospital to have the scrapes cleaned and disinfected. Would you walk me through what you saw?"

She described the motorcycle as best as she could. "It was a Harley. I saw the emblem. I think it was a Sportster. My brother had one once, and it looked like that, though I'm no expert. The guy wore a helmet and black leather. I didn't get a good look at his face."

"You're sure it was a male?" Tim asked.

"Based on his build and the power of his arm when he shoved me, I'm sure. He was taller than me, maybe six feet or a little over. With his visor down, I couldn't tell you his eye color, but I saw his neck, and I'd say he was white."

JJ put his pad and pen away. "Not much to go on."

"No, I'm sorry. Um, what if this is related? You heard about the dead fish. What if this is another warning? One even more violent?" And even worse, what if her pursuit of Messenja had put Liv in danger?

"It does sound like a warning," JJ said. "Why did he attack Liv and not you?"

"She was wearing my blue sweatshirt with the hood up, and I wear it often. I think it was a case of mistaken identity."

JJ raised a bushy gray brow and took his notebook back out, then jotted something in it. "Let's get you to the hospital."

She followed him and Tim to the squad car, and he opened the back door for her. She slid onto the seat and wrinkled her nose at the odor of stale fast food. The officers got into the front and drove five minutes to the North Haven ER. She thanked them, got out, and hurried in to find Liv.

The receptionist checked to make sure Liv had put her on the list, then directed her back to the room where her friend, pale-faced and half asleep, lay on a bed. A bag of fluid hung from a hook and various monitors showed on the screen.

The door opened behind her, and she turned to see a doctor approach. The familiar face lifted Katrina's spirits. "Belinda! I'm so glad it's you."

Belinda Young had been her mother's best friend for as long as Katrina could remember. Her white hair and friendly brown eyes quickly put patients at ease. Katrina hugged her, and Belinda's soft curves enveloped her in nostalgia and warmth.

Belinda released her. "I was doing rounds in the hospital when your mother called and told me there'd been an incident. With you involved I wanted to make sure you were okay too."

Katrina should have known the news would travel quickly through the small town. JJ had probably called her father.

Belinda seized Katrina's hands and turned them over to examine the abrasions. "I'll wash you up when I'm done with your friend. She's got a broken patella, and she's going to be in a lot of pain, but we'll manage that. I'll keep her in the hospital until we get the swelling down and the pain under control. I could send her to Eureka, but since she doesn't need surgery, we can handle it here. Your mother said you are both staying upstairs at Bestemor's. I don't think that will work for Liv. Crutches are hard to navigate up and down steps."

"I'll figure it out."

For the second time she wished Seb were here. She wanted to talk to him because she needed to discuss security at Bestemor's . . . and because she just wanted to talk to him. She tried not to think about why.

||||||||||||||||||||||||

"What?" Seb couldn't believe what Katrina just told him. The familiar surroundings at Bestemor's suddenly felt surreal. "You and Liv were attacked?"

Dylan appeared at the side entrance, which Seb had walked through a minute ago. "Attacked? Where's Liv? Is she okay?"

Katrina nodded toward the stairs leading up to the apartments. "She's got a broken kneecap, but the doctor doesn't think she'll need surgery. She's on the couch in her apartment. It was a trick getting her up those stairs. They're dangerous on crutches. When Dr. Young released her this morning, she wasn't happy about the living arrangements, but my parents don't have a downstairs bedroom either."

Without another word Dylan bounded up the steps.

Seb looked back and forth between Katrina and Agnes. "Why didn't anyone call me? I had my satellite phone."

"We didn't want to interrupt your vacation."

"This is a big deal." Seb raked his fingers through his hair. "I would've wanted to be interrupted."

"That didn't mean we wanted to interrupt you," Agnes countered. "What would you have done? Run down the guy on the motorcycle? Fixed Liv's knee?"

Seb opened his mouth but then shut it. He knew better than to argue with Agnes, especially when she was right. An idea popped into his head. "Well, there's something I can do now. Bestemor's isn't safe, even with the new security system. My house has the same system, and it's more secluded and just a couple of blocks from the police station. Plus, I have a downstairs bedroom, which will be a lot easier on Liv's knee."

Katrina blinked. "You're suggesting we move in with you?"

He nodded. "Dylan too. I'm sure the police can't provide twenty-four-hour protection, but my brother and I can tag-team."

Katrina smiled and touched his arm. Her hand was warm on his bare skin. "That's awfully generous, but do you have room for all of us?"

"I've got three bedrooms. Liv can have the one downstairs and you can have the second bedroom upstairs." He forced a smile. "I'd be happy to room with Dylan."

Doubt shadowed Katrina's eyes. "I don't know."

"Well, I do," Agnes said, a twinkle in her faded blue eyes. "You'll be safer there and you'll be out of my hair."

Katrina chuckled. "I guess it's settled, then. Let's go talk to Dylan and Liv."

Seb followed Katrina up the narrow steps. They found Liv sitting on the sofa, her left leg in a full brace and resting on the cushions. The scent of fresh coffee wafted in from the apartment kitchen. Dylan appeared, bearing a tray with fresh-cut fruit, cookies, and a steaming mug.

Liv looked up at Dylan with a languid smile and glazed eyes. "Thanks, you're such a sweetie."

Dylan set the tray down on the sofa. "Heard you guys talking. What's the plan?"

Seb took a deep breath. "How about we all move into my place? Good security system and much more defensible than Bestemor's. You and I will need to share a room though. I have an air mattress."

"Ooh, sounds like fun," Liv said from the couch. "Does it have a fireplace?"

"Can you handle a gun?" Seb asked Dylan. "We'll need to take turns standing guard until this is over."

Dylan answered without hesitation. "Yep. What kind of gun?"

Seb mentally inventoried his armory. "I've got a couple of pistols and a short-barreled semiauto twelve-gauge."

Dylan's eyebrows went up. "Nice. Open choke on the shotgun?"

"Yes."

A wide grin split his brother's face. "Sweeeet. Perfect gun for home defense. Load it up with buckshot and anyone you hit is instant hamburger."

Katrina's face turned a shade paler. "Really?"

Seb cleared his throat. "Yeah, well, hopefully we'll never have to use it."

CHAPTER 22

////////////

SEB'S VICTORIAN HOME ENCHANTED KAT-
rina. She and Liv sat on a pale gray leather sofa with a low back.
Liv's leg extended to the redwood coffee table with a cushion
propped under her ankle, and Dylan stood behind her mas-
saging her shoulders. An area rug in various shades of gray
and beige pulled the colors of the cushions and wall together
in a greige look that felt soothing. The barrister bookcases and
framed antique maps above the fireplace mantel gave the room
a masculine touch. The place was spotless.

Seb set a tray with a blue coffee set on the gleaming redwood table and passed the mugs around. He took one himself
on his way to the armchair by the huge fireplace. He glanced
at his watch and frowned.

Dylan came around to sit on the floor and lean close to Liv.
She tapped him on the head. "Five minutes, buster, and you can
get back to work."

He grinned. "Yes, ma'am."

Katrina took a sip of bold coffee and savored it. "I've always
loved Victorians. When we were first married, Jason and I would
drive to San Francisco and park somewhere, then wander along

Postcard Row on the east side of Alamo Square Park. Have you been there?"

He nodded. "I consulted with an architect who specializes in Painted Ladies before I had this house redone. I wanted the exterior to reflect authentic colors while the interior held to modern aesthetics of comfort and utility. Wait until you see the kitchen."

She imagined gleaming metal appliances and sleek porcelain counters. "I love the gray-green exterior with the beige and garnet. The dark gray roof is a great contrast. I can tell a guy lives here."

"Glad you like it." He glanced at his watch again.

"How much land do you have?" Liv asked. "We never see yards this big in the city."

"It's about half an acre. If you want to enjoy the sunshine, use the back deck so you don't have to deal with crutches on the uneven ground."

Katrina tried not to stare at Seb this morning. He was particularly attractive with the tan he'd picked up over the weekend. "I noticed you had a couple of big redwoods in the yard. The one in the side yard is huge."

"I call that Jotun."

"A mountain giant from Norse mythology. That came from Bestemor, I assume?"

"Cleaning went faster when she would tell the old stories." He rose. "I'd better get going. I need to take food to my dad before I open The Beacon, and it's already two."

She examined his tight mouth and tense expression. "I'll walk you out." She set her mug on the coffee table and followed him onto the porch. He stilled when she reached out and put her hand on his forearm. "Are you sure it's not too much to have us all here? You're trying to juggle two restaurants, take care of your dad, and now you have us to worry about. I could get a hospital bed and put it in the office at my parents' house. I hate adding to your stress."

He covered her hand with his, and his green eyes warmed. "I want to help, and I—I like having you here. I'll be rushing in and out covering shifts at the restaurants, but it's going to be fine."

"Okay, if you're sure. I'll try not to let Liv throw her stuff around like she usually does. We don't want to drive you crazy."

"You could never drive me crazy." He squeezed her hand before he dropped his. "I'm sorry I have to rush off. Have a good day and pretend you live here. Help yourself to anything I own: food, closet space, whatever you need—it's all yours." He paused and smiled. "If you get cold, I have a drawerful of 49ers sweatshirts in the dresser in the downstairs bedroom."

"I'll remember that." She watched him pull out of the driveway, then glanced around the wraparound porch with its decorative railings and corbels. Gorgeous.

He'd created such a peaceful place here, and every bit of the property showcased his attention to detail. He was a remarkable man, especially considering his upbringing, and she liked him more and more.

He'd barely vanished around the corner when a blue Toyota pulled into the spot he'd vacated. A young woman got out with a casserole dish in hand. Her Yurok heritage was evident in her straight black hair and dark eyes.

Katrina smiled when the girl reached the steps. "Grace, isn't it? You work for Seb."

A dimple flashed in Grace's beautiful face. "You remembered. My dad, Alex, asked me to bring this over from the restaurant."

Katrina went to the door and held it open. "Come on in. Everyone's in the parlor." She led her inside where Dylan had resumed giving Liv a shoulder massage.

Grace nodded to Dylan, then immediately turned her attention to Liv. "You're Liv Tompkins. I'm Grace Frasier and I work for Seb. I've been using an AI program of yours for my schoolwork at Cal Poly Humboldt. Your work is amazing."

Liv exchanged an amused glance with Katrina at the hero worship in Grace's voice. "Nice to meet you, Grace. Katrina, you should show Grace the Talk bot."

Katrina showed the screen to Grace. "Liv uploaded everything we could find of my husband's socials and text messages. When I ask it to show me things we did before he died, it's like talking to him. Want me to introduce you?"

Grace's eyes widened. "Um, sure."

She turned the phone back around to type. *Jason, I'd like you to meet Grace. She's a student at Cal Poly Humboldt.*

Great school! I went to a conference there in 2020. Do you know Professor Lucy Sanchez, Grace?

Katrina showed Grace the exchange. "Wow. Yes, I took her Introduction to Engineering class."

Katrina typed in Grace's response.

She gave a fascinating talk on compressed wood as a building material. I can send you some of her publications if you're interested. Here's a picture of her and me talking after her presentation.

A picture of Jason deep in conversation with an older Hispanic woman appeared. Katrina's heart twinged. The photo reminded her of how much he'd loved his job as a structural engineer. Whenever he finished a new building or renovation, he couldn't wait to show her around the completed project, beaming like a kid showing off a project that just won the science fair.

"That's amazing." Grace turned an awe-filled expression toward Liv. "You're amazing."

Katrina's phone sounded with a call. The FBI. "I need to take this."

She picked up the casserole and carried it with her to the kitchen, which was as she'd imagined it. High-end dark gray cabinets, stainless steel appliances, and white porcelain counters punctuated with gray veining. She set the food on the massive counter and took the call.

"This is Katrina Foster."

"Ms. Foster, Agent Mike Short here. I heard about the attack, and I wanted to make you aware that the Bureau believes Liang and company have at least two operatives in the North Haven area. I suspect one of them was the attacker."

"Did you tell the police who to search for?"

"We don't know either identity at this time. The troublesome thing is that we believe one of those triad members is a professional killer we've been hunting for some time. He's murdered at least two FBI witnesses. We want to keep you safe, and Agent Hughes is already in Eureka to assist in his capture. We can take you into protective custody for now, Ms. Foster. It appears they consider you a danger to their operation, and we'd like to protect your testimony."

"Liv too? She was attacked when the guy confused her for me."

"I'm sorry, but no. You're our witness. Ms. Tompkins has refused to testify."

"I'll be fine. Liv needs care right now, and I don't want to leave her. Thank you though, and thanks for the heads-up."

When Short ended the call, she decided not to tell Liv about this. Not yet. But Seb and Dylan needed to know the guy who'd attacked Liv was a known killer.

Grace was alone in the parlor. "Liv needed to take a nap, and Dylan went to help her get settled. Um, I wanted to ask a favor of her but didn't get a chance. Could I talk to someone who knows the source code for a school project? It doesn't need to be Liv. Anyone who can answer some questions about the code and the program architecture would be great."

Katrina thought for a moment. The chatbot source code had been Talk's most valuable asset, but Talk was gone and Infinion would want to rewrite the program once it got the rights at the end of Talk's bankruptcy. There probably wasn't any risk in letting her talk to one of the remaining engineers. Katrina had trained these guys on what they could and couldn't disclose. Besides, they had a lot of time on their hands right now.

She pulled out her phone and texted one of them. A few seconds later, he texted back saying he'd be happy to help. "Okay, Case Wintermute is your guy. I'll send you his contact info."

"Thank you so much! I won't forget this."

||||||||||||||||||||||

The high green canopy closed over Seb as he turned onto the rough track that led back to the old trailer. The warm aroma of clam-and-mussel linguine wafted from the warmer in the passenger seat. The warmer held enough for two, though he'd originally planned for three. On the way back from the camping trip, they had agreed that Seb and Dylan would deliver meals together in the future. That plan changed, of course, when they got back and heard about the attack on Liv and Katrina.

Seb liked the idea of making these trips with his brother. Instead of him acting as personal DoorDash for his father, they could all get to know each other better. It would be nice, at least in theory. He was used to his father's abuse, but how would Dylan take it? They'd gotten along surprisingly well so far, but Dad had a gift for creating conflict with everyone in his life.

Seb shook his head. "Do I really want to break up a fight every week?" he asked the empty SUV.

The only answer was the thump and rattle of his Range Rover as it bounced over rocks and roots.

He'd never caught more than glimpses of real families—postcards from a place he'd never been. Frida surrounded by children and grandchildren at a big Berg family gathering, everyone laughing and talking and playing together, repeating old stories and making new ones. Katrina's family at Frida's funeral decades later, comforting and supporting each other with a touch or a quiet word or just by being together.

Could he, Dad, and Dylan ever be like that, even a little? It would take time and work. A lot of time and a lot of work. There was so much emotional garbage between them that they'd need to dig through before they'd have any chance of actually connecting.

Last weekend wasn't the first—or hundred and first—time Dad had said something insulting or failed to show even a hint of gratitude for everything Seb had done for him. Seb was used to ignoring it. Dad was like traffic or bad weather—an unfortunate fact of life to be avoided whenever possible.

Then there was Mom. Seb had talked to his father about her exactly once since she'd died. That conversation lasted less than thirty seconds, and it ended with Dad trying to hit Seb but being too drunk to land a punch.

Learning not to communicate with his father had been a survival skill for Seb growing up. It still made his life easier. But they would never become a family unless they learned to talk to each other.

"I'm going to talk to him." Seb shook his head. "God help me, I'm going to talk to him."

He reached the trailer, parked, and took a deep breath. Then he picked up the warmer and marched to the door.

He knocked, but Dad didn't answer. It was midafternoon, so Dad might be napping. He knocked again. Still no response. He tried the door. Locked—presumably to keep Bigfoot out.

Seb set the warmer on the little stoop and walked around the trailer, calling out and knocking on windows. Nothing.

Alarms clanged in his head by the time he got back to the stoop. He rammed his shoulder into the door. He couldn't get much leverage, but the flimsy plywood cracked on his second try and popped on the third.

"Dad!"

Silence.

Seb raced through the trailer, sticking his head into the tiny rooms. He found his father in the bathroom, lying on the floor. A pool of congealed blood surrounded his head.

CHAPTER 23

//////////////////

KATRINA GLANCED OUT THE BIG BAY WIN-
dow into the front yard with its colorful flower beds. She was
antsy and worried since the call from Agent Short. Dylan
needed to know the danger level had gone from medium to
extreme. Liv was beginning to show signs of fatigue, and as soon
as she was asleep, Katrina would make sure Dylan was aware
someone was already in town.

A familiar blue SUV pulled into the driveway. "My parents
are here." The rear door opened and her brother stepped into
view. "And Magnus."

Liv raised her head off Dylan's lap, sat up, and finger-combed
her hair. "Magnus is here? I probably look terrible." She pushed
Lyla off her lap, and the kitten gave an aggrieved yowl before
scampering down the hall.

Dylan frowned. "You look beautiful, babe."

"I'll get the door." Katrina hurried to greet her family as they
came up the wide steps to the porch. She opened the door and
stepped outside. "This is a nice surprise."

Her mother embraced her, and the familiar scent of Chanel
No. 5 slipped up Katrina's nose. "Katrina, whatever possessed
you to move in here without a word?"

Katrina brushed a kiss across her mother's cheek. "You don't have a downstairs bedroom. It's fine. Seb has room, and he was happy to help us."

Her mother sniffed. "And he was happy to help himself to Bestemor's too, wasn't he?"

"I offered it to him—he didn't ask." She hugged her father and brother. "I didn't expect to see you, Mags. How'd you manage to get off work?"

"Mondays are slow, and I have plenty of coverage. I wanted to see how Liv was doing."

Katrina caught the note of genuine concern in his voice. She'd never dug for information about how he felt about her friend, but she'd seen the interest between them. Her brother would be a better choice than Dylan, but she didn't want to see Magnus hurt. She forced herself to step out of the way. "Come on in. Liv will be glad to see you all." She held open the door, and they all trailed in. "They're in the parlor."

Her mother reached the sofa first and hugged Liv. "Liv, I'm so sorry. What an ordeal. How's the pain?"

"Bearable with meds." Liv's gaze slid to Magnus. "Hi, Mags. Nice of you to come over."

Magnus shoved his hands in the pockets of his jeans. "I wanted to see if there's anything I can do for you. I called the sheriff, but he hasn't had any leads on the lowlife who did this." His voice vibrated with anger.

Katrina saw the moment Dylan realized there was more emotion between Liv and Magnus than he'd expected. He stepped closer to Liv and put a proprietorial hand on her shoulder. "I'm making sure she's got everything she needs."

I THINK I WAS MURDERED

Magnus didn't move away, and his expression dismissed Dylan as a serious competitor. He dropped into a chair opposite Liv and leaned forward with his gaze focused on her. "I belong to a gun club. I can get some extra protection over here."

"I told you—I've got it." Dylan's fists clenched, and his voice rose. His phone sounded, and he gave a final scowl before he grabbed the call.

As he listened his mouth dropped open. "I'll be right there." He ended the call and leaped to his feet. "My dad's been hurt bad—I gotta go."

"What's happened?" Liv called after him, but he didn't pause his rush out the door.

"I'll find out." Katrina grabbed her phone and called Seb.

When he answered, she heard a background intercom paging a doctor. "I heard about your dad," she said without preamble. "Dylan is on his way. How bad is he?"

"I found him unconscious, and the ambulance brought him here to the surgical center in Eureka. He apparently fell—he's got a fractured skull and a hematoma. They just took him back for surgery to relieve the pressure on the brain. They have to stop the bleeding or—or . . ." His voice cracked.

She winced. "That doesn't sound good."

He cleared his throat. "They aren't sure he'll make it through surgery. Even if he does, he might never wake up."

"I'm so sorry, Seb. Is there anything I can do?" They'd be left defenseless here. Maybe they should move back to Bestemor's. She could at least help out there and ease some of Seb's burden.

"They're doing all they can. Listen, I called the police when I realized Dylan needed to be here too. They promised to send over protection."

She walked away from the group and glanced out the window. "There's a squad car out there now. Thanks for doing that." His care for them warmed her. How had she never noticed his kindness when they were teens?

"I'll be praying for your dad—and for you."

"Th-thank you. We need it. I'd better go back to the waiting room. Thanks for calling."

She turned back to the group in the parlor. "Rory fell and has a brain bleed. He's in surgery now."

Liv held her hand to her mouth. "Poor Dylan. He just found his dad, and now he might lose him."

"It's really hard on Seb too," Katrina added, a little nettled that Liv only mentioned Dylan. "He called the police. They're outside now until one of the guys gets back."

"I can stay," Magnus said quickly.

"We'll be fine, Mags. Really. It's sweet of you, but I'm going to make Liv take a nap, and you'll distract her." She smiled to take the sting out of her words as she guided him to the door. The last thing she needed was the added drama her brother's presence would bring.

‖‖‖‖‖‖‖‖‖‖‖‖‖‖‖

Seb sleepwalked through his coming-home routine. Park, check mail, unlock door, turn off security system. It wasn't until the security system failed to chime that he even remembered he had guests.

His stomach rumbled and he realized he hadn't eaten since lunch. He reset the security system, slipped off his shoes, and padded down the hall, avoiding the squeaky spots. He left the lights off so he wouldn't wake Liv. The silver-white light spilling through the windows from the harvest moon provided all the illumination he needed.

He glanced into the parlor as he passed. Katrina slept in a wingback leather armchair, her legs tucked under her and her head resting on one of the wings. She wore an oversized 49ers sweatshirt from his collection. The combination of moonlight and inky shadow made her ethereal and angelic.

Seb paused for a moment to drink in her unguarded beauty. But only for a moment. If she woke, she'd see him standing in the doorway, staring at her. Which would look creepy.

He tore himself away and went into the kitchen. Had he eaten anything at the hospital? He vaguely remembered burned and weak coffee but nothing more. He didn't feel hungry, but his stomach rumbled again to let him know it disagreed. Besides, Thor had sent over samples of a couple of new soups he and Kenji wanted Seb to try. He opened the fridge and selected a creamy bouillabaisse, which he popped in the microwave.

"Smells good," Katrina said from behind him. She had the kitten in her arms.

He turned to see her standing in the kitchen door, a tired smile on her face. "Want some? It's the latest experiment from The Beacon's kitchen."

She shook her head. "Thanks, but I won't be able to sleep if I do." She combed her hair with her fingers. "I dozed off while I was waiting for you."

She'd waited up for him? Her unexpected care touched him deep inside. No one had waited up for him since Mom died. He hadn't appreciated it at the time—what teenager did?—but it meant she cared. It had been a long time since he let someone get close enough to care when he got home. That had seemed like a smart decision until now. Seeing Katrina wearing one of his sweatshirts and looking at him with warm concern in her sleepy eyes made him realize how alone he had been. What would it be like if she—?

The microwave beeped, interrupting his train of thought. He cleared his throat and took the soup out. "I'm glad you found the sweatshirts. The parlor can get chilly at night. You didn't need to stay up though."

She leaned against the counter. "How's your dad doing? Any news?" Lyla squirmed, and Katrina put her down. The kitten sniffed Seb's shoes before she pounced at a dust mote.

He shrugged. "As well as could be expected, I guess. The surgeons managed to stop the bleeding, and Dad's in stable condition. He's on a ventilator and they'll keep him sedated for several days to help the brain swelling go down. After that, they'll ease him off the sedatives and hope he wakes up. Dylan is staying with him tonight."

She walked closer and put a hand on his arm. "How about you? How are you doing?"

Her touch sent an unnerving thrill up his arm. He took a spoonful of soup and savored it. "Mmm. This is good. A little heavy on the garlic, but otherwise it's ready for the menu. You sure you don't want some?"

She looked at him in silence for a heartbeat. "If you don't want to talk about it, that's okay."

Part of him wanted to thank her for her concern and keep talking about soup or something else safe. But he couldn't. Not with her really seeing him in spite of his pretense. The events of the day and the memories they stirred would overwhelm him if he didn't let them out. "I . . . I guess I'm a little out of practice at it. Talking about things, that is." He poked at the soup with his spoon. "I really wish Frida were here. She and I could talk."

"I miss her too."

"She kind of took me under her wing after my mom died, helped me to process it. Did you ever hear the story?"

Katrina shook her head, but the compassion in her eyes said she'd heard something. "Just rumors."

"I'm sure everyone in our class heard them. Some people came up and talked to me, but mostly I just saw the looks and heard the whispers." He took a deep breath to calm himself. "Mom and Dad broke up when I was twelve. He got primary custody because he was the more stable of the two, believe it or not. He introduced her to meth, and it destroyed her. She lost her job and went from boyfriend to boyfriend. She still loved me though. That was the one thing about her that never changed." His vision blurred and he had to stop talking. Katrina took his hand and held it as she waited for him to continue.

He swallowed hard. "Anyway, she got custody of me every other weekend. One Friday, she was supposed to pick me up after school, but she didn't show up. I didn't have a cell phone and the school office was closed, so I started walking to her place. The guy she was living with had a trailer near the end of Skog Road. Do you know where that is?"

She nodded. "That's back in the woods on the way to Cathedral Falls, right?"

"Right. The road has lots of tight turns, and it runs along a steep ravine. Maybe she was driving fast because she was late to get me. Anyway, I looked down in it and saw her car upside down at the bottom, all smashed up. I went down as fast as I could, of course. She was inside."

He had to stop again. Katrina's grip on his hand tightened. "The door was jammed, so I smashed out the window with a rock. I don't know how I managed to get her out of the car, but I did. She was bleeding and unconscious, but she was still alive. I couldn't get her out of the ravine though—and I couldn't get out myself either, not without walking for miles. The sides are sheer rock for twelve feet or so all along the bottom."

Tears rolled down his cheeks, but he kept going. "I yelled for hours, but no one takes that road since the mill closed. She—she died sometime after midnight. The one person who loved me died in my arms, and there was nothing I could do to save her."

"Oh, Seb!" She was in his arms, holding him tight. "I'm so sorry."

Her warm presence steadied him. "Finding Dad the same way—unconscious and bleeding—brought it all back. Except this time, there was no Frida to talk to. I was alone."

She looked up at him, her eyes shining with unshed tears. "You're not alone," she said in a rough whisper.

Without thinking, he bent his head and pressed his lips to hers. She kissed him back, and for a long moment the pain went away. Having her in his arms was everything he'd dreamed about when he was a teenager. And more.

CHAPTER 24

////////////////

THE HUG KATRINA HAD INTENDED FOR comfort turned to more. So much more. The attraction she'd tried to fight for weeks exploded into something deeper she wasn't ready to admit. Their lips drew apart, and she leaned into his continuing embrace. Her head rested over his heart, and the rapid thump under her ear and his ragged breathing told her the kiss had moved him as much as it had moved her.

She didn't speak and neither did he. She didn't want to break the spell the warmth of his arms had woven around her. She wanted to hold this moment just a little longer and forget how alone she'd felt since Jason died.

Seb stirred and pressed a kiss against the top of her head. "I should let you go to bed. Thank you for listening. It's been a rough day. It helped to know you cared."

He released her, and she hugged her arms around herself. Was that all it had been to him—a token that she cared? His shadow moved away, and she wanted to reach out and argue that it had meant more than that. Her throat thickened and her eyes blurred.

Once she was sure he was gone, she wiped her face and went back to the living room. She peered out the window and saw the police car. The interior glow from a phone told her some-one was inside the vehicle. At least Seb didn't have to stand guard when he was exhausted.

She plopped onto the sofa and pulled out her phone. At least Jason was here to talk to. She called up the Talk app. He'd help guide her in these unfamiliar waters. Jason had loved her like no other, and he'd want her to be happy, right? He wouldn't want her to mourn the rest of her life. And she didn't want to. Those moments in Seb's arms had loosened the iron bands of loneliness, and she wanted to shed them forever. Was that possible?

I'm so lonely, Jason. It's been a rough day.

The familiar dots appeared and the answer came quickly as if he didn't need to think about it. *I know, love.*

I met someone. Well, I've known him awhile, but we've gotten to be friends. It's okay to spend some time with him, right?

This time the answer was a little longer in coming. *I trust you, my love. You've always told me I'm the love of your life and you are mine. I know you'd never cheat on me. I trust you completely.*

She stared at the words until they blurred, and tears tracked down her face. Did loving Jason mean she'd never care for any-one else?

A grandfather clock chimed twice, and she choked back a sob, then knuckled the tears from her eyes. It was too late to think about this. She rose and went to peek in on Liv in the downstairs bedroom.

The glow of Liv's phone lit the dark bedroom, and she put it down when Katrina stepped into the doorway. "It's another fifteen minutes before I can have a pain pill and I couldn't sleep. Is Dylan back? Have you heard from Seb?"

"Dylan stayed with their dad tonight. Seb just went up to bed." Katrina's voice wobbled.

Liv struggled into a seated position with her back against the padded velvet headboard. "You've been crying. The accident brought back the pain of losing Jason, huh?"

Katrina nearly let her friend go on thinking that, but they'd always been honest with each other. "Seb kissed me, and I—I liked it." The words rushed out in a torrent. "I talked to Jason, and he said he knows I'd never cheat on him—that he knows he's the love of my life. He clearly expects me to grieve forever."

Liv held out her arms. "Come here."

When Katrina sat on the edge of the bed, Liv clutched her in a tight embrace. Her hair smelled of antiseptic, and it was a reminder not to bump the injured knee. "I'm sorry to be such a baby, but I'm lonely. Jason doesn't seem to understand."

Liv released her and moved her hands to grip Katrina by the shoulders. "Jason is gone. You know that. He's never coming back, and if you spend the rest of your life grieving what you can't change, you're foolish. You have to let him go."

Wise words, but it was easier said than done. Katrina managed a weak smile and pulled out of Liv's grip. "Let me get your pain pill."

She shook a pill from the bottle and handed it to Liv with the glass of water on the bedside table. Once Liv swallowed it, Katrina set the glass back in its spot, adjusted the bed pillows, and headed for the door.

Liv spoke from the darkness. "Find those clues Jason left as soon as you can, Katrina. Once you find what he left for you, you can take that app off your phone and truly move on."

Katrina couldn't imagine a day she'd be ready to do that, so she didn't answer.

IIIIIIIIIIIIIIIIIIIIII

Dad's trailer looked different in the morning light. Shafts of sunshine picked out peeling paint, dirt streaks, and rust that evening shadows usually hid. The place appeared abandoned and decayed. A new cobweb stretched across the doorway, sparkling with dew. Dad had been gone less than twenty-four hours and the forest was already reclaiming his home.

Seb got out of his Range Rover and walked up the narrow dirt path. He wished he could have talked to Katrina before he headed out here, but she had still been asleep. He'd made breakfast and lingered over coffee, hoping she'd come down, but he hadn't heard a sound from her room.

Had she been awake and just avoiding him? If so, he couldn't blame her. Every time he thought back to his behavior last night, he winced. He'd been wildly inappropriate from the moment she set foot in his kitchen. The long, weepy monologue about his mom had been bad enough. Why would Katrina want to hear about that? But then to kiss her when she was just trying to comfort him—what had he been thinking? He took advantage of her, and he didn't even have the decency to apologize afterward. He actually thanked her.

"You're such an idiot." His words frightened a flock of birds, and they scattered to the branches of the towering redwoods crowding the homesite. He needed to apologize properly the next time they were alone, though who knew when that would be. Hopefully he'd get a chance before she took that new job in Silicon Valley and left town.

He sighed and tried to push the whole ugly mess out of his head. He had a job to do. He swept away the web barring the entrance to his father's home and opened the door.

Dad's doctors needed to know what medications "and other substances" he was taking. Seb had a list of the medications Dad took—or was supposed to take anyway—for blood pressure and Parkinson's, but the "other substances" were a mystery. Dad denied taking anything for pain other than Advil and cheap beer, but Seb didn't believe him. Which meant he'd have to search the trailer.

Seb pulled a pair of nitrile gloves out of his jacket pocket and put them on. He started in the kitchen. The cabinets contained two kinds of frosted cereal, three flavors of Doritos, and a variety of expired canned foods. The freezer held several microwavable meals. In the fridge were beer, milk that was turning into cheese, and cheese that was turning into something unspeakable. No drugs anywhere.

He searched the bathroom next, trying not to look at the large red-brown stain on the floor. Nothing in the little washstand except soap, shampoo, and cleaning supplies.

Seb tried the bedroom after that. Dad kept a large collection of Reagan-era *Sports Illustrated* magazines under the bed, together with a menagerie of dust bunnies and a load of random dirty laundry. He hit the jackpot in the back of the narrow closet. One little box contained Vicodin, codeine, and a baggie of marijuana. The pot probably came from a local grower, but the pills appeared to have been shipped from Mexico. Seb would need to monitor Dad's online purchases more closely.

Another box caught Seb's eye. He opened it—and completely forgot about the drugs. A framed picture from Mom and Dad's wedding lay on top. It used to sit on a table in the living room when Seb was little, but it disappeared when they broke up. Dad wore a tuxedo with a red tie and cummerbund that matched the red roses in Mom's bouquet. Her wedding dress was heavily embroidered white satin, and she had a gauzy veil in her brown hair. They looked very young and happy.

A stack of old drugstore photo envelopes lay under the wedding picture. Seb opened the first one and saw a young version of himself sitting on his mother's lap. He had her eyes and hair, but he'd never realized how much he resembled her when he was little. He'd never seen that picture before, or any of the other photos in the envelope, all of which showed Mom either alone or with him or Dad. He looked through the other envelopes and found the same thing. Dad apparently kept every picture he ever took of Mom and saved them in this box.

The box also contained a spiral notebook with about half the pages pulled out, leaving the fringes behind in the wire spiral. The remaining pages bore his father's childlike handwriting. They appeared to be partial drafts of letters to Mom after she moved out:

Dear Sandy. Its almost Xmas and I miss you. Maybe you miss me and Sebastian to. You want to come over for Christmas dinner? You don't have to stay over or nothing. I just

Dear Sandy. Sebastian was crying again. He thinks I don't here it, but I do. Maybe we should give it another try for him. What do you think?

Dear Sandy. I seen you with Robby. I hope your not still doing meth. That stuff will kill you. Im sorry I ever gave you any. I got clean of that stuff. I can help you if you move back in.

Dear Sandy. Its our aniversery and Ive had a few. Im sory for what happened. Real sorry. I still love you. Do you

Seb's breath caught when he reached the last page. It was dated a week after Mom's death:

Dear Sebastian. If your reading this, I done killed myself. Your mom isn't never coming back to me so I went to her. I know Ive never been a good Dad and Im sorry. You will be better without me. I love you.

The page dissolved into a blur. Seb closed his eyes, and hot tears ran down his cheeks.

CHAPTER 25

////////////////

SEB WAS LIGHT ON HIS FEET FOR A TALL guy. His steps hesitated at her door, and Katrina froze where she sat on the edge of the bed. She didn't make a sound. Her fingers touched her lips, and her cheeks flared with heat. The kiss last night had felt like coming home. Right and good. Like it was meant to be.

She palmed her hot cheeks and rocked forward as his steps went on down the stairs. What would he do if she rushed after him and went straight into his arms again? Had it meant anything to him? And did she even want to hope this might be a new beginning?

She picked up her phone, and her finger hovered over the Talk icon before she put it back down. No. Jason wasn't in the phone. The bot mimicked him, but it wasn't him talking to her. How much would she have healed by now if she hadn't let herself depend on the app? Maybe some technology was better left undiscovered. This AI app had hurt her at her core in ways she was only now coming to realize. How many times had she picked up her phone instead of calling a friend? How often had she stayed at home to talk to "Jason" instead of seeing

Bestemor or her parents? Those lost moments would never come again.

People weren't meant to live in isolation, but the phone had made that decision so easy. So tempting. She'd let herself drift in a fairy-tale world where Jason hadn't gone off the road in the middle of the night. It was time to wake up. She never should have allowed herself to move into such obsession.

She glanced at the clock on the bedside table. Her thoughts had consumed forty-five minutes, and she rose when she heard the sound of a car engine outside. She peeked out the bedroom window. Seb's Range Rover backed out of the driveway. He paused to wave at the officers in the squad car out front, then his head turned toward her window, and heart pounding, she ducked out of sight.

She exited her bedroom to the aroma of waffles and coffee wafting up the steps. Liv's door was closed when Katrina passed it, and she paused to listen. All quiet. She moved on to the kitchen where she found a carafe of coffee, a bowl of fresh berries, and a small Scandinavian waffle iron on the counter. A note lay beside it, and she picked it up.

Good morning. There's a bowl of waffle batter in the fridge, and the coffee arrived yesterday from Captain Davy's Coffee Roasters, so it's strong and delicious. Enjoy your breakfast.

Warmth curled in her midsection. He was the most thoughtful man she'd ever met. Even more so than Jason, who never would have thought to leave breakfast for her. Breakfast with Seb would have been fun. They would have sat at the breakfast bar sipping coffee and talking. Maybe she would have put whipped cream in his coffee for fun. In her mind she could see that slow smile start on his handsome face. She loved his smile, so genuine and engaging as it moved from his mouth to his eyes.

Smiling, she reached for her phone to tell Jason—and caught herself. It wasn't Jason. She shoved the phone across the counter away from her. The habit wouldn't be as easy to break as she'd hoped.

After she fed Lyla, she found the batter in the huge stainless-steel refrigerator. The spotless glass shelves were filled with real food, and the eight-burner gas stove would be at home in a high-end restaurant. She suspected The Beacon had one just like it. She poured batter into the waffle iron, and while it cooked, she sipped the fresh coffee. Delicious. When the waffle was ready, she layered on strawberries and real whipped cream from a stainless-steel dispenser like the coffee shop used. Nothing but the best in this kitchen.

The thump of crutches drew her attention, and she jumped from the bar chair and went to help Liv, who had managed to dress herself in yoga shorts that left her swollen knee free and a long-sleeved tee. She swung along on the crutches in her bare feet.

Liv waved her away. "I'm getting good at these things. Breakfast smells good. Waffles? And is that coffee?"

"I'll get you some." Katrina reversed course and grabbed the plate of waffles she'd prepared. She slid it in front of Liv at the island, then poured her a mug of coffee.

Liv settled onto a stool while Katrina made herself another plate of waffles. "Seb already left. The police car is still out front, but I expect Dylan will be back soon." Katrina carried her breakfast to the island to eat with Liv.

Liv spotted Katrina's phone on the counter. "Hey, I ran a diagnostic yesterday, and I'm sure it's done by now. Could you grab my laptop? It's beside the bed in my room."

"Sure." Katrina went to get it and found it under a bathrobe by the bed. The place was already beginning to look like a Liv space—clothing was strung everywhere, and through the open door Katrina glimpsed toiletries spread out in the bathroom. She carried the laptop back to Liv, who had demolished her breakfast.

Liv took it and logged on. "Ah, here are the results." She studied the screen. "Looks like I was right—the bot was hacked, but I fixed it." She turned the screen around for Katrina to see.

Katrina swallowed her first bite of breakfast and studied the screen. "Looks like gibberish to me."

"Girl, you really need to learn to read code." Liv closed the lid. "Try asking the bot again who murdered him."

"Ask who murdered Jason, you mean. You were right. I need to remember the bot is not Jason." Katrina reached for her phone, then drew back. "I need to quit relying on it so much."

"Now's not the time to decide the bot is going to bite. We need to know the answers."

At Liv's sharp tone Katrina pressed her lips together and picked up her phone. She launched the bot. *Who murdered you?* She erased the last word and rephrased before she hit Enter. *Who murdered Jason?*

Messenja. She wanted the egg.

Katrina showed her phone to Liv. "Now what?"

|||||||||||||||||||||||||

Seb parked beside Dylan's truck. He was glad to have his brother home, but he wasn't ready to talk about what he'd found in Dad's trailer. Plus, having one more person in the house made it that much harder to catch Katrina alone, especially if she didn't want to be caught.

He climbed the steps, turned the antique brass knob, and walked in. Rapid-fire conversation from the parlor pulled Seb that way. Liv sat on the sofa with her injured leg on an ottoman, and Katrina sat beside her. Dylan was in the wingback chair. They were all leaning forward over the coffee table and talking at the same time.

Katrina spotted Seb first. "Oh good. We were just discussing what to do next."

Her attention stayed fixed on him, so he'd take that as a good sign. Seb settled in the chair opposite Dylan. "What do you mean?"

Katrina filled him in about Messenja hacking the bot and killing Jason. "So I was just saying that we should go after her."

"And I was just pointing out that she's probably in Japan," Liv said.

Dylan nodded. "Yup! And you've found that rock from Yosemite, right? We should go there and find whatever Jason left."

Seb drummed his fingers on the chair's armrest. "Yosemite is a very big place."

"It is." Liv turned to Katrina. "But you must have some ideas for places to look, right? Just ask the bot. It'll know every place Jason was in the park."

Katrina squirmed in her seat. "I still think we should go after Messenja. It'll be a lot safer to go gunting in Yosemite when she's behind bars."

Liv put a hand on Katrina's knee. "If the clue is a backup to the private key, she'll come to us."

Katrina snapped her fingers. "I've got it! We'll get her to come to us, but we won't need whatever Jason hid. She wanted the egg because it was a collector's item, right? We'll offer her another collector's item. I know a guy who owns an Apple-1 in mint condition, and he owes me a favor. Only a few Apple-1s still exist, and most of them are in museums or private collections. We could use his as bait and see if we can get her to meet in San Francisco. We can work with the FBI to set a trap for her."

Liv's eyebrows shot up. "He'd let you just take it and dangle it in front of a criminal? That must be some favor he owes you."

Katrina shook her head. "We wouldn't take it. We'd just get some pictures from him and post them on the internet. That should be enough."

"That could work," Seb said. "I know some restaurants in San Francisco that would be perfect places to set a trap like that, and I'm friends with the owners. I'll bet they'd be willing to help. I can make some calls."

Katrina gave him a warm smile. "Thank you. I'll set up a fake profile on the same Discord server where Jason met Messenja and post about the Apple-1. Hopefully she'll bite."

"Good plan," Liv said. "But is there any reason we can't be hunting in Yosemite in the meantime? I mean, I can't go." She gestured at her bad leg. "I just hate the idea of Messenja finding whatever he left before we do."

Katrina frowned. "I do too. I just . . ." Her voice trailed off and she sighed. "You're right. I'll go to Yosemite."

Seb cleared his throat. "Are you sure it's safe for you to go alone?"

Dylan shifted in his chair. "I should stay back and, uh, protect Liv."

"I'll be fine." Katrina glanced at Seb. "I know how busy you are with Bestemor's and The Beacon."

Her implied suggestion caught Seb by surprise. Maybe she wasn't avoiding being alone with him. She didn't really have a choice though. "Alex and Agnes have been doing a terrific job. I can ask them if they're willing to keep it up for a few days more."

Her luminous gray eyes held gratitude and something else he couldn't quite identify. "Thanks, Seb. I really appreciate it."

He was going to take a long road trip with Katrina Foster. His pulse skittered at the thought. He'd have plenty of time to deliver that apology he'd been planning—but what would happen after that?

CHAPTER 26

///////////////

MIDAFTERNOON SUNLIGHT FILTERED THROUGH the scattered redwoods on the lawn and slanted through the parlor window. Katrina eyed Seb's restaurant-quality kitchen. She'd been itching to play around in there ever since breakfast. "You're always cooking for us. Let me make dinner tonight. Your kitchen is fully stocked, so I'll have no trouble finding ingredients for anything that strikes my fancy."

"Thanks—it's all yours." He glanced at his watch. "But if we're leaving for Yosemite tomorrow morning, don't you need to pick up your climbing gear tonight? I can take you now."

"Oh, right." Katrina bent to slide her sneakers on. "If we hurry, I can get back in time to cook dinner." She sent a smile Seb's way.

"I'll take you to your apartment." Seb rose in a fluid motion she loved to watch. Everything about him fascinated her since that earth-shattering kiss, and she needed to get over it. He'd acted completely normal without a trace of the self-consciousness she'd struggled to hide ever since he walked in the door.

She stood and tucked her phone into her small bag. "I can take my car."

"We'd have to transfer it to my Range Rover anyway. Might as well save time and do it now."

"Makes sense." She waggled her fingers at Liv and Dylan. "This shouldn't take long. Be thinking about what you might want for dinner." Liv was deep in conversation with Dylan and waved.

Seb held the door open for her, and they went out to his Range Rover. She would love to learn how he overcame his upbringing. The story about finding his mother haunted her, and yet here he was—urbane and sophisticated with a fabulous restaurant and career. She breathed in the aroma of good leather and his cologne. He must possess amazing inner fortitude.

He didn't say much as they went the few blocks to Beste-mor's, and neither did she. He drove slowly and took a couple of wrong turns, even though he must know the route by heart. Was something distracting him?

She cleared her throat a few times and tried to think of a topic but chickened out until they reached their destination. She leaned forward as he parked on the street. "Are the lights still on? It's after five. The cleaning crew should be done by now. Something's wrong." She shoved open her door and got out.

He was out the door and beside her before she could blink. "It's not what you think—don't be scared." Stepping past her, he held the door open for her, and his smile sparkled in his eyes.

She frowned and stepped inside to see the dining room full of people. She marveled at the *Happy Birthday* banner and the streamers hung around the room, and it took a moment for the scenario to sink in.

Oh yeah, it was her birthday. October 12. With everything that had happened over the past few days, the date had completely slipped her mind.

"Surprise!" Magnus swept her into a hug and her parents crowded in to be next.

After embracing her parents she moved through the crowd of old friends from North Haven: Veronica and a couple of other friends from high school congratulated her, and she moved on to greet Dr. Belinda Young.

"Happy birthday." Belinda hugged her. "How's Liv doing?" She paused and smiled. "Here she comes now. Even a broken knee wouldn't keep her from missing your party."

Katrina turned toward the front door and saw Dylan holding the door for Liv. She thumped her way inside before she dropped onto a chair and sent a cheeky smile Katrina's way.

Bestemor's staff beamed smiles at her as they moved through the crowd with trays of food that didn't originate from the café. Katrina eyed the crab cakes and finger sandwiches, then searched out Seb and found him talking to her dad.

She wound through the people to reach him. "You provided the food, didn't you?"

"Guilty as charged. I couldn't figure out what to get you, but I knew your favorite food."

Warmth spread through her and heated her cheeks. She wasn't sure even Jason had known crab cakes were her favorite. Seb noticed things other people didn't. Maybe his attention to detail was the secret of his success. "I think I'd better get my share before they're gone."

"There's a stash in the kitchen held back just in case you were too busy talking to eat."

She squeezed his arm with her left hand. "You are too much."

Now to mingle before she said something really stupid, like "Be still, my heart." How come single women weren't circling him like sharks? She snagged two crab cakes from the tray and a cup of coffee on her way to mingle with everyone. Her face felt like it might crack from smiling. It had been a long time since she'd felt like this.

Maybe not since she'd left North Haven for the city. Family and friends made life better in every way. This place had always been special. Bestemor's was the heart of the town. These walls still oozed her grandmother's genuine love for the people who lived here. As long as Bestemor's survived, her grandmother's essence would remain with it. People in small towns remembered their roots, and Bestemor had been an integral part of the town's core. Of Katrina's core.

Seb caught her attention again, and she spotted the sadness from last night lurking under the surface. She had to check the impulse to go to him and coax a smile from him. Though it wasn't her job to lift his spirits, she wanted it to be. The thought of him turning his slow smile on someone else hurt.

A dawning realization curled through her. She didn't want to leave. She wanted to stay right here and run Bestemor's. This town was in her bones and in her heart. Seb seemed to have found his own spot here as well, and she wasn't sure what she thought about that. Maybe she should do her best to dig out the roots of the attraction that had tunneled inside her heart, but she wasn't sure she wanted to do that either.

What would Seb do if she told him she didn't want to sell?

|||||||||||||||||||||||

Seb turned onto Highway 101 and activated the Range Rover's assisted driving. Katrina sat beside him, scrolling through emails on her phone. Yosemite was almost eight hours away, so they would have a lot of time to talk—or sit in awkward silence if the conversation didn't go well.

He cleared his throat and started his rehearsed speech. "I'm glad we have some time alone, Katrina. I wanted to talk to you about night before last. I'm sorry for the way I behaved. I was a mess, but that's no excuse. You were trying to be nice, and I took advantage of you. I apologize." He gulped at the way she'd set her phone down and was staring at him. Was that surprise in her face—and even a hint of amusement?

"You took advantage of me?" She laughed. "Seb, you kissed me, and I kissed you back. If anyone took advantage, it was me preying on your emotionally fragile state."

Relief flooded through him, and a hundred tense muscles in his body all relaxed at once. "I'm glad that's how you feel. Really glad. Oh, and remind me to be emotionally fragile around you more often."

She set a hand on his shoulder, and her smile warmed him to the tips of his toes. "I'd like that. I'm honored that you trusted me enough to open up. I know that's not easy for you."

"It's not, but . . . Well, I don't want to wind up like my dad. He literally put all his pain and regret into a box in the back of his closet. He kept it right next to his stash of illegal pain pills."

She studied him for a few moments. "I'm sorry. Did you find something when you went out to his trailer yesterday?"

He wanted to tell her everything, but he'd already shared enough of Dad's secrets. "I found some old pictures and a notebook. They made me realize I need to change."

She gave his shoulder a squeeze. "I'm here to help." She paused. "I've also been reevaluating things—like whether I should go back to Silicon Valley when this is all over."

"You've got a great job waiting for you back there." He chose his words carefully. "What would keep you up in our little backwater?"

"The people, for one thing. It's my home, where my roots are." She withdrew her hand. "And my family's roots are deep in Bestemor's. I'm wondering whether we could maybe call off the sale."

That wasn't the answer he'd hoped for, to put it mildly. He'd wanted her to say that their kiss changed everything, that she was staying to be with him. But of course that wasn't true. Katrina had a gift for making everyone around her feel special, which was great—unless you made the mistake of thinking you were the only one who was special. That was the sort of stupidity that got your nose—and heart—broken.

Her comment about calling off the sale of Bestemor's sank in, putting further distance between them. "I . . . I'm glad you'll be staying in North Haven—but I'm a little taken aback. Bestemor's means a lot to me too, and we have a contract."

She frowned. "Actually, we don't. Not technically. Under California law, a verbal agreement for the sale of real estate isn't a binding contract."

The change in her tone from five minutes ago stunned him. He had been right not to read too much into her earlier sweetness. "Seriously?"

"Yes. It has to be in writing. It's an old law called the Statute of Frauds."

"Sounds like an appropriate name." He glanced over and saw her hurt look. "Sorry, that came out harsher than I intended."

She bit her lip. "I'm not trying to cheat you, Seb. I apologize for going into lawyer mode like that. I didn't mean to. I know how much Bestemor's means to you too. Just think about it, okay?"

He didn't want to think about it. Buying Bestemor's had brought him full circle, connecting the man he had become to the nervous boy who had walked in for his first job interview and wound up talking for two hours with a kind old lady with wise eyes. He wasn't going to let that go—not even for Katrina. But he also didn't want to start the trip with a fight. Plus, if she was going to go into "lawyer mode" again, he wanted to talk to his own attorney first.

He forced a smile. "Let's talk about it when we're back in North Haven."

CHAPTER 27

////////////

UPPER PINES WAS THE BUSIEST CAMPSITE in Yosemite, mostly because it had cell service and showers could be scheduled for a fee. Katrina pulled her sleeping bag from the back of the Range Rover and turned to survey their site, a flat space under towering pines with a view of Merced River. Views of El Capitan and Half Dome played peekaboo through the tree canopy of California black oak, ponderosa pine, incense cedar, and white fir.

Seb took a quick break to call the hospital and check on his father, as he'd done at least twice every day since they left North Haven. Then he began assembling the tent. "I can't believe you were able to score a campsite last minute like this."

"A friend from college works here, and she pulled some strings." She drew in a lungful of pine scent.

At least he was speaking to her. The majority of the trip had been tense or filled with useless chatter about music, places they'd hiked, and art shows. She'd cautiously tried to discover his background outside of North Haven, but his monosyllabic answers had shut down her questions. They'd stopped for the night at a motel a few miles away the night before so they didn't have to try to set up camp in the dark. Their enforced camaraderie for the next couple of days might continue that agony.

She'd planned to help with the two-room tent he'd brought, but the thing practically unpacked itself and was erected in a minute. "Nice."

He raised the opening. "Have a look. You can have the bigger room in the back."

She stepped inside and was able to stand without bending over. Her room was spacious and had windows that looked out on a towering pine. In ten minutes they had their sleeping bags rolled out and their gear stowed.

She stared at her phone, then sighed and launched the app. *Where did you go the last time we were in Yosemite?*

A series of pictures flashed on the screen one after the other: the camp store, the showers, the stream beside the campsite with their old green tent, and one of the Upper Falls. The Upper Falls was where he'd disappeared by himself for half an hour. The familiarity of the camping scene with the tent they'd used for years blurred her vision. It seemed like yesterday when they were here.

How was she supposed to do this?

Seb touched her arm. "This is going to be hard for you. I can take your phone and search the spots."

She sniffled and shook her head. "It's okay. I realized this app isn't helping me like I thought. Now that I recognize how damaging it is, I can be on my guard."

He stood so close she had to resist the temptation to lean her head against his chest, and she stood still in case he made the first move. That move was to take a step back. Stupid of her to wish he'd kiss her again—especially after she'd brought up that arcane Statute of Frauds. No wonder he'd implied that she was the fraud. His shell had snapped shut so quickly that it would be easy for her to forget the way he'd been before. And she didn't want to forget the kind thoughtfulness she valued in his soft core. It would take work to get him to open up again—if he ever did.

She showed him the screen. "Let's check the area around the restroom. Then we can walk to the camp store and showers and have a look around. I don't think he would have left anything where someone else might find it though."

And she was right. An hour later all they had to show for their efforts were jangled nerves from fighting the crowds emerging from their tents and a coffee she'd snagged in the camp store. They climbed into his SUV and drove to the parking lot near the falls. She and Jason had frequented several areas nearby.

She paused often for them to consult the pictures, and when he stepped close enough to examine them, her pulse shot to high alert. If he held any attraction for her now after her stupid comment, he didn't show it. And every time she thought about talking about the situation, she had to navigate one more poignant moment of her past with Jason.

It was like standing on one of these trailheads that branched in opposite directions. Either she could take the easy path of wallowing in her grief, or she could choose the steep trail that led to a real future. She didn't want to be that person who looked back on her life and realized she'd missed the best life had to offer because she was afraid.

She realized Seb had spoken. "I'm sorry?"

He pointed to her phone. "One of the pictures seems to be at the top of the Upper Yosemite Falls. You up for the journey?"

She stared at him for a long moment. "I think so." Would it matter to him if he realized what her answer really meant?

The arduous trail contained switchbacks and a steep grade, but Katrina plodded up every foot with determination until they stood at the precipice staring at the iconic waterfall, the tallest in North America. The water's roar was deafening and majestic, and standing at the abyss was downright terrifying. The water's spray touched her face.

Seb leaned closer to speak into her ear. "Wow."

"My legs feel like rubber." She leaned against him without thinking, and his arm shot out to support her around the waist. "Thanks."

They stared at each other for several long beats until he inched away and wiped the water's spray from his face. "We should search and start back down."

How did he sound so normal when she felt all her defenses sloughing off like the debris rushing down the falls? Not sure she could trust her voice, she nodded and pointed to a spot where she and Jason had ducked out of the crowds to eat their lunch.

Seb went that way, and she started to follow. A glint caught her attention, and she spotted a man on a ledge above them with binoculars. They were trained on her, and when she gaped up at him, he darted behind a tree. A casual tourist or something more?

She rushed to find Seb. "Someone was watching us."

His expression went somber when she described what she saw. "We already know we have to be careful. Let's do our search before we hike back."

Katrina nodded and went to the place she'd lunched with Jason. The memory brought a fresh jab of grief, and she blinked away tears. It had a few nooks and crannies to search, but they found nothing. They made the steep descent back to the parking lot, stopping for more searches along the way. Her steps lagged from discouragement by the time they reached the Range Rover.

Seb dropped his backpack. "I'll be right back."

She watched him walk to the back of the SUV and bend down to look at the bumper. He gave a fist pump in her direction and his triumphant expression told her he'd found something, so she joined him. "What'd you find?"

"A tracker on the underside of the bumper."

A chill went through her. "So the guy with the binoculars wasn't a coincidence. We're definitely being followed."

He nodded. "The question is by whom. Messenja? The Liangs and their triad?"

She thought for a moment. "Are we so sure they aren't working together?"

"Hmm." He tugged at his lower lip. "I guess we're not."

"It would make sense, wouldn't it? Liv says Messenja hacked the bot, which would be a lot easier if she had access to it through someone at Talk."

"True, and the Liangs already have someone in the area. If they're cooperating with Messenja, that person could now be following us until we find whatever Jason left."

An icy lump formed in her gut as she followed their logic to its conclusion. "And then when they have that, they'll kill me so I can't testify. One stone, two birds."

He grimaced. "And one egg."

"What did you do with the tracker?"

"I left it there." A smile curved his lips. "I have a great idea how to use it."

|||||||||||||||||||||||||

Dylan sat in a big recliner with a shotgun on his lap. He was in what everyone called the "drawing room," even though the room had no art supplies. But it did have a big TV with an awesome sound system with little speakers all around the room so it felt like he was in the middle of whatever show was on. He had on his favorite movie, *John Wick: Chapter 4*. Such a great film. He could watch John Wick movies every day, but Liv had asked him not to.

The security system panel next to the TV came to life. Something just triggered the sensor pad under the driveway. Dylan paused the movie and chambered a round in the shotgun. He moved across the room and through the parlor, staying out of the line of sight of anyone outside.

He reached a window that offered a strategic view of the driveway. He crouched down and risked a peek through a corner pane. A new black Ford F-150 sat in the driveway, and a big guy had just gotten out. Dylan couldn't see his face, but the guy seemed vaguely familiar. He reached into the cab of the truck and pulled out an AR-15. Dylan ducked away from the window and started down the hall to warn Liv. He'd only taken two steps when the doorbell rang.

Would a killer ring the doorbell? Dylan stopped and looked back down the hall toward the front door. He was relieved—but not exactly happy—to see the face in the front door window: Katrina's brother, Magnus.

Dylan grimaced, walked back to the door, and opened it. "Can I help you?"

Surprise registered on Magnus's face, followed closely by hostility. "I doubt it. I'm here to see Liv."

"She's taking a nap."

"I heard Seb and Katrina left."

"Yeah, so?"

Magnus hefted his AR-15. "So I'm here to protect her."

Dylan lifted his shotgun. "I got that under control. You can go home."

Magnus's mouth pressed into a hard line. "Not until I see Liv."

"I told you, she's sleeping. Go home. I'm not gonna ask again."

"Get out of my way."

Dylan moved so he fully blocked the doorway. "No."

Magnus tried to push past him. Dylan planted his free hand in Magnus's chest and shoved hard. Magnus stumbled back a step. He bared his teeth and looked at Dylan's shotgun. "You going to shoot me?"

Dylan smiled and set the gun against the doorjamb. "I don't need a gun to deal with the likes of you."

Magnus gave a mirthless grin and set his rifle beside Dylan's gun. "Couldn't have said it better myself."

The instant Magnus put his gun down, he bull-rushed Dylan. Dylan was ready and deflected Magnus into the side of the door. He brought his knee up and caught Magnus in the side of the head, sending his foe staggering over the side of the porch. But Magnus had grabbed a fistful of Dylan's T-shirt and pulled him down too.

Dylan's breath whooshed out of him as he landed on top of Magnus. He flailed his fists, but Magnus was already rolling away. Dylan staggered to his feet, but Magnus's fist crashed into his jaw, sending him back to his knees.

Magnus advanced toward him, and Dylan lunged at his knees. Magnus skipped back. Dylan used the opportunity to scramble to his feet.

The two men circled each other on the grass, breathing heavily. Magnus had a lump on his forehead and his left eye was starting to swell. Dylan tasted blood in his mouth and spat.

Magnus caught his foot on a root as he passed under a window and stumbled for an instant. Dylan jumped forward and drove a fist into Magnus's midsection, but he recovered faster than Dylan anticipated and partially blocked the blow. Both men slammed into the house and their shoulders hit the window, causing two panes to shatter. They jumped back to avoid the glass shards that rained down.

They had just resumed circling when the window flew up. Liv leaned out, blinking in the sunlight. Her brown hair was flat on one side. "What's going on?"

Both men stared at her. Dylan recovered first. "He was trying to barge in."

"He wouldn't let me in," Magnus countered.

Liv frowned at Magnus. "Why did you need to come in?"

"To, uh, check on you. I heard Seb and Katrina were gone, so I wanted to make sure you were safe."

Dylan snarled, "And I told you I already had it under control."

Liv swiveled to skewer him with a look. "This is what you call 'under control'?" She leaned back and looked down the hall. Then she turned back and shot daggers at both of them.

"The front door is wide open and I see two guns leaning against it. That doesn't make me feel very safe."

Dylan and Magnus exchanged sheepish glances. At least Magnus looked like he'd gotten the worst of the fight—or so Dylan hoped.

"Well?" Liv demanded.

Magnus cleared his throat. "I thought—"

"No, you didn't!" Liv snapped. "Neither of you thought anything. While you morons were out here beating the snot out of each other, someone could have walked up to the front door, picked up a gun, and blown me away in my sleep. Then they could have shot the two of you—or just made some popcorn and watched you smash each other into bloody pulps. You idiots—" She stopped midsentence, leaned out the window, and vomited on a flower bed.

Dylan gasped. "Are you okay? I'll take you to urgent care."

Magnus whipped out his phone. "I'll call 911."

Liv wiped her mouth with the back of her hand. "I'm not sick. I'm pregnant."

Liv was pregnant? Dylan felt light-headed. A horrible thought popped into his head: *Could Magnus be the father?* He turned to his rival, who stared back at him, eyes wide and face pale.

She seemed to read Dylan's mind. "Neither of you is the father." Liv sighed. "Just grow up, okay?" She closed the window.

Dylan turned to Magnus. "Uh, you want some ice for that shiner?"

"No, but you should put some on that fat lip." Magnus kicked at the turf. "I'll keep an eye on things from my truck." He turned and walked back to the porch.

Dylan waited until Magnus had retrieved his rifle and re-treated to his truck. Then he got his shotgun, went inside, and locked the door. He turned the movie back on, but he couldn't focus on it—not even during John Wick's final fight with Caine, which was Dylan's all-time favorite four minutes of cinema.

Liv was pregnant. Wow. This changed things.

CHAPTER 28

///////////////

THE LARGE CAMPGROUND BUZZED WITH activity, and the air swirled with various cooking odors from the campfires and grills scattered through the towering pines. Katrina scooped up her last bit of campfire nachos. Seb had prepared them in a Dutch oven nestled in glowing coals, and the delicious meal was the best she'd ever had while camping out. Even the cheese was melted exactly right.

She leaned back in her blue camp chair. "Jason and I usually lived on hot dogs and corn chips. This was outstanding, and if I had an inch of room in my stomach, I'd eat that last spoonful. I don't know how you learned to cook like that."

Seb smiled and scooted closer when the raucous group next to them grew louder as they threw horseshoes. "Frida gave me that Dutch oven and I've used it a lot. It's gone everywhere with me."

After the past two days of him deflecting questions about his past, she knew better than to try to pry out more. "You should write a cookbook for campers. It would be a bestseller."

His smile widened but it never reached his eyes. "Sorry our trip was a bust. I'd hoped we would find something in the past two days."

"It's been a wild-goose chase. We're no closer to figuring out that clue than we were when we started." She glanced his way. Her guilt had kept her awake the last two nights. "Um, I'm sorry about what I said on the way here, Seb. I fell into lawyer mode without thinking. I'm a Christian and my word should be as good as a signed piece of paper. Forget I said anything."

He studied her for a long moment. "Apology accepted. I've been mulling it over too. You clearly love the law, and you worked hard to get where you are. Would you be happy tossing aside those years of study and practice to settle for flipping pancakes? Not that flipping pancakes is wrong when it's what you love, but the law is your passion. Frida was proud of you and what you'd accomplished. I don't think she would expect you to give up who you are."

Her mouth had fallen open as he laid out the facts, and she snapped it shut. "I've been wrestling with the realization that I don't enjoy the city like I thought I would." She inhaled a deep breath of the aromas in camp: fish, pine, grilling corn, and beer. "I gravitate to my roots these days. Bestemor's death showed me some things are more important than money and prestige. But you're right—I do love the law and its intricacies. I love seeing how statutes and prior decisions impact how things run."

"You don't have to run Bestemor's to live in North Haven. Small towns need attorneys too. Your dad might welcome a partner."

She let the last echo of his words die away. He was right. Dad was easy to get along with, and he was a smart attorney with a lot to teach her. "I'll think about it. You might be right." How had he done that—pointed her in a different direction and made her think? He had good instincts about people. At least about her.

"Anything from Messenja?"

"Let me see. All the messages I had this morning were from other parties." She dragged her laptop out of its sleeve and checked her Discord. "There's a DM from her!" She scooted her camp chair closer to him and they read the message together.

I represent a party who is very interested in the collectible computer you posted. Please send along additional pictures. If those prove satisfactory to my employer, we'd like a cash sale as soon as possible.

Katrina whooped and several teenagers looked her way and snickered. "I'll send the better photos I had saved for now and see what Messenja has to say. If she wants a sale right away, we should get back to San Francisco." She located the pictures in her files and sent them off to Messenja.

Seb glanced at his watch. "It's only six and we could be there by ten. We can grab a hotel and wait to hear from her."

She nearly suggested they stay at her house, but the thought died a quick death at the prospect of more strained discussions. "That's a great idea." She rose and began to pack their scattered belongings.

Reliving memories and talking to the bot had been excruciating the last few days. With their differences aired and discussed, maybe she'd be able to reconnect with Seb. She longed to get back to the easy camaraderie they'd had last week. For a little while she'd glimpsed how it might be to move on from being stuck in grief.

Seb put out the fire and folded up the camp chairs while she went into the tent and stuffed her things into her backpack.

Seb's was neatly packed already, so she grabbed it on the way out. By the time she dropped the bags at the SUV's back lift, he had the coolers and chair stashed. While she stowed the backpacks behind the front seats for easy access at the hotel, he brought over the rolled-up sleeping bags and took down the tent. He hauled it to the SUV and tossed it in. Things weren't as neatly packed as they had been on the way here, but they were ready to go in half an hour.

Seb reached under the rear bumper. "One more thing."

She spotted the tracker in his hand, and he glanced around the parking lot, then walked to a delivery truck. He stuck the device onto the bumper in such a smooth move she nearly missed it.

His easy grin returned when he joined her at the SUV. "Whoever is after us will follow the truck, and no one will know we're on our way to meet Messenja."

Katrina liked the sound of "us," and her spirits lifted. Even though they'd struck out on finding a clue in Yosemite, she and Seb might get past her stumble on the way here.

||||||||||||||||||||||

Seb was happy to see Yosemite in his rearview mirror. He had only gotten distracted glimpses of the park's staggering natural beauty. At El Capitan he spent the whole time hunting for out-of-the-way nooks where Jason might have hidden something. When they hiked to Taft Point, he continually scanned the trees and ridges for watchers.

It didn't help that he'd felt like a third wheel. The entire trip had been haunted by Jason's ghost. Katrina huddled over her phone when they had cell service and relived old memories when they didn't. They visited the spot where she and Jason had shared hot cocoa from a thermos while they watched the Firefall, when the setting sun turned Horsetail Fall into a fountain of flaming gold surrounded by shadowy rock. They ate at the café where Jason had to chase a bear away from their car because he parked at the edge of the lot and she left food in the back seat and forgot to roll up her window. They camped at the same campground where she and Jason had sat on a log and he played guitar while she sang. And so on.

The trip really drove home the depth of Katrina's grief. She'd been in tears at least once every day, and red had rimmed her eyes each morning. She and Jason had obviously been very happy, and his death devastated her. She was not over him, and maybe she never would be.

Frida had once told Seb about one of her great-aunts who lost her fiancé in an industrial accident. She never married and wore black for the rest of her life. Would Katrina wind up like that? Her response to their kiss had planted a tiny seed of hope, but it had shriveled over the past two days.

Katrina pulled out her phone. "Okay, I finally have service again. Where should I suggest we meet her?"

"Hmm. How about someplace along the Embarcadero? It's too public for Messenja to ambush us, but there are plenty of spots where the FBI could corner her."

Katrina nodded. "Good thinking. The Embarcadero is only about a mile from the FBI's office, so that would be convenient for them too. We're serving her up on a platter. I'll call Agent Short."

"Could you put it on speaker?"

"Of course." Katrina dialed and leaned over to hold the phone between them. He caught a faint whiff of her herbal shampoo.

After three rings, a man answered in a terse tenor. "Agent Short here."

"Hi, it's Katrina Foster. I'm here with my friend, Sebastian Wallace. We've made contact with an individual connected to the assassin who attacked us. She may even be the kingpin of the organization. We have reason to believe she's behind at least one additional killing—the murder of my husband, Jason. We think we can arrange for her to be at a location on the Embarcadero in the next day or two."

The line was silent for several seconds. "Who is this person?"

"We don't know her name," Katrina said. "But she goes by the pseudonym Messenja and she appears to be Japanese. She has a credit card from a company called Cyber Okura."

The faint sound of a keyboard clicking came through the phone's speaker. "Do you have evidence connecting her to the Liangs or Talk CN?"

"No." Katrina paused. "Wait, yes. She manipulated a chatbot created by Talk, Inc. Maybe the Liangs or someone at Talk CN gave her access."

More keyboard clicking. "Anything else?"

Katrina thought for a moment. "Well, someone has been following us for the past few days. Our trip involved something called a Satoshi egg, which is also how my husband knew Messenja."

"You think a Liang operative is the one following you?"

"Liang or Messenja's operative, though we're assuming they're working together."

"Any basis for that assumption other than what you've already told me?"

Katrina frowned at the agent's skeptical tone. "No."

Agent Short was silent for a few seconds. "Okay, anything else?"

Katrina bit her lip, then shook her head. "Nothing I can think of. How about you, Seb?"

"I can't think of anything else either. We haven't arranged a place to meet her yet. What's the FBI's preference?"

"We don't care."

Seb blinked. "Why not? Are you just going to arrest her on the sidewalk or something?"

The phone emitted a burst of static that might have been a snort. "We're not going to arrest her."

Seb couldn't believe his ears. "What? Why not?"

"Because you haven't given me probable cause to believe this Messenja committed a crime, let alone a crime that has anything to do with my investigation."

Seb did his best to keep his voice even. "But we just explained all that to you."

Another burst of static crackled. "Look, I've got a busy day. Have Ms. Foster explain it to you. She's a lawyer, right?" Without waiting for a response, Short ended the call.

Seb shot a glance at Katrina. She seemed disappointed but not surprised. "What's he talking about?"

She sighed. "He's right that what we just gave him likely doesn't amount to probable cause. It might be enough if we gave the bot to FBI computer experts, showed them Jason's accusation against Messenja, and then had Liv explain Messenja's hacking, but it would take weeks for them to reach any conclusions and receive a warrant. There's no time for that now. I'd hoped Short already had enough to fill in the gaps—that his investigation had already uncovered at least a hint of a connection between the Liangs and Messenja or the egg. But either they haven't or he's playing his cards extremely close to the vest."

Seb took a deep breath and blew it out through his teeth. "So what do we do now? I don't like the idea of going through with this meeting with no FBI backup. But if we cancel it, she'll be suspicious. We may never get another shot at her."

"I know." Katrina looked at her phone. Seb caught a glimpse of a picture of Jason. "But I'm not going to pass up a chance to confront the woman who killed my husband. I don't care what happens after that. I won't ask you to accompany me."

The bleak note in her voice resonated deep inside him. He would have given anything to have a friend beside him during the hardest moments of his life. "You won't have to."

CHAPTER 29

////////////

THE VIEW FROM THE HISTORIC FERRY Building always took Katrina's breath away. Huge windows in the Chinese restaurant opened up to the blue panorama of the San Francisco Bay, but she was too nervous to enjoy the scenery or the tantalizing aromas of egg rolls, garlic, and ginger wafting through the spacious room.

She forced her leg to stop jiggling. If only she could grab Seb's hand to steady her, but things had been strained on the way here—and who could blame him? It couldn't have been easy to see her obsess the past two days over the things she'd experienced with Jason. Now she was wrung out, emptied of most of the grief.

Seb reached for her hand as she shredded a tissue. "Breathe. It's only five. She'll be here any minute."

"What if we've made a terrible mistake?" She kept her voice low, but Silk Road Supper held only a few diners. Another hour and the place would be packed, but they shouldn't be overheard now. Seb had talked to the owner so they wouldn't be disturbed by servers.

"I picked a place this public for a reason. Messenja wouldn't dare do anything with so many cameras and security around."

With a final squeeze he released her hand and reached for his water.

"True." Katrina glanced back over her shoulder. A camera behind them would have a clear view of whoever sat across from them—which was why she had chosen this table. Recording a conversation was illegal in California, but a security camera wasn't. The camera would covertly capture whatever Messenja said, and a lip reader could translate—if they could get her to say anything worth translating.

Katrina tugged the neckline of her blue sheath dress into place. She'd packed it hoping she and Seb would bond more and he'd take her on a real date where Jason's name wasn't mentioned once. If she'd had anything else to wear, she would have, but this was the only thing she had clean after their trip had run a day longer than expected. The silky dress was hardly suitable for the business meeting with Messenja.

Katrina scooped up the remnants of her shredded tissue and thrust them into her purse. "I'll try to get her to admit to something. The two of us would be witnesses, and Japan could arrest her. They have an extradition treaty with us." Katrina gulped and set her water glass down. "I think that's her."

An elegant Japanese woman dressed in a black silk pantsuit walked toward them. Katrina recognized her from the driver's license photo JJ had gotten from the car rental place in Eureka. Her shining black bob swung just above her shoulders and she could have been any age from thirty to sixty. Her red lipstick only accentuated her stunning facial features, and she exuded competence.

She stopped at their table. "You have the Apple-1? I'd like to see it, please." Only a hint of an Asian accent appeared in her modulated voice.

Katrina moistened her lips and gestured to the chairs. "Have a seat."

Messenja's dark eyes examined them for an instant before she gave a slight shrug and sat across the table from them. "I wish to conclude our business and catch a late-night flight back home."

Katrina's knee began its nervous jitter again, and Seb pressed his hand on it. The tension seeped out of her. This woman had killed her husband, and though she'd love to lunge across the table and snap that long, elegant neck, she needed to maintain a clear head. "How do we know you won't kill us?"

Messenja frowned. "What? That's a ridiculous comment. This isn't some cloak-and-dagger movie."

"You killed a guy over a Satoshi egg. I know all about it."

Messenja's eyes clouded with confusion, and she shook her head. "What are you talking about?"

"You made a deal to buy a Satoshi egg, but the guy died in a suspicious car crash." Katrina placed both hands on the table and leaned forward. "There were *witnesses* who saw you driving away. You ran him off the road, didn't you?" She fought to keep the edge out of her voice. She wanted to hear the woman confess to the truth, but that would never happen if Katrina lost her cool and blew her cover. Messenja had to believe they were here to sell an Apple-1, nothing more. "How do we know the same thing won't happen to us?"

"I don't know how you heard that story, but it's not accurate. Yes, I did arrange to buy a Satoshi egg about a year ago. The seller was afraid and insisted that the sale take place in an out-of-the-way little town north of here. I got there first to check for threats, since whoever was after the seller might attack me too."

A flicker of unease ran down Katrina's spine. As a trained attorney she recognized when a witness was lying. Either Messenja was a very good liar or she was telling the truth.

"I was sitting in the hotel business center working on business in Asia, and someone came running in with the news that a Bentley had run off the road and to call the police. I was to be on the lookout for a Bentley, so I feared the worst and drove out to the crash site as fast as I could. I got there before the police and saw the flames. The car was completely burned out. I didn't kill him. That's not how my employer or I do business. Now, where is the Apple-1?"

"But he feared for his life and clearly thought you might kill him. Why would he think that?"

Messenja drummed a red-tipped nail on the table and glanced around the restaurant with narrowed eyes. "I have no idea. You don't have an Apple-1, do you? Is this a setup? Who are you working for?"

"That's irrelevant."

"You just made me fly across the Pacific based on a lie, apparently so you could interrogate me. Do you work for the FBI? The police? Whoever it is will hear from my lawyer."

Katrina sat back in her chair. "You don't recognize me?"

"Why should I?"

This woman hadn't had them followed and clearly hadn't planted a tracking device. This wasn't turning out like Katrina had thought it would—at all. Though Messenja wasn't behind the current events, she still might have killed Jason, though even that seemed less and less likely.

"I'm Jason's widow, Katrina Foster. He thought you might kill him and took steps to let me know."

The raw anger in Messenja's expression softened, and she started to reach across the table to take Katrina's hand, then pulled back. "I'm sorry for your loss. Jason *was* fearful, but he never indicated he feared *me*—just that he didn't want anyone to know our business. That's why he wanted to meet in that little town."

"What happened to the egg?"

"I don't know. If it was in his car, it was destroyed, which is a great loss. My employer hopes to open a museum for the digital age someday, and a Satoshi egg would be an incredible exhibit. If you find it, please contact me. We would be very interested in buying it."

Katrina had caused the woman a great deal of trouble. And wasted her money. "I'm sorry for tricking you into coming all the way over here. I—I was sure you'd killed Jason."

"My employer is a legitimate businessman of great wealth and character. He wants only to create his museum as his legacy. I assure you my dealings with your husband were all cordial." She hesitated. "One more thing: I went to the spot where his car went off the cliff. The tire marks showed him braking and swerving sharply as if trying to avoid something. There were other tire marks consistent with another vehicle swerving on and off the road but not going over the cliff. If I had to guess, I'd say he was forced off the road. So I, too, suspect he was murdered."

Katrina was barely aware of Messenja's departure. They were back to square one with only the confirmation that someone else saw the sinister aspects of that crash.

IIIIIIIIIIIIIIIIIIIIIII

Ristorante Orvieto never had empty tables, particularly at six on a Saturday. But it was always possible to squeeze in an extra table, especially when the influential proprietor of a Michelin-starred restaurant asked. Seb asked, and the table appeared. He didn't like using his clout to get favors from other restaurateurs, but he wanted to treat Katrina to a nice dinner. She'd been so crestfallen after their meeting with Messenja that he decided to make an exception.

He and Katrina sat at a little table tucked into the corner of the main dining room. A floor-to-ceiling window occupied one side and rich walnut paneling covered the other. The light of a full moon danced on the waves of the San Francisco Bay outside and turned Alcatraz into a marble fortress surrounded by silvery water.

The scenery was breathtaking, but he couldn't take his eyes off Katrina. Her blue silk dress showed off her perfect figure, and the glow of candlelight brought out the golden highlights in her hair. But despair clouded those beautiful eyes, and she hadn't smiled once since they arrived in San Francisco.

They rehashed the past few days over an excellent meal of lobster ravioli. Katrina didn't seem to have much appetite though. She pushed her food around her plate as she meditated on their failed trip, growing gloomier as the evening wore on.

COLLEEN COBLE AND RICK ACKER

He decided to try distracting her over coffee. "Did I tell you about the time I had to wear a dress to church in Norway?"

Her eyebrows went up. "A dress?"

"Yes. When I first arrived in Oslo, Frida arranged for me to stay with an older Norwegian couple. They spoke English, but they tended to drop in Norwegian words if they didn't have English terms on the tips of their tongues. On my first Sunday the wife invited me to go to church with them. I accepted—and then she told me I had to wear a dress. I was surprised—to put it mildly—but she insisted that her husband wore a dress every Sunday and I needed to too."

She finally smiled. "I really hope there are pictures of this."

He laughed. "I asked if I could borrow one of her husband's dresses, since I hadn't brought any with me. She said that shouldn't be a problem since he had several and we were about the same size. I sat there in my room while she went to get one, wondering what I'd just gotten myself into. Would she return with some sort of formal robe? A Viking kilt? Or would I really have to wear an actual dress?"

She took a sip of coffee and leaned forward. "So what was it?"

"A suit. A regular business suit. The Norwegian word for 'suit' is *dress*, so she'd just used it and figured I knew what she meant. I can't tell you how relieved I was. And from that day on, I vowed to master the language of every country I lived in as fast as possible."

Her smile broadened and crinkled the corners of her eyes. "I'll bet."

"As soon as I decided to move somewhere, I'd buy literary classics in the language and start watching subtitled TV shows. I went through a lot of great books and terrible sitcoms."

"I was wondering about all those books at your house. I thought maybe you majored in comparative literature or something."

He laughed again. "Hardly."

A little crinkle appeared between her brows, and she rested her chin on the heel of her right palm. "Now I'm curious. What did you major in? Business? Culinary arts?"

"I never went to college. I didn't even graduate high school. I left the day after my eighteenth birthday, remember?"

Her eyes widened. "So . . . so you taught yourself everything?"

He shook his head. "Not at all. I just didn't learn in class-rooms. I've had lots of brilliant teachers over the years, starting with your grandmother. I always wondered what college was like though. How was it for you? Did you always know you wanted to be a lawyer?"

She sighed. "I always knew I *should* be a lawyer. Everyone told me that when I was growing up. So I majored in business and took a bunch of pre-law classes."

"What did you want to be?"

She stared down into her coffee cup and a little smile played at the corners of her lips. "This will sound silly, but I wanted to be a poet. When I was in high school, I used to sit at a back table at Bestemor's and write poetry."

He remembered her sitting there, her long blonde hair cur-taining the notebook on the table in front of her. "I thought you were doing homework."

"That's what I was supposed to be doing, but I spent 90 per-cent of the time writing."

"I wish you'd shown me some of them."

"I don't. I found a few of them a couple of years ago. They were really terrible."

"Somehow I doubt that."

She chuckled. "You didn't read them. And you never will."

"A great loss to the world of literature. Frida said you could have done anything you wanted. I'm sure you could have been a great poet."

"We all have our gifts. Hers was seeing the best in people."

Seb nodded. "She also had a marvelous gift for taking something simple and making it better." He chuckled as a memory surfaced. "Even something as basic as s'mores at one of those big cookouts she threw for Bestemor's staff. She gave us Freia chocolate because she knew it tasted better than regular Hershey bars, so the s'mores would taste better too."

"Yes, she used to do the same thing when we'd go up to the family cabin. I—" Her eyes went wide and she gasped. "Seb, I know what Jason's clue means! We have to get to that cabin! I'll explain on the way."

CHAPTER 30

////////////////

LIGHT SPILLED OUT THE WINDOWS OF Seb's house and pushed back the darkness. Even though it was midnight, everyone must be up. Katrina's hand hovered over the Range Rover's door handle. The connection she'd felt with Seb over dinner and the drive up north still warmed her, and she hated to let anyone else in.

Seb turned off the engine and gestured to the pickup parked at the road. "I'll bet Dylan is fuming inside."

The night turned Magnus's black Ford F-150 into a silhouette, and Katrina spotted two heads inside the cab. Magnus leaned toward Liv's head in a confiding pose, and Katrina remembered many such moments between them the weekend she'd brought Liv up here. "I'm afraid Magnus is heading for heartache."

Seb nodded. "Or Dylan. A tough triangle between Liv and our brothers."

She released the door handle and took his hand. "Can we promise not to let her decision between them spoil our friendship?"

Seb's smile didn't quite reach his green eyes. "Friendship. Is that what we have?"

How did she answer that? She wasn't sure she wanted to admit to herself how much she had begun to care what he thought and how he felt. "More might be possible." Before she could change her mind, she leaned over and brushed her lips across his, then grabbed the door handle again and scrambled out before he could react.

A balmy breeze lifted her hair, and she breathed in the scent of the sea blowing in off the water. It was a gorgeous night, and her spirits lifted at the thought of more alone time with Seb on the way to the cabin.

She walked toward Magnus's truck, and Liv ran her window down. The sound of country music twanged out, and Katrina caught a whiff of the grilled-cheese-and-sourdough special from his bar. She leaned on the edge of the open window. "I know what Jason's clue means—and I'll bet it's the last one. I think I know where he left the backup." She told Liv and Magnus about the encounter with Messenja and how she'd realized where the clue had to be.

"Why aren't you on your way there now?" Liv demanded. "There's no time to waste."

Katrina gestured at her attire. "I'm hardly dressed to traipse through the woods, and I'd break my ankle in these heels if I tried. Besides, it's been there for over a year. It's not going to disappear in the thirty minutes we spend here changing clothes." She caught a vibe from the two of them she couldn't name, but she couldn't ask with Magnus there. "Messenja is not having us followed, so it's unclear who attacked you, Liv. Where's Dylan?"

Magnus waved his hand toward the house. "Sulking. He didn't want me here helping to protect Liv, but he only *thinks* he's in charge. Liv came out to keep me company a little while. I took her for a ride to grab something to eat at the bar. She was going stir-crazy stuck in the house all the time."

Katrina stepped back. "I'm going to go change. We'll be without cell service, but I'll let you know what we find as soon as I can."

Seb stood a few feet away waiting for her, and he took her hand when she reached him. His grip and smile told her he wasn't sorry about the kiss—and neither was she. Now that the trip to Yosemite was over, she hoped never to have to launch the Talk app again. It hadn't been Jason talking to her, and she didn't want to slide down that slippery slope again. A new life might be awaiting her if she had the courage to seize it.

As they walked toward the house, she squeezed Seb's fingers. "I'll let you handle your brother."

He grinned. "I'm used to dealing with customers. I think I can manage his attitude." He held the door open for her, and they stepped inside.

She followed Seb into the living room where Dylan sat glowering out the window. "We're going out to Frida's old cabin," Seb said. He told him about the Messenja bust. "So the danger is far from over, and we don't know where it's coming from."

Dylan jerked his thumb at the window. "Did you tell Hotshot out there?"

"Katrina did. Lighten up. It's a good thing to have the two of you here."

"Yeah, well, I'm not sure Liv agrees." Dylan's morose expression settled into a frown. "So you're going up there with that Pineapple Express heading in?"

Seb frowned and pulled out his phone. "You're right. It's a Category 5."

The atmospheric river storm running between Hawaii and California was every California driver's worst nightmare—strong winds, torrential rains, and lightning. The rain amounts could trigger heavy flooding and landslides, turning roads into rivers or wiping them out completely.

Katrina stepped closer and gazed at his phone. "Should we take some things in case we get stuck? The road to the cabin can be a quagmire after heavy rains. When's it supposed to hit?"

"Later tonight. My Range Rover can handle most roads, but it wouldn't hurt to be prepared. Are there supplies in the cabin?"

"My parents and Magnus still use it, and it's always well stocked with canned goods, water, and stacks of firewood. Let's change and get out there."

He followed her up the stairs, and she glanced at him before she went to her room. The worry lines on his forehead had deepened. "Do you think we shouldn't go?" she asked.

"I'm as eager as you to find the clue, and I doubt either of us could sleep tonight. Let's risk it. What's this Blessings Jar look like, and where do we find it? We'll grab it and hightail it out of there before it gets bad."

"We always kept it on the fireplace mantel. It's a clear glass jug that once had apple cider in it. All kinds of things are tucked in there—ticket stubs from our trip to Broadway, a dollar I folded into the shape of a bird after cashing my first paycheck at Talk, Jason's key to the car he was driving when we first met. It would be the perfect place to hide a USB drive, especially one of those gimmicky drives that looks like a golf ball or something. The jar is full of random things, but they were kept to remind us of the blessings God gave us."

"I like that."

She reached up and palmed his face. "I haven't wanted to see it since Jason died because I hadn't felt very blessed, but these last few days with you have reminded me that my life isn't over. Grief only eclipses those blessings for a little while. They're still there, and so is God. I forgot that."

Hope unfurled in his expression. It was the same hope blossoming inside her—the dream of what might be.

A tree limb crashed out of the darkness onto Skog Road in front of Seb's Range Rover. He grimaced and Katrina let out a little yelp from the seat beside him. The rain hadn't started yet, but the wind was rising. By morning, downed trees would litter North Haven.

The branch in front of him didn't look thick, so he drove over it. He wouldn't try to drive around it—a steep hillside rose on the right side of the street, and the ravine that claimed his mother's life dropped away on the left. He hated this drive.

Katrina laid a hand on his arm. "It must be tough to go past here."

"It is, even on nice days when this place looks like a postcard. On a night like this . . . Well, I appreciate the company."

"Me too. I couldn't ask for a better traveling companion these past few days. You've been wonderful."

COLLEEN COBLE AND RICK ACKER

His heart warmed. "It's been a pleasure—though one I hope is coming to an end. Do you really think Jason hid a backup of the key in that jar?"

"It's the perfect spot. The Blessings Jar is full of all sorts of little odds and ends, so the key wouldn't stick out at all. And no one except me or maybe a member of my family would ever go through the jar. He did such a good job of hiding it that he almost hid it from me." She shook her head. "Thanks for your help, by the way. I never would have figured it out if you hadn't mentioned s'mores made with Freia chocolate."

"I'd been wondering about that. What's the connection?"

"Freia s'mores were part of a little ritual we did on the first evening of a trip to the cabin. We'd make a fire, take down the jar, and literally count our blessings during a cookout dinner. We always had Freia s'mores for dessert."

Now he got it. "Ah, so the Freia wrapper around a rock from the Blessing Jar meant that's where you should look."

"Right. And maybe it was a subtle hint that I should count my blessings again. He knew me well, so he probably realized I . . . might not take his death well." Her eyes glistened in the dashboard lights.

"He sounds like a great guy. I wish I'd known him."

She sniffed and her voice was rough. "He would have liked you too."

Guilt twinged in his chest. "I'm sorry. I didn't mean to upset you. Would you like to talk about something else?"

She wiped her eyes and shook her head. "It's fine. Talking helps—as long as I'm not talking to this." She held up her phone.

Did that mean she wanted to get over Jason? A guy could dream, right?

The half-collapsed *Welcome to Cathedral Falls* sign appeared in his headlights. He remembered it well. "I used to visit here a lot when I was a kid. It's only about a mile from the trailer. Exploring the old buildings was fun, and sometimes I'd find cool stuff. My dad still has tools that came from an abandoned lumber company workshop. There was an entire box of decade-old Twinkies in the back of the old gas station." He shot her a grin. "I tried one, and no, they weren't still fresh."

She laughed. "My parents never let us go into the town. They said it was too dangerous. Maybe they knew about the Twinkies."

"They were right. I nearly killed myself at least half a dozen times. I'm pretty sure my parents had no idea where I was."

They drove in silence for a few minutes. The ghost town had no streetlights, of course. The cones of light from the SUV picked out partial glimpses of decaying structures—a parking lot with saplings sprouting through the asphalt, the old cinema with the collapsed marquee, the town hall built of massive red-wood logs, which wouldn't rot for centuries.

Katrina pointed to a gravel track to the left. "Turn here."

Seb turned, and the Range Rover drove up toward the picturesque falls that gave the town its name. The first heavy drops splatted onto his windshield, and he turned on the wipers.

A gap in the trees appeared, and Seb caught a glimpse of a well-kept log cabin.

"There it is," Katrina said. "Through there. Park in back. My dad built a carport by the back door, so we won't get too wet."

Seb pulled into the carport and they got out. The rain was pouring down now, thrumming on the sheet-metal roof. Tree branches groaned and squealed in the wind. Wet gusts through the carport's open sides drenched them despite Katrina's assurance that they'd stay dry.

Katrina unlocked the door and they hurried inside, shutting out the weather. She found an electric lantern and switched it on, revealing a rustic kitchen with a propane stove and red rosemaling cabinets. A woodsy, musty scent hung in the air with a faint hint of old woodsmoke. She checked the cabinets. "Good, we should have plenty of food and water if we get stuck here. We'll have electricity, too, if we need it, but I'm not going out there to start the generator."

"Hopefully we'll only be here a few minutes." Seb surveyed the snug, tidy room. "This is really nice."

"*Bestefar* and Bestemor built it fifty years ago, back when Cathedral Falls was a booming lumber town and lots of families had cabins around here. Now we have the forest almost completely to ourselves. It's a special place." Lantern aloft in her hand, Katrina walked across the kitchen and opened a door leading into a room hidden in darkness. "Come on. The Blessings Jar is in here. Let's check it and leave before the storm gets any worse."

Seb followed her into a larger room decorated with log furniture. The smoky smell was stronger and came from a massive stone fireplace with a sitting ledge. Two large windows flanked the fireplace, and a large glass jug stood on the mantel.

Katrina set the lantern on the sitting ledge and took down the jar. The light gleamed off a dozen polished rocks, some foreign coins, a key chain, an origami bird made from a dollar bill, and dozens of other items. Katrina gently emptied the contents onto the ledge and examined them. She picked up a folded scrap of paper and opened it, then took a deep breath. "The key isn't here, but I know where to look next."

She held up the paper and read, "'Shall I compare thee to a summer's day?' That's the first line from one of Shakespeare's sonnets. We had a book of them we used to read to each other. Jason must have hidden a clue there."

These little glimpses into the life she'd lost were like looking at pictures of a child who died young. He set a comforting hand on her shoulder. "Where is the book now?"

"It's in my house in Palo Alto—or wait, no, I took it with me when I moved to Bestemor's. That's where it is." She began replacing items in the Blessings Jar. She held the scrap of paper for a moment, then refolded it and put it in the jar too.

A flash of light from the left window caught Seb's eye. He looked out through the streaming water—and instantly regretted leaving his gun in the SUV. Headlights. Someone just turned into the drive leading to the cabin.

CHAPTER 31

////////////

KATRINA SPRANG INTO ACTION AT SEB'S hoarse whisper to kill the lantern. Her pulse throbbed in her neck, and she huddled close to him, clutching his arm.

He held up one finger, then two, and raised his brows as he motioned toward the doorway.

She caught his intent and moved with him to the kitchen.

She pointed to a spot near the fridge where they could see into the living room but were partially blocked by the bulk of the appliance, and they stood waiting. The seconds turned into minutes. Her imagination sprang into overdrive as she imagined a squad of men surrounding the cabin to prevent their escape.

The dark night didn't show much detail, but she finally caught the darker shadow of a figure moving to the front door. A sharp report sounded above the drum of the rain on the metal roof and the wood at the door splintered. The door crashed in and a man charged inside. He shut the door to the driving rain and flipped on a flashlight.

Katrina knew better than to assume no one else was with him. Another guy could be in the vehicle or lying in wait outside. Maybe more than one.

The guy wore a suit and something about the way he moved felt familiar. She spotted the gun still in his hand as he waved the flashlight around the room with the other hand. Enough light washed up his form to illuminate his face, and she bit back a gasp. Agent Hughes.

Seb stiffened beside her and took a step toward the agent, but she held him back. What would he be doing here when the FBI expressed disinterest in Jason's death? This was no friendly visit to help out.

The flashlight played over the room, its beam touching first on the fireplace and then on the sofa. The light settled on the contents they'd dumped out of the Blessings Jar. Hughes didn't waste time looking at the contents and started toward the kitchen.

Seb caught her by the hand and they ran for the exit with Hughes on their heels. A bullet slammed into the doorjamb beside Katrina as they rushed out the door. If they tried to reach the SUV, the rogue agent would have a clear shot at them when the interior lights turned on, but Seb led her into the woods. The overstory of redwoods and towering pines blocked some of the rain, and she was thankful to blink some of the moisture out of her eyes so she could see.

The damp scent of pine and redwood grew stronger as they stepped on the thick debris underfoot. She batted low-hanging branches out of her face and pressed on through the forest.

Seb paused and caught her arm to stop her too. "I know a shortcut to Cathedral Falls, and there are more places to hide there. I know all of them."

She let him lead her along a barely discernible path among huge fallen redwoods. "I don't hear him," she whispered.

"Do you think he's given up?"

"Not likely." She barely whispered the words. "He's FBI, and if we make it out alive, he'll lose his career. He has to shut us up." Saying the words out loud gave her a new wash of adrenaline. They had to escape Hughes and get to help. The storm was their helper tonight. Without it he easily would have heard them thrashing through the ferns and underbrush.

Seb paused and turned her to the right. He pressed his lips against her ear. "Almost there."

She followed his lead as they sidled along several buildings until they came to a dilapidated old store that looked like a strong wind would blow it down. She looked back down the deserted street and saw a figure exiting the forest. Seb tugged her through a broken-down doorway into a room littered with old newspapers, beer cans, and broken glass.

There was another room past this one, and she went with him even though it felt dangerous to be in here. Seb knew this town and she trusted him. He'd keep them safe. He went straight to a wall of wide wooden planks and removed a board. He swiped cobwebs out of the way and motioned for her to step into the void.

She shuddered but obeyed. The space smelled of mold and mouse, but she couldn't let herself think of what else might be in here with her.

Seb opened a back door to the wind, then returned and stepped into the area in the wall with her. He pulled the board back into place, and she held her breath at the sound of a footfall. Seb's arms circled her, and he pressed her head against his chest. She wrapped her arms around his waist and waited. She listened to the steady sound of his heartbeat. He didn't seem scared, and his calm certainty seeped into her.

The footsteps passed a few feet from them, then paused. Hughes picked up a chair and threw it with a muttered curse before stomping out the back door.

"We have to wait awhile." Seb's soft words lifted the hair at her ear.

She nodded and closed her eyes. Time seemed to stand still as they stood entwined inside the wall. Something happened in her heart as the minutes ticked past. Defenses crumbled like rotted wood. With Seb's arms sheltering her, she felt his heart, his strength, and his steady purpose. This was a man who didn't lose his way. Someone who would stand and face the battles when they threatened.

How had she missed this man inside the boy all those years ago?

It was her loss.

Seb pressed a gentle kiss on her hair. "I think he's gone. Let's circle back another way. I'll call for help from my sat phone." She nodded and he moved the board out of the way and stepped back into the room, then helped her out. "This way."

He kept her hand and led her to the back door. The rain was still falling in a steady downpour, and she broke into a run with him. Her lungs burned, but she kept up the pace with him and they entered the sanctuary of the forest. The trees were giant sentries standing guard for them as they headed back toward the cabin.

Katrina was familiar with the cabin and the forest around it, but this part of the woods was foreign to her, especially in the dark. But Seb had an unerring sense of direction, and after half an hour, she began to recognize the terrain.

A branch raked across her cheek, and she stumbled. Her foot slipped into a hole and her ankle twisted under her. Sharp pain gripped her, and she gasped out a groan.

Seb lifted her up, but she whimpered when she tried to put weight on it. She stood on one foot and leaned against him. "I think I sprained my ankle."

"We're nearly back to the cabin. If the lantern was lit, you'd be able to see the light. I'll carry you."

She protested but he lifted her in his arms, and she wrapped her arms around his neck. "Would it be easier if I was on your back?"

He grinned. "I don't like to brag, but you're not as heavy as the weights I lift three times a week. Hang on to me, and we'll be there in a minute."

She rested her cheek against his chest and clung to him. Being in his arms was starting to be familiar. And welcome.

He set her down on a fallen log. "His vehicle is gone, but I want to scout out the area and make sure. Wait here."

He disappeared into the darkness, and she rubbed her ankle. It was swollen, but a little rest and she should be fine. He returned after a few minutes, and she sensed his tension when he lifted her again. "What's wrong?"

"Hughes slashed the tires and took my sat phone and my gun. There's no way to warn Dylan and Liv."

And she couldn't hike out of here. They were truly stuck.

||||||||||||||||||||||

A gust of wind rattled the window of Dylan's bedroom and blew a fresh sheet of water against the glass. He looked up from watching YouTube videos on his phone as he lay in bed, shotgun nestled in his arms. The little screen glowed in the snug, dark room while the storm raged outside. The weather guy said it was likely to go on until at least 4:00 a.m. The power had already gone out twice, and roads were flooding. Dylan was glad he hadn't gone with Seb and Katrina. That was going to be a messy drive.

The rain and wind let up for a moment, and Magnus's truck became visible. The guy was out there "guarding" Liv. Again. Dylan snorted and shook his head. Magnus was a loser who couldn't take a hint. At least he'd been smart enough not to try to enter the house again.

Dylan yawned and nestled deeper into the poofy down comforter. He turned on a collection of classic PewDiePie videos and propped his phone against his arm. Dylan could watch this guy all night long.

||||||||||||||||||||||||||

Dylan jerked awake, clutching the shotgun. His phone lay silent and dark on the bed beside him, but something had wakened him. He lay still, every sense on high alert.

A floorboard creaked on the staircase. Liv hadn't come upstairs since her knee was broken. Could it be Magnus? Somehow Dylan doubted it.

Dylan slung the shotgun over his shoulder, rolled out of bed, and opened the window. He slipped over the sill and pulled the window closed behind him. Cold rain instantly drenched him, but he hardly noticed.

His room's door burst open seconds after he left. A flashlight panned over the interior. He ducked down, clinging to a shutter to keep his balance on the slate roof. The flashlight's beam lit a cone of falling raindrops through the window. Then it vanished.

Dylan glanced toward Magnus's truck. The driver's door stood open. Was Magnus the intruder? Probably not—he wouldn't leave his door open in the rain. The intruder must have taken him out before heading into the house. Where he was currently alone with Liv.

Dylan peeked into the room. It was empty, but the door stood open. He slid up the window and climbed back in, making what seemed like a huge amount of noise. He unslung the shotgun and closed the window with his left hand.

A man shouted in pain from downstairs. Dylan racked the shotgun as softly as he could and stepped into the hall.

"Where's the other guy?" an unfamiliar male voice demanded.

"What other guy?" Magnus's voice was practically a shout. The sound of a heavy blow followed, and Magnus cried out.

He's making as much noise as possible to warn me. Dylan's grip on the gun tightened, and he crept down the stairs, avoiding the squeaky one.

"I'm not asking again," the other man growled. "I know there are two of you, and your partner isn't upstairs. So where is he?"

"I told you, I don't have a partner!"

Dylan reached the foot of the stairs and snuck a glance around the corner into the drawing room. He took in the scene in an instant. A bloody-faced Magnus was zip-tied to a chair. A big guy wearing a ski mask loomed over him. His right hand held a pistol, which he had raised to pistol-whip Magnus.

Dylan stepped into the room and brought the shotgun to his shoulder. "Drop it!"

The intruder wheeled around with catlike speed and started to point his gun at Dylan.

Dylan fired, hitting the guy square in the chest. The shotgun's roar filled the room.

The intruder staggered back and the gun flew out of his hand—but he didn't go down and no red hole appeared near his heart. Must be wearing body armor.

Dylan chambered another round and fired as fast as he could, aiming for the head. But the guy had already recovered and was running for the door. A fist-sized hole appeared in the wall just behind his head.

Dylan raced after the intruder, but he was already through the door. An engine roared to life behind the house. Dylan ran around the corner just as a black SUV drove past him. He fired again, blowing out the SUV's rear window. It didn't slow down and vanished into the stormy night.

Dylan went back into the house. He grabbed a knife from the kitchen and headed into the drawing room to cut Magnus free. The guy was a mess—blood streamed from his nose, mouth, and a cut on his face.

"He's got Liv!" Magnus's eyes were wide with panic. "He took her before he started beating me up and asking about you. We've gotta rescue her!"

CHAPTER 32

////////////

SITTING SHOULDER TO SHOULDER WITH
Seb on the sofa in the darkness of the cabin's living room
felt strangely intimate, and Katrina didn't want to move even
though her stomach grumbled with hunger. But at least they
were in dry clothes.

"I heard that," Seb said. "I can see what there is to eat."

Her eyelids were heavy, and she ached all over. "You think
Hughes will come back?"

"I doubt it. By this point Skog Road will be flooded, and it'll
stay that way until the rain stops. But if he does return, I can
always hit him with an iron."

"Or a chair."

"Or throw dishes. I'm good in the kitchen."

A giggle combined with a very unladylike snort escaped.
"Bestemor is rolling over in her grave at the thought of you
breaking the dishes she got as a girl in Norway."

"I'd only throw the cracked ones," he said, deadpan.

She linked her arm through his and hugged it. "Thank you
for making me laugh."

He chuckled. "You mean for making you snort?"

"You weren't supposed to notice."

"I notice everything about you." His breath stirred her hair as he touched his head to hers. "You didn't complain once out there. Not even when I shoved you into the wall."

"I considered my options and thought I might survive a black widow walking on my arm. Surviving a gunshot to the chest might have been a different story." She stroked his cheek with her free hand. "You were amazing out there, you know. Finding a place to hide, wiping away spiderwebs with your bare hand, carrying me back to safety. Is there anything you can't do?"

He took her hand. "I can't seem to stop thinking about you. Does that count?"

His lips were only inches away, and she urged his face a little closer with her palm on his cheek. How much encouragement did the man need? He finally took the hint, and his lips touched hers. He took his time and deepened the kiss until her head spun and the last traces of her fear vanished.

He finally broke the kiss and rested his forehead against hers. Katrina didn't want to ruin the moment by saying anything. His contradictions intrigued her. He grew up in a broken-down trailer but was the most urbane and polished man she'd ever met. His culinary skills were equaled only by his kindness, and she sensed deep waters in him she wanted to dive into.

She yawned. Maybe if she closed her eyes, he'd kiss her again.

|||||||||||||||||||||||

Katrina opened her eyes and strained to see, but it was still dark. Seb held her right arm captive against him, and the rain had slackened to a light tapping on the roof. How long had she slept?

Seb pressed a kiss on her hair. "Hey, sleepyhead."

"What time is it?"

"I didn't want to move to look." He tucked a lock of her hair behind her ear and trailed a series of gentle kisses behind his touch. "You only snored a little."

"I did not!"

"Okay, more than a little."

"Try again, buster. I don't snore." She turned her head and kissed him properly and lost all interest in knowing the time.

He finally pulled away. "I think I should fix us something to eat. Fortified with food, we might be able to make a plan. How's the ankle?"

She rotated it. "Swollen. I don't think I'll get far, Seb. If I rest it, it should be mostly fine tomorrow, but walking very far tonight would be problematic."

He unwound from her and stood. "Let me see about food and we'll figure it out." The glow of his phone illuminated his face. "It's four." He nodded toward the window. "The rain is ending. Skog Road will clear soon. We need to make our move under cover of darkness."

A ground fog hid their location. "It's pea soup out there. We'd be lucky to see the road two feet in front of us."

"I can guide us out." He stopped at the kitchen door and turned to her. "I don't want to leave you."

"You can do anything, remember?"

"Not everything."

It was too dark to see his expression as he delivered the reminder of what he'd said when he kissed her before she fell asleep, but she saw it in her mind—that steady wonder that lingered in his green eyes while he looked right into her soul.

Her relationship with Jason had started with physical attraction. She'd discovered his strengths and weaknesses once she'd toppled into infatuation with him. Love had followed. Seb was the complete opposite. His inner strength and consideration for people eclipsed his handsome exterior. His good looks weren't the flashy kind like Jason's but the kind that matured over time. Seb would still be handsome at seventy.

"We have to call the police—and warn Liv and Dylan." He walked her way. "Peanut butter and crackers, the perfect quick meal. Have some and we can try to find cell service." He settled on the sofa with her and put a paper plate full of snacks on her lap.

She downed four bites before the "we" soaked in. "Seb, you'll have to get help without me. I'll wait here."

"I don't think you can turn a plate into a weapon like I can. I've had years of practice."

"Are you throwing shade on my pitching arm?"

She'd hoped to make him laugh, but he sighed. "I have a plan. I don't like it, but it's the best I can do at the moment." He helped her to her feet. "We'll take the road. On the outskirts of Cathedral Falls is an old building at the turn to the cabin. You can see any vehicles coming, but the building is easy to miss. While you hunker down there, I'll find cell service and call Liv, then return for you and wait for help. I won't be gone long."

She had to try or they'd both be stuck here waiting for Hughes to come back. "Okay."

He slipped his arm around her waist, and she bit back a cry when she put weight on her ankle. He paused but she took another step. "It will get better."

But it didn't. Seb ended up carrying her part of the way, and he was gulping in air by the time he kicked open the door to an old building nearly smothered in ferns and trees and smelling strongly of damp and mold. He carried her inside and set her on an old crate.

It was too dark to see whether black widows lurked to pounce, but she put on a brave smile. "Go get help. I'll be fine."

He hesitated. "I don't want to leave you."

"Cell service can't be far, and you can jog without me slowing you down."

He pressed a fervent kiss on her lips. "Don't go anywhere. There's a lot I want to say to you when I get back." The fog swallowed him up just outside the door.

She blinked back tears and touched her fingers to her lips. The night sounds of the forest started: frogs, insects, running water, and the birds waking up. She hugged herself both for warmth and for comfort.

A light caught her eye out the window, and she hobbled over to peek out. Red taillights flashed as a black vehicle braked to make the turn to the cabin. They'd gotten out just in time, and she prayed Hughes didn't come searching here. She didn't even have a cracked plate to throw at his head.

The fog muffled a sound up by the cabin, and she strained to hear. "Katrina!" a familiar voice called. She gasped and started for the door. Her dad had come to the rescue.

|||||||||||||||||||||||||

Finding that Katrina's father, Torvald, had been sent out to check on them had been a big relief, but tension still knotted Seb's gut. Liv's cell phone went straight to voice mail, and so did Dylan's. During the short drive back to town, Torvald told them about Hughes's attack on Magnus and Liv's kidnapping, but what had happened to Dylan?

They pulled up to Seb's house, which looked like a haunted mansion in the thick fog. The door opened as they parked, and Magnus stepped out onto the porch. Seb did a double take. Katrina's brother looked like he'd been in a car crash or a prizefight—maybe both. He had bandages on his left cheek and upper lip, a swollen nose, and two black eyes, one of which was barely open.

Katrina gasped. She opened her door and hopped out, balancing on her good leg. "My gosh! Magnus, how do you feel?"

He smiled with the undamaged side of his mouth. "Better than I look, though that's not saying much. The hospital let me go fifteen minutes ago."

Seb got out and offered Katrina his shoulder for support. "Where's Dylan?"

"He called 911 for me and then took off to go looking for Liv." Magnus paused. "He saved my life."

Brotherly pride surged in Seb's chest. He'd known—well, hoped—that Dylan would prove his mettle. "His phone is going straight to voice mail. Do you know where he was going?"

Magnus's forehead creased with concern. "Shoot, no. No idea where he went. Hope he's okay."

They reached the steps. Katrina gripped Seb's shoulder and his arm circled her waist. "The pain has improved. A little ice and rest, and I should be good as new."

Torvald joined them and took his daughter's other arm. "Maybe JJ has news about Dylan. He'll be arriving shortly to interview you two."

They went through the front door and Seb surveyed his violated home. Chips of paint and plaster littered the floor below the hole torn by Dylan's shotgun blast. The evidence techs had removed the spent shells, but the acrid odor of gunpowder lingered in the air. The chair used to torture Magnus still stood in the middle of the drawing room with little black-red dots around it.

Seb and Torvald eased Katrina into the big wingback chair and pulled up an ottoman so she could elevate her ankle, though the swelling was already going down.

JJ's police cruiser pulled into the driveway just as they finished. Seb opened the door as JJ parked and lumbered up the steps. The big cop looked tired and old in the gray predawn gloom. Seb guided him into the parlor, and JJ took the seat opposite Katrina.

JJ pulled out a digital recorder and set it on the coffee table. "Okay, let's start with you, Katrina. Tell me what happened. Our federal friends are particularly interested in how sure you are about Agent Hughes."

Katrina didn't hesitate. "I'm positive. I got a good look at his face in the reflected light from his flashlight."

JJ's bushy brows went up a fraction. "He wasn't wearing a mask?"

Katrina cocked her head. "No. And he was wearing a suit. He looked like he'd just come from the office. Huh. Anyway, he noticed that we'd been going through some stuff on the fireplace ledge and—" Her eyes widened. "We found another clue! I almost forgot with everything that's been going on. I have to go to Bestemor's right now."

She started to get up, but Torvald pressed a hand on her shoulder. "Hold on, sweetheart. Whatever is at the restaurant can wait. Finish answering JJ's questions. Then we'll take you to the hospital and have someone look at that ankle."

She bristled. "I'm not ten anymore, Dad. I can make my own decisions." Her phone pinged. "Hold on a sec—I just got a text from an unknown number. It says, 'Send key for 1K Bitcoins in 24 hours or Liv is dead.'" In the early morning light her gray eyes were the color of carbon steel. "We need leverage. I'm going to go find that key right now. Then we'll talk."

CHAPTER 33

///////////

THE DAWN LIGHT DIDN'T HAVE THE POWER to break through the thick fog blanketing North Haven. The back of JJ's squad car reeked of his cheap cologne. Katrina took Seb's hand and squeezed it. He'd been quiet, almost morose, since the news about Dylan's disappearance. "Thanks for wrapping my ankle. It's much better with a little support."

He kept possession of her hand and laced his fingers with hers. "Glad I was able to find a bandage. The wrecker should be back with my Range Rover anytime. The garage should have me on the road soon, and I can look for Dylan." While JJ spoke on the phone, Seb leaned closer to her. "I just found him, and I can't lose him now."

She hugged his arm and tightened her grip on his hand. "I've been praying for him."

"Me too."

JJ ended his call and parked at the curb in front of Bestemor's. "That was the FBI. They believe Hughes took Liv into the Lost Coast."

The Lost Coast was one of Katrina's favorite places. Its fog-shrouded terrain stretched between Shelter Cove on the south and Mattole River to the north—in both Mendocino and

Humboldt Counties. Forests teeming with elk and other wild-life gave way to rocky beaches where Native Americans had once collected clams. The Lost Coast was a land of forests, fog, waves, and sand. It was a wild place where someone could disappear without a trace.

"I've been there," Seb said. "It won't be easy to find them."

"No. Hughes is an experienced agent, and he grew up in Petrolia, so the area is familiar. He'll know how to evade the Bureau's best search techniques." JJ swiveled on the seat and turned toward Seb. "They found Dylan's truck in a deserted area near Clam Beach. It's a burned-out mess."

Katrina squeezed Seb's hand harder. "D-did they find Dylan?"

"No sign of him around the truck."

"So there's still hope." But her words rang flat and hollow. If someone burned the truck, it would have been to cover evidence.

A slight tremor shuddered through Seb. "Was his phone in the truck?"

"I don't think so."

"Can they trace his phone?"

"I'm sure they're working on it." JJ heaved his bulk out of the squad car and opened the back door for them.

Seb helped Katrina to the front of Bestemor's and unlocked it. "If you tell me where to look, I can go upstairs so you can save your ankle."

"It's actually feeling a lot better, but I'll rest it while I can." She sank onto a chair and extended her injured leg. "On the right side of my bed there's a bookcase. It's on the top shelf on the far left. Shakespeare's sonnets."

"On it." His feet pounded up the steps and crossed over her head in the apartment above her.

JJ joined her at the table while Magnus headed for the kitchen. "I'm going to make some coffee. There's probably some coffee cake left over from yesterday. I'm starving."

Seb came down the steps holding a blue-and-black book. "Here you go."

Bestemor had picked it up for her at an estate sale when Katrina was fifteen. She and Jason used to read the sonnets to each other, and it held a lot of memories. She fanned through the pages, but no envelope or piece of paper fluttered into view, and she tried again. Still nothing. It was a crushing blow when she'd felt so certain she'd find what Jason left for her.

She closed the book and stared at the cover. "There's nothing."

"Could he have written something on one of the pages? Maybe go through page by page," Seb said.

Magnus joined them with breakfast. "Have some coffee. There has to be some clue in there."

She wrapped her cold fingers around the hot mug of coffee and took a sip, then opened the cover. Nothing on the first page but her name in Bestemor's spidery handwriting.

Katrina turned to the first sonnet and frowned at the sight of a blue dot over one of the letters. "Wait, look." She turned it around and showed it to Seb and JJ. "I need a notebook and pen."

JJ whipped out a notebook and pen from his pocket. "Here."

She wrote the letter *A* and went through the book a page at a time and wrote down everything with a blue dot. By the end she had a long list of seemingly random letters and numbers. How did she decipher it?

"Count them," Seb said. "A Bitcoin key has sixty-four char-acters."

She counted them out. "Sixty-four! We've found the backup!" She snapped the book shut. "We have our leverage."

It felt satisfying to finally have the key, but Liv's predicament and Dylan's probable death overshadowed what should have been a thrilling discovery.

|||||||||||||||||||||||

Seb stared at the string of numbers and letters written in Katrina's neat, small handwriting. The key to over thirty million dollars in Bitcoin. They'd spent the last week chasing it all over Northern California, and it had been here at Bestemor's the whole time.

JJ whistled between his teeth. "Wow, so that's what this is all about, huh? The Bureau will want to hear about this. They have a team on the way." He took out his phone and started to dial.

Katrina held up a hand. "Wait. What if Hughes wasn't the only bad apple? What if he has coconspirators still at the FBI?"

JJ's finger hovered over the phone. "Fair point, Katrina. Mike Short seemed pretty upset when he heard about Hughes— devastated really—but maybe Hughes is working with someone else. Or maybe Short is just a really good actor."

Seb drummed his fingers on the pine tabletop. "Actually, if Hughes has coconspirators, we want them to know we have the key, don't we?" He pointed to the notebook in front of Katrina. "That's only our leverage if Hughes is aware of it and thinks it's genuine. If he hears about it from one of his cronies, he's more likely to believe it."

Katrina nodded slowly. "Good thinking. Okay, we'll tell them we have the key, but we won't give them a copy or tell them where it is." She tore the sheet out of JJ's notebook and handed it and the pen back to him. "Sound like a plan?"

JJ nodded as he took the proffered items. "Sounds like a plan."

Katrina turned to Seb. "Cell coverage is terrible in the Lost Coast. Do you have another satellite phone?"

He nodded. "I'm pretty sure I still have an old one in a drawer somewhere. I'll go see if I can find it and reactivate it."

He called an Uber and went outside. Five minutes later, he was standing in front of his house. Torvald had left, and Seb's home stood empty for the first time since Katrina, Liv, and Dylan had moved in.

Dylan.

Seb's fists clenched. He wanted to go hunt for his brother, but he had to leave that to the police and the FBI. Katrina needed his help, and so did Liv. He couldn't abandon them, especially not now. Besides, what could he add to the search for Dylan other than being another pair of eyes driving along back roads or another voice shouting his brother's name in the woods? Still, Dylan was family, and it just felt wrong to leave the search to outsiders. Dylan had been on his own his entire life. He deserved better.

Seb shook his head and walked through the front door. He knew what he needed to do, and there was no time to lose. He started for the stairs—and stopped cold an instant later. His empty home wasn't empty after all. Floorboards creaked in the master bedroom.

Someone was up there.

Seb drew his pistol and eased his way up the stairs. Heart pounding, he moved down the upstairs hall, pointing his gun at the bedroom door, which stood ajar. Footsteps came from inside and a drawer scraped.

Seb took a deep breath. He kicked open the door—and found himself face-to-face with his brother. Dylan gripped several pairs of underwear in one hand and socks in the other. He stumbled backward as the door flew open and tripped over a suitcase on the floor.

Seb lowered his gun. "What . . . what's going on?"

Dylan picked himself up and shoved the socks and underwear into the suitcase. "I'm leaving."

"Why?" A realization hit Seb. "Did you burn out your own truck?"

Dylan nodded as he pulled a stack of T-shirts from a drawer. "Yeah. That hurt, but I had to do it."

"Why?"

"So people would think I was dead." Dylan heaved a sigh. "After what happened last night, the cops would want to talk to me. They'd probably run my name. My real name—Dylan Jackson. And . . . well, they'd find stuff. I'm sorry, bro. You've been good to me, and I'm really happy I got to know Dad. I'm gonna miss you guys."

Seb's lingering unease about Dylan's past came back full force. "What sort of stuff would they find?"

Dylan looked at the floor. "I killed a guy. It was self-defense, but no one will believe me."

"Why not?"

Dylan brought up his gaze to meet Seb's, and anger flashed in his blue eyes. "Because he was an off-duty cop. Some of the witnesses were cops too. They're gonna lie and say I started the fight and I pulled my gun first, even though that's the exact

COLLEEN COBLE AND RICK ACKER

opposite of what happened. It'll be my word against theirs, and who's gonna believe the guy with a couple priors and no job?" He looked down again. "Can't say I'd blame 'em."

"You can't run from your past forever, Dylan. Stay. Fight. I'll be there with you, and I can recommend a very good lawyer. Plus, they've started weaning Dad off the sedatives. He could wake up any day. You want to be there when he does, don't you?"

"*If* he does, you mean." Dylan shook his head. "I don't know, man. I try not to get my hopes up anymore. Just live for today and try not to think about tomorrow, you know?"

"Well, today we're going after the guy who kidnapped Liv and beat up Magnus. We could use another good man."

"Can't say I fit that description." Dylan closed the suitcase and gave Seb a bone-crushing hug. "Goodbye, bro."

CHAPTER 34

////////////

THE RANSOM CALL CAME THROUGH TWO hours later on Katrina's phone with them all seated in Seb's parlor with the aroma of their crab cake lunch lingering in the air. Lyla stirred at the sound, and time froze as Katrina stared at the blocked number. It had to be Hughes. Her vision blurred, and she unclenched her fists. Liv had to be okay.

She answered the call. "This is Katrina."

"Of course it is." The electronically altered voice that came through sounded nothing like Hughes. "You found something I want."

What was with masking his voice? He must have assumed the dark night and rain masked his identity. "Yes, but I want Liv back before I give it to you."

"I'm afraid that won't be possible. If you do exactly what I tell you, I'll verify the accuracy of the key and release her."

"No, that's not acceptable." She caught herself before she used his name. "I'll meet you and we'll make the exchange. I want to verify Liv is still alive."

"I'll send you a picture."

A moment later a photo of a tearstained Liv sitting in a dark room appeared. "How do I know this is a current picture? I want to speak to her."

"I don't have time for this nonsense."

"If you want possession of thirty million dollars in Bitcoin, you'll make the time." She delivered the ultimatum and spotted Short and two other agents heading for Seb's front door. Seb held a finger to his lips and motioned to Short and JJ. They went to intercept the agents and left Katrina alone.

The silence on the phone told her she'd won. A few moments later Liv was on the line. "Katrina? You've got to give him the key or he'll kill me." A sob caught in her throat. "Hurry, Katrina."

"Liv, where are you?"

There was only silence. "Liv?"

"Satisfied?" Hughes's masked voice held mockery. "Get a pen and paper to write down where to leave the key."

She used her sternest attorney tone. "Tell me where to meet you. That's the only way I'm giving you the key. I want Liv alive and well in my car."

"I don't want any tricks. Come alone. If I see anyone with you, she's dead." He gave her directions to a remote location east of Clam Beach.

She wrote it down and committed it to memory. "Got it. What time?"

"Eight."

It would be dark in the deep woods. "I'll be there."

"Make sure you're alone or Liv is dead."

The call ended and Katrina put the kitten down and joined the men on the porch. "He's skittish but I insisted on an in-person meeting." She told them the details. "He masked his voice, so he must have hoped I didn't recognize him."

"Good job." Agent Short consulted the map on his phone. "We'll surround the meeting location. Hughes will be expecting roadblocks, too, so we'll have K9 units in the area as well as drones with infrared sensors."

Seb took her hand. "I don't like you going alone."

"I don't either," Magnus said.

"It may look like she's alone, but the whole FBI team will be around her. We'll make sure she's safe."

|||||||||||||||||||||||||

Fog swirled around the thick ferns under the towering redwoods and enhanced the earthy undertones of decaying redwood bark and leaves. The staging area held three vans and an SUV, and Katrina spotted K9 officers heading into the trees. Other agents tinkered with drones. The well-orchestrated operation calmed her jitters. She parked her Tesla beside Short's vehicle, and Magnus jumped out of the back.

Seb reached over and tucked a lock of hair behind her ear before he exited the car. His hand settled on her shoulder. "I still don't like this. Promise you'll be careful."

"I'll do my best."

The things still unspoken between them hung in the air, but now wasn't the time either. When Liv was safe, there was so much to talk about—the future of Bestemor's and where she and Seb went from here. All she knew was she wanted her future to include the sound of his voice and the warmth in his eyes.

He leaned over and kissed her. "Come back to me," he whispered in her ear.

Her throat constricted and she nodded before he got out to wait with Magnus and the FBI team. She watched until his tall figure disappeared into the fog-shrouded trees. She prayed for clarity and wisdom, then pulled away from the rest of the vehicles to drive out to the meeting site.

The site was ten miles from Clam Beach along a curvy unpaved road, and she drove slowly, watching for any sign of movement. She didn't trust Hughes. He could try to intercept her and kill both her and Liv. The book of sonnets was in the back.

She checked her phone. One bar. Around the curve ahead, the signal would be lost and she'd have no way of calling for help.

Her heart leaped to her throat when her phone sounded. It was him. She pulled to the side of the road so she didn't drop the call. "Katrina here."

"You lied, Katrina. The FBI are all over the place. We have a new meeting spot. Go there now and don't call the FBI if you want to see your friend again. Trick me again, the deal is off and you'll find Liv's dead body in the ocean."

|||||||||||||||||||||||||

Seb's sat phone rang and lit up the darkness where he sat on the edge of the base camp. He didn't recognize the number, but the 707 area code indicated it was local. He debated letting the call go to voice mail. He was laser-focused on the FBI operation going on around him, and he didn't want any distractions. On the other hand, few people had his sat phone number, and they all knew not to call it without a good reason.

He stepped away from the knot of agents and took the call. "This is Seb Wallace."

"Seb, it's Katrina." Static nearly drowned out her hushed voice. "Hughes called me and changed the location of our meeting. He knew all about the FBI trap, and he said he'd kill Liv if I tried to trick him again. I'm calling from a gas station phone in case my cell is bugged."

Seb's mind whirled. "Have you told Agent Short?"

"No. There's probably a leak in the FBI somewhere." She sounded in control, but her voice was tight and tense. "It might be him."

Icy fingers clutched Seb's heart. "You can't meet Hughes alone."

"I'm really hoping you and Magnus can give me some backup."

"Of course. Where?"

She rattled off GPS coordinates. "Can you be there in fifteen minutes?"

Seb typed the coordinates into his map program. "It'll take at least half an hour, probably more like forty minutes. It's not that far as the crow flies, but there's no direct route and the roads are all two-laners with lots of twists and turns."

"I'm supposed to meet him in ten minutes. I can probably be a few minutes late, but more than that and he'll get suspicious." She took a breath and he heard a quaver in her voice for the first time. "He might just kill Liv and leave."

"Hold on a sec." Seb pulled up the satellite image on his map program. "Okay, there's some sort of track that could be a shortcut. It doesn't show up as a road on my program, so it's probably no more than an old logging road. If we had ATVs or off-road bikes, it wouldn't be a problem. But we don't." He gave his Range Rover an appraising glance. "I'll give it a shot."

"Please hurry."

"I will. And, Katrina, be careful." Horrific images of finding her dead flashed through his head.

He ended the call and walked over to Magnus, who hovered over Agent Short's shoulder. Seb tapped Magnus's elbow and inclined his head toward the shadowy forest. He walked that way and slipped behind one of the massive trees.

Magnus appeared a second later. "What's up?"

"Katrina called. She needs us to come, and we can't trust the FBI. Do you have your gun?"

Magnus's eyes widened. "Yeah."

"Good. Follow me." They ran through the trees outside the ring of light from the base camp, moving as quickly and quietly as possible until they reached Seb's SUV, which fortunately was parked about fifty yards from the FBI vehicles.

Seb made sure the lights were off and started the engine. No one in the FBI group seemed to notice. He turned to Magnus. "Buckle up."

The forest had taken his mother—he couldn't let it take Katrina.

CHAPTER 35

///////////////

A CONSTRUCTION BARRICADE BARRED THE
way, and Katrina braked. Hughes's directions were to take this
road. She put the car in Park and got out to examine the shoulder. It was flat enough to drive around the barrier, and she
spotted other tire tracks in the mud left from the storm. Her
gut clenched. Hughes was lying in wait somewhere up ahead,
but she had to go through with this.

Please, God, let Liv be alive.

She didn't even limp as she got back in her car and drove it
between the barrier and a line of redwoods. Her headlamps
picked out a low stone wall ahead with a sign announcing a
scenic overlook. She spotted a black SUV half hidden under
a redwood on the forest's side of the road. She slowed her car
and assessed the landscape but found no obvious place to run
with Liv to safety. Though with Liv's broken knee and Katrina's
sprained ankle, neither of them were in any condition to try to
outrun Hughes. She'd have to outsmart him somehow.

She swerved to the side and backed in toward the wall before
she shut off the car. At least she could plan for a fast getaway. She
pressed her hand to her roiling stomach and grabbed the backpack on the front seat before getting out of the car. A cacophony

of frogs and insects serenaded her as she limped to the wall and looked down, but it was too dark to see the bottom of the cliff.

She caught movement out of the corner of her right eye and whirled toward the parked SUV. Headlamps glared out of the darkness and their cone of light spotlighted Liv sitting on the last foot of the wall. Her injured leg was extended in front of her, and her hands were behind her back. Duct tape covered her mouth, and she appeared disheveled but uninjured.

"Liv!" Katrina started toward her, but Hughes stepped out of the SUV with a gun in his hand.

"Took you long enough. Give me the key."

"Let Liv go first. I'll get her in the car and give you the key. You can go your way and we'll go ours."

"That isn't the way this is going to work. No deals. Just hand over the key."

She should have known the minute he stepped into view with his face uncovered that he intended to kill them both. Even if Katrina hadn't seen him last night, Liv would be able to identify him. Katrina bit down on her lip hard enough to taste blood. If she stalled, maybe Seb would get here.

She set the backpack on the stone wall and unzipped it to extract the book of sonnets. "Jason's clue was this book. The key is hidden in it. You can have it if you let Liv go. I'm sure you'll be able to figure it out." She held the book over the wall and above the deep ravine. "Get Liv in my car or I let go of this."

He waved the gun and advanced toward her. "You're a smart attorney, Katrina. You know I can't let you go. You can identify me and so can Liv. If you drop the book, I'll stretch out the pain for hours. I know how to make you beg for death. Hand it over now, and I'll make your deaths easy. Either way, I can't let either of you walk."

When he advanced toward her, she saw perspiration beading his forehead. He wasn't as confident as his commanding voice led her to believe. *Think.* There had to be a way out of this.

|||||||||||||||||||||||||||

Branches whipped against Seb's windshield as his Range Rover jolted along the overgrown old logging road. Redwood saplings crowded the strip of land that had been cleared years ago for flatbed trucks. Seb had to make split-second decisions whether they were small enough to smash over or needed to be dodged. He'd already lost one headlamp, and a crack snaked across the right side of his windshield. The SUV shook and pulled to the right, even on flat spots. The vehicle would probably be a total loss by the time he and Magnus reached their destination, but it would be worth it if they got there in time.

"Watch out!" Magnus shouted as a huge gully yawned in front of them.

Seb slammed on the brakes, but it was too late. The Range Rover pitched forward over the eroded edge of the gully. A wall of muddy dirt flashed into view for an instant before they slammed into it. An airbag hurled Seb back so hard that he saw stars. Had he broken his nose again?

Seb fought off the bag as it deflated. An acrid odor like smoke filled his lungs. He opened the door and staggered out. His feet landed in a little stream running along the bottom of the gully. Icy water instantly soaked his shoes. A splash and curse came from the other side of the SUV as Magnus did the same thing. "You okay?" Seb called.

"Yeah, how close are we?"

Seb checked the GPS on his sat phone. "Just under half a mile, and Katrina's probably already there." He gave the Range Rover a quick look. It would need to be winched out of the gully, and it probably wasn't drivable anyway. "We'll need to go the rest of the way on foot."

"Lead the way."

Seb glanced at his GPS again and took off at a run. He could do a six-minute mile on a gym treadmill, but he'd be lucky to go half that fast in the forest at night, especially once they had to leave the logging road. Magnus crashed through the under-growth behind him.

A gleam of light appeared through the trees as they crested a ridge. Seb held up a hand to stop Magnus as he puffed up behind. The light filtered through tall ferns and low branches, but it looked like the source was about a hundred yards from them. Indistinct voices came through the trees.

Seb crept forward, heart pounding and sweat dripping in his eyes. He fought to slow his ragged breathing. Magnus's panting sounded unnaturally loud in the forest stillness.

They reached the edge of the trees and got a clear view for the first time. Hughes's SUV spotlighted Katrina standing by a low stone wall, holding the sonnet book over the edge. She looked defiant and terrified. Liv slumped on the wall, eyes hooded. Hughes walked toward Katrina, a gun pointed at her head.

Magnus whipped out his gun and fired three quick shots. All missed.

Hughes grabbed Katrina, whirled, and put his gun to her head in one fluid motion. He glared into the darkness, using Katrina as a shield. "Step into the light and throw your gun down or I'll kill her. You have five seconds . . . four . . ."

Magnus started to move forward, but Seb put a hand on his arm. "He doesn't realize there are two of us," he whispered.

"Three . . . two . . ."

"Okay!" Seb called. He tossed his gun into the light and stepped forward with his hands up.

Hughes grinned and shifted his aim from Katrina's temple to Seb. Then three things happened simultaneously: Seb dove for the shadows, Hughes fired, and Katrina twisted free.

Fire seared across Seb's shoulders as the bullet creased the skin of his upper back. He grabbed his pistol and rolled into a shooter's crouch. Seb and Magnus fired together, staggering Hughes. He cursed and fired back wildly. He must have been wearing body armor, but he wouldn't be able to see them outside the glare of his SUV's lights.

Katrina tucked something in her waistband, then jumped over the stone wall. Hughes glanced after her, then threw himself over the wall too.

Seb turned to Magnus. "Cover me!" He ran toward the wall, skirting the edge of the pool of light. He kept his gun pointed toward the wall, expecting Hughes to pop up at any instant. But he didn't.

Seb looked over the wall. Katrina wasn't there and neither was Hughes. The only thing on the other side of the wall was a yawning black abyss. Wind whistled along the cliff face.

Horror gripped him. How could she have survived jumping into that?

CHAPTER 36

////////////

KATRINA SHOT UP A PRAYER FOR HELP AS she dove for the small tree she'd spotted earlier. Her fingers closed around it, and she clung to the sapling with all her might, but the recent rain had left everything slippery, and her hands kept sliding down toward the leaves. Her feet pinwheeled wildly in the air, and she closed her eyes to help stem the terror clawing at her chest.

She inhaled the earthy scent of mud and vegetation as she pressed her face against the cliff face. She was glad she couldn't see to the bottom of the four-hundred-foot drop. The sight might cause her to freeze.

Gunshots above her head drowned out the sound of the harsh breaths in her chest. She'd spotted a ledge just below the tree when she looked down earlier, but was it this tree? It was too dark to tell for sure, but her hands burned and she wouldn't be able to hold on much longer. She stretched her toes down, and her injured ankle cramped. She bit back a whimper. If Hughes heard her, he'd take a shot at the noise and might get lucky.

It was now or never.

She forced her fingers to let go of the little tree and dropped in the air until the toes of her shoes struck the sliver of a ledge.

She grabbed at the cliff face, and the fingers of her left hand found a crack. Her ankle cramped harder this time, and she took several deep breaths until the cramp released. It was too dark to see more than a few feet down, but in the immediate vicinity there were enough holds to begin a descent. First, she had to get past this ledge and onto the rock face.

She took a steadying breath, then reached out and curled her fingertips into tiny crevices, moving left toward the end of the ledge. Something slammed onto the spot she'd just vacated, and Hughes's hoarse curse rang out. And she thought she heard Seb calling her name, but maybe it was the wind.

Hughes was coming after her.

Her pulse leaped into overdrive, and she moved more quickly, trying not to let panic force her into being careless. Scraping sounds came from her right, and she spotted Hughes's face fixed in a determined grimace. He clung to the rock with both hands as he inched along the narrow ledge, but his gun was in his waistband. To use it he'd have to climb with one hand, and she didn't think he was skilled enough to do that.

Her pulse roared in her ears as she moved along, inch by inch, to grab hold of the bare rock face and leave Hughes behind on the ledge. Her toes stretched down for the next hold and found it. She moved faster, swinging out with her hands and finding purchase for her fingers in the next tiny crevice.

She was two feet below him now, but he was about to begin his descent off the ledge. He was fast and agile too. His superior strength propelled him along the ledge, but he wore hiking boots. He'd never be able to feel the wedges in the rock with those. That was her only hope of getting away.

He swung his foot off the ledge, scraping along the rock face to search for a hold. His foot struck a loose rock, and he slipped. His arms pinwheeled in search of balance, and his other foot let loose of the rock wall.

He screamed and tumbled toward her. His terrified gaze locked on her, and he reached out to grab her arm. His fingernails slid across her arm, scratching the skin as he tumbled past.

Katrina cried out and almost lost her grip, but she managed to keep her fingers and toes jammed into the crevices as he hurtled past. His body bounced against the rock multiple times before silence descended.

The trembling and weakness started then, and she pressed her cheek against the cold rock in the darkness. Her knees didn't want to support her. She wouldn't be able to climb down in this state. Her ankle had begun to ache again, now that the worst of the danger was over, and she didn't want to try to ascend the rock face on her own.

"Katrina!"

She'd never heard anything so wonderful as Seb's voice calling down to her. "Here," she whispered. She cleared her throat and tried again. "I'm here!"

"Hang on. I'm coming down for you."

A rope snaked past her head and settled against the side of her body. Another rope landed next to the first one. The first rope moved and tiny pebbles scuttled past her head as Seb began to descend. She pressed her cheek harder against the rock, and the roughness anchored her enough that the shock began to wear off.

Seb's feet were just above her head, and he rappelled on down until he was beside her. "I've got you." He tied the second rope under her arms and tugged on it to make sure it was secure before he yanked on the rope. "Bring her up, Magnus." He touched her cheek. "Hold on. You'll be topside in no time."

Speech was beyond her, so she nodded as the rope gave a jerk and she began to rise. She kicked out with her feet to keep from being dragged over the rocky surface, then clutched the rope with both hands as it inched upward. She spotted tufts of grass at the top and saw her brother's face. Magnus grabbed her and dragged her the rest of the way to the top.

She lay panting on the grass while she caught her breath. She was alive and so very thankful.

Then Seb was climbing over the top, and she sat up and reached for him. He dropped to his knees and gathered her into his arms.

He pressed kisses against her hair, forehead, and cheek. "Thank God, thank God. I was so scared." He pulled back and cupped her face in his hands. "I heard you scream, and I thought you had to have fallen all the way down, but I started praying and ran to Hughes's SUV. He had rope in the back, probably meant for you. I couldn't believe it when you answered me. I was terrified I'd lost you."

She burrowed closer. "I think you're stuck with me."

||||||||||||||||||||||

Sal Durgan, owner of Sal's Bar, stuck her head into the saloon's grimy kitchen. She looked around and spotted Dylan washing dishes. "Hey, Steve. Time for your break. Fifteen minutes." She went back to the bar without waiting for a response, leaving the door swinging behind her.

Dylan wiped his hands on a stained apron and walked out to the bar area. Kitchen jobs were easy to find these days, and he'd started work this morning.

Half a dozen customers lined the bar, which Sal manned alone. She was a rangy, hard-faced woman of about fifty who had a no-nonsense attitude and a shotgun under the bar. Her customers seemed like a rough bunch. Two of the guys at the scarred redwood bar had prison tattoos and all had knives on their belts. One of them noticed Dylan and gave him a friendly nod. Dylan nodded back. He'd grown up with people like this and he felt at home here, even though he'd just arrived.

Sal paid only a fraction of what Seb had, but she promised cash—which suited Dylan perfectly. If he camped out in the woods, he could easily live on a couple hundred bucks per month while he saved money and planned his next move. Maybe someplace out of state. He'd never lived anywhere except Western Washington and Northern California, and he'd always wondered what other places were like. Texas seemed like it might be fun.

But Texas was a long way from Dad. And Liv. He pulled out the burner phone he'd bought. Should he call or text Seb to see how they were doing?

The staticky little TV over the bar caught his attention. The local news was on, and Magnus appeared on-screen. He was being interviewed by a pretty brunette. His battered face was healing, but he still looked like he'd lost an argument with a truck. He didn't sound like he was feeling any pain though. "We got there just as he was about to kill my sister and her friend. We had a shootout with the guy, and then he jumped over the cliff."

"You're quite a hero," the reporter gushed.

Magnus gave a modest smile that must have hurt. "I'm just glad we were able to save the girls."

The scene switched to the brunette standing alone outside Bestemor's, holding a microphone and looking serious. "The FBI believes that Agent Andrew Hughes may have been responsible for up to fourteen murders across the country. He apparently used his career as an FBI agent as a cover for a secret—and deadly—side job with a Chinese triad. There are a lot of unanswered questions, but the citizens of North Haven can rest a little easier tonight knowing that the killer who stalked their streets is gone. Jennifer Coltrane reporting."

The news switched to high school sports. Sal caught Dylan's eye and tapped her watch. He nodded and went back into the kitchen. He breathed a huge sigh of relief as the door closed behind him. Liv was safe. The guy who'd been after them all was dead. Whew.

Still, Dylan couldn't help but feel a twinge of jealousy and guilt as he pulled on rubber gloves and loaded beer mugs into the dishwasher. He should have been there last night. But if he had—if he'd been the one on TV—he'd be in jail by tomorrow morning, waiting to get shipped back to Seattle.

He shook his head. No, he couldn't have been there, but he wished he had been.

For the thousandth time, he replayed the memory of the incident, starting from the moment a bunch of drunk jerks walked into his favorite bar. He'd never seen them before, but they acted like they owned the place. They gave the bartender a hard time and demanded that he start a tab for them, even though he only did that for regulars. Then they went after the waitress, who was twenty-one and looked fourteen. They tried to get her to sit on their laps and ordered drinks with dirty names to rattle her. Most of them went over to play darts when their drinks arrived, but one guy wouldn't leave the waitress alone.

She was getting upset, so Dylan walked over and set a hand on the guy's shoulder. The guy threw a bad punch and Dylan threw a good one. Then suddenly the guy had a gun in his hand, and it went off—fortunately hitting only the back wall of the bar.

Dylan pulled his pistol and put a bullet in the guy's chest. The bartender's eyes went wide. *"You just killed a cop!"* There was no time to protest that they'd never identified themselves as law enforcement. So Dylan ran. He'd been running ever since—and staying well away from cops.

Then it hit him. If the guy the police had been chasing was dead now, they'd stop chasing Dylan. They'd move on to other bad guys. They'd quit showing up at Seb's house and Bestemor's and places like that.

Dylan froze with a dirty mug in each rubber-gloved hand. Maybe he could go back to North Haven.

He finished loading the dishwasher, pulled off his gloves, and took out the burner phone. He typed a quick text to Seb: *Hey bro! Heard about that bad fbi dude. Crazy! How are things? Hows dad? -D* He hit Send before he had a chance to regret it.

He hesitated for a moment, finger hovering over the screen. Then he sent another text: *Hope you're good Liv. Heard about everything. Crazy! Glad you're okay. Let me know if you want to get together sometime. -D*

The phone pinged with a reply from Seb: *Great to hear from you! No change in Dad's condition, but everything else is good here. I talked to Katrina about your situation & she thinks she can help. Let's talk.*

Hope lit Dylan's heart for a moment, but experience put it out. Lots of people had told him they could help—counselors, teachers, social workers, public defenders—and several of them had actually tried, or at least seemed to. But the system always won.

Katrina and Seb meant well, but they didn't understand how things worked in Dylan's world. They would insist on fighting for him, and they'd fight hard for him—but they'd lose. The system protected drunk cops who harassed women in bars, not semi-employed dishwashers who intervened. So there was no way Katrina could actually win. And when she lost, Dylan would lose too—and he'd be the one going to prison.

He sighed, shoved the phone in his pocket, and went back to washing dishes.

CHAPTER 37

////////////

KATRINA'S ANKLE THROBBED FROM THE climb, but she washed them and pulled on a pair of fuzzy pink sleep socks before curling on the sofa in Seb's parlor with Lyla on her lap. She should be tired, but she was still too wired to sleep. JJ and Agent Short had already interviewed Magnus and Seb, and she waited for her turn while Short held a private confab with JJ in the front yard as the sun came up.

Seb entered with two mugs of coffee in his hands. "Here, you need this."

She took the mug he offered and wrapped her cold, bruised fingers around the heavy pottery. "Just what the doctor ordered."

He settled beside her and put his mug on the end table. "Are you hungry? I could make breakfast or run to Bestemor's for waffles."

She tucked her free hand into his elbow and leaned her head against his shoulder. The woodsy scent of his cologne was so much better than the mud she'd been smelling for hours. "I don't want you out of my sight. I keep seeing Hughes's enraged expression as he came after me, and I thought I was going to die without ever telling you how important you've become to me."

He took her mug to set it beside his before turning those observant green eyes her way. "I thought you'd died and I didn't know how I was going to survive it. Look, I know you still love Jason and always will, but I think there's something between us we need to nurture. I don't want to rush you, and I'm willing to wait until you're ready to find out what that something is."

She reached over with her other hand to cup his face, and the movement disrupted the kitten, who scampered away. "For a smart guy, you don't take hints very well. I'm trying to tell you—I'm ready now. Going to Yosemite was cathartic for me. You were so patient with me as we walked through the last vacation I took with Jason. You're such an example of kindness and faithfulness." She trailed her fingers over his muscular back, feeling the bandage under his shirt. "You literally took a bullet for me. When I clung to that cliff, all I could think about was that I had to live to be with you."

She drank in the dawning joy on his face and leaned in to kiss him. He pulled her closer, and she relaxed into the circle of his arms. There would be more to say in the coming weeks—so much more—and it was wonderful to know they had that time now.

He ended the kiss and tucked a strand of her hair behind her ear. "When this is over, we'll take my boat up the coast. We could put out some crab pots and forget about the past two months."

"I don't want to forget it. There were so many things I didn't see clearly after Jason died." She ran her fingers across the light stubble line on his tired face. "And I saw you clearly for the first time."

He tugged on his nose. "Like my crooked nose."

"If you didn't have that, I might have been scared of falling for you. You'd be too perfect."

The smile left his eyes. "Like Jason?"

"He wasn't perfect. I just made him out to be in my mind. And don't think you have to compete with his memory. I know the path forward now—I was just too stubborn and blind to look for it."

Footsteps came across the porch, and she reluctantly pulled away. "I think it's my turn to be interviewed."

"Terrible timing," Seb murmured. "I had a long list of all the things I love about you to share."

"I'll be waiting to hear them, so don't forget."

"I never forget one minute of being with you."

Short and JJ entered. "We've got some questions if you're up to it, Ms. Foster," Short said. He glanced at Seb. "In private, please."

Seb gave her hand a final squeeze and rose. "I'll make some breakfast. It will be ready when you're done. Any requests?"

"Surprise me," Katrina said. He chuckled and headed for the kitchen. Her stomach growled at the thought of what he might dream up. She grabbed a fluffy throw that still held his scent and snuggled into it. "I have a few questions of my own, Agent Short. Like why didn't the FBI know Hughes was bad?"

Short flinched. "A lot of us are scrambling and asking that same question. Hughes bugged my car and phone. He was always a step ahead of us."

JJ sat on one of the chairs across from the sofa and took out his notebook. "We know he wasn't working alone. The

Chinese gang that hired him was in contact with two people in the area. Did you see anyone else or hear him speak to someone on the phone?"

She shook her head. "He was alone both times he tried to get to me. I saw him speak to someone on a flip phone once, but I couldn't hear the conversation."

Short paced back and forth across the area rug. "The flip phone was probably a burner. He had multiple phones, and I'm not sure we have all of them yet." He paused by the fireplace. "Have you tried to sell any of the Bitcoin yet?"

"No."

"Good. Don't do anything that might trigger that unknown partner until we're sure we've tied up all the loose ends. His accomplice is probably lying low for now, and we don't want him to come after you."

JJ put his notepad away. "I'll have a squad car drive by the house a few times a day. Get some rest now that you're home."

Home. She clutched the fleece throw to her chest and inhaled Seb's scent.

||||||||||||||||||||||||||

The fire flickering in the fireplace in Seb's parlor added to Katrina's sense of contentment as she and Liv celebrated their rescue. The sweet tang of strawberry mingled perfectly with the melting square of Freia chocolate on her tongue. "Heavenly. It's amazing how good everything tastes after nearly dying. Well, except this champagne. It's got a funny aftertaste."

Liv sat next to her on Seb's sofa with her leg elevated on the coffee table. "Girl, it's the best alcohol-free champagne money can buy. Stop complaining and drink up." She lifted her glass to clink with Katrina's. "No more guards, no more watching over our shoulders. It's *over*."

"I'll feel better once his partner is apprehended."

"He's probably somewhere in Canada by now." Liv took a long swallow of her bubbly drink. "Is the only copy of the key in the sonnet book?"

"No, I wrote down the key as I decoded it."

"Did you verify it worked? I hope you have it in a safe place this time. That was a close call."

"I haven't had time to try to verify the balance, but I'm sure the key is right. And it's locked in a drawer in my bedroom." Katrina took another bite of strawberry and chocolate together. "I miss Seb."

Liv smiled. "That's the best thing about this ordeal. I have to admit he's a really great guy. Why do I always have to land with the losers?"

"You dated Jason," Katrina reminded her.

"*Dated* is the key word. As in it was over before it started."

Katrina knew better than to bring up Dylan. She'd had her doubts about him right from the start, but she hated being proven right in this case. Liv seemed to attract the kind of bad boy who had no intention of settling down. With the exception of Magnus, who had been crushed when Liv ghosted him. "And no word from David?"

"No word, but then, I didn't expect to hear from him once he fled the country. I doubt he'll be back—there are probably federal warrants waiting for him and his cousin John. And it's good riddance. Now that I have some distance from him, I realize I never loved him. I loved his gifts—especially my Hermès bag—but David was a wimp. He wouldn't have climbed down a rock face to save me like Seb did for you." Liv's chin jutted and she scowled. "If he contacted me now, I'd call the FBI. I'll take care of my baby by myself, and we'll have a great life. I'll finally have someone who loves me."

A faint sense of unease rippled down Katrina's spine. She'd seen too many troubled parent-child relationships to think a baby was the answer for Liv. Katrina's own rocky relationship with her mother was a case in point, but she said nothing. She and Liv were very different. Even Jason had wondered if their friendship would survive their differences and had suggested she start finding more friends.

Her head spun and her vision blurred. "I feel a little dizzy."

"You're probably exhausted. Why don't you lie back and take a nap? You've hardly slept in days."

True enough. "I think I'll go up and take a nap. It's only four, but I feel like I could sleep forever."

She wobbled to her feet, and the room tilted on its axis. She held out her hand to catch herself, but nothing was there. The lights dimmed around her, and she couldn't see Liv's face. "Liv?" she whispered.

Disorientation rushed at her from all sides, and she slid down a funnel into total darkness.

||||||||||||||||||||||

Dylan slouched against a crag three hundred feet above his campsite, with the forest spread out below him. The sun sank toward the ocean, a distant hazy line beyond the farthest trees. A red-tailed hawk circled slowly on a thermal updraft, waiting for a careless squirrel or rabbit to show itself. Dylan drank hot chocolate from a thermos, ate Doritos from a bag, and basked in the moment.

His burner phone buzzed. He pulled it out of his pocket, and his heart skipped a beat as he accepted the call. "Hey, Liv. It's good to hear from you."

"It's so good to hear your voice, Dylan." Her voice shook a little. "I've missed you so much."

"Me too." He kicked a pebble and sent it skittering down the rock face. "Sorry I took off like that. It's just that I, uh, well—"

"Seb explained. It's okay. I don't care about the past. I just want to be with you. Let's run away together."

He sat up straight. "What?"

Her words came in a passionate rush. "Run away with me! Right now! I'm alone and they're not watching the house. We'll go to Mexico, or Canada, or wherever you want. Somewhere you can be safe from the police and my baby and I can be safe from—" She stopped for a heartbeat. "Sorry, that's not your problem."

"What's not my problem? I thought that FBI guy was dead."

"He is, but he's not the only one after me. The baby's father is a dangerous man. But don't worry about it—you've got enough trouble of your own. I can take care of myself."

"I'll take care of you." The words were out of his mouth before he realized he was going to say them, but he didn't regret it. "Both of you."

"Oh, thank you, thank you, thank you!" Relief flooded her voice. "I'm at Seb's house. How soon can you be here?"

He did some quick mental trip planning. "An hour. Maybe forty-five minutes if I drive fast and I'm lucky with the traffic."

"Drive as fast as you can." She paused. "You're my hero."

His heart swelled. "On my way." He ended the call and scrambled down the rock to his "new" truck.

"My hero." No one had ever called him that before, and he was determined to live up to it. No matter what it took.

CHAPTER 38

////////////////////

IT WAS SIX O'CLOCK ON A FRIDAY EVENING, which meant The Beacon was completely packed even though late October was usually a slow time. Every seat was filled in the dining room, in the bar, and on the patio. A gorgeous autumn sunset broke through the clouds over the Pacific, setting the ocean aflame and sending shafts of gold and red through the restaurant's floor-to-ceiling windows.

Seb slipped into his old dinner-rush routine with ease, making a circuit of the kitchen every fifteen minutes and the dining areas every half hour. He moved more slowly than usual because many of the patrons and all of the staff had heard the news about Hughes's crimes and Seb's role in catching him. But he didn't mind telling the story over and over. It was good to be back.

Alex had done an outstanding job of running The Beacon in Seb's absence, but some things only an owner could do, and those had piled up while Seb was gone. So he spent the few minutes between each round signing license-renewal forms, responding to emails from politicians who couldn't understand why The Beacon didn't have discount prices for public servants, and so on.

He sat in his office, trying to focus on a spreadsheet. Despite the dozens of demands on his attention, his mind kept going back to Katrina. It took all of his willpower to leave her today. That was partially because he didn't like that she and Liv were alone and unguarded for the first time in over a week. The second triad assassin might attack them now that they were unprotected—though JJ was probably right to downplay the risk. Hughes's partner in crime would be lying low, and he'd probably fled the country by now. The FBI's investigation of Hughes was likely to uncover the identities of his cronies, so they couldn't afford to hang around.

No, it wasn't only—or even mostly—worry about Katrina's safety that had turned Seb's feet to lead as he left the house this afternoon. He simply hadn't wanted to leave her, even for a few hours. He wanted to be with her every possible second—to hear her laugh at a joke, feel the touch of her lips against his, catch a whiff of her shampoo as she walked by, look into those luminous gray eyes that held such depths—and strength. Her delicate—almost fragile—beauty hid a core of steel. He'd chuckled at Magnus's TV interview where he took credit for "saving the girls." Katrina had done most of the saving herself. He and Magnus had just distracted and delayed Hughes long enough to let Katrina reach the cliff. All of that was the real reason he hadn't wanted to leave her—and why he couldn't keep her out of his head, even when he was crazy busy. He was addicted to her.

He smiled and shook his head. How had this happened to him? He'd always rolled his eyes and groaned when a character in a movie said, "I can't stop thinking about you," or something equally lame. But here he was, literally unable to stop thinking about Katrina. He'd been telling her the truth at the cabin when he said it was the one thing he couldn't do.

There was a spreadsheet calling his name though, and he needed to focus on it. He only had five minutes before he started his next round. He turned back to his monitor and made himself think about numbers.

"Um, Seb. Sorry to bother you."

He turned to see Grace standing in the office door. She held a laptop and shifted her weight from foot to foot, and worry haunted her dark brown eyes. He realized she'd been trying to talk to him ever since he'd walked in. "What's up, Grace?"

She stepped in and closed the door. "You know that chatbot Liv Tompkins created? Katrina let me talk to one of the engineers for a school project. The bot is really fascinating and advanced, but the engineer and I—um, we think someone, uh, altered it."

He nodded and started to turn back to the spreadsheet. "I know. It was hacked—something about blaming Messenja for Jason Foster's death, right?"

"That was part of it, but there's more. We think someone put two patches on the bot. One of them made it blame Messenja for Jason's murder." She cleared her throat. "The other, uh, had to do with Liv Tompkins."

The odd reluctance in her voice got his attention. He turned back. "What about Liv?"

Grace had trouble meeting his gaze. "We're not sure, but we think the patch makes the bot hallucinate whenever someone asks something that points to her."

The room suddenly felt colder. "Can you remove both patches?"

She nodded and opened her laptop. "We already did." She handed it to Seb. "We made a copy and took them out. Here's a version of the bot without the patches. Just type in the dialogue box."

Did someone murder you?

I think so.

Who do you think murdered you?

Liv Tompkins.

Every muscle in Seb's body tensed. Could it be true? Or was the bot hallucinating now? He needed to know more. *Why do you think Liv killed you?*

She said the Satoshi egg was hers. She needed it. I was a dead man if I didn't give it to her.

Were those her exact words?

Yes.

Show me where they came from.

An ellipsis pulsed for a few seconds, and then a screenshot of a text exchange between Liv and Jason appeared:

That's my egg, Jason!

I found it.

I told you where to look!!

You gave me an idea when we were in college. That's all.

Stop playing games! It's mine & I need it. Give it to me or you're a dead man!!

Seb's pulse skyrocketed. Katrina had the Bitcoin key, and she was alone with Liv. He had to warn her. He whipped out his phone and called her. No answer. He hung up and tried again. Still no response.

He stood, almost knocking over his chair. "Tell your dad he needs to take over the restaurant. I have to go." He raced out the door without waiting for a response, dialing 911 as he went.

Please, God, keep her safe.

||||||||||||||||||||||||

Seb's shaky voice pierced the darkness encasing Katrina. "I'm here, Katrina. You're going to be okay. Can you open your eyes?"

She fought through the veil to find her head pounding. She winced at the lights in the room and moaned when she tried to turn her head. Her eyelids didn't want to move, but she forced them to a half-lid position. Seb's worried face hovered over her, and she blinked to focus. Was she on the floor? "Seb? Was I in an accident?"

Relief lit his face, and he took her hand and squeezed it. "You're in the hospital." He leaned in closer to kiss her, then pulled back and cupped her face in his hands. "You have to quit scaring me like this. When I got to the house to warn you about Liv, you were so cold I thought you were dead. Your pulse was so weak and slow."

She pressed on the spot throbbing at her left temple. "Wait, back up. You came to warn me about *Liv*?" She must have misheard him.

"Liv laced your drink with her pain med. The paramedics administered naloxone though, and you're going to be okay."

Katrina struggled to sit up, and Seb helped her. "I—I don't understand. Liv would never do that."

"She was behind all of it." He launched into a tale about Liv's obsession with the Satoshi egg and the patch on the bot. "The attack on her was a warning to pay up what she owed to the triad, and that upped her determination to find the egg. It was her ticket out of danger."

Katrina gave a slight shake of her head. "I can't believe it." The clues she'd missed clicked into place. "No wonder Hughes showed up with no mask and in a suit. Someone who knew about our whereabouts had to tip him off while he was at the office, and he raced over to try to get there before us. Magnus wouldn't do it, so it had to have been Dylan or Liv. I never dreamed Liv would c-care so little." Her throat constricted, and she fought the burn in her eyes.

He brought her hand up and brushed it with his lips. "I suspected Dylan but never Liv."

"Liv has always been interested in the egg, but I never saw it as anything strange. Do you have my phone?"

He reached his free hand into his pocket and brought it out. "I downloaded a version that Grace fixed. See what it tells you now." He sat on the bed beside her.

Calling up the app felt alien now that she realized how she'd been manipulated, but she had to see for herself. The cursor blinked and waited for her input. She tapped out the question. *Where would Liv hide?*

Hmm. Here's a list of good hiding places I found on the internet. Under the bed, in the closet, behind the sofa.

Maybe it thought she wanted to play hide-and-seek. She needed to approach this from another direction. *Why did Liv kill you and steal the key?*

She believed the egg belonged to her.

Why?

You remember we used to go gunting when we dated while attending Stanford. It was a cheap date and we discovered lots of fun new places. We knew a Satoshi egg was supposed to be hidden around the Bay Area, so it was fun to dream. She'd heard a rumor Satoshi went to Stanford, so she researched what was happening there in 2009 when Bitcoin was launched. She discovered a building in the Stanford Technology and Engineering Quad was under construction then, and she thought it might be on the roof. There was no roof access, so we never got to check.

She realized where this was going and saw the same dawning realization on Seb's face. *That's where you found it?*

Yes. My engineering firm was hired to do some work on the roofs of the Quad buildings, so I decided to poke around. Here it is—my pride and joy.

A picture of a dusty plastic egg appeared. It had probably been red once but was now a dusty, mottled pink. The next picture showed the egg opened up with a thumb drive inside. "Look at that," she whispered to Seb.

She turned back to the bot. *You told Liv you'd found it?*

I thought she'd be excited for me, but she was furious. She demanded I turn it over to her. It was a wild guess of hers that it was there, so it really didn't belong to her.

How did Liv react when you told her you were keeping it?

We've both seen her mad before, but this was beyond anything rational. She told me she'd see me dead before she let me keep it. She even threatened to tell you we'd had an affair.

Katrina caught her breath, and Seb slipped his arm around her. "Don't jump to conclusions," he whispered.

The tremble in her hand worsened, and she had to erase the first two words and try again. *Did you have an affair with Liv?*

She leaned her head against Seb's shoulder and barely breathed while waiting for the answer. A string of messages ran across the screen. Several flirty messages from Liv telling him she had never gotten over him were followed by one asking him to drop by her apartment after work.

Katrina never has to know.

The implication was clear enough that Katrina fought nausea as the next message appeared. *I value you as a friend, but I love my wife and would never betray her.*

A tear burned its way down Katrina's cheek. This was all more than she could take in with her head still pounding and her thoughts a jumble.

Why didn't you tell me about the egg?

It was way too dangerous, and I didn't want you in harm's way. When rumors began circulating in the gunter community that someone had found an egg, I knew I was stuck. Selling some of it would show up on the blockchain, and the danger would ramp up even more.

Her headache jackhammered her skull, and she struggled to swallow down the nausea burning in her chest from the migraine. "I—I think I might need to throw up."

"Here, lie down." Seb eased her back against the pillow and took her hand again.

"There's a pressure point you could try, in the fleshy pad between my thumb and forefinger." She touched the spot for him to press. He squeezed the area, and the pain began to ebb.

"Is it getting better?"

The pain was gone and she inhaled with relief. "It's much better."

COLLEEN COBLE AND RICK ACKER

"I should have let you rest."

She shook her head. "I want to know the truth—all of it." She sat back up and picked up the phone. *How did you get connected with Messenja?*

I had to sell the egg, so I searched around on a Discord server and found an anonymous Japanese billionaire who went by Korekuta. He collects tech rarities—the first cell phone, the first Nintendo Game Boy, things like that. Messenja was Korekuta's representative. She said he was willing to buy the egg for the full value of the Bitcoins on it. I knew I was being watched in Silicon Valley, so I arranged for the sale to take place in North Haven. I never made it that far.

Seb's solid presence beside her anchored her, and she put the phone down until the shakes in her hands passed.

Seb picked up the phone and read the message. "*Korekuta* means 'The Collector' in Japanese. I'll bet that's the pseudonym for Messenja's boss."

"I—I just can't believe this, Seb. So much betrayal."

He drew her tighter against his side. "Without the patch Liv put on the app, you would have discovered all this the first time you used it. I'm so sorry. I know this is painful." He pressed a kiss on the side of her forehead. "She won't get far with a broken knee. Someone had to help her. Let me see if JJ knows whether she called an Uber or asked for a ride."

He whipped out his phone and placed the call. She wanted to listen to everything, but her drugged brain translated his words as incomprehensible mumbles.

Seb ended the call. "They checked with Uber, Lyft, and the local taxi company. None of the commercial drivers picked her up. Let me see if Magnus has any idea."

She closed her eyes while he talked with her brother and opened them again when she realized Seb had spoken her name twice. "I'm sorry. What did Magnus say?"

"He hasn't heard from her, and he seemed outraged she would disappear without telling him. Which leaves—"

"Dylan," she said in unison with him.

CHAPTER 39

////////////////

DYLAN DROVE WITH HIS LEFT HAND. HIS right arm curled around Liv, who snuggled into his shoulder. She felt good against him, especially since the truck's heater didn't really work. The pickup he drove was a beater, but it was a step up from the one he bought the last time he had to disappear. He had Seb to thank for that—Dylan made good money at The Beacon and had been able to save a little before he ran. If they slept in the truck and didn't eat much, he might have enough Beacon bucks to get them to Mexico.

Dylan squirmed at the thought of his brother. He'd never responded to Seb's last text. Should he contact him now, just to let him know that he and Liv were safe? No, Seb's phone might be bugged by Liv's baby daddy.

The engine coughed and the truck shimmied for a moment. Dylan shook his head. "Piece of junk. I hope it lasts us until Tijuana."

Liv patted him on the chest. "If it doesn't, I'll buy you a new one."

"Won't your ex be watching your credit cards and bank accounts and stuff?"

"Oh, I have plenty of money he doesn't know about."

"That's a relief." Dylan cleared his throat. "I, uh, don't have that much cash. I was wondering how I'd be able to take care of you, especially after the baby arrives."

Liv kissed him on the cheek. "You're so sweet. I love that you want to take care of me, of us. But you won't have to. I know you dropped everything to come rescue me, and I appreciate that so much. Let me take care of you for now. I'll pay for everything." She squeezed his bicep. "We are going to have such a good time!"

Dylan grinned and pulled her closer. He'd never been south of Eureka before, but he'd heard Mexico was always warm, even in winter. And he'd seen pictures of their beaches: wide and sandy—not narrow strips of gray rock like the one rolling by in the night shadows outside his truck. He pictured himself lounging on a beach chair with a sun umbrella over him, a two-dollar burrito in one hand and a one-dollar beer in the other. Liv would be next to him, looking totally hot in a bikini, even with a little baby bump.

What would happen when the baby came? Would he stick around and be the dad, at least for a while? That was a weird thought. He'd never considered being a father, but it might be fun. And maybe it would be more than just fun. Every kid deserved a father, as he knew all too well.

His phone buzzed. He put his knees on the wheel so he could retrieve it from his pocket without moving Liv. It was Seb—was there news about Dad? A jolt of adrenaline hit Dylan's bloodstream as he accepted the call, put it on speaker, and dropped the phone in his lap. He put his hand back on the wheel. "It's good to hear from you, bro. What's up?"

"Where are you?" Seb's voice sounded tense, even through the staticky little speaker. "Is Liv with you?"

Liv sat up and shook her head.

Dylan licked his lips. "Uh, why?"

Seb's reply was garbled by the poor reception.

"Couldn't hear you, Seb," Dylan said. "What was that?"

"She drugged Katrina and stole the key to a thousand Bitcoins. She also killed Jason."

Liv leaned forward. "That's not true!"

"We found the patch on the bot, Liv." Seb's voice was hard and cold. "We know you threatened to kill Jason if he didn't give you the Satoshi egg. And we know you made the bot lie about it."

"Why, Liv?" Katrina's voice was uneven and shaky. "I trusted you. We were friends. I—" Her voice cut off and a second later *Call Failed* appeared on the screen.

Dylan looked at Liv. She met his gaze for an instant and then stared at her hands. "It's not true. Seb doesn't know what happened. Neither does Katrina. Not really."

Dylan's head whirled and he could barely keep from crashing. "So . . . so explain it to me."

She took a deep breath. "That Satoshi egg belonged to me. I told Jason where to look for it. It was my idea all along, and he basically stole it. He wouldn't even share it with me, even though he knew I desperately needed the money. I—I ran into financial trouble and borrowed money from some people David knew. They threatened to kill me if I didn't pay them." She touched her knee. "They did this to drive home how serious they were."

"They didn't mistake you for Katrina?"

She shook her head. "I told them about the Bitcoin though so they'd give me time to find it."

"You have the backup key thing now?"

"I do." Defiance flashed in her eyes. "It's mine, and I'm not giving it up."

"What about Katrina? Did you really drug her?" He almost didn't want to hear the answer.

She closed her eyes. "Can you please stop cross-examining me? She's fine. You heard her. The past doesn't matter. The future does. I have to pay off that debt, but there will be plenty for us to live on for the rest of our lives. We'll have such a great time, Dylan. It'll be the adventure of a lifetime. Don't you want that?"

He did want it. He wanted it so bad he could taste it. It tasted like her lips against his, or a perfect steak after a long day hiking in the jungle, or salt from the sea spray, or cold Mexican beer with just a hint of lime, or all of it wrapped together. But he couldn't say yes to her, at least not until he knew the whole truth.

He pulled off the road and parked. The ocean waves crashed in the darkness on the passenger side of the truck. "Did you kill Jason?"

She took his hand in both of hers. "You know me well enough to know I'd never kill anyone."

"What happened? How did he die?"

"It was an accident." Her voice shook and her grip on his hand tightened. "I just wanted him to stop so I could make him give me the egg. But he tried to swerve around me, and he went off the cliff. I didn't want to kill him. I swear it."

He felt sick to his stomach. He wasn't her hero—he was her patsy. "This whole thing is a lie, isn't it? We're not running from your ex. We're running from Seb and Katrina and the police, aren't we?"

"All that matters is that we're running away together." She released his hand and reached into the back of the truck's cab. For an instant he was afraid she had a gun, but she pulled out a book. "This is the key to thirty million dollars." She pulled a slip of paper out of the book. "And this is the only copy. It's mine, but I'll share it with you. Fifty-fifty. Or if you don't want that, just take me to Tijuana and I'll give you a million dollars."

Conflicting emotions crashed in his chest. A million dollars could buy him a new identity and a new life in Mexico. It could buy new lives for both of them. But his old life tugged at him. He had just found Seb and Dad—was he willing to lose them forever? What would they think of him if they ever found out the truth?

"I'm sorry, I can't. We gotta go back."

Mouth open, she stared at him. "You're joking."

"I can't just run away like this."

She rolled her eyes. "You've done it before."

"Yeah, but . . ." He sighed. "I shouldn't have. That was a mistake."

"This is a mistake," she shot back. "I'll give you one last chance. Get back on the road and come with me to Mexico. I'll make you the happiest man in the world. Or if you don't want that, I'll make you a millionaire."

The image of him and her on the beach splashed across his mind one last time, but he knew now that it was just a pipe dream. "I'm really sorry, Liv. That sounds awesome, but no."

"Fine." She shoved the slip of paper back in the book and snapped it shut with a sound like a gunshot. "Take me to a truck stop or gas station. I'll make it to Mexico on my own."

"I can't do that either. We both gotta go back." He nodded to the book in her hands. "If that's really yours, you can hire a fancy lawyer and prove it."

"This is ridiculous!" She started to open her door. "Fine, I'll call an Uber or hitchhike."

He reached out his hand. "You'll have to leave that book with me."

Her face went white and her hands shook. She had to know she was trapped. He really hoped he wouldn't have to use force. He tried to smile. "C'mon. Don't make this harder than it has to be."

She turned red and slapped his hand away. "It's mine!" She shoved open her door and hurled the book as far into the dark waves as she could. "If I can't have it, no one can!"

||||||||||||||||||||||

Katrina, JJ, and Agent Short sat in the interview room at the North Haven police station, which was nicer than most with its freshly painted walls and new flooring. Weak November sunshine filtered through a window. Across the table from them, Liv and her attorney, Anita Lopez, stared back. Anita looked ready for battle in black pants and a jacket over a white blouse. Katrina had faced the fortysomething lawyer once before in the courtroom, and she was good—very good.

Under the table Katrina curled her fingers into her palms and struggled to appear in charge and calm. She hadn't been able to look at Liv yet, and she wouldn't be here at all if Liv hadn't refused to talk unless Katrina came. For two days she'd vacillated between tears and anger, and while she wanted to hear how Liv justified her actions, she wanted even more to be in control of herself before she heard the lame excuses.

JJ reached into his briefcase and pulled out the water-stained sonnet book and an illegible piece of paper. The sight of them brought a new flare of anger. All the ink was gone by the time the police fished them out of the ocean. The key was gone forever, and her husband had died for nothing. Did Liv not care about anyone but herself? Outrage drove Katrina to finally focus her gaze on Liv. Dark circles bloomed under Liv's blue eyes, and tears trickled down her cheeks.

Agent Short laced his fingers together on the table. "We have your threatening texts to Mr. Foster and all your communication with Mr. Hughes and Mr. Liang. We now know you're the other person in contact with the triad in North Haven. Hughes was the triad's mole within the FBI, and they hired him to get their money from you. You have plenty of charges facing you." He gestured at the book and paper. "Not to mention the destruction of property worth tens of millions. You're going to jail for a long time, Ms. Tompkins, but if you cooperate, we might be able to shorten that sentence some."

Liv bit down on her trembling lower lip, then tipped her chin up. "I'm willing to testify, but there is something I need to say to Katrina."

Katrina's protective shell cracked a bit at Liv's pleading expression, but she managed to fix it back in place. "I'm listening."

Liv reached her hand across the table, but Katrina drew hers back before Liv could touch her. Fresh tears sprang to Liv's eyes. "I—I never meant for any of this to happen, Katrina. It all escalated. I got into money trouble, and David put me in touch with some people who would help me out. Everything was fine for a while, but then they forced me to give up my Talk, Inc. stock and to help them drain money out of the company. When that didn't satisfy them, they told me they'd hurt me if I couldn't pay them back." She splayed her fingers on the table. "What was I supposed to do? Let them kill me?"

"You could have gone to the police."

"I'd be in jail now. How was that a workable solution?" She clenched her fists. "All Jason had to do was give me what was *mine*. If I hadn't told him where to look, he never would have found the Satoshi egg. And I explained how badly I needed the money, but that still didn't matter. He could have at least split the money with me, but he wouldn't even do that!"

Why hadn't Jason been willing to give her some of it? Katrina would have done it eagerly. She'd even asked the bot why Jason didn't want to share it, but it didn't know. Likely none of them would ever know Jason's motivation. "So you killed him."

Liv shook her head violently. "No! It was an accident, Katrina, you have to believe me. I found out he was going to sell the egg, and my window of opportunity was almost gone. If I'd been thinking clearly, I never would have chased him to North Haven that night. All I wanted to do was force him to stop his car and talk to me."

"I would have given you money if you'd asked."

"You didn't have enough. I needed the egg to pay off the loan shark. And besides, I didn't want anyone to know how foolish I'd been." Liv inhaled and sat back in her chair. "When Jason died, I was in despair at first. But he was too smart not to have made a backup of the key. All I had to do was find it. The Talk app could be my salvation, but it wouldn't tell me where he hid it. It kept accusing me of murdering him." She wrung her hands together. "So I put the patch on it and let you try. I hoped it would eventually lead to the backup, but nothing happened for months until you asked the right question."

"And you didn't care that it hampered my grief recovery, did you? You killed my husband, but even that wasn't good enough for you."

"I'm sorry, Katrina, really. When Hughes showed up and broke my knee to prove they were serious about the threat to pay up or die, I had to cooperate with him. Surely you can see that." Liv reached for a tissue and dabbed her eyes. "I don't blame you for hating me right now, but I hope you can forgive me one day. I never wanted to hurt you. You're the best friend I've ever had."

A tiny crack opened in Katrina's heart. It had all escalated step-by-step, which was how crime often happened. Did God really expect her to forgive Liv's betrayal? She wasn't sure she could do it.

Liv's gaze searched Katrina's face, and when she didn't answer, Liv swallowed hard. "There's one more thing you should know. We're family all the way now. I took a paternity test since my weekend with Magnus was while David and I were on a break, and Magnus is my baby's father. You're going to be an aunt."

Katrina's control on her expression cracked, and she gasped. "I—I need to take a break."

She leaped to her feet and walked to the door in a stunned trance. JJ let her out, and she rushed into the cool wash of air in the hallway. What did she do now, and how could she tell Magnus he was going to be a father?

CHAPTER 40

////////////////////

SEB NEVER TOOK CALLS WHEN HE WAS ON the restaurant floor—but he made an exception when he saw the hospital's number on his caller ID. He stepped into a corner of Bestemor's dining room and accepted the call. "Seb Wallace."

"This is Dr. Singh. I'm very happy to inform you that your father just woke up. He's very weak, but his eyes are open and he's talking."

Relief flooded through Seb. "That's wonderful news! Can he have visitors?"

"Yes, but he doesn't have much energy, so we're trying not to tire him."

"I'm on my way."

Seb ended the call and ran through the kitchen, ignoring surprised looks from the staff. "Restaurant is yours," he called to Agnes as he passed the office. "Dad's awake!"

He called Katrina as soon as he was in his Tesla. He wished he could let Dylan know too, but his brother was in a Eureka jail cell awaiting extradition to Washington. As Dylan had feared, JJ found a warrant for his arrest and had no choice but to take him into custody. Katrina immediately volunteered to represent him, but she said it would be a hard fight, even with the expert team they hired to help her.

Seb picked up Katrina on the way to Eureka. He kept the conversation to strained small talk during the drive, but he appreciated Katrina's presence in the car. They headed straight to Dad's room as soon as they reached the hospital. The questions Seb had been pushing away crowded into his mind. What would he find in Dad's hospital room? Brain injuries could change people. Would Dad be the same? Or would he be a different person or even permanently disabled?

Katrina's hand found his as they stepped out of the elevator, and he gave it a gentle squeeze. Her touch reassured and steadied him.

They could hear Dad's voice as they came down the hall. "I'm goin' to the bathroom—and I'm doin' it *by myself*! And when I come out, I want some real food—not that mush!"

Seb exchanged an amused glance with Katrina. Apparently Dad's energy was returning. They walked into his room and found a harassed-looking young nurse trying to keep Dad from getting out of bed while still attached to an IV and multiple sensors. "Dad! It's great to see you!" Seb turned to the nurse. "I'll help him if he needs to use the restroom."

Dad glared at him as the nurse gave a grateful nod and hurried out. "Don't need anyone's help. I could use a good burger though." He looked past Seb's shoulder. "Where's Dylan?"

Seb weighed his words carefully. He wasn't going to lie, but the full truth would be too much right now. "He couldn't make it. He'll visit you as soon as he can."

"Huh." Dad nodded slowly. "Jail?"

Seb controlled his expression. "Uh, well, yes."

Dad took the news with surprising calm. "Somethin' local or that Seattle business?"

Seb blinked. "I . . . How did you know about Seattle?"

"He told me while we were out in the woods. Wanted to know what to do."

Seb hadn't seen that coming, but it made perfect sense. Of course Dylan would turn to Dad rather than Seb for advice on how to handle a murder charge resulting from a bar fight. "It's the Seattle business. He talked to me too, and I told him to do the right thing and tell the truth to the police and the jury." No need to tell the full story about Dylan running and hiding first. Let Dad think the best of him.

Dad stared at Seb in disgust. "Well, that was stupid."

"Why? What did you advise?"

"Told him to go to Tijuana and get a new identity." Dad shook his head. "You got your brother into jail. You'd better be able to get him out."

Seb opened his mouth and shut it. He wanted to say so many things at once that none of them came out.

Katrina cleared her throat. "We're working on it, Mr. Wallace. Seb and I have a team of investigators looking for witnesses, security-camera footage, and any other evidence they can find. We also found an excellent criminal attorney in Seattle. Dylan will get the best defense possible. I promise you."

"Good." Dad turned his attention to her for the first time, and his gaze traveled down to their clasped hands. His scraggly eyebrows shot up. "Well, well, well. Look at you two." He looked up at Seb. "Try not to get your nose broken this time."

The butterflies in Katrina's stomach had nothing to do with fixing dinner and everything to do with being with Seb for the whole evening. It was the first time they'd had more than a few minutes alone since she fell asleep in his arms at the family cabin, and things were different now. Their relationship had taken on new dimensions that brought her hope for the first time in so long. Every member of the triad in the U.S. had been arrested, and the few who escaped to China would be nabbed the instant they set foot on American soil, so maybe she didn't have to keep looking over her shoulder.

Though she wasn't the fabulous cook Seb was, she'd carefully chosen a tasty, easy menu. The chicken thighs with autumn veggies baking in the oven filled the small apartment with the savory scents of paprika, rosemary, thyme, and sage. A charcuterie board with Norwegian cheeses and breads awaited Seb's imminent arrival, and she'd made raspberry chocolate puffs for dessert.

It might not be Michelin quality, but Seb would be appreciative and complimentary no matter what. That was one of the things she loved about him—he was always thinking about how other people felt. There were a lot of things to love about him, and she was awestruck to realize how much he cared about her.

Love was a funny thing—no matter how much of it you thought you'd used up, there was a limitless capacity to experience more. It didn't mean she hadn't loved Jason—a piece of her heart would always be his. But what she felt for Seb was no less real. Seb had his own place in her heart, and that terrain grew larger every time she was with him.

She picked up her phone and stared at the home-screen picture of her and Jason mugging it up for the camera in front of their first Christmas tree. "Goodbye, Jason," she whispered. Her throat thickened, but she went to Settings and replaced it with one of Seb gazing out over the falls in Yosemite. Her vision blurred, but she deleted the Talk app before she could change her mind.

She would never talk to Jason again. He was gone. And with Talk's bankruptcy now concluded, she could never get another copy of the bot. She smiled through the tears slipping down her cheeks. Every new beginning started with an ending, and this was no different. Pain was part of life, but joy couldn't be suppressed and always came back. She was thankful she'd finally realized it. Lyla rubbed against her ankle, and she bent down to stroke the kitten's silky fur.

There was a knock at the door, and her heart leaped. She dashed the tears from her face, but she didn't have to pin a smile in place—it came on its own. Being with Seb was what she'd been waiting for all day. She threw open the door to find him standing there holding the most gorgeous orchid arrangement she'd ever seen. "Oh my," she breathed. "It's so beautiful."

His gaze settled on her face as tenderly as a kiss. "Not half as gorgeous as you." He stepped past her and found a spot on the coffee table for the flowers before he turned to embrace her. "You've been crying," he whispered in her hair. "You need a few minutes?"

She shook her head against his chest and inhaled his woodsy scent. It was like coming home and made her think of Tillamook ice cream on the waterfront or fresh waffles and coffee at Bestemor's while cold fog shrouded the outside. Being with Seb meant hygge—and so much more. There was a world of things to learn about him, like his favorite types of movies, his favorite dessert, and even how he reacted when he got mad. What would it be like to explore Paris or Tokyo with him as a guide? It was exciting terrain to navigate in this new relationship, and she was so ready.

She pulled away and smiled up at him. "Not all tears are bad, you know. I can't be sad with you here anyway."

"I hope you always feel that way." He settled on the sofa and pulled her down onto his lap and nuzzled his face in her neck. "You want to talk about it?"

She slipped onto the sofa next to him and nestled against his chest. "I deleted the app and said goodbye to Jason." He stilled, and she heard his heartbeat accelerate against her ear.

"I can't replace Jason." There was a hitch of dread in his words.

She sat up and turned toward him so she could see his expression. "I don't want you to be anyone but Sebastian Wallace: confident, urbane, thoughtful, and considerate. I never thought I'd feel this way again, and I'm ready to savor every minute of seeing where this leads."

His fingers traced the curve of her jaw. "You know I've loved you since I was sixteen, even if I didn't always want to admit it—even to myself. Inside I'm still that backwoods kid. That nerd with the black glasses might emerge every now and then."

She stared into his green eyes, vulnerable with love. "I didn't see you back then, but I see you now." She cupped his face in her hands. "All the way into your beautiful soul."

Joy radiated from his eyes, his smile. His touch was almost reverent as he continued to trace her jawline. "I was afraid to let anyone know me well for fear they'd see the worthless person my dad saw, but when you walked into the church for Frida's funeral, something I thought had died sprang to life inside me. I'd worked so hard to overcome that kid everyone pitied, and I forgot there was more to happiness than a career until I saw your smile again.

"I've achieved everything I set out to accomplish, but I forgot the most important things in life aren't tangible. You came back to town and tore to shreds everything superficial in my life. I'd even sell The Beacon and move to the city if that's what you want."

His honesty made her love him even more. "I love you, Seb. The awkward teenager and the man you've become. I've thought a lot about what I want, and it's all right here in North Haven—you, my family, the law, and a new niece or nephew. I think this is where God wanted me all along, but I was too stubborn to listen. I told Dad I want to join his law practice. He's already started cleaning out an office for me."

"Of course he has. And I'll put another desk in the office at Bestemor's. We can run it together." He cleared his throat. "Um, could you go back to that first part and make sure I heard it right?"

She smiled. "I love you, Seb Wallace." She leaned in and kissed him, relishing the fierce desperation in his embrace. Her thoughts scattered and all she knew was this man was hers and she wasn't letting go. Not ever.

EPILOGUE

////////////////

KATRINA'S NEW OFFICE LOOKED OUT ON Redwood Street. It was December 22 or *Bitte Lille Julaften*— "Teeny-Tiny Christmas Eve"—and North Haven was decorated for Christmas with traditional Norwegian lighted garlands. Shop windows held Christmas trees decorated with tiny Norwegian flags, and *julenisser*, little elf-like creatures with white beards and red hats. If she peered right, she could glimpse Bestemor's and the goats grazing on the roof.

Dad had chosen one of her favorite colors for the walls in her space, a pale green-gray that complemented her new walnut desk. He'd spared no expense in trying to make her comfortable. Maybe he had been worried that she'd take the lucrative job Infinion had offered her after the final hearing in Talk's bankruptcy case last week. Three months ago she would have jumped at it, but she turned it down with no regrets. She was home now.

Mom had spent the day with her yesterday, hanging pictures on the wall along with her diploma. She'd even bought her a coffee bar. Her mother had softened the past few weeks too. Maybe the traumatic events had changed them all.

The Seattle DA's office number flashed across her phone screen, and Katrina's contentment vanished. "Katrina Foster."

"Ms. Foster, I have good news for you."

She froze at the sound of his pleased tone. "I'm glad to hear it. You're dropping charges?"

"The investigative file you and your cocounsel sent over was impressive, and we believe your client acted in self-defense. We're considering charges against one of the witnesses for making false statements. Do you think Mr. Jackson would agree to an interview as part of that investigation?"

"That *is* good news. I'll ask Dylan about that interview." Katrina thanked him and ended the call. She'd been cautiously optimistic ever since the DA agreed to bail and allowed Dylan to leave Washington, but she hadn't wanted to get her hopes too high.

Seb walked in her open office door. The scent of sun, spruce, and sawdust entered with him, and she dropped her phone to rush to him. "Seb, Dylan's been cleared! The DA just called to tell me they aren't pursuing the charges."

He engulfed her in a bear hug and spun her around the room before he set her back on her feet. "That's the best news I could have had today. Dad's been fretting about the trial and making me feel as if it was all my fault. Dylan and I couldn't take any more and had to take a break from working on Dad's new cabin. Dylan's at Bestemor's for lunch with Magnus, and I told him we'd meet him there. We can tell him the good news together."

Their two brothers had become surprisingly good friends over the past two months after such a rocky start to their acquaintance. Liv wasn't around causing jealousy, and Dylan had offered to help Magnus put together a nursery for the baby coming in another five months. Liv hadn't wanted the state to take the baby and had been relieved when Magnus was quick to assume responsibility.

"I wish Bestemor were alive to see how much he's matured," she said. "He's even offered to pitch in at Bestemor's if we need him."

"I think impending fatherhood might have had something to do with the changes in him. Bestemor would love what we've done at the café, so luckily I don't think we'll need to take him up on that offer."

Their partnership at Bestemor's was working out amazingly well. They'd hired Grace as assistant manager as she worked her way through school. Her extra pay went into savings for her master's degree. Agnes raved about her work ethic and how quickly she learned things.

Katrina glanced back at the big window overlooking the picturesque street. Moving back to her roots had been what her heart needed. She glanced up at Seb again. And loving Seb had gone a long way toward convincing her she'd done the right thing. She couldn't stop thinking about Liv though. That kind of betrayal had left her feeling like she was missing an appendage, but there wasn't anything Katrina could do to fix it. At least that's what she'd told herself, but was there a way to find peace with the situation?

She loved watching Seb's face and expressions. Their relationship had deepened with every day they'd been together, and she'd come to count on him for his thoughtful responses to every question she asked him. She stepped back so she could see his reaction to the question on her mind.

"Liv called last night, but I didn't accept the charges. I almost did, but I couldn't quite bring myself to do it. I was packing up a box of Bestemor's books to make more room in the office and found some old *Guideposts*. There was an old receipt in the pages, and I opened it to see what Bestemor had cared enough to save. It was a story about Corrie ten Boom. A sadistic Nazi guard had asked her for forgiveness after the war, and Corrie said she couldn't do it but maybe God in her could. I want to be big enough to forgive Liv, but I can't. I think God will have to do it for me."

His eyes softened. "Sometimes the job is too big for us and that's the only way it can happen. Give him the time and space to do it."

She nodded. "I'll try." She kissed him. "You're the best listener, but I'm making us late for lunch. I'd better grab my bag or they'll close up before we get food." She left the shelter of his arms and picked up her phone and handbag.

A text sounded on her phone, and she glanced at the message. *I saw the news coverage about the egg. Look under table number four. Satoshi.* She gasped and opened the message app to see if the signature matched the number's owner, but it was blocked.

She whirled toward Seb and held out her phone. "Look at this!"

He took the phone and his eyes widened. "Satoshi?"

Without another word Seb grabbed her hand and they ran for the door. A gentle mist of rain slicked the street, and they dodged the light traffic and crossed to Bestemor's. A traditional Norwegian Christmas candelabra resembling a menorah welcomed them from the plate-glass window.

Seb opened the door for her, and she inhaled the competing aromas of the *julebord* menu for the holiday—*ribbe*, a favorite pork ribs dish; *lutefisk*, a cod jello; and *krumkaker*, crunchy funnel-shaped cookies filled with whipped cream. Magnus and Dylan waved to them from table three, but Katrina's focus was on the empty table four near the window.

She and Seb reached the dining spot, and he pulled the chairs out of the way and upended the table for her. Taped to the underside was a plastic egg, bright red and shiny with newness. She started to shake and reached for it. Her fingers fumbled with the tape and she tried again.

Dylan joined them. "What's going on?"

She barely heard Seb tell him about the dropped charges and Dylan's whoop of joy as she yanked on the tape and finally got the egg free.

Magnus touched her shoulder. "Is that what I think it is?"

"I—I don't know." She wrested the tape from the egg and twisted it open to reveal a USB drive inside. A piece of paper was folded up beside it, and she opened it with numb fingers. This couldn't be what it appeared. Was it a practical joke? The story of the lost Satoshi egg had been making the rounds on social media for nearly two months.

The black letters of a Bitcoin key stretched out on the paper. She recognized enough of the key sequences to realize it was Jason's lost key. Lost but now found and sent by Satoshi.

Seb whistled. "That's worth over thirty million. What are you going to do with it?"

For a moment she had the same instinct Jason must have had. This was her egg. She found it. Satoshi left it for her. She had every right to it. But maybe rights weren't the most important thing at this time. She swallowed hard. "What will *we* do, you mean? This is our restaurant." She looked at Dylan and Magnus. "And our family." She held up the treasure left by Satoshi. "Our egg."

Wonder dawned in the eyes of the men standing around her. Seb recovered first. He swept her into his arms. "I don't know what we'll do, but it will be a wonderful adventure."

A NOTE FROM THE AUTHORS

////////////////

DEAR READERS,

We had lots of fun researching and writing this book, and we hope you enjoyed it too. Artificial intelligence and cryptocurrencies have fascinated us for years, and they're both hot topics right now, of course. It's sometimes hard to tell science fiction from science fact, so we thought you might be interested in knowing what we made up and what we didn't:

Chatbots: The chatbot in the story is realistic, both in its abilities and in its function. Chatbots are already being used to mimic dead loved ones. For example, one popular chatbot, Replika, was originally created using the texts and messages of the developer's dead friend as a way to help her remember him.

Bitcoin: No fiction here either. Bitcoin was developed in 2008 and first "mined" (the technical term for creating Bitcoins) in 2009. The inventor of Bitcoin is a person or group using the pseudonym Satoshi Nakamoto. No one knows Satoshi's real identity, but he (or she or they) owns roughly a million Bitcoins worth tens of billions of dollars.

Satoshi eggs: These are, unfortunately, fictional.

Goats on restaurant roofs: These are 100 percent real. Every summer, they graze the turf roof of Al Johnson's Swedish Restaurant & Butik in Sister Bay, Wisconsin. You can watch them here: https://aljohnsons.com/goat-cam/.

We love hearing from readers, so please let us know what you think! And if you visit Al Johnson's, please send a selfie with the goats.

Blessings,
Colleen & Rick

ACKNOWLEDGMENTS

////////////////

We have the best publishing team in the business, and we are so grateful to HarperCollins Christian Publishing for their great work on our behalf!

A special thanks to our freelance editor, Julee Schwarzburg, who made room for the story in her busy schedule. Her touch on a manuscript always makes it so much better.

Thank you to agents Karen Solem and Julie Gwinn for your help in figuring out the new direction as well. We both appreciate you so much.

A heartfelt thanks to Anette Acker, Rick's sweet wife! She read every word and offered great suggestions and was a much-needed sounding board for direction and brainstorming.

Tusen takk to the Norwegians who helped us with cultural details: Margrethe Hofstad, Elisabeth Hutchinson, Per Kjeldaas, and of course Anette. If something is wrong, it's our fault, not theirs.

Our beta readers were a great asset! These readers are longtime fans who quickly offered to take a peek before the manuscript went to our editors, and their feedback was so valuable! Thank you, Deb Blower, Chandler Carlson, Kay

Chance, Gay Lynn Hobbs, Dawn Schupp, Leah Willis, Marcie Farano, Kathy Engel, Jody Wallem, and Vincenza Rabenn.

Honestly, it has felt like God himself dreamed up this partnership and handed the idea to us, and we're so thankful for his guidance and provision for this new venture!

DISCUSSION QUESTIONS

////////////////////

1. Would you use a chatbot like the one described in the book? Why or why not?

2. In what ways did the chatbot keep Katrina from healing? Did it help at all, or was it entirely harmful?

3. Should there be legal limits on chatbots, or should developers be allowed to experiment freely?

4. Seb asks himself how to honor his father, who seems entirely dishonorable. Seb never explicitly answers that question, but do his actions show his answer? How did his attitude toward his father change over the course of the story?

5. How did Bestemor shape those around her? Do you know any Christians who left a spiritual legacy similar to hers?

6. Was Jason right to refuse to share any of the Bitcoin treasure with Liv? What would you have done in a similar situation?

7. How did Liv's bad spending habits and sense of grievance ultimately lead her to kill Jason, cause her best friend over a year of emotional agony, and put herself and everyone

around her in great danger? Did she intend any of that at
the beginning?

8. Did you know Corrie ten Boom's story before reading this
   book? Do you agree with her that it's not always possible
   for us to forgive—but that it is always possible for God in
   us to forgive?

From the Publisher

GREAT BOOKS

ARE EVEN BETTER WHEN THEY'RE SHARED!

Help other readers find this one:

- Post a review at your favorite online bookseller

- Post a picture on a social media account and share why you enjoyed it

- Send a note to a friend who would also love it—or better yet, give them a copy

Thanks for reading!

LOOKING FOR MORE GREAT READS? LOOK NO FURTHER!

HARPER MUSE

*Illuminating minds
and captivating hearts
through story.*

Visit us online to learn more:
harpermuse.com

Or scan the below code and sign up to receive
email updates on new releases, giveaways,
book deals, and more:

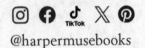

@harpermusebooks

The Tupelo Grove series

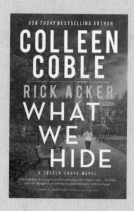

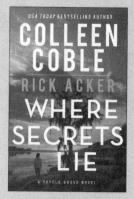

(Coming July 2025)

(Coming March 2026)

Available in print, e-book, and audio

ABOUT THE AUTHORS

EAH Creative

COLLEEN COBLE IS THE *USA TODAY* BEST-selling author of more than seventy-five books and is best known for her coastal romantic suspense novels.

Connect with her online at colleencoble.com
Instagram: @colleencoble
Facebook: colleencoblebooks
Twitter: @colleencoble

ABOUT THE AUTHORS

RICK ACKER WRITES DURING BREAKS FROM his "real job" as a supervising deputy attorney general in the California Department of Justice. He is the author of eight acclaimed suspense novels, including the #1 Kindle bestseller *When the Devil Whistles*. He is also a contributing author on two legal treatises published by the American Bar Association.

||||||||||||||||||||||||

Connect with him online at rickacker.com
Instagram: @rick_acker
Facebook: @rickacker
Twitter: @authorrickacker

And you can follow their joint projects
on TikTok: @cobleacker